DEMONSTORM

Also by James Barclay

Chronicles of The Raven
DAWNTHIEF
NOONSHADE
NIGHTCHILD

Legends of The Raven
ELFSORROW
SHADOWHEART
DEMONSTORM

DEMONSTORM
LEGENDS OF THE RAVEN
JAMES BARCLAY

an imprint of **Prometheus Books**
Amherst, NY

Published 2011 by Pyr®, an imprint of Prometheus Books

Cover illustration © Raymond Swanland.

Inquiries should be addressed to
Pyr
59 John Glenn Drive
Amherst, New York 14228–2119
VOICE: 716–691–0133
FAX: 716–691–0137
WWW.PYRSF.COM

15 14 13 12 11   5 4 3 2 1

Library of Congress Cataloging-in-Publication Data

Barclay, James, 1965–
    Demonstorm / by James Barclay.
        p. cm. — (Legends of The Raven ; 3)
    First published: London : Gollancz, an imprint of Orion Publishing Group, 2004.
    ISBN 978–1–61614–252–0 (pbk. : alk. paper)
    1. Raven (Fictitious characters : Barclay)—fiction. I. Title. II. Series.

PR6102.A76D46 2011
823'.92—dc22

                                                                    2010044347

Printed in the United States of America on acid-free paper

For Simon Spanton, a great friend and great editor,
and without whom there would have been no Raven.

BALAIA

NORTH BAY

Sunara's Teeth

TERENETSA

Sethe River

TornWastes

PARVE

Baravale Valley

WESMEN HEARTLANDS
(Uncharted)

Arch-Temple
of the
Wethsites

EyeLake

•LEIONU

N

SkyLake

W   E

Garan
Mountains

S

Southern Force

SOUTHERN OCEANS

Cast List

THE RAVEN

Hirad Coldheart   BARBARIAN WARRIOR
The Unknown Warrior/Sol   WARRIOR
Thraun   SHAPECHANGER
Ry Darrick   CAVALRY SWORDSMAN
Denser   XETESKIAN MAGE
Erienne   DORDOVAN MAGE

THE COLLEGES

Dystran   LORD OF THE MOUNT, XETESK
Sharyr   DIMENSIONAL MAGE, XETESK
Suarav   CAPTAIN, XETESKIAN COLLEGE GUARD
Chandyr   COMMANDER, XETESKIAN ARMIES
Vuldaroq   TOWER LORD, DORDOVER
Heryst   LORD ELDER MAGE, LYSTERN
Pheone   HIGH MAGE DESIGNATE, JULATSA

THE ELVES

Cleress   GUILD OF DRECH
Rebraal   LEADER OF THE AL-ARYNAAR
Auum   LEADER OF THE TAIGETHEN
Evunn   TAI CELL OF AUUM
Duele   TAI CELL OF AUUM
Dila'heth   ELVEN MAGE

BALAIANS,
WESMEN,
DRAGONS,
AND DEMONS

Blackthorne   A BARON
Ark   AN EX-PROTECTOR
Diera   WIFE OF THE UNKNOWN WARRIOR
Tessaya   LORD OF THE PALEON TRIBES
Riasu   LORD KEEPER OF UNDERSTONE PASS
Sha-Kaan   GREAT KAAN
Yasal-Naik   GREAT NAIK
Ferouc   MASTER STRAIN
Drenoul   MASTER STRAIN

CHAPTER 1

"Again!" Tessaya swept his arm down. "Again!"

The Wesmen charged the walls of Xetesk once more, tribal banners snapping in the breeze, voices mingling to a roar. The ladders drove into position, his warriors stormed up their rough rungs. Below them, archers tried to keep the defenders back from the wall. A difficult task over such a distance.

In the deep night shadows of Xetesk's walls, tribesmen pivoted more ladders. Along a four-hundred-yard stretch of wall they arced up. The best of them just rough cut and bound, the worst little more than shaved trunks of the tallest trees they could find. In earlier attacks, some had not been tall enough. He saw the ladders catching the light of the torches on the battlements before they thudded into place, warriors already swarming up them two abreast.

This time he had his enemy. This time, the Wesmen would break through the defences. He could feel it. In the daylight, many had died. Spells and arrows had ripped into wood and flesh. Burning warriors had tumbled to the ground screaming. Ladders, charred or frozen, had cracked and collapsed in heartbeats.

Yet the tribes had not faltered. Urged on by their lords who could see victory so close they had continued to press. And while hundreds scoured the land for the wood to build more ladders, hundreds more died at the walls doing exactly what had to be done. They exhausted the spell casters.

Tessaya saw the outlines of men running along the battlements to prepare their defence. Below them, holding shields above their heads, came his warriors. It was the fourth attack of the day. The night was just passing its zenith, and the spells no longer deluged them.

In desultory fashion, the odd casting blew away the top of a ladder and the men that scaled it. But that was all. Tessaya had foreseen this moment and had kept back his greatest force. Xetesk no longer had the magical power to stop them. Now it came down to who was the stronger with sword, axe and spear. And that was a battle he knew the Wesmen would win.

He watched for a moment longer. Arrows still peppered the warriors streaming up the ladders. His people still fell in their dozens. He breathed the night air deeply. The smells of ash and fear mingled with the freshness of grass in the breeze. He heard the voices of the Wesmen, their tribal songs echoing from the walls of Xetesk. They were the anthems of strength and victory, swelling in volume with every heartbeat.

He turned to Lord Riasu. The man's small eyes sparkled in the darkness and his heavy-set features had reddened with excitement.

"You can feel it too."

"I can, Lord Tessaya," said Riasu. "We are so close."

"And what is your desire now?"

Riasu nodded in the direction of the walls. More and more Wesmen were higher and higher up the ladders. Arrows alone were not enough and the spells had all but stopped falling. One deep blue flash to their left served as a reminder of the diminished threat.

"My men are on those ladders," he said. "I would join them. Lead them onto the walls."

Tessaya smiled and slapped Riasu hard on the back. "It is a wish I share."

He looked quickly about him. Six other tribal lords stood with them, their warriors, a thousand and more, ready to charge forward. Their shouts of encouragement to those already engaged sounded across the open ground. Beyond them, the fires of the camp burned and the Paleon guard stood watch over the Shamen while they prayed for guidance and strength from the Spirits. Prayers that had surely been answered.

The group of lords was close to him. All wanted just one thing but waited for Tessaya's word. Ten tribes and their lords had been unleashed already. The glory of being the first to make the walls outweighing the risk of death. Three of those lords had joined the Spirits as heroes. Four more would join them shortly. The remaining three were at the walls now.

"It is time," said Tessaya. He unhitched his axe and held it in one hand. "My Lords, let us deal the greatest blow."

He raised his axe high above his head, roared a Paleon war cry and led the charge to the walls. Behind him, the lords invoked their tribal Spirits and came after him, a thousand warriors with them, voices raised to a deafening crescendo.

Tessaya ran. His braided silver-grey hair bounced on his shoulders; his arms and legs pumped hard, the breeze was on his face. He couldn't remember ever feeling more alive. Not even leading the Wesmen out of the shadow of Understone Pass matched this. Then, they had so much still to accomplish and had failed. Now, their goal was within his grasp.

His forgotten youth surged back into his middle-aged veins. His heart thumped life through his body. His mind was clear, his eyes sharp. The Spirits were with him and within him. Nothing could stop him. He laughed aloud and upped his pace.

The darkness deepened in the lee of Xetesk's walls. Seventy feet high, with a slight outward slope. Imposing, menacing and never before breached.

Here, the noise of the fight intensified. Tessaya could hear the thud of bow strings, the creaking of the wood against its bindings and the calls of the Wesmen above him, silhouetted against the flare of torches.

As they had been ordered, the Wesmen, barring those bracing and those about to climb, did not cluster around the ladder bases. They were scattered across the field, waiting the shout to approach. No dense targets for the magcs, no easy masses for the archers.

Tessaya ran past the waiting warriors, his name being taken up and spreading across the field quicker than a scrub fire. And by the time he had run through the waiting warriors and had his path cleared to the base of the ladder, all he could hear was the chanting of his name.

He thumped onto the bottom rung, exhorting those around and above him to push harder. Riasu was right behind him, yelling in a tribal dialect Tessaya could barely understand. Not that he had to. The message was clear enough.

Tessaya climbed fast, feeling the timber give beneath his feet and the ladder shake and bow. But the bindings were firm and would hold. Left and right, Wesmen hurried up their ladders. Energy was pouring into the assault now Tessaya had joined. Those in the fight knew they would not fail.

"Keep close to the rungs," ordered Tessaya. "Don't give them a target."

A shame not all of his men heeded that advice. Arrows were still streaming by. One thudded home into the exposed neck of a warrior who risked looking up to see how far he had to go. Screaming, he plunged past Tessaya and bounced dead on the ground below.

"Keep moving!" he shouted.

There was a man right above him. Tessaya unashamedly used him as a shield. He noted how far he had climbed by the closeness of the wall behind the ladder. Not far now.

Another spell flashed across the night sky. To his left, ice howled into flesh and wood, expanding into cracks and splitting bindings and rungs. The ladder shattered, spilling survivors onto the long drop to death. Tessaya cursed. But the roar was intensifying above him and he heard the first glorious sounds of metal on metal, his warriors finally face to face with the Xeteskian defenders. A smile cracked across his face.

"Still with me, Riasu?" he called.

"I am, my Lord," came the slightly breathless reply. "I can smell their fear."

"Then let's not delay you seeing it in their eyes," said Tessaya. "Push!"

Now Tessaya looked up. He was only ten or so feet from the battlements. The arrows had stopped now. His men were climbing faster and he along with them, desperate to reach the walls before the small bridgehead was closed. One body fell to his right. Sparks flew as weapons collided and the songs of the Wesmen grew still louder, instilling in them all the desire to fight harder. For the tribes, for themselves, and for all those who had died to bring them to this place.

Those above him were still moving too slowly for his liking. Holding his axe outside the right-hand edge of the ladder, he shifted as far as he dared to that side and began to shout warriors from his path.

"Left, go left. Let me through. Go, go!"

He could sense Riasu right in his tracks. Using his left hand to steady himself, Tessaya surged up the rungs, using the ladder's angle against the wall to give him momentum. The breach was still holding. His men were breasting the walls scant feet from him. He could smell the stone, cold and ancient.

The sounds of the fighting came slightly muted to him. The individual battles. Grunts of exertion, cries of pain and shock. The thud and clash of weapon on leather and chain. The squeal of blades thrust together. The drop of bodies on stone and the scrabbling of feet desperate for purchase and balance.

Right at the head of the ladder, the reason for the slow progress above became clear. One warrior clung fast to the top rung. He had been sick over his hands and his weapon was still sheathed. Tessaya paused by him, swallowing his disgust at the cowardice when he saw the warrior's age.

"Stand with me, boy," he said. "Live or die you will know glory."

The boy gave him a terrified look but nodded minutely.

"Good lad."

Tessaya grabbed his collar and hauled him up the final step. In the next pace, they were on the walls and surrounding them was bedlam. Even Tessaya found the surge in volume of noise and the closeness of the action hard to take in. His charge wobbled at the knees. Urine poured down the boy's leggings and he vomited again. But in the midst of it all, he drew his blade, a short stabbing sword.

In the light cast by torches and braziers, the small breach was under concerted attack. Three other breaches could be seen left and right. Xeteskians were running in from the right and were packed left but coming under pressure from Wesmen on both sides. The parapet was no more than five feet wide, was unfenced and had never been built to defend in this fashion. Tessaya saw the game at once.

"Push out!" he yelled and jumped from the wall onto the bodies of the dead and into the backs of the living, shoving hard.

The Wesmen in Tessaya's way were forced off balance, able only to try and brace themselves against their enemies. In front of them, the reflex backward pace was fatal. With nowhere to go, the three Xeteskians nearest the edge stepped out into nowhere, grabbed at those nearest and at least half a dozen fell into the city far below. One of his warriors went with them. Two others saved themselves.

"Keep the breach open," he ordered. "Fight, my tribes, fight. Hold right, push left. Let's isolate those bastards. Someone get these bodies over the edges."

They obeyed. Tessaya was with them and they would do anything he asked of them. He looked back to see where the boy was and saw him fighting and killing; terror replaced by the desire to live. He would not.

Riasu breasted the battlement and howled a battle cry, circling his axe above his head.

"Riasu, pass the message back down the ladders. I want clear wall between the two nearest gatehouses. Do it!"

Without waiting, Tessaya plunged into the fight. His axe carved down between two of his warriors, splitting the skull of an enemy. Blood fountained into the torchlit night. The first Xeteskian blood he had spilt in years. He drew back his axe to move into the space his warriors left him.

Before he focused on his next victim, he stared out over the city of Xetesk. The towers of the college stood stark against the sky, light blazing from every window and wall.

"I am coming," he growled. "I will cast you down."

"Get back to the walls!" ordered Dystran, Lord of the Mount of Xetesk. "Wesmen are standing on them. I look at my senior commander and do I really have to wonder why?"

Dystran had intercepted Commander Chandyr in the dome of the college tower complex having seen his most decorated soldier thundering through the streets on his horse. The otherwise empty dome echoed to raised voices. Chandyr's battle-scarred face was pale and angry. Dystran knew exactly how he felt.

"No, my Lord," said Chandyr. "You have withdrawn too many mages to the college. Give them back."

"I will not exhaust every mage I have."

"Then do not expect me to hold the walls much longer."

"Ever the poor soldier blames lack of resource and support."

Chandyr's eyes narrowed. "Three thousand men against a few hundred, and many of those only just returned exhausted by forced march from Julatsa. What would you have me do, Lord Dystran?"

"I would have you do your job."

"I am doing it," said Chandyr quietly. "I am before you trying to prevent a massacre."

"Then how is it Wesmen have scaled my walls?"

Chandyr snapped. Dystran saw the shadow cross his eyes and felt the sharp prod of the commander's gauntleted finger in his ribs.

"Xetesk's walls, not yours," he said, menace in his tone. "And they are there because the defence to keep them away was taken from me by you at dusk. You have a responsibility to this city which you are shirking. What use is the college if the city is burning around it, eh?"

Dystran did not speak for a moment, allowing Chandyr to lower his hand.

"The college is the city," he said. "And as ruler of the college, all the walls are mine. I shirk nothing, Chandyr. Indeed I should be applauded for taking mages from the slaughter over which you are presiding. They at least will be able to strike back."

"Another of your indiscriminate dimensional spells, Dystran?" Chandyr scoffed. "You will kill more innocents than enemies."

"I will stop the Wesmen," said Dystran, feeling his patience expire. "And you, Commander Chandyr, will remember to whom you are speaking and, if you take my advice, will choose your next words very, very carefully."

A half smile flickered across Chandyr's mouth. It didn't touch his eyes. He nodded and took a pace forward, coming so close Dystran could barely focus on him.

"Never accuse me of being a poor soldier again."

"Men are judged by their actions," replied Dystran mildly, though his heart was beating faster.

"You only get one warning," said Chandyr.

The commander spun on his heel and strode from the dome, shouting for his horse. Dystran watched him go, letting his anger build. He had no wish to suppress it and enjoyed the heat it generated in his mind and body.

Chandyr did not understand, he reflected, hurrying out of the dome toward the base of his tower. His guards saluted him on his approach. Something else Chandyr had failed to do. A typical soldier. Blind to the bigger picture. Fit only to accomplish the task set before him and sometimes not even that.

"I want Sharyr in my reception chamber right now," he ordered. "He'll be in my hub rooms."

"Yes, my Lord," said both men.

Dystran began to climb his stairs. He replayed Chandyr's words, the tiny claws of doubt scratching at his self-confidence. That they had underestimated the Wesmen was not in question. This had been no disordered attack. There were brains and tactics behind it along with brimming determination and a willingness for self-sacrifice that had been breathtaking. Tessaya was out there somewhere.

What taxed Dystran most was not that the Wesmen lord had managed to marshal his warriors into very effective decoy and draw units. The issue here was that he plainly knew Xetesk was poorly defended by mage and soldier and had deliberately kept up his attack waves to force stamina exhaustion. Where had he got his intelligence?

Tessaya's aim had been obvious earlier in the day. It was why Dystran had withdrawn a core of mages to join the dimensional team and prepare for the next casting window. A window that had better be open.

Chandyr had been unable to hold the Wesmen back, though. He was surprised and disappointed by that. Xeteskian soldiers and archers should have been able to deal with a few ladders. How was it then that Wesmen had done that which no one should have been able to do?

Perhaps he should have probed further.

By the time he reached his reception chamber on the third landing, he could hear running footsteps behind him. He threw open the balcony shutters of the dimly lit room to reveal an uncomfortable picture of the threat to his city. He augmented his sight with a quick casting to sharpen the fine detail.

Lights blazed in a wide ring around an area over two hundred yards in length. It was bustling with Wesmen but not thronged. They were attacking left and right toward the nearest turrets and had built a shield wall, fresh-cut wood for the most part, toward the city. Archers were having some success but it was not affecting the advance along the battlements.

Chandyr had defended the turrets heavily. The Wesmen were suffering significant casualties but without a solitary spell to force them back to their ladders their weight of numbers would ultimately tell. How soon was hard to say. Before dawn in all probability.

"Dammit," he breathed. "Where did I go wrong?"

"My Lord?" queried a voice behind him.

"Sharyr," said Dystran, not turning to face his new head of dimensional magics. Barely more than a student but the best he had left. "Come here. Tell me what you see."

He heard a nervous shuffle then slightly laboured breathing mixing with snatches of noise from the walls. Dystran looked across to Sharyr and watched the balding young man scanning the night, anxious to pick up whatever he was supposed to see. He shifted uncomfortably and gave a half shrug.

"Wesmen on the walls?" he ventured, voice tremulous.

"Excellent," said Dystran. "Does that scare you?"

"Yes, my Lord," said Sharyr. "I have family in the city."

"Then they are fortunate because you will personally be keeping them safe, won't you?"

"Me? I—"

Dystran turned to face his nervous student.

"The distance between the walls of the city and those of this college is slight for a rampaging Wesmen army. Less than a mile, wouldn't you say?"

"My Lord."

"This is not a big city," said Dystran. "When do you think the Wesmen will take either of those turrets?"

Sharyr stared at him blankly.

"You see," continued Dystran. "When they do, they will have access to our streets and more importantly, the south gatehouse. And there are thousands of them just itching to get in."

"Yes, my Lord."

"The point is that this undefined but quite possibly short length of time is how long you have to be ready to cast the spell of your choosing."

"I—" Sharyr backed up a pace into the room.

Dystran turned to follow him. "You do understand that none of those men will reach the college, don't you? If Chandyr can't stop them, you will. Won't you?"

"The—the alignment isn't going to be complete until this time tomorrow night," managed Sharyr.

"Oh dear," said Dystran, putting a hand to his mouth. "Whatever will you do?"

"Well, I don't know, my Lord," replied Sharyr, missing Dystran's sarcasm completely.

Dystran bore down on Sharyr, forcing the younger man to back away across the room.

"Then let me enlighten you." His voice barely above a whisper carried all the menace of long practice. "You will be ready to cast because you and I both know that the alignment can be forced for the purposes of the casting. I have written at great length on the subject. The spell will be difficult to control and you will instruct your charges how to handle the forces and inform them of the personal consequences of failure. Backfire from a dimensional casting is very, very messy."

Sharyr fetched up against the mantle of the fire. Fortunately for him, there was no heat from the embers.

"The risks to our city . . ." he began.

Dystran leant in further. "The Wesmen will take this college if they are not stopped. That is the risk to our city. You will stop them or you will die in the attempt. Any of your team who feel they are not up to the task can report to me to discuss it."

"I—"

"Do not fail, Sharyr." Dystran straightened and stepped back a pace, seeing the terror in the student's expression, the sweat beading on his brow and the darting of his eyes. He chose to smile. "You have heard the shout, 'Death or glory'? Bet you thought it only applied to soldiers, didn't you? Think again, get down to the catacombs and be ready. When the time comes, I will call you personally to the walls of the city. Go."

Sharyr had the presence of mind at least to bow his head and mutter, "My Lord."

But the door to the reception chamber opened before he reached it and an old man with tears on his face stood in the brazier light from the stairway. It was Brannon, Ranyl's manservant of decades.

"Please, my Lord," he said. "You must come quickly."

Dystran felt his world dropping around him and fear shiver though his body.

"Oh no," he breathed, already starting to run. "Not now. Not now."

Chapter 2

Hirad Coldheart sat on the steps of Julatsa's refectory. The night was warm and peaceful. From outside the college, he could hear the odd snatch of life. A cart rattling over cobbles; horse hoofs echoing against buildings; a voice raised in greeting. He breathed in deeply, feeling his chest wound pull under its bandages. It was a stubborn one. Magic had knitted the muscle but his skin was still sore and tight. A mark of age, he supposed. A little like the grey flecks he'd found in his long braids.

He knew he shouldn't but he felt released. All the problems that Balaia still faced and for the first time in so long he and The Raven were not bound by honour or contract to do anything about them. He knew he should still care but he found he couldn't. Not at the moment. Not ever, probably.

There was tension in Julatsa as those who had fled began to return. The city's rulers still hadn't had the guts to come to the college. There would be trouble, he was sure of it. And beyond this city, Dordover, Xetesk and Lystern presumably still fought. They'd battle themselves to a standstill. All too proud to sue for peace before the maximum blood was spilt.

He knew he should worry about where the country he loved was going but something was missing. Looking over at the Heart of Julatsa, around which would soon be constructed a new tower, he knew exactly what it was. It wasn't the country itself that was great and worth saving. It was the people he loved that wanted to live there. And they were dead or leaving. All of them.

Ilkar might have been the final straw for him but there were Sirendor, Ras, Richmond, Will and Jandyr too. All dead despite everything he had tried to do to save them. And The Unknown, Denser and Erienne were all thinking of their families across the ocean, alive or dead. Thraun would go with them because The Raven were his family. Either that or return to the pack. He would not be drawn on the subject. That left Darrick. Hirad chuckled. If there was one man more wanted than the rest of The Raven, it was Darrick. He really had little choice.

So they would all be travelling back to take ship near Blackthorne with those very few elves that could be spared from the effort to shore up the college now the Heart was risen. Rebraal had to go. The Al-Arynaar needed their leader on Calaius. The same was true of Auum and the TaiGethen and of course, where he went, so did his Tai. Finally, Hirad would have bet everything he owned on the single ClawBound pair returning to the rain forests. They had been mourning for those of their kind lost since the end of the siege. That they missed their homeland and their kin was something he could read even in the eyes of the panther. They were outside now, staring up at the stars and knowing their positions were all wrong.

Hirad drained his goblet of wine and looked down at his plate. It was empty of the bread and meat he'd taken. Thinking it was probably time to turn in, he picked up the plate and turned to rise. Denser and The Unknown were just coming out of the refectory, a wineskin and goblets in hand. He smiled at them both, the sharp-featured mage and the shaven-headed warrior.

"Where do you think you're going, Coldheart?" said The Unknown.

"For a refill?" ventured Hirad.

"Correct answer," said Denser.

The two men sat either side of him. Denser filled his goblet.

"What's this, some sort of deputation?"

"No," said The Unknown. "We just thought it's a long time since we'd sat and drunk wine together. The others'll be out soon."

"Time to toast the dead and move on, eh?" Hirad nodded at the Heart.

"Something like that," replied Denser.

"Well, no sense in hanging about." Hirad raised his glass. "Ilkar. An elf without peer and a friend I will miss forever."

The goblets clacked together. Hirad drained his in one and nudged Denser for more.

"He'll be proud of us, you know," said Denser, rubbing a hand across his neatly trimmed and still jet-black beard.

"He'd bloody better be. Almost saw the end of the lot of us, dragging that piece of rubble from its hole."

Denser laughed loud. Out in the courtyard, the panther turned her head lazily. "Ah, Hirad, ever able to bring everything down to its most basic level."

"Best thing is, though, whatever happens to us, this is a memorial to him, isn't it?" said Hirad. "I mean, it's only raised because of what he started us doing." He sighed, heart heavy for a moment. "Should have been here to see it though, shouldn't he?"

There was a silence, each man lost in memories.

"You ready to go?" asked The Unknown.

Hirad shrugged and looked up into The Unknown's flint-grey eyes. "Well, it's not as if I've got much to pack."

"That isn't what I meant."

"I know."

The Unknown punched him on the arm. "So tell me."

"That hurt."

"Not as much as the next one will."

Hirad eyed the bunched muscles beneath the smile. "Actually, I was thinking about it before you two interrupted me. There's nothing keeping me here now. And I'm tired of fighting. Really. Look at all we've done. And the only monuments are those we have built for our dead friends. Nearly everyone else wants us dead too. Ungrateful bastards."

"We thought we'd go tomorrow. First light," said The Unknown.

Hirad raised his eyebrows. "Are we fit for that? I'm talking about Erienne, of course."

"She's fine," said Denser. "Physically at any rate. I think she just can't make up her mind which part of arriving back on Herendeneth she is looking forward to least. Seeing Lyanna's grave or getting taught about the One by Cleress."

"We'll get south all right, will we?" asked Hirad. "There's still a war on, you know."

"Nothing escapes you, does it?" said Denser.

"Darrick picked a route. I agree with it," said The Unknown. "It'll see us back to Blackthorne without much problem. Then all we have to do is wait for the *Calaian Sun* to put into the Bay of Gyernath."

"So long as you're happy," said Hirad.

"I am," said The Unknown. "But you know how it is. We don't move until you say."

Hirad felt that familiar surge. Even on their way out of the country they'd fought to save from itself for so long, even on their way to retirement, The Raven was still working. He nodded.

"There's no reason to stay if we're all fit to travel." He smiled and looked across at The Unknown. "Thanks for asking."

"You know how it is."

"Yeah." Hirad stood up and looked down into his goblet, seeing the ripples in the dark liquid. "Where are the others? I feel the need for another toast to someone or other."

Sha-Kaan turned a lazy roll in the air. Below him, the mists enveloped the valley of the Kaan Broodlands. Ahead of him, the plains of Domar and the dense steaming forests of Teras fled away beyond the encircling mountains of Beshara from which the dragon dimension took its name. The mountains that made his valley so rich and humid, trapping the moisture and heat.

He could hear the calls of his brood in flight, operating the patterns that kept intruders from entering the Broodlands. Now more than ever, they must not fail. Now more than ever, they were prone to attack.

Sha-Kaan blessed the strength of Hirad Coldheart and The Raven. He blessed their belief and determination, their energy and their courage. Without them, he would not have been here to lead his brood at this most critical time and their own belief would surely have faltered. And without Hirad in particular, he would not have been able to spend these last days in the healing streams of interdimensional space. To relax in the Klene, the melde corridor that was anchored at one end by the brood consciousness and at the other by the remarkable barbarian's, and there be tended by the Vestare. His servant race. Faithful, steeped in awe of their masters and living to serve under their protection. It was a pleasure he had thought denied him forever.

Sha-Kaan felt the frightened excitement of a dozen brood at spawn. Their time was upon them. The next cycle of light and dark would see new births for the Kaan to celebrate and protect. The energy of a birth could be felt far beyond the Broodlands, in the minds of their enemies. Such was the danger linked to the joy of every birth. It was the reason the brood flew now, securing their borders, and would fly in even greater numbers very soon. The Kaan were ageing. They could not afford to lose any of their young.

Sha-Kaan pulsed out with his mind to his brood. His return had been like a birth to them and now of course they looked to their Great Kaan for guidance as they had done for so many cycles. He pulsed orders to be wary, to ensure the flight patterns were kept tight, and to keep the Kaan in flight changing and so keep them all fresh. And he pulsed harmony, calm and his confidence in living births to the brood at spawn.

Driving his wings hard for a dozen beats, he swept upward, meaning to look down on his lands from the outer markers where his patrols circled, eyes and minds alert for early signs of enemies. He greeted them with barks and a pulse that warned against complacency.

Reaching his desired height, he turned into a gentle downward-spiralling glide, feeling the rush of the wind over his scales and fully extended wings. His eyes searched below, looking for anything he had missed, any gap that should be closed. He counted just on a hundred Kaan above the mist layer. There would be an equal number below it and twice that many at rest in chouls across the Broodlands.

It looked an impressive defence but it represented the immature and the very old in addition to those of fighting age. The Naik were strong. They knew Kaan birthings were close. He wondered whether they believed an attack worth the probable losses. They had so often proved an impossible brood to gauge. At once utterly dismissive of rival broods' rights to land in Beshara and surprisingly concessionary and honest in alliance.

The Kaan had not experienced alliance with the Naik themselves but knew their ways from the Veret, a dying brood threatened and now defended by the Naik in a bizarre turn of attitude.

An attack depended on the Naik ability to defend their own homelands while trying to take the Kaan's. That meant new alliances would have to be made. Sha-Kaan wished he had the time to visit the Veret to get some indication of likely force but they were too far distant.

Satisfied his flight organisation left no unseen access for their enemies, he sailed down faster. A rest in a choul was what he needed now to further ease his ageing muscles, not yet healed by his rest in interdimensional space; its coolness, darkness and companionship would be very welcome. But before that, he probed Hirad Coldheart's mind. Across the uncertainties of interdimensional space and into Balaia, he let his consciousness wander.

He could sense the enemies that probed its enclosing membrane, looking for a way in. The Arakhe. Demons, the Balaians called them. An ever-present danger to every creature that inhabited the countless dimensions; and besides enemy broods, the only threat to the Kaan. Balaia was calm. The dimensional magic that had alerted the Arakhe had caused no lasting damage. The tears in space had been small and short lived. And Hirad Coldheart was sleeping, his mind free though he did not know it.

Sha-Kaan withdrew, satisfied. Yet the density of the Arakhe surrounding Balaian space bothered him. Like they anticipated something. He could feel their minds like thorns in flamegrass. Unpleasant, unwelcome and unnatural.

He would keep close watch on them. Once the birthings were complete and the disruption to the brood psyche settled, he would have more time. Perhaps then he might build alliances of his own, do something about the Arakhe. Something terminal.

Barking his approach, he flew to a choul.

Dystran tried to calm himself before he entered Ranyl's private chamber. He took a moment to readjust his shirt and be sure his hair was smooth against his head. He slowed his breathing and hoped his face wasn't too red from his run. He nodded at the guard on the door who opened it for him. A wave of heat washed out from the dimly lit interior. He walked in.

To the left, the fireplace glowed hot, yellow and orange flames spreading beguiling shadows over walls and drapes. To the right, the light from a hooded lantern revealed Ranyl's bed and the woman sitting beside it. She had one arm resting on the bed, her hand gripped by Ranyl's. At her side on a low table, a bowl and cloth.

Dystran had expected to hear the rasping of a man near his end but the room was quiet. Yet the atmosphere was thick with expectation, smelled sweet from bowls of infused herbs and petals and was hardly supportive of Ranyl's longevity. He moved quietly toward the bed.

"Thank you, my lady," he said. "Your tending has been most welcome these last days."

After a moment's hesitation, the woman stood. She moved Ranyl's hand from hers, squeezed it briefly and leant in to murmur a few words before kissing him on the forehead. With head bowed, she hurried past Dystran, who did not miss the tracks of tears on her cheeks reflecting the firelight.

As he sat, Dystran had the overwhelming urge to run. Not to face what he knew he must. The sounds of fighting echoed across the dark city. Everything he knew and treasured was under threat. And here, breathing so quietly he could hardly be heard, the man he needed most was slipping away from him.

He took Ranyl's hand in his and felt the fingers move weakly in his palm.

"Feeling tired, old dog?" asked Dystran quietly, concentrating on keeping his voice steady. So few days had passed since Ranyl had seemed strong, able to walk, sit up, eat. The suddenness of the change was brutal to see.

In the gloom, Ranyl's eyelids flickered and opened. His eyes, so recently bright and full of determination, were dull and sunken. His mouth moved, breath a sibilant hiss over which his words were barely audible.

". . . can't bear to see Xetesk attacked. Keep them from us."

"The Wesmen won't make it off the walls," said Dystran gently. "Rest easy. Hold on. See us victorious."

"No, young pup. I'm tired." He managed a brief smile. "I will leave it to younger men. I was . . . I was really only waiting until you came to say goodbye."

Ranyl's voice was fading such that Dystran had to lean closer and closer. His words chilled the Lord of the Mount. He gripped the old man's hand, shaking it.

"No, Master Ranyl," said Dystran. "I need you to guide me. There is no one else I can trust."

"You have been such a friend," said Ranyl. "And you are a great leader. You need no one."

"No, Ranyl. Hold on. This pain will pass. You'll soon feel stronger."

But the words weren't true, he knew that. He could see it in the pallor of Ranyl's complexion, ghostly in the gloom. And he could smell it in the air.

Ranyl coughed weakly. "Mourn me, but don't miss me."

Dystran nodded, accepting. He smiled and placed a hand on Ranyl's cold forehead. "Everything I have achieved is because of you. I will be in your debt for eternity."

Ranyl chuckled. "A fitting epitaph," he said, his eyes brightening just briefly.

And then he was gone.

Dystran walked to the balcony shutters and opened them, admitting the cool air of night. He saw fires toward the walls and could hear the sounds of battle and of panic beginning to grip the streets. He even fancied he could taste blood in the air.

Mostly, he felt isolation. Only one man could save Xetesk now. Unfortunately, it was him. For a time he let the tears fall, his mind focusing on the tortured screams of Ranyl's familiar as it faded to death after its master.

The prize was so close Tessaya could almost touch it. Men were bred tough in the Heartlands and he felt proud to fight next to them. The Xeteskians were falling back before him and his heart sang victory.

He had led his warriors in a hard drive right along the battlements. His axe ran red and his arms and chest were cut by his enemies. But now the turret was theirs. In front of him a warrior fell, skull crushed by a mace. Tessaya grabbed his collar as he went down, dragging him back. He strode into the space, axe carving through an upward arc left to right across his body. Its blade caught his enemy under the chin. His helmet flew off, his jaw shattered and his head snapped back, taking his body with it and striking those behind him.

Warriors surged forward, the noise intensifying in the enclosed space.

"Hold the far door," ordered Tessaya, pushing men at it. "The rest of you, let's take these stairs."

Handicapped by the direction of the spiral, the Xeteskians were forced back quickly. Tessaya led his warriors down, taking the inside himself. His axe was in his right hand, sweeping in front of him.

As Tessaya knew it would, the Xeteskian retreat stopped at a landing. Orders were shouted up the stairs. In front of him, the terrified boys, for that was all they were, squared up. Outside, he heard the rare impact of a spell. He snarled and stepped away from the centre of the thread and gripped his axe in both hands. A warrior stood to his right, the pair of them filling the stairwell. Behind and above, the fighting continued on the battlements. He heard his warriors chanting as they drove onward, their voices echoing down to lift his spirits even as they crushed those of whom he faced.

"You will die, boy, if you lift that blade against me," said Tessaya into the impasse. He pitched his voice to carry further than the whelp he addressed; a quivering youth whose helm sat too large on his dirt-streaked face. "But at least you will know more courage in death than those who command you. Where do they stand, eh?"

"Who . . . ?" The Xeteskian didn't know whether to ask or not, caught between fear and awe.

"I am Tessaya, Lord of the Paleon tribes and ruler of the Wesmen," he replied. "And what a prize should you beat me. The time has come. Lay down your blade and be spared. Or die dreaming of being a hero."

Tessaya didn't think the boy even had the courage to lift his sword in attack and in that at least he was mistaken. But in everything else, he was not. Deflecting the ill-learned strike and chopping downward through the poorly armoured shoulder, he muttered a prayer that the boy be respected by the Spirits.

He stepped across the body, a chant erupting from his lips and taken up by the men around him. Invoking the Spirits of strength, of true aim and keen edge, it was a guttural sound, its rhythm in time with the strokes of his axe.

Tessaya paced forward, chopping up through the defence of one Xeteskian, sweeping left to eviscerate a second and back right and down to hack into the arm of a third. The warrior next to him, voice booming in song, moved in closer, forcing his enemy's guard down and butting him on the bridge of the nose. The Xeteskian sprawled backward, flailing his arms, more of a danger to his comrades than the Wesmen.

Tessaya saw the fear in their eyes and the tremble of their limbs. Blood slicked the walls, the floor was covered in gore and the bodies of fallen Xeteskians and the air stank and steamed. The Lord of the Wesmen licked his lips and drove on, breaking them further with every step.

CHAPTER 3

None of Chandyr's experience had prepared him for this. He had fought Wesmen before but of course there had been the backing of mages able to break lines and obliterate enemies at will. And in combat with enemy colleges, the balance of spell power gave the warfare a symmetry that he could understand.

But here tonight, hand-to-hand and face-to-face, he was seeing ferocity that was simply awesome. The Wesmen were indefatigable. They were skilful. And they were cutting through his men like paper.

On his horse outside the lost turret, he saw men spill outward, regroup and push in again. He heard the turret captain yelling for order and getting precious little. The faces of those few around him were lined with fear. Either side, high up on the battlements, the Wesmen taunted his toothless forces. He had so few mages and the spells cast recently had been wasted. Now the chastened casters awaited his order in an arc around the turret. They wouldn't be kept long.

Chandyr had thought about riding back to the college again. But the mood was fragile and he couldn't afford to be seen leaving the battlefront. Instead he dismounted and turned the reins of his horse over to the nearest messenger.

Before he spoke, he took in the fires burning on the walls and those buildings onto which the Wesmen had managed to cast torches. He saw more and more join those already behind their makeshift wooden barricade on the battlements. And he didn't have to imagine the number who waited outside for the gate to be taken.

In the streets around him, the confidence of many city folk had given way to panic. People thronged the main roads, heading for the north gate and the college, no doubt to demand escape or sanctuary. Dystran would not give them the latter. But by the Gods burning, he could buy them time to achieve the former.

His messenger waited expectantly, wincing as roars of triumph sounded from the Wesmen advancing toward the south gate tower along the battlements.

"Ride back to the college," said Chandyr, handing the messenger his badge of command. "Use my authority and speak only to Dystran himself. Tell him this:

"If he is to cast his spells it must be now. We are losing the battle for control of the south gate. He must give us more mage support or they'll be at the college before dawn. Got all that?"

"Yes, sir."

Chandyr grabbed the messenger's arm. "One more thing. Tell him he does not need to cast his dimensional spells. We can hold on without them, at least. Go."

Chandyr watched him mount up and ride away before turning to add his strength to the fight for Xetesk.

Spring nights could be chill and the hours before dawn were the coldest. But Sharyr hadn't known how lonely they could be until now, particularly not in the company of so many friends and enemies.

Of course it wasn't just this that set him alone. It was the awesome expectation placed upon him to succeed and the enormity of the risk he was being forced to take to achieve that success.

He and the dimensional team of twenty—hardly enough anyway—had rested in shifts while they made their calculations. They were looking for any edge they could give themselves. Something to provide focus yet minimise exposure to the power with which they toyed. By the time Dystran ordered them to the walls, they had found precious little. Hardly surprising. So little time had passed.

The urgency of the orders had frightened him and he'd led the team at a run from the catacombs. Much of the rest had been a blur of impressions. Voices clamouring. Armour clanking and grinding as soldiers ran beside them. The glare of fires against dark buildings. People running toward them, pushed aside to speed their progress. The smell of wood smoke. The cobbles beneath his feet. The extraordinary din of battle that grew with every pace they took nearer the walls.

The college guard brought them to the roof of a building with clear line of sight up to the embattled walls. Commander Chandyr had joined them almost immediately. Sharyr missed his first words, transfixed by what he saw in front of him. A mass of warriors on the battlements, bodies choking the street below. Fires in two guard turrets. And desperate defence on the ground. Xetesk under threat.

". . . are not who I wanted here. Why are you here?"

"My Lord Dystran ordered us here in response to your messenger."

"I don't want your dimensional spells, Sharyr. You know my feelings."

"Commander, Ranyl has died. Dystran wants to make a statement. We're all you have and we have instructions about which spells we will use."

Chandyr nodded. "Fine. Then do so carefully. Take out that turret. Destroy the stairway."

"Commander, that kind of focus is not possible. The minimum strike area will cover left and right for twenty yards. And that assumes we can keep it tight. The dimensional alignment is not right."

Chandyr regarded him blankly. "You're talking to me as if I should care or understand. Fifty yards either side is Wesmen. Take them down too." He shrugged. "I asked for mage support and here you are so do what you have to do. But don't hurt a single Xeteskian."

"Have your mages shield our forces," said Sharyr. "It's the only way to keep them safe."

Chandyr spun round at a renewed roar from the turret. Xeteskians spilled into the street once again but this time could not drive back in. The first Wesmen set foot on Xetesk's soil.

"And you'd better do it quickly," said Chandyr. "Or they'll be up here too. Don't let me down."

Sharyr watched Chandyr stride from the rooftop then turned to his team.

"You can see the target. You know the risks. Shut out everything. We cannot afford to slip. Are you ready?" The chorus of assent was loud but anxious. "Then we will begin."

Sharyr felt a charge race through his body and lodge in his gut. The mage team gathered about him. He tuned to the mana spectrum and could see through the chaotic streams the dark outline of the walls. He began to focus, constructing the shape to pierce the fabric of the Balaian dimension to access the raw energy beyond.

One by one his mage team joined him. In the stark colour contrasts that made up the Xeteskian mana spectrum the deep blue mana stream gained intensity. Power surged through every strand.

Like all base magical constructions, this one was essentially simple. The shape was a shifting octagonal column no more than ten feet wide. At its head, gossamer threads wove a complex pattern that mimicked the flows of interdimensional space, allowing them to lock onto the chaos outside the Balaian dimension.

The column itself acted as direction for the power they were tapping and as a seal against that power spilling out uncontrolled. Where the column attached to the dimensional fabric was entirely at Sharyr's discretion. And because this spell was statement as well as destruction, he drove it high into the night sky, issuing the command that activated the threads just beyond a layer of thin cloud.

They felt the backward surge along the column, saw the shivers in the mana light. And that was just the start. With the threads fast on the fabric, Sharyr began to feed energy into the column. Half the team followed his lead.

"Brace," he warned, his words carrying to them across the spectrum in sound and light. "And expand."

They pulled. And in the fabric of Balaia was torn a hole. Immediately, they felt the rush of the forces of interdimensional space, apparently grabbing at the hole, trying to force it wider. It was purely a reaction as chaos and order clashed. The mages were ready for it and used it. They allowed the tear to grow to optimum size and only then stiffened the borders, feeding in mana energy and locking it tight.

"That was the easy part," said Sharyr. "Column team, prepare. You know this isn't going to be easy to handle. Alignment team with me, keep your concentration if you keep nothing else. Let's go looking."

The information given Xetesk by the Al-Drechar and Sha-Kaan had allowed mages to draw a new dimensional map. They could predict with some accuracy the movement of those dimensions closest to Balaia. They also had some perception of the enormous number of dimensions crowding space. The old notion that all dimensions were somehow occupying the same small area of space had been disproved beyond reasonable doubt. Now it was about alignment. And the more dimensions aligned with Balaia at any one time, the more powerful the spell effect.

Sharyr's problem was that there was no alignment. Almost, but not quite. And while it was still possible to cast, the streams of energy would not be as focused and would be difficult to control.

Sharyr, using the combined energies of his team of nine, pushed the seeker pulse into the void, already knowing roughly what he would find. They were awaiting a four-dimension alignment. It was expected to begin the next midday. What Sharyr was presented with was a confusion of power streams, still in partial conflict though with a common broad direction given them by the partial alignment in which they were caught.

He could feel the pull of the distant dimensional shells and imagine their ponderous movement. Every heartbeat that passed brought the alignment closer but at this moment there was a problem.

The first and third shells were about in line, the latter moving slightly faster than the former. But the second shell was still way out of place though travelling quickly in relation to its peers. Currently, he couldn't sense the fourth shell at all.

"This is going to hurt," he said. "Brace yourselves."

Lacking the natural focus alignment would bring, the mages would have to channel the power themselves while holding the sheath spell construct in place to avoid a casting without control. Without a certain end.

On Sharyr's command, the alignment team poured mana energy into the seeker pulse, changing its polarisation from repulsor to attractor. At once, the part-aligned streams fed into the seeker pulse. Sharyr felt the force thunder through his mind, a sudden and prolonged deluge of crudely directed energy. The seeker pulse bulged under the strain.

"Hang on!" Sharyr gasped, sensing the tension in those around him. There was a roaring in his ears, reminiscent of a distant waterfall. "Right, let's use it."

The alignment team shortened the seeker pulse, dragging the inter-dimensional power with it. Sharyr knew that there was too much to control safely. It raged through his mind while he struggled to hold his concentration.

With the sound of air rushing to fill a void, the interdimensional force met Balaian space. It coalesced into thin discs, trailing smoke in their wake. Shaped by the minds of the mages and set spinning by nature. Tens, hundreds of them, cobalt blue and travelling at extreme speed, fled down the octagonal mana corridor. They bounced hard against its surface, the collisions increasing the stress on the structure further, to emerge from its protection to slam into ground, walls and men.

The Wesmen could see the spell approaching. Those at the base of the tower had some route of escape but they were the only ones.

The discs sheared into the tower, the ground surrounding it, and any flesh in their way over a sixty-foot spread. With a sound like a thousand metal spikes hammered into rock, they bit into the stone. Sparks flew, lighting up the night in garish relief. Dust was projected into the air, sections of the stonework cracked and crumbled. The tower shook under the impact.

On the ground, those Wesmen who hadn't reacted instantly were cut to pieces in moments. In front of them, the Xeteskian shield over the defenders bucked and twisted, its mages driven to their knees by the effort to keep it together.

Sharyr exhorted his mages to maintain their focus. Below them, their casting was scything the tower apart, shredding its stone, sending lethal fragments to every point of the compass. He fought the forces channelling through his mind, kept the polarity of the seeker pulse firm. It was he and his team who were responsible for reversing the flow when the time came.

But the drain on the alignment team was greater than any of them had imagined. The discs were further out of control with every heartbeat, crashing into one another and increasing their impacts on the column, which bulged under the pressure. And though the tower wasn't down, Sharyr felt he had no choice but to order the disconnection of the spell. He was the blink of an eye too late.

At the base of the column, multiple discs collided and scattered into its sides, threshing it with enough force to break the shape. Tattered in an instant, the base of the column was flayed apart. Wisps of mana clung to order for a few moments and were engulfed again in the mass. The sides of the column rippled and ripped upward, chasing back toward the hole into space.

And spewing out unconfined, came the discs. Along a front hundreds of feet wide, they gouged into Xetesk's walls and buildings or collided in midair to scream away back into the city.

One plunged into his mage team, chopping two men down. The other mages lost their concentration. The column vanished completely and Sharyr clung desperately to the seeker pulse, feeling its power weaken.

"Reverse!" he shouted. "Reverse!"

He tried to ignore everything around him. The wails of dying men on the walls and right by his side. The clouds of dust billowing into the night sky. The unfettered discs of pure cobalt brutality destroying the walls.

Dragging in everything he had left, Sharyr forced his will on the seeker pulse, switching its polarity. "Push," he gasped. "Damn you, push."

The building shook. Dimly, he heard a deep rumbling. The dust was in his nose and mouth and had forced itself into his eyes. He could feel the irritation and the tears but had to ignore them. He pushed against the tide of interdimensional energy, those that remained with him taking his lead. Around them, the storm continued. Next to the tower, the parapet collapsed, spilling Wesmen seventy feet to the streets. A series of detonations sounded. The discs had bulged into huge, harsh teardrops and they poured into the walls, the street, the tower and buildings all around. Only luck was keeping Sharyr and his team alive.

Sharyr gathered himself again, feeling the seeker pulse finally move under his control. "Got you."

Quickly, the movement gained momentum. Sharyr and the remains of his team pressed. The pulse whipped up into the night sky. Ahead of it, the teardrops lost their strength, unable to fight against the opposing force. Up to and through the hole went the pulse. And the tear itself, without the energy flowing through it and with no spell keeping it open, shut hard.

Sharyr had no strength in his legs. He sagged to his knees, staring at the point in the night sky where the tear had been. It glittered blue. He frowned.

"Someone check that," he said, gesturing upward. "That isn't right."

He became aware that the silence following the end of the spell had given way to a growing tumult of voices and action. He dragged himself back to his feet and walked unsteadily toward the edge of the building to see what he had wrought in the name of Xetesk and its Lord of the Mount.

His heart chilled at what he saw through the clouds of dust and smoke blowing all around him. Bodies lay everywhere, few moving and many burning. Around them, Xeteskian soldiers hurried to fulfil Chandyr's barked orders. In front of him, the target tower was gone, rubble was all that remained. It had taken with it the parapets to either side. Stone had fallen clear across the street to destroy other buildings.

But there was far, far worse and the reason for Chandyr's urgent shouts became all too clear. And all Sharyr could do now was watch.

Truly the Spirits kept Tessaya alive for a greater purpose. *The* great purpose. That much was evident now. He had been blown from his feet when the first screaming lights from the sky had struck. Catapulted out of the tower doorway to sprawl in shadow under the parapet.

He had watched the Xeteskians' spell break their own walls and kill their own men even as it took brave warriors to the glory of death in battle. But he had once again been spared.

He had heard the crack of the failing walkway above him and scrambled to safety in a doorway while chaos descended. Mute, he had seen it collapse with the deaths of so many. He had seen the tower shiver and slide to the ground. He knew he shouldn't smile as the smoke and dust cleared in front of him. Indeed Riasu was surely among those dead. But in their attempts to break the Wesmen spirit, they had sealed their own dooms.

The walls of Xetesk were breached.

CHAPTER 4

His head fuzzy with the aftereffects of too much red wine, Hirad led The Raven from the college and city of Julatsa with the sun climbing high into a beautiful, clear spring sky.

He had made his peace with Ilkar. His anger at his friend's death was much diminished. It was time to move on and, despite the knowledge of their immediate destination, he wasn't sure where he wanted to move on to.

One thing he felt well able to do, though, was put as much distance between himself and the war as was physically possible. The Raven felt the same way, a feeling shared by many in Julatsa. But not all had their choice. Almost all of the elves were staying on for the time being. The threat from outside, though not as potent, was still present. And with the mage strength that much greater and the Heart beating strong once more, there was much restorative work that could now be done.

Some, though, had to return to Calaius. It was as he had surmised sitting on the steps of the college refectory the night before. Rebraal to gather together the remnants of the Al-Arynaar; and Auum to tackle the enormous task of rebuilding the TaiGethen order. With him went Duele and Evunn, ever his shadows. To complete the odd assortment came the one ClawBound pair to survive Balaia. They yearned for the touch of the rain forest and the calls of their kind. No one invited them to travel south. No one questioned them either. Hirad was just glad to have them nearby.

Their route to Blackthorne and thence to the Bay of Gyernath to await the *Calaian Sun* was of necessity going to be, initially at least, circuitous. They had decided to travel due east for a day and a half before turning south. Even then, they would have to travel carefully through the forests, what was left of them, and low hills that made up the eastern border of the mage lands. Darrick considered that even though the focus of aggression would once again fall on Xetesk, Dordovan patrols would be looking for The Raven, and Erienne in particular. And they might well be backed by Lysternan forces. Once beyond the mage lands south, they would be able to breathe more easily but that was days away.

Hirad shook his head. The Raven, hunted by those they had fought so long to save. At least ordinary Balaians would still hold them in high regard, those that even knew who they were. He let a smile cross his face. Their fame was countrywide and no doubt embellished in story and verse in places they had never even been. But he wondered how many actually knew what they looked like.

It was a question that would be put to the test later in the day. Darrick knew of a hamlet that they should reach by late afternoon or early evening. A comfortable place to sleep and the chance to buy supplies before ten days in the open was an attractive prospect. They had taken very little from Julatsa. The Gods knew the city was struggling even to feed its own people let alone groups of ex-mercenaries.

With the ClawBound pair of tall, black-and-white-painted elf and sleek black panther ranging ahead and southeast, The Raven felt able to ride in the open, making good time over easy ground. Beside them ran the elven quartet, their regular long strides conserving energy and making the pace for the horses.

The first hours of their journey were peculiar for the almost complete silence in which they were conducted. There was none of the banter Hirad associated with The Raven riding to their next job, running from enemies or returning home from a fight. In every face he saw reflection, and felt a sense of loss himself.

Erienne was deep within herself as she had been for much of the time after the battle to lift the Heart. The fact of Cleress's continued survival had been a source of great comfort but scared her more than she would admit. The elven Al-Drechar mage was instructing her even now in points of the One magic. It would mean exposing herself to more danger and Denser wasn't sure his wife was ready for it.

Erienne's introspection led Denser to the same state. He barely left her side when she was awake. And Thraun, who could sense so much more than he could say, also rode close. Hirad had joked that he'd have shared Erienne and Denser's bed if he'd been allowed. No one had laughed.

Darrick, when left alone, descended to an anger he refused to let loose in word or action. But Hirad could see it in his eyes. He felt betrayed by those he had served so faithfully. He had placed the security of his college, city and country above his own for years and they had expressed their gratitude by giving him a death sentence. Hirad knew how he felt.

Only The Unknown carried anything approaching a good mood and the big man was riding by Hirad with a half smile on his face.

"Not long now, eh, Unknown?"

"I hope not," said The Unknown. "You know when we left Herendeneth and I waved them goodbye, I didn't think I'd see them again. It seems so long ago but so little time has passed."

"Cleress has told them we're coming?"

The Unknown shook his head. "No. And not because I want it to be a surprise. It's just that until we're on board ship, I won't let them believe we'll actually make it." He turned to face Hirad. "How hard it would be to know something was so close but then have it snatched from you."

Hirad nodded. "It's your choice."

"And what about you, Coldheart? You're quiet. We've learned to worry about that. And this group could do with some more of your ill-chosen comments, I think. Not a great mood, is it?"

"That's because you don't know why, Unknown. You're heading for something. You have a target." Hirad paused. "You know how it was when we had retired at Taranspike Castle before Denser and Dawnthief buggered things up? Well, for me it's like that except I have no desire to fight. It's odd. I've got no clear idea what I want to do bar travel with you to Herendeneth but I know it's the right thing to do this time."

"So it isn't like Taranspike at all, then, is it?"

Hirad chuckled. "I don't think I said it right. I mean it's the end of The Raven, isn't it?"

"And you never thought you'd live to see the day."

"No, Unknown, I always thought I'd live to see the day, I just didn't ever know when the day would be. Funny thing, even when we were apart for those five years after we closed the noonshade rip, I somehow didn't think that was the end."

The Unknown smiled. "And now there's no prospect of anyone wanting us, is there?"

"That's it exactly," said Hirad. "I'm just not sure how I should feel."

"Let me ask you something. Was it the prospect of fame and fortune that kept you fighting?"

"At the start, of course it was. But not lately. Now it's all about being with The Raven and fighting for the people I love, dead or alive."

"And had you wanted to fade into gentle retirement or did you want to be fêted everywhere you went?"

Hirad shrugged. "A bit of both, if I'm honest. Not much chance of being fêted now though, is there?"

"Not here," agreed The Unknown. "But on Calaius they respect us for what we did. And elves have longer and better memories than Balaians, it seems."

"Think I should go and live there?"

"It's a thought. Put it this way. Our time, The Raven's time, is over. We have to face the fact that we're a little creaky, not as fast as we were. More than that, we're unpopular with Balaia's power brokers. But we've never reneged on a contract and we've never been beaten. We've preserved all that we can both here and on Calaius. We've made a difference. No one can take that from us. So I'm saying go and live somewhere you can have peace but keep in touch with your memories. The elves will provide that for you. Besides, I think Herendeneth would bore you rigid. You and Darrick both."

Hirad laughed. "Yeah, can't see us tending the gardens till we die."

"Exactly. You aren't cut out for a quiet life. Something will find you, mark my words."

"So long as it isn't sharp."

Dystran's head ached with lack of sleep. That and the sound of EarthHammers destroying every building surrounding the college for forty yards beyond the cobblestones. His familiars, those that were left, were harrying the Wesmen who had no defence against them. But they were so few and could do little more than irritate. They seemed to have lost their capacity to terrify and Tessaya—he had seen the Wesmen Lord prowling the shadows at dawn—had quickly worked out that what could not be killed could at least be caught and trapped. Already the stones and timbers of Xeteskian houses were pinning two of the thralled demons to the ground.

With the sun halfway to noon, Dystran stood on the walls of the college above the gatehouse, having just completed another circuit. Wesmen surrounded his college. Unbelievable. The spells and arrows kept them at a safe distance for now; and the CobaltFury had made them wary, but Tessaya would wait until he deemed them weak enough and attack again.

When the tower had collapsed, tearing holes in the walls, the city defence had quickly folded and terror had gripped the streets. Every soldier and mage had fled back to the college, Wesmen chasing them down. The south gates stood open, under the control of the enemy. The other gates to the city were also in Wesmen hands though they remained closed.

The city populace had nowhere to run. The Wesmen had herded them away from the gates, the spell barrage had kept them from the college and so they cowered in their homes, not knowing whether they would live or die. Dystran knew the answer. The attitude of the Wesmen had changed. The only people Tessaya wanted dead were inside the college.

Dystran turned to the duty officer standing by him.

"Marshal your spell reserves well. When he attacks, I don't want to find all my mages having to rest."

"My Lord."

The Lord of the Mount hurried down the steps from the gate tower and across the courtyard to the tower complex. Those he had ordered to provide him with their current situation awaited him in the cavernous banqueting hall. Three men, two exhausted, one in old age, awaiting his pleasure in the chill room. They sat at one end of the high table near a fire hours dead. Light streamed through the dark stained windows but provided precious little in the way of warmth. Dystran's footsteps echoed hollow as he approached them. They stood on seeing him but he waved them down impatiently, taking the steps to the platform two at a time.

"I seem to be holding such meetings with monotonous regularity," he said. He sat in his chair and laid a hand on the arm of the one adjacent, squeezing its upholstery. Ranyl's absence made the room truly cavernous.

"May I add my condolences to those of the mage community for the passing of Ranyl. He was a great man," said Chandyr, his head bandaged, an oozing cut on his left cheek.

"And I would consign him to the next life in peace!" Dystran thumped the arm of his chair.

"We will prevail," assured Chandyr.

"Will we?" Dystran snapped. "And what leads you to that happy conclusion? Our astonishing defence of our city walls or our ability to demolish our own warehouses and civic offices? Commander Chandyr, we have exchanged one siege for another and I must say that I found the former far more agreeable. More spacious. I fear that our chances for victory lie not in arms but in spells. Prexys, what of our casting strength?"

The old Circle Seven mage scratched his head and allowed a small smile to cross his face. "As Ranyl would undoubtedly have said, we have had easier times for our stamina reserves and for the security of our dimensional gateway for their replenishment."

Dystran nodded. "But he is not here, though your thoughts are welcome. How long do we have before Tessaya knows we are spent enough for him to attack?"

Prexys sighed. "He is a clever man. He probes close enough to force casting almost continually but he is not losing men at the rate we need. You know how depleted our mage strength is. We can cast at our current expenditure for another day at the most before it becomes apparent we are struggling. And with the dimensional team out of the picture temporarily, we have nothing else to throw at them except our few remaining soldiers."

"I see." Dystran sucked his lip and turned to face Sharyr. He and fifteen of the team had made it back to the college. All were resting bar him and he was fit to drop, his face not washed clean of the dust of the walls. "And why are you out of the picture, Sharyr? I would have thought a day plenty enough to ready yourselves for a decisive casting."

Sharyr's eyes widened. He shivered. "You can't ask us to do that again. You saw what happened. The alignment isn't there. We cannot contain the energy."

"They are already through the walls, Sharyr," said Dystran. "Scatter the power wherever you choose. Destruction of buildings is a small price to pay for all of our lives, surely?"

"With respect, my Lord, you don't understand."

"I understand that alignment closes with every passing heartbeat. I understand that fifteen rested men can and will cast on my command if it becomes necessary. I understand that there is no price I am not willing to pay for the survival of this college."

"Even its destruction?" Sharyr raised his voice.

"Well now, Sharyr, if it were destroyed, it would hardly survive, now would it?"

"Damn you, don't patronise me!" shouted Sharyr, shooting to his feet. "We were not enough before and we are not enough now."

"You will not—"

"There is residue where the connection with interdimensional space was made. Something of the tear remains, I'm sure of it."

Dystran paused and frowned. "What are you trying to tell me?"

"That we may have caused permanent damage, my Lord," said Sharyr, calming a little and sinking back into his chair. "And that casting again might cause us serious problems. You see, my Lord, if there is still the residue of a tear, I have no idea how to close it."

"We had a tear in our skies once before, as you will recall. It could have led to an invasion of dragons. Please tell me this is different."

"Oh, quite different, my Lord," said Sharyr. "There is no hint of a link to any other dimension at this stage. I'm just currently at a loss how to deal with it."

"Then I suggest that you rest now, Sharyr. And when you are rested, see that you investigate what you have left in my sky. I will have my spell ready, with you or without you. Because when I pay my last respects to my dear friend Ranyl tomorrow night, I will have peace and not a horde of Wesmen vermin battering at my door." Dystran smiled thinly and saw the fear in Sharyr's eyes. "I trust I make myself clear."

The village of Cuff was a settlement of probably fifty houses and farms nestled in a shallow and sheltered, tree-lined valley. Grazing animals ranged free up and down its length, crops were sprouting through fertile earth. To look at Cuff, it was clear the Nightchild storms had hardly touched it. The scene before them was at odds with much of the rest of Balaia given war and so many displaced people.

While farmers worked their land and the odd fisherman netted the free-flowing river on which the village stood, others on horseback patrolled its borders and guarded the crests of the valley east and west. Two rough watchtowers had been built, visible at either end of the village, looking out north and south along its single track.

The Raven approached at an easy trot, the elves running beside them in the late afternoon sun. The ClawBound had disappeared. Hirad's guess was they were already downwind of all the livestock and horses. In the trees to the south, hunting.

"Times are hard and people are desperate," said The Unknown. "We'd be the same. Let's tread carefully, Raven."

"What do you think about the guards? Mercenary or local?" asked Hirad.

"Soldiers," said Rebraal. "Well armed. Used to armour."

"We probably know them," said Hirad.

"That's not necessarily a good thing," said The Unknown. "Let's be prepared. Just don't look like you are."

There was a price on The Raven's capture and return to Lystern or Dordover. Probably a very high price at that.

"I'll keep my hand just far enough from my sword to be of no use if there's trouble," said Hirad.

"You know what I mean."

Hirad smiled. He glanced meaningfully at the TaiGethen moving fluidly by him. Even without their faces painted, he found it hard to imagine them anything less than fully prepared. Readiness oozed from every pore.

They watched the mercenaries gather at the head of the village to meet them. It wasn't an overtly threatening gesture but a statement of intent nonetheless.

"There are seven. Four swordsmen split two and two on horses. Three behind. Two mages, one archer," said Rebraal.

"Hirad, watch the right-hand side. Rebraal, Auum, look for others joining. I'll watch left. Thraun, back me up, Darrick to Hirad. Denser, prepare HardShield, Erienne, SpellShield."

The Unknown's words calmed them to focus. No one moved a muscle in response. No hand strayed toward a weapon yet they all had their targets. It was enough.

At twenty yards distance, a strong voice sounded out at them. In the fields and on the river, all action had ceased.

"Dismount and walk, strangers."

A moment's hesitation.

"As he says," said The Unknown. The Raven dismounted. His voice lowered to a mutter. "Mark the far left, hand to his sword. Archer is loaded and tensed. No reaction, Raven. These are not our enemies. Yet."

They slowed, the elves falling naturally into narrow order with them, sensing the threat they might otherwise pose. The Unknown brought them to a halt five yards from the first mercenary, who they took to be the leader.

"What would you have us do?" asked The Unknown.

"State your business."

"Rooming and food for the night. Stabling for our horses and supplies for the journey in the morning. We have coin for all we need."

The man in front looked them over slowly, appraising. He lingered over the elves. Hirad took the opportunity to weigh up the mercenaries. They appeared capable enough. Confident, at ease. Hirad raised his eyebrows. One of the mages was an elf. Echoes of the past.

"Food is short, costs are high," said the mercenary leader. He was a large man, carrying a two-handed sword across his back.

The Unknown shrugged. "We can cover your costs."

The leader nodded. "We'll see. Enter. Find rooms where you can though I would suggest Ferran's barns and house over there is your best bet. You'll pay in advance for everything. We don't appreciate late-night chases, if you understand me."

"Perfectly," said The Unknown. He relaxed his face. "We're no threat to you. We are just passing."

"See it stays that way. One more thing. You will not unsheathe swords in this village. We are a peaceful community."

"But it hasn't always been that way, I take it?"

The leader shook his head, indicating his men move aside to let them through before he replied.

"A lot of refugees have passed this way from the mage lands, and before them we had them from as far east as Korina and as far south as Arlen." He paused. "Not all of them would take 'no' for an answer. That's why we're here now."

The Raven led their horses into the village, angling for the indicated farm on its eastern edge. The elves followed them, their suspicion plain.

"What do you make of it?" asked Hirad.

"Well, they aren't faces I recognise," said The Unknown. "And they clearly don't know us, which is a blessing. I think we shouldn't get involved."

"I don't know," said Hirad. "I don't like the setup. Think about it. Mercenary teams are being paid very good money to fight for the colleges or side with baronial defence. This lot? How can they possibly earn enough from a place this size to make it worthwhile?"

"Ask the farmer, why don't you?" said Denser.

"I will. Let's get sorted out first though."

There was precious little space but it served them well enough. Denser and Erienne had the one empty room in the farmhouse. Ferran spread it with straw and blankets. The rest of them were given shelter in the two barns, one for grain storage, the other part stables, part hayloft. It was serviceable though the price was ruinous.

The Raven plus Rebraal gathered around Ferran's prodigious kitchen table once the horses were unsaddled and Auum and his Tai had taken their leave. Not all of them had seats but there were enough places to rest and enjoy the thick vegetable stew and tough rye bread served by Ferran's daughter, a girl barely into her teenage years but with eyes that had already seen a long hard life.

Ferran was a humourless middle-aged man. His hands were callused and split from many years working hard cold earth. His chest was a barrel and his eyes were deep set in a weathered face.

"Long journey, is it?" he ventured of his guests.

"Long enough," conceded Darrick. The ex-General still managed to look neat despite their time on the road, his young face already clean of grime and his brown curls shaken free of dust.

Ferran nodded, apparently gleaning everything he needed from the General's brace of words. "Well, it'll be a comfortable night. No trouble." His eyes glinted. "We're protected."

"So we see," said Hirad. He leaned forward, arms resting on the table, hands clasped together in front of his bowl. "Treat you well do they?"

"I'm begging your pardon?"

"You've bought their services," Hirad explained. "Are you getting what you expect?"

Ferran thought on the question, aware all eyes were upon him.

"They keep us alive," he said. "We'd been raided. Three times. They offered us protection for a consideration."

"Which is?" asked The Unknown.

"Well now that's a deal between—"

"Which is?"

Recognise him or not, no one refused The Unknown Warrior.

"They keep us alive," he repeated. "And safe. We carry on, they take the rest. It's right."

"They take *all* your profit?" Denser blew out his cheeks. "There's your answer, barbarian."

Ferran nodded.

"And no doubt food and lodging is part of the deal," said Hirad. "This is some easy deal."

"It goes without saying."

"But the war is as good as over," said Hirad. "When were you last threatened or attacked?"

"They say there is still danger," said Ferran. "They keep us alive." That sparkle was in his eyes again. "And you don't question the best."

"And that's what they are, is it?" Hirad couldn't help but smile.

"Well yes," said Ferran. He looked at them all, imploring them to understand. "Don't you recognise them?"

"Should we?"

"Of course." He stood tall. "They are The Raven."

"Oh," said Hirad, feeling his skin crawl. "Are they indeed?"

CHAPTER 5

"Hirad, sit down," barked The Unknown Warrior. "Let's decide how to deal with this."

"I'll tell you how we deal with it," said Hirad. "We go outside, call them out and take them down."

"Calm down, Hirad," said Darrick. "We can't just run out, swords waving. It's an unnecessary risk."

"It might not mean much to you, General, but these bastards are trading on our name to bleed this village dry. I will not see our reputation ruined by bandits."

Hirad's head was thumping, his body tense with the frustration boiling within him. Outside, people who believed in The Raven were being taken for everything they had when, more than ever, they needed every scrap of fortune they could lay their hands on. Perhaps their fortune was about to change. But what really made Hirad seethe was the bad taste that would be left in the mouths of these people whenever The Raven was mentioned again.

"We can't just walk out there and kill them," said Denser.

"Why not?" Hirad jabbed a finger at Ferran. The farmer and his daughter had frozen at the exchange, their mouths slack and eyes widening. Their disbelief at what they were witnessing grew with every heartbeat. "These people have been made to think that it's right that The Raven should take from them anything they want because of who they are. That's never been our way. It's a betrayal of all that we stand for. Someone needs to be taught a lesson."

"We were mercenaries too," said Denser.

"Yeah, and we were paid a fair price to fight. A good price because we were the best. People who hired us understood the rules. But this . . . this is robbery and I'm not having it."

He moved toward the door.

"Hirad, where do you think you're going?"

"I'm going to demonstrate who The Raven really are. Back me up, why don't you?"

"I know the hurt you feel," said The Unknown. "I feel it too. We all do. But we do things a certain way. That, as you are so fond of telling us, is why we're still alive. And now it's your turn to play by the rules. Sit down and listen. Whatever we do, we do as The Raven."

The Unknown didn't have to raise his voice to command complete authority. Hirad paused, nodded and returned to his seat.

They did not emerge until dusk. The last vestiges of the day's light clung to the tops of the valley but the village was cast largely in shadow. The Raven had talked while the afternoon waned, not letting Ferran light lanterns or a fire in his kitchen. They had seen the impostors patrolling the streets, still on horseback. And from the rear windows of the house had watched them trot past regularly. While not exactly prisoners, it was clear The Raven were not to be given licence to roam Cuff at will.

The leader had visited them once, to check they were settled in and to ask after the whereabouts of the elves. The Unknown had simply shrugged and intimated they had continued on southward. Without evidence to the contrary, the man had withdrawn.

Ferran had confirmed that there were indeed seven of them, the number popularly associated with The Raven. Hirad wasn't sure they had convinced him that they were the genuine article. What he did know was that the moment they left the house, Ferran was running for his neighbours to set the rumour spreading, his daughter heading in the opposite direction. They were fulfilling expectations perfectly.

The Unknown led them, Hirad to his right, Darrick and Thraun left. Erienne and Denser were behind them. The track through the village was quiet but the four men who had been paying particular attention to the farmhouse now rode in from front and back, intercepting them as they reached the street. Thraun dropped back to cover any threat from the rear.

Neither pair of riders had any presence. They were uncertain, nervous and looking to each other to make the first move. The Raven made it for them.

"Better call your leader down here," said The Unknown. "You've got a problem."

The Raven had weapons sheathed but both Erienne and Denser were ready with shield spells should the need arise. In front of them, a heavy-set man with both hands on the pommel of his saddle spoke.

"He'll be along presently, I have no doubt. Now, what is this problem we have?"

"You all need to hear what we have to say. All seven," said The Unknown.

Hirad smiled unpleasantly. "Yeah, six men and an elf. You're a little behind the times."

"Listen, you don't need to test yourselves against us," said the heavy-set man, frowning in Hirad's direction. "It isn't worth your while and we have no wish to spill your blood."

"Well, that's comforting," muttered Denser.

The second pair of riders rode around to the front of the standoff. Hirad could hear more hoof beats coming up the village. To his left, a door opened and a man ran across the street, not pausing to knock on the door of the house opposite before barging in.

"Which one are you, then?" asked Hirad of the heavy-set man.

"I am Hirad Coldheart," he said without hesitation.

"I'd heard he was better looking," replied Hirad, no humour in his voice.

"Stop it, now," said The Unknown, turning to him.

The remaining impostors rode up along the street, doors opening with regularity behind them now. The archer unslung his bow as soon as he reined in, the leader trotting calmly to the front of the group.

Looking at him again, Hirad could see immediately who he had modelled himself upon. In fact, he was surprised he hadn't already noticed, the likeness was that obvious. He supposed he just hadn't been looking. Shaven-headed, broad-shouldered and strong-faced. The two-handed blade on his back was something else that should have pricked his memories.

"Don't fancy yours much, either," he said.

The Unknown glared at him.

"What is it I can do for you?" asked his double in a passable impersonation.

"Several things," said The Unknown. He glanced around him, looked past the impostors and along the street. "Seems we've drawn quite a crowd. Good. Here begins the lesson."

"Get back to the farmhouse," said the leader.

"Be quiet," said The Unknown. "And listen. It might just save you."

The sounds of swords being pulled from scabbards echoed across the instant's silence. The Raven followed suit instantly, forming up into their trademark chevron.

"Shield up," said Denser and Erienne together.

"I suggest you lower those weapons," said the bandit leader, the only man among them whose sword was not drawn. "You will prove nothing by taking us on."

"On the contrary," said The Unknown. "We will prove what we must."

"Which is what? That you can beat The Raven?"

"No, my apparently blind double. That we *are* The Raven."

A ripple ran around the villagers close enough to hear and spread quickly to those who could not. The crowd, now more than forty, bunched and moved forward a pace. But the men, women and children still kept a respectful distance.

Hirad watched the impostors stare at them, trying to gauge if The Unknown could be telling the truth.

"Look hard," growled Hirad. "Believe."

The leader snorted, straightened in his saddle. "Look at you," he said. "Just six. One a woman. No elf. And you," he pointed at The Unknown Warrior. "A little old aren't you? And if you had heard the stories, you would have a two-handed blade. A pale imitation. It's been fun. Now it's time you left before we run you down."

"But that's the trouble with stories, isn't it?" said The Unknown, his face a mask, while Hirad felt his own burning with renewed anger. "They don't take account of the passage of time. We have not fought in line for six years and in the troubles that have followed, even we have lost friends."

"There is no elf because Ilkar is dead," said Hirad, staring down the elven mage. "No one lives on his name. No one."

"All right, Hirad," said The Unknown. "So you see the problem we have. We cannot let you simply walk away. You have taken our name and used it for profit. And that is not the worst of it. You have betrayed what The Raven stand for and believe in. We were mercenaries, not parasites."

"And you expect these people to believe that you, not we, are The Raven?"

"I don't much care who they think we are," said The Unknown. "All they need to know is that *you* are not The Raven."

His voice was pitched to carry to the villagers. Hirad heard the mutterings of conversation. The impostors' heads all turned, their anxiety rising.

"You surely don't believe them, do you?" demanded the leader.

Unexpectedly, Ferran stepped from the small crowd.

"We pay you to keep our village free of undesirables," he said. "If they are such, do your jobs. Get rid of them."

His words were greeted with assent from those around him.

Hirad grinned. "Yeah, Hirad," he said. "Take me on. Run me out of the village." He spat on the ground in front of him, enjoying the tension that grew in the space between them.

"I'll tell you what's going to happen," said The Unknown. "You're going to give back every coin you have taken from this village. You'll also leave them your horses because you are walking away from here. Your return will be to your graves."

"Not a chance," said the leader, tone dismissive but fear edging into his expression. He was eyeing The Unknown ever more closely, the doubt eating at him.

"Your alternative," said The Unknown, "is not to leave here at all. Mind you, since you're The Raven, that threat won't impress you much, will it?"

Hirad saw the band wavering. He knew why. In front of them was unshakeable belief born of fifteen years of winning. The Raven, standing quite still, did not and would not flinch. Their adversaries, even with the advantage of being mounted, were losing the battle of wills. It was what separated The Raven from everybody else. Always had.

"There is only one Raven, and you aren't it," said Hirad.

Tap. Tap. Tap.

The Unknown's blade struck the ground in front of him.

"No time to debate," he said. "Get off your horses now."

"Boss?"

There it was, the first vocal crack in the façade. The impostors' leader scowled. Then he swallowed and looked back at The Unknown, hesitant.

"You're out of time," said The Unknown. "Dismount."

Tap. Tap. Tap.

"Go," snapped the leader.

He kicked the flanks of his horse. Startled, the animal sprang forward. The Unknown reacted instantly, diving forward and left. Hirad mirrored him right, both men rolling to their haunches. The Unknown was confronted by a wall of horseflesh on the move. Two others had followed their boss and were right on top of Thraun and Darrick. Hirad surged to his feet and grabbed at the arm of the mounted man in front of him. He pulled hard.

"Mage casting," warned Darrick.

"Shield down," said Denser. And in the next instant, "Got him."

Men tugged hard on reins, horses reared and whinnied, dust was kicked into the air. Swords flashed in the dying light. Thraun roared. Metal clashed. A single arrow flew. There was a shout of pain.

Hirad kept on pulling, unsaddling the man. His horse turned sharply, its head butting Hirad, sending him stumbling. The man scrambled to his feet to face his smiling double.

"So, *Hirad*," he said, beckoning him on. "Let's see if you measure up to the real thing."

The man lunged forward, thrusting to Hirad's open side. The barbarian switched his blade between his hands, blocked the attack aside and drove an uppercut into his enemy's exposed chest.

"Didn't think so."

Hirad left him to bleed to death and turned back to The Raven, slapping the riderless horse away. From the back of the group, the elf had detached and was spurring his horse toward the gathered villagers.

"Oh no you don't," breathed Hirad and set off after him.

The mage cast, his ForceCone meeting Erienne's implacable shield. Denser's focused Orb drove him from his horse to die screaming in flame on the dry earth. Thraun and Darrick had stopped the fledgling charge of two of the group, and, like The Unknown, had hands on reins or bridles, keeping themselves out of strike range in front of their enemies' horses.

The last rider broke and galloped away to the north of the village and open ground, abandoning his comrades to their fates. The Unknown beckoned the leader down and waited while he drew his sword. Beside him, Darrick and Thraun killed effortlessly.

"Are you who you say you are?" asked the leader.

The Unknown nodded, his sword tapping again. "At least you will have faced me."

The leader brought his sword to ready. The Unknown ceased his tapping, made nonsense of his double's ponderous defence and skewered his heart. "But not for long."

Hirad sprinted through the crowd and after the elf. "Get back here, you bastard. Face me! Face Ilkar!"

He would never catch him but he ran on anyway, hoping for a slip, anything. A shadow moved against the buildings at the end of the village and leapt unerringly. The riderless horse galloped on a little way before losing momentum. On the ground behind it, Hirad saw Auum's single thrust. He stopped running, smiled and walked back to The Raven.

"What about the other one?" asked Hirad.

"Leaving one to tell the tale can't hurt."

He stooped and cleaned his blade on an impostor's clothing, sheathing it and walking toward the villagers. Hirad glanced around. So easy. So effortless.

"Not much of a security force, I wouldn't have thought," he said to Darrick.

The General, one hand pressed against his opposite shoulder, tried to smile.

"No. Can you help me with this?"

He lifted his hand. The arrow had struck him just under the collarbone. Darrick had snapped off the shaft to leave a couple of inches remaining.

"That was careless," said Hirad.

"Denser let his shield down," said Darrick. "No blame intended."

"Indeed I did," said Denser, coming to his side. "The least I can do is sort you out. Hirad, why don't you talk to our new friends or something?"

Hirad shrugged and wandered off after The Unknown. Some of the villagers were walking into the combat area, staring dumbly at the bodies and blood.

"Looks like you've got yourselves some new horses anyway," said Hirad. "Hope you don't mind clearing up. Think of it as payment."

He saw the odd nod and smile but there was wariness amongst the villagers.

"Hey," he said. "You didn't need them. And they weren't who they said they were. They deserved it. They were damaging the reputations of friends I have lost."

The Unknown was standing with Ferran. The farmer was frowning.

"And what will you do now, take their place?"

The Unknown shook his head, smiling. "We'll move on in the morning, like we said."

"Are you The Raven?"

"Does it matter?"

"We have tales to tell," said Ferran.

"Fair enough." The Unknown looked across at Hirad, who shrugged. "Yes, we are The Raven. Very different from the tales you've been told, I expect. We're tired, we're wanted by both sides in the war and all we want to do is leave Balaia and hang up our swords."

"Leave?" Ferran's eyebrows raised.

"We've done all we can," said Hirad. "And there are too many out there who will thank us by having us locked up or executed. Draw your own conclusions."

Around them, the crowd stood mute. Not quite believing what they were seeing, what they had heard, or what they were hearing right now. Hirad couldn't help but chuckle.

"None too impressive looking, are we?" he said. There was a little laughter in the crowd. On an impulse, he continued. "But we couldn't let them go. We couldn't. So many of those they were mimicking are dead friends. And I will not stand by while their memories are sullied by this sort of filth, and while the deeds of those with us now are ignored." He gestured at the corpses. One, his double, still breathed. Hirad hoped he was being heard. He continued.

"We lost Ras at Taranspike Castle, Sirendor Larn was poisoned by a Xeteskian assassin and Richmond died in Black Wings' castle. All more than six years ago now but they are the names you have been told, are they not?"

There was a murmur in the crowd. Heads were inclined. They hung on his every word.

"Yet there were so many more. Jandyr, who died on the fields of Parve; poor Will Begman, terrified from his life by the touch of a demon. Aeb, the Protector who sacrificed his soul to The Raven. And Ilkar. Ilkar who even in the act of his death, saved the rest of us. That is what The Raven is. That is who we are and what those of us who remain represent." He indicated them one by one. "Erienne; Denser; Thraun; Darrick; The Unknown Warrior. And me, Hirad Coldheart, lucky enough to have stood with them all."

He stopped, aware that he was welling up and that his voice was in danger of breaking.

"So," he said and clapped his hands together, smiling as he swallowed at the lump in his throat. "Do you have ale and wine here?"

"That we do," came a voice from the crowd.

"Good. Then anyone who wishes, join me in raising a tankard to The Raven, all of us. I'm buying."

The Unknown turned to Ferran as the crowd broke into excited conversation and set off as one to the tavern. "Is that a good enough tale for you to tell?"

Ferran nodded. "His heart speaks, doesn't it?"

"Always," said The Unknown. "Hey, Coldheart, get over here."

Hirad strode toward him and found himself enveloped in The Unknown's arms.

"Well said, Hirad. Well said."

CHAPTER 6

Tessaya ducked as another FlameOrb smashed into the rubble of a building behind him, its deep blue flame gorging on whatever wood it could find. The garish light it cast threw harsh shadows on the walls and ground around him. He ordered another attack on the gates.

Conservatively, he reckoned he had lost a third of his men to Xeteskian sword and spell; most of them when the tower and parapet had collapsed the previous night. Riasu was dead, so were at least two other tribal lords. Tessaya himself was bandaged along one arm, cut and burned in four places he could feel and probably others he couldn't.

But the belief of the Wesmen was unwavering. Here they stood, in front of Xetesk's college gates, night full around them and the defenders increasingly desperate as their strength ebbed away.

Tessaya concentrated much of his efforts on the gates though he had tribesmen all round the walls under command of their tribal lords. The tactic was simple. Hit and run. Force them to use spell and arrow. Keep them from consolidating in one place. Fear nothing. Not even the winged demons, impervious to the kiss of metal. Even they could be dealt with if the will prevailed.

Tessaya glanced right. One of the creatures was piniored beneath the rubble its masters had created. It cursed and spat, struggled and shifted. But the four warriors guarding it simply piled on more stone. It would not escape and its humiliation undermined it. Without fear as a weapon, it was diminished.

His warriors charged the gates with the battering ram they had built outside the walls of the city. An oak trunk with branches thick as a man's leg. Beside the twenty who carried the ram ran twenty more carrying thick bark shields above their heads. And beside them, archers fanned out, four on either side. And all around the walls, more teams with trunks and ladders, roared on by their tribes.

The noise of song and shout sent a thrill through Tessaya every time he heard it. It was the call of the Wesmen to victory and it filled him with joy. On the walls, the defenders responded. But as it had been with every attack through the night, they were holding back because they didn't have the spells or arrows to do anything else.

The ram clattered into the centre of the doors, his tribesmen flailing at the familiars who flew in amongst the arrows. Splinters flew, timbers groaned and the spells that strengthened the doors sparked. Arrows and rocks poured down. Three men fell. The ram reversed and simultaneously the familiars withdrew. FlameOrbs and IceWind drove into the bark shields. Warriors screamed and toppled among the fallen of earlier raids. There was no quarter here. The dead would lie uncollected.

The ram went in again and this time Wesmen archers were close enough to fire. Shafts skipped off the walls, chipped shards from the crenellations. Some found their targets. Since the zenith of the night, the defenders had not had the capacity to shield their own men with magic. It was one more indication of their weakening. And every blow of the ram, every spell they were forced into using and every arrow fired from the walls weakened them further.

Tessaya nodded, satisfied. He flexed the muscles of his thigh and felt the pull where a Xeteskian arrow had punctured it. Never send your men where you were not prepared to go yourself. But by the time he was called upon to carry the ram again, he thought the gates would already be down. Soon it would be dawn. It was fitting that the new day should see the fall of Xetesk.

He took another look at the college's seven towers, soon to be toppled. Men were gathering high up on the tallest of them. Tessaya sniffed. The air tasted suddenly sour. Xetesk's evil was about to be unleashed once more.

Dystran stood with his dimensional team. Dawn was just below the horizon. He and they had spoken at some length and watched the Wesmen cycle their forces, never giving the defenders a break. Dystran's mages were close to exhaustion, his archers were almost spent and his commander was at the end of his tether, desperate to get out and fight in the streets. Swordsmen were idle, Chandyr had said, while Wesmen went unchallenged. Dystran wanted them fresh. If this last gambit failed then every sword would be required to defend the tower complex. There was still scope for victory, but timely deployment was crucial. Dystran felt Chandyr was running on emotion, not logic.

He had argued long with Sharyr about the risk. He knew the alignment was incomplete. But the Wesmen had to be knocked back. The moment couldn't be delayed.

"Make me proud," he said to the team as Sharyr readied them for the casting.

"Either that or I'll make you dead," said Sharyr sharply.

Dystran respected his strength of belief. It made him a man with whom he could identify; and perhaps one to bring onto the Circle Seven where he could be kept more firmly in control.

"Just get started," said Dystran. "You'll be fine."

He heard the thud of the Wesmen ram on the gates once more and felt the sharp spike in the mana spectrum indicating stress on the binding spells. All around the college, spells flew out, carving lines of dark blue in the predawn sky. Fires burned in a ring and everywhere he looked Dystran could see Wesmen.

"Sharyr, if this spell only stops one thing, make it stop that damn chanting. It is as distracting as it is tuneless."

Sharyr almost smiled at that. He turned to those he could see of the fifteen that encircled the Tower and the casting began. Dystran sent a short prayer to whatever God might be listening. StormFront was a dangerous casting, barely developed and never live-tested. But it was the only one that would break the Wesmen in time. It required accurate construction, visualisation and placement. It needed the power of interdimensional space to drive it. And it needed huge mental strength to hold it while the storm coalesced. Everything went into the formation. After release, they could all stand and admire while it washed out to every point of the compass.

Dystran smiled. The situation to test the casting was ideal; the desired formation circumference was just within the boundaries of the theoretically possible; and they were surrounded by enemies. StormFront was designed for exactly this scenario. Its successful casting would complete the suite of interdimensionally powered spells and defeat the Wesmen at the same stroke. It would be a most satisfying outcome.

Sharyr was an efficient mage. No fuss. He managed his team closely. Dystran felt the pull of the mana and the order of a focused casting. He almost wished he had joined them. Almost.

The first indication of the casting was an impressive slit in the sky. Blue-edged, it appeared directly above his head and moved out to the periphery of the college where it stabilised. To begin with it was a slice of silk only a few feet long, alluring and delicate. It hardened then, taking on the shape of the spell: an arc, glimmering deep blue and ragged at its height. Abruptly, the arc lengthened. It ran away left and right, faster than the eye could follow, tracing the circumference of the college.

The circle completed. White flashed briefly in the blue mana light. The air hummed. Up on the walls, archers straightened and mages moved to standby, letting their casting constructs disperse. The Wesmen were withdrawing. Dystran didn't blame them.

The slit opened downward slowly as the StormFront coalesced. To Dystran's left and right, mages gripped the balcony rail, steadying quivering legs while the energy washed through them and they fought to first contain it and next, feed it into the casting. He heard Sharyr's suddenly ragged breathing.

"Hold on," he was urging his team. "Hold on. Breathe easy."

Inside the widening front, forks of bright blue light flashed. There was the roaring of a hurricane punctuated by the bass rumble of rolling thunder.

On its lower edge, descending fast now and almost out of sight, the front boiled and bubbled in the Balaian air, hungrily grabbing at the elements to blend with the raw power of interdimensional space.

"Holding steady," muttered Sharyr. "Focus. Focus."

The nature of the front changed slowly. It thickened. Its colour turned a deepening grey, muting the flashes within it. A wind whipped up around it. Even at this distance, it picked at Dystran's cloak. Down on the walls, soldiers hunched behind the battlements. Outside the college, Wesmen ran to the edge of the cobbles by the first rubbled buildings where their fires burned. They thought the spell was a shield but they were gravely mistaken. They had not retreated far enough.

Dystran sampled the construct. Felt its solidity and the effort of the mages keeping it secure while the forces poured in. It was the textbook shape. The casting would be a triumph. All he could do now was wait. The field strengthened further, discordant noise filling the air. The Wesmen had stopped singing.

Next to him, Sharyr stood with every muscle tensed. His forehead was damp with sweat that trickled over his closed eyes and down his cheeks. Dystran became aware of the murmuring of the casting team. Their words were barely distinguishable as they spoke to each other across the construct and used command words that opened up new pathways in the shape, closed off others or bled away excess power.

A frown passed across Sharyr's face.

"Instability. Base level. Lock it down."

To Dystran's right, a mage gasped with the effort, his teeth grinding. He swayed. Across the surface of the front, chaotic blue light surged and flashed.

"Spreading," said Sharyr. "Something's wrong. The alignment isn't firming, it's failing. How can that be . . . prepare to release."

"No," said Dystran. "Believe. Hold on for full term."

The top edge of the front rippled violently. Dystran was buffeted by a sudden howl of wind. From the opposite side of the tower, he heard a cry of pain.

"One out, one out!" called Sharyr. "Release on my mark."

Dystran pursed his lips. Before him, the StormFront bucked and twisted. Its grey colouring was shot with dark lines. Bolts of pure energy seethed across its surface or grabbed at the ground. The intensity of noise grew sharply, battering at the ears. It was the sound of a thousand dragons breathing fire.

"Release!"

A moment's pause and the StormFront surged outward, precisely as designed. An expanding wall of Balaian elemental destruction, focused and powered by the energy of interdimensional space. It would dissipate in no more than seventy to a hundred yards, minimising the risk to ordinary Xeteskians. But before it became little more than a puff of air, it would obliterate everything in its path.

Scant feet from the walls, the StormFront guttered and halted. Dystran staggered under the weight of the backwash through the mana spectrum.

"What—" he began.

It guttered again, rippled across its surface then the whole front delivered a blistering white light that scoured the night from the city in an instant. Through the patterns across his tortured eyes, Dystran saw the StormFront blink and suck back toward its starting point, the constant light casting harsh day over Xetesk. At dreadful speed, the circle wound back. The entire construct reversed until just a twinkle of blue mana light remained in the air just above and outside the college gates.

Blackness flooded the void left by the light. Dystran blinked hard, trying to shift the shapes that flowed across his vision. In monochrome, he could just pick out the sparkle of light over the gates, the fires indicating the Wesmen and, too bright to be anything other than a problem, the glimmer from the previous night's CobaltFury that had never dissipated.

Hypnotised, he watched a strand of blue emanate from the glimmer above the city walls and trace across the sky toward the college. It was pencil thin and quite steady but Dystran sensed such menace inside it that it made him shudder.

There was no sound he could hear above his own breathing and the crackle of fires and hiss of lanterns and torches. Every waking eye would be transfixed by the line being drawn above the city. Every voice was mute.

"Sharyr?" hissed Dystran. "Answers. Quickly."

"I have none," said Sharyr, his voice weary.

Dystran would have looked at him but he was reluctant to leave the spectacle. The points of light were almost joined now and the sense of foreboding growing.

"It's going to be a gateway," said Dystran. "But to where?"

"You can't be sure," said Sharyr. "It's probably just something caused by the meeting of our elements and interdimensional space." Sharyr's tone suggested he didn't believe what he was saying.

The line of light reached the walls of the college. Alien sound abruptly split the nervous quiet. From the windows of towers, open doors and shadowed recesses, familiars flew. Two dozen and more, all that remained in the college. Gone was the mischievous laughter and the chittering contempt to be replaced by hollow keening and long, high-pitched and querulous wails.

Shivering, Dystran watched their flight pattern. It was tightly formed, one leading all the others in a helical pattern around the beam of light. They dispersed back into the sky after a few turns, rising in graceful arcs before plunging back toward the college, voices changed, sounding warning and alarm.

One by one, they disappeared back where they had come but the last diverted and flew to the balcony where Dystran stood. It hovered in front of him. Dystran considered he had never seen a familiar display fear before.

"Prepare," it hissed. "Save the masters. They are come." And it dropped from sight.

Dystran's eyes snapped back to the beam.

"Oh dear Gods, what have we done?" he breathed.

Already, the first signs of panic were evident in the grounds of the college. People were running and shouting to no discernible purpose. Dystran fancied he could hear doors slam and lock. As if that would make any difference. Around him, the alignment team were pressing toward the balcony doors, eager for an escape.

"I tried to warn you," said Sharyr. "The alignment was never favourable enough for the power we had to use. A breach was surely inevitable."

"They must have been waiting," whispered Dystran.

"Ever since we first cast BlueStorm, I expect," said Sharyr. "Congratulations, my Lord Dystran. You have killed us all."

Fierce cold washed out from the beam. Teeth ached in chilled gums, hair frosted and eyes dried out and stung. Through the frozen mist filling the air, Dystran could see the beam move. Edges appeared along its length and blue light spilled out. Not the deep blue of Xetesk but the livid colour of the demon dimension.

And out they spilled in their tens, hundreds and thousands. Multiple shapes and innumerable sizes and colours. Dystran saw demons the size of small birds flit off on buzzing wings. He saw others that would tower over houses, floating. He saw tails and tentacles. He saw necks like those of dragons, the heads of disfigured men, animals and other forms totally alien. Snakelike demons shimmered in the sky, bulbous-skulled demons roared across the firmament.

Still they poured out on a wave of blue demon light. And when they had finished their cavorting, they grouped together. Four main groups and dozens of smaller ones fizzing and diving, setting off to every point of the compass, or so it seemed.

Dystran couldn't move. His mouth was dry and his body shook.

"Do something!" yelled Sharyr.

"Nothing," mumbled Dystran, gesturing uselessly. "There's nothing to do."

"Organise, damn you!" Sharyr grabbed his lapels and shook some sense back into his mind. "We have to work together or we'll all die, do you understand?"

"Yes," said Dystran. "Yes. ColdRooms. Make ColdRooms. And work. Research. We must fight. Muster in the mana bowl."

Thousands of demons descended on Xetesk. Their approach was soundless and awesome, on a wave of freezing air. Others were surely on their way to Dordover, Lystern and Julatsa. They were the centres of mana energy and life force. The jewels the demons had craved for so long.

"Go," said Dystran. "Let me face them. They will want to talk."

"Talk?"

"Yes, Sharyr. Demons always want to talk."

At the head of the advance, three detached themselves and floated toward the tower. Sharyr took the remnants of his team and fled. Dystran, his heart thrashing in his chest, his consciousness threatening to desert him, faced the new enemy. The three were monstrous. Better than thirty feet tall, they had roughly human torsos but beneath their trunks tentacles writhed. Colours flashed across their sexless bodies, rainbows chasing each other to nowhere.

"You are not welcome here," managed Dystran. "Respect the ancient laws and treaties. Return to your dimension and seal the rift you have made."

"The time of humans has passed," said one, chest rippling and writhing. The voice was deep and carried far and wide. "We rule here now."

CHAPTER 7

Hirad awoke with the sense of unease he had learned to trust. He lay where he was for a time, breathing in the rich scent of hay around him in the barn loft, seeing the rays of the dawn sun through the gaps in the planked walls and hearing the sounds of horses. Quite a number of horses.

He hurried to his feet and looked around for The Unknown. The big warrior was already standing at a small window, Thraun and Darrick by his side, looking down onto the village's single street.

"Trouble?" asked Hirad.

"See for yourself," said The Unknown. "Dordover has arrived."

Through the window, Hirad could see at least twenty horsemen in college livery. Next to them was the one impostor that had escaped the previous evening along with several villagers. They were grouped at the bottom of the path that led up to Ferran's farm and there was no doubt at all where their attention lay. While he watched, Hirad saw small bags being tossed to the impostor and each of the villagers, who were then waved away.

"They're paying our ransom," he said.

"Yeah," said The Unknown. "A little premature, don't you think?"

Hirad heard the sound of a sword belt being buckled on.

"Damn right," said Hirad. "Ideas?"

The Unknown looked out of the window once more. Hirad broke away to pull on his boots, and belt on his own sword. "Ferran isn't with them, I see. We can presume he's innocent. That means that while they know we're in his buildings they won't know who's where necessarily. But we aren't going to get to the farmhouse without being seen and I think a little surprise is what we need."

"I wonder if Denser and Erienne know what's happening."

"I don't doubt it," said Darrick. "What we have to worry about is that we're unshielded. And I disagree with you, Unknown. Surprise is not what we need. After all, we've got a little help coming."

He pointed to the left toward the southern edge of the village. Figures were racing in from the forest just beyond the last houses, disappearing into shadow to reappear far closer than they had any right to. And very much adjacent, a panther roared. The predatory sound scared the horses. A couple reared, the rest shifted, backing away. Riders began to dismount.

"Well, even if our loving couple were asleep, they aren't now," said Hirad. "Let's go, Raven, there's work to do."

Thraun hung back. "I will run with the panther one last time on Balaia," he said.

"You sure?"

The blond warrior nodded, his yellow-tinged eyes bright. Hirad didn't wait for him but led the way down the ladder to the empty horse stalls. At the barn's double doors, The Unknown halted them briefly.

"Remember, if they want to arrest us, we can talk. Buy time. Just like last night."

"I doubt they'll be as incompetent as last night," said Darrick.

"Take my lead," said The Unknown.

He pulled open the doors and strode out into the cool air of early morning. Darrick and Hirad were at either shoulder. Thraun was still inside. Not two paces into the sunlight and FlameOrbs arced toward them.

"Run!"

The Raven trio scrambled back inside, the Orbs crashing into the barn and the ground where they had been standing. Loose hay ignited, timbers flared and the ageing structure groaned and protested the impact. Fire took swift hold of the village side of the barn. It raced up the lintel where tongues licked down, daring them to attempt escape. It ate across the floor, finding ample fuel. Darrick, joined by the others, kicked a makeshift firebreak while behind them Thraun prowled, growling nervously.

"How strong are the walls d'you reckon?" asked Hirad. "You know, just in case."

"Not strong enough," said The Unknown.

Smoke fled across the underside of the roof, choking the timbers and carrying sparks to the hayloft. Already, flames threatened the thatch high above them.

"We don't have a lot of time," said Darrick.

"Patience," said The Unknown, coughing.

"Raven!" came a voice. "Surrender immediately or we'll burn you where you hide. You have—" He made a choking sound. Hirad fancied he heard a dry thud.

"Auum," said Hirad. The panther roared into the teeth of another spell detonation. Men shouted. There were running feet.

"Hirad, shoulder at the edge of the flame, we'll break through there. Roll and split outside. Don't give them a target." The Unknown sheathed his sword. "Raven with me!"

Hirad and The Unknown sprinted for the fire's edge which was advancing along the wall at frightening speed, its heat drawing sweat from their brows. The warriors launched themselves on the last pace, shoulders connecting with scorching timbers. The impact of their combined weight on weakened wood was predictable and they punched through to fresh air in a shower of sparks and splinters.

Both men rolled on the packed earth, drawing swords as they regained their feet and running at angles toward the enemy. Thraun howled and charged. Darrick moved up in their wake. From the left, the TaiGethen and Rebraal advanced carefully behind accurate bowfire that skipped off a Hard-Shield but kept its caster concentrating hard. The ClawBound were sprinting in a wide arc to reach the back of the Dordovans, their horses beginning to panic and split.

Already, one of their number lay with a shaft through his throat. Others circled and ran to defensive positions. Mages, one still on horseback, were either casting or held shields in place. The Raven's betrayers were backing off north. Hirad noted them and was just wondering if Denser and Erienne were with The Raven when the Xeteskian announced that he was.

Two focused columns of HellFire speared down from the clear sky. Rich blue and targeted at two standing mages, they struck with unstoppable power. A shield flared briefly orange and collapsed. Beneath it the two victims vaporised, not even having the time to scream.

"Let's take them, Raven!" yelled Hirad, changing the angle of his run to strike the centre of the demoralised and confused Dordovan force.

Thraun was past him on the next heartbeat, leaping to take the remaining mage from his horse. Blood fountained into the air and his horse bolted.

"They're open!" shouted The Unknown. "Keep firing!"

Arrows flew. Two men were struck. From behind, the ClawBound elf strode in and buried his fingers deep into the face of a terrified conscript. His panther was by his side.

Half the remaining Dordovans turned to run and found themselves facing The Raven. Hirad was in no mood for games. The man in front of him recognised him and had all but resigned himself to death before Hirad struck. He raised a guard. Hirad stepped inside it, blocked away the sword arm with his left and buried his blade deep into the Dordovan's gut, driving up under the rib cage. Blood exploded from his mouth, spattering Hirad's face. The barbarian dragged the blade clear, turned to find his next opponent and crashed a fist into his face above his sword guard. The soldier staggered back. Hirad paced after him, punched him again, square on the chin. The soldier's sword dropped from nerveless fingers. Hirad growled and sliced out his throat.

Darrick had already downed two men who mistakenly thought him the easier target, while beside them one hapless soldier had met the full force of The Unknown's sword and had been all but divided in two at the midriff. The sword had caught in his splintered ribs. The Unknown struggled to drag it clear, another soldier closing on him, looking to carve himself a piece of history.

"Your right, Unknown," called Hirad, blocking away a quick attack from one of a duo he faced.

The Unknown swung round, straight-punched the soldier on the nose with his right fist, paced in and butted him hard. The man stumbled backward and The Unknown finished him, driving his blade deep into his gut.

Hirad pushed away his closest attacker and backed off a pace, smiling.

"Shame for you," he said. "Because you'll never know what hit you."

In front of him, the soldiers hesitated. And Auum's Tai hit them with a speed that made Hirad gasp. Duele kicked head high, snapping the neck of one man, Auum and Evunn scything into the legs and chest of the other. Hirad looked about him. It was over. The one remaining impostor leaped onto the back of a horse and kicked it into frenzied action. His limbs flailed as he urged it desperately toward a gallop.

"Not this time," said Hirad. "Thraun!"

The wolf looked up from the throat of a victim, blood covering his muzzle.

"The rider!" Hirad pointed. "Quickly. Betrayer!"

Thraun barked once and set off, the panther quickly at his side. The impostor looked over his shoulder and screamed at his terrified mount for more speed. But instead of that, all he got was a stutter and a half turn on the gallop. Thraun closed the distance quickly, nipping at the animal's heels. It kicked out and bucked and in the same instant the panther leaped high and bore the impostor from his saddle. Fangs ripped and tore.

Hirad looked away. Straight into the eyes of one of the village betrayers.

"You," he breathed and began to advance.

All five of them were in a group twenty yards from the fighting, all set to run.

"Reckon you can outrun the wolf or the panther, boy?" snarled Hirad at one, a youth of no more than sixteen, freckled and ginger haired. Urine coursed down his legs. "Don't you move a fucking muscle."

The villagers froze, caught between the advancing barbarian and the knowledge of the two wild animals behind them.

"Hirad," warned The Unknown. "Don't you do it."

"Do what?" asked Hirad, not breaking stride.

"You know what I'm talking about."

"Damn you, Unknown, you know me better than that." He dropped his sword to the ground, unbuckled his sword belt and dropped that too, complete with its sheathed daggers. He stopped and turned, arms outstretched. "All right now?"

"Still hardly a fair contest," said The Unknown.

"There isn't going to be a contest."

Hirad marched up to the five men. They all looked so small though at least two were bigger than he was. Strong farmers and farmers' sons. But where it mattered, they had no strength at all.

"I don't know," said Hirad. "I really don't."

He stood close to them, looking from one to another in turn, seeing scared eyes beneath shamed brows. He could barely control the fury coursing through his body. The Unknown had been right to make sure he was disarmed.

"I would cut you all down and piss on your rotting corpses but it would be a waste of my edge and my water."

He saw them cower and it gave him no pleasure. He struggled to understand what they had been prepared to do. These were ordinary Balaians. His people. The people he had been fighting forever since the discovery of Dawnthief more than six years ago.

Hirad pointed at one, a broad-shouldered man with a thick thatch of unruly brown hair and a long nose.

"I drank with you last night. We bought each other ale. Exchanged names. And you." He jabbed the freckled youth's chest, forcing him to back up a pace. "You pestered me all night for stories."

He shook his head sadly.

"And I told you everything you wanted to hear and every bit of it was true. And did you count the number of times The Raven stood against the enemy and saved your lives? We'd never met you and still we wanted you to live.

"That's honour. That's wanting what's best for the people of your country. We spent six years fighting battles we didn't start to give you the chance to grow your crops and tend your cattle.

"Yet you meet us for one night and decide to help another man betray us."

His voice, carrying strongly, rose to a shout as his control finally broke.

"My friends died for you!" he stormed. "Saving you so you could turn round and sell us for a few pieces of fucking coin."

Hirad bit back bitter tears.

"If you ever had an elven friend and he's alive today, that's down to The Raven. You are not a pile of dragon-fired ash because of The Raven. Because the Wytch Lords don't own your souls, you should be thanking The Raven. And my friends died in that time. Ilkar the last of them. A sacrifice to stop those who would dictate how you thought about magic.

"You are free because of us. Yet you would sell us. For how much, eh? What's in those purses of yours? What are The Raven worth?"

They fidgeted, looked to one another. Like last night, the village had assembled to see the spectacle. Hirad held out his hand.

"Show me. Now."

The youth fished in his pocket and dropped a small purse in Hirad's palm. The barbarian eyed him meaningfully and poured the contents into his other hand. A few gold coins. Little real value in today's market where produce was king. He emptied them onto the ground.

"I could multiply that by five and still it would come to bugger all, wouldn't it? That's the price you put on everything The Raven have done for you is it? The price you put on Ilkar's death?"

The youth didn't see the left hook that laid him flat. Hirad rounded on the four still standing.

"Purses. Now. On the ground."

They hesitated.

"You were paid a reward. But unless you are planning on arresting me yourselves, I suggest you hand it over. You have not completed your contract."

A second hesitation was ended by a significant growl from Thraun who had padded up silently behind them. With great reluctance, hands reached into pockets. Four purses clinked to the ground. Hirad kicked them away and turned at last to face the villagers. To the left, Ferran's barn, wrapped in flame, began to collapse. Smoke boiled into the air.

"We didn't ever demand much. Payment for our services. Sometimes not even that. Mostly we just wanted a country where we could all live in peace.

"What you do with these behind me is up to you but personally I wouldn't be happy if they were part of my village. They are barely part of the human race. The money we'll take, barring what Ferran will need to rebuild his barn."

He turned to walk back to The Raven but a final thought struck him.

"You know the thing that really makes me sick to my stomach? It's the fact that next time Balaia is threatened, the same people who betray us today will call for us to help them. Well, we won't be hearing you. Perhaps you'll think on why that is before the enemy kills your children in front of you. Find yourselves some new heroes. Because we're leaving and we won't be coming back.

"The Raven will not ride again."

Dawn's light had brought little real respite in Lystern. The demons had flooded through the city and into the college two hours before. Heryst had lost a third of his mage strength then and there, their life energy and souls feeding their attackers; their deaths mere prelude to lingering purgatory if the myths were true.

Heryst and the council had reacted smartly and enough mages were holed up in the great council chamber to keep a ColdRoom casting going almost indefinitely. The spell, which banished mana from within it, was their only effective defence against the mana-based demons which quickly suffocated without it. Any that tried to attack within the ColdRoom were easily dispatched because swords were also affected by the spell and carried no mana in their steel.

Heryst, Lystern's Lord Elder Mage, prayed for the souls of any not within similar sanctuary. He could not Commune from within the ColdRoom. Mana would not coalesce. Indeed the only strands of mana were those that led from the five casting mages that fed the spell construct.

Latterly, the demons had seemed content to walk or float just outside the transparent spell. It was enough to keep the one hundred and sixty-three mages, soldiers and assorted college staff on edge. Heryst knew he couldn't let the situation stagnate. He could feel the anxiety in the chamber and sense all of them begin to add up the practical problems they faced.

He squeezed the arm of his most trusted aide and friend. A man who he was so pleased to have with him now.

"Kayvel, it's time to get organised. Check on the casting team will you?"

Kayvel smiled through his own fear and climbed onto the council table. The casting team, surrounded by swordsmen, were in its centre, as far from accident as was possible. Heryst watched Kayvel walk rather awkwardly across the intricately designed wood and kneel by the team to exchange soft words.

"People," said Heryst, clapping his hands and stilling the quiet hum of conversation. "Let's gather ourselves. Over here, please. We've got work to do."

He could see it so clearly in all their faces. From the most senior mage to the youngest serving girl or kitchen lad. Incomprehension edged by terror. Loss. The war had been hard enough though it had never touched them. But this. Most of these people had gone from knowing about demons only from text and story, to the staggering certainty that nothing would be the same again. And that everything they had known and taken for granted was gone. Heryst had worse news for them.

He waited while they assembled. Every eye was on him, needing him to help them find a way back. If they could only but sample the desperation he felt. Too much knowledge could sometimes be considered dangerous. But he felt that he had to tell them what they were up against. But first, a little balm.

"We are safe here," he said. "I know you don't all understand what we have created but, as you have seen, it keeps the demons at bay and those who try to breach it are easy targets. Remember that because it is as good as our position gets."

A murmur went round the crowd in front of him.

"There are things you have to know. And because I need you all if we are to survive, I will not hide anything from you. Outside this spell, we cannot fight them for any length of time. Though they are vulnerable to spells, they will barely be harmed by swords because of the mana in the air and over everything."

A hand went up. It was a young girl that Heryst recognised. She was attached to the staff of the tower kitchens. In her early twenties, dark haired and slim built.

"Please my Lord, I don't understand. What are these things?"

Heryst smiled. "I'm sorry, yes, let's start at the beginning. I'll be brief though so anything you don't quite get, ask a mage later. Mages, you will answer all these questions. This is no time to feel you are somehow above helping ordinary Lysternans.

"These demons are from a dimension other than our own. We have had contact with them for many hundreds of years. Enough to know that they covet our land because of its richness and the vitality of life here. Demons need mana in the atmosphere in order to breathe and maintain their natural armour and that is why we are cocooned in the ColdRoom spell. But they live on the life force of other creatures. You'd call that their souls, I guess, and it is as good a word as any. They can drain your soul in an instant or feed off it over the course of years. They can choose to keep you alive while they drain you. It would be a drawn-out death. And we understand that the souls of those they take can be kept in existence in their own dimension, stimulated by pain to pulse out life for years."

He paused and looked around the room. Tears were running down the cheeks of men and women alike. He saw others shivering. And yet more looking to the edges of the casting, into the corridors beyond the council chamber where demons hovered. A hand was raised. Heryst nodded for the soldier to speak.

"Can we beat them back?"

Heryst shrugged. "I don't know. I have to say I have my doubts. We can only guess at the numbers they have in the city and beyond. Fighting them one to one is probably not worth it. What we have to do ultimately is find out where they are coming from and literally close the door."

"How are we going to do that stuck in here?" shouted someone.

Heryst held up his hands. "Calm, please. That is why we are talking now. Here is what I want us to consider. First, the practical. We have no food, water or latrine facilities and we have to work out ways to get them."

"My Lord Heryst," said Kayvel. "I can partially solve the latter."

Kayvel's voice was like a cool breeze over hot skin. Heryst smiled. "Then let us hear you. I have managed only to depress people so far."

A fractional easing of the tension was evidenced by the odd chuckle.

"The spell's coverage is a little wider than we thought. It does cover the latrines beyond the north doors. Only just, but it does nonetheless."

"Thank you," said Heryst. "But it isn't enough for a long-term siege in here. They will fill and we have no way of clearing them. But for now, it is a piece of genuinely good news. As soon as I've finished speaking, Kayvel, who I am putting in charge of soldiers and nonmages, will organise a rota. No one is to visit the latrines without an armed guard. Remember, the demons will watch our every move and try to counter it.

"Right, food and water. We all know where our stores and wells are. The question is, how do we reach them without being taken by the demons? Mages, I need you to work out if it is possible to effect a moving ColdRoom. Kitchen and cleaning staff, identify every place where there is a bucket, a basin, a barrel . . . anything we can use to carry food, water, clothes, bedding up here. Assume we are going to be here for some time while we decide how to strike back. When Kayvel is ready, he will hear what you know.

"Any questions?"

"My Lord?"

"Yes, Oded, speak up," said Heryst to the young council mage.

"Thank you, my Lord," he said. "Do you think we can expect any help from the outside?"

Heryst noted the concentrated gaze of all present on him. It was a hope to which all had been clinging.

"No, I don't think we can," he said quietly. "I'm sorry. I'll come back to why in a moment but before I forget, Oded, I want you to take a team of three and think hard about how we can communicate. I know there is no Communion from within the ColdRoom but consider this. There are strands of mana feeding the ColdRoom construct. Is there any way you can piggy-back those to reach the mana spectrum? And if so, what can you do when you get there?

"Now, back to your question. We don't yet know where the demons are getting into the Balaian dimension but we were attacked from the north. I suspect Xetesk was the focus. But we have to assume that the demons have attacked all colleges, and other centres of population will no doubt follow in due course. If we're lucky, mages in all the colleges have gathered together like we have. Elsewhere on Balaia, I fear for our people, I really do.

"I expect that at some stage the demons will make their plans known. Whoever is leading them in Lystern will come here and want to talk to me.

That is when we will perhaps know the extent of what we face. But we have to face facts.

"The demons control Balaia."

With a growing sense of incomprehension, Tessaya and the Wesmen had watched the events taking place in the air above Xetesk. They had watched the line being drawn in the sky and had seen the extraordinary creatures spill out of it like entrails from a slit gut. With a collective furrowed brow they witnessed them group up and fly off to all parts of Balaia. None, he noticed, directly toward the Blackthorne Mountains. Tessaya had gathered his men as it became obvious that the threat from Xetesk's defence had gone in the face of whatever it was that attacked them. He didn't want any of his people anywhere near it.

Initially, the Wesmen had cheered and sung as the creatures in every possible hue, and on a tide of purest blue light and cold, attacked within the walls. Spells had flashed and flared into the predawn sky. But so quickly, it had quietened. The songs had died in their throats and all they could hear were the occasional shouts of men, the swish of a thousand bodies swooping in the air, and the shuddering sound of Xeteskians screaming and wailing. It was a sound that would live with him forever. He had heard frightened men before but this was something so much worse. Like the opening of a gulf into unending despair.

He was at a loss. To all intents and purposes, Xetesk's new enemy had done their work for them. That should have made them an ally. But Tessaya was not about to offer his hand to any of those that he saw and that still emerged from the slit in the sky, scattering through the city and the lands beyond.

Not one of them had shown the slightest bit of interest in the Wesmen gathered outside Xetesk's college gates. And for that he was glad. Because something was badly astray with what he was seeing. This wasn't the work of mages. The cold in the air was unnatural and it smelled bad. And there was an evil in the way the creatures moved and attacked, in the way they sounded and in the cries of the Xeteskians as they died, if die they did.

Part of him wanted to remove his men from the area, return to the Heartlands. But in all truth he could not. He refused to turn and run from the new invaders; and indeed felt that would be futile, so fast did they travel. Far more than that though, he was in sight of realising the dream of the Wesmen. To throw down the Towers of Xetesk. Their defiance had been comprehensively broken but what had replaced it was clearly a power of considerable strength.

For the first time in many years, he did not know what he should do. So he waited. Waited while the noise died to a whisper within the walls and the screams that had echoed through the city had ceased. And while the chill in the air deepened, the glow of blue light from the slit in the sky spread and the sense of evil pervaded the walls behind him and the mind of every warrior standing with him.

They spoke in low tones, sang tribal songs and stared at him and the college. He knew they were scared but not one would run, not even in the face of an enemy they had no idea how to fight.

"My Lord, look!" shouted a warrior.

A renewed hush fell over the two thousand. From behind the college walls arose six of the creatures. One, huge, half as tall as the walls and truly awesome, was at their head. It had the body and head of a man but was tentacled from the waist down. The tentacles wavered like an anemone, propelling the creature through the air. Those grouped around it all had wings, tails and flat features in cold dead faces. All of them were hairless and had adopted blue colouring though flashes of reds and greens rippled across their flesh.

Tessaya drew his blade and gripped it hard.

"Don't flinch," he shouted. "We are the Wesmen. We fear nothing."

He heard his words shouted back at him and he nodded, a fierce smile cracking his features. He watched the creatures which approached fast, on a wave of cold. The giant one settled onto its tentacles in front of him. It was completely odourless.

"We are the new masters here," said the creature. "You will submit to our rule. You will not bear arms and you will offer all your subjects for sacrifice. We will take as we please. It is the way."

"No one rules the Wesmen. We will fight you and we will prevail."

Tessaya struck out with his blade. He saw the sword cut deep, he felt the resistance of the creature's flesh, but when he ripped the blade clear the wound healed while he watched. Pain flickered momentarily across its face.

"You cannot fight us," said the creature. "You will be the first. Your people will learn to respect us. There is no other way."

The creature reached out and touched Tessaya above the heart, gripping. A frown creased its face. It pushed harder. Tessaya stumbled a pace and was pushed back upright by the men behind him.

"What is this?" hissed the creature. "Your soul is mine. All your souls are mine."

Tessaya laughed loud and in its face.

"Demons." He spat on the ground, recollecting the Easterner word from the stories and rumours. "Do you really know so little? You cannot touch the Wesmen. The Spirits protect our souls."

"Then we will break the Spirits before we break you."

"It is a battle you cannot win."

The demon stared at him for a moment, turned and floated away back to the college. An uneasy calm fell over the Wesmen. Tessaya looked back to the towers of Xetesk.

They were clever, these Xeteskians. The demons were susceptible to magic but stamina for offence was finite and the enemy had overwhelming strength. But they had worked out quickly what it was the demons feared and had set it in front of them as a barrier. And for all their force of numbers, the demons respected it and had backed off.

Whatever the casting was, demons died within it and so remained outside of it. There had been very few times in his life when Tessaya had wished he understood magic but this was one such. He envied the potential it gave them and he was filled with a curious impotence. The fact was that these Easterners could kill the demons, or damage them at the very least, while he with all his passion and strength could not.

The sun was dipping behind the towers before he had seen enough. There came a moment when the barrier had sapped the wills of the demons for the time being and they had turned their minds to the recently enslaved populace. Tessaya had no desire to join them.

"The mages will not die easily or quickly," he said to his nearest lieutenant. "Our opportunity for today has passed."

"And perhaps forever," said the warrior.

"There will be other days and the demons fear us," replied Tessaya. "But for today, we are finished. Call the tribes. We will withdraw. The city belongs to the demons."

"Camp at Understone?"

Tessaya nodded. "But with a forward camp within sight of the walls. We must not lose touch. Something extraordinary is happening. Sound the fall-back."

Dystran watched the Wesmen go and felt deserted. The ColdRooms deterred the demons for now but he needed his every ally and his erstwhile enemy had surely become one.

They had something, they must have. Because the demons didn't, or more likely couldn't, take their souls. Dystran was damned if he knew what it was. But their departure marked the passing of the last vestige of what could laughingly be described as normality on Balaia.

He wondered what they would do. How far they would go. However far, it would not be enough. Strange. He almost felt sorry for Tessaya. Know it or not, the Wesmen lord's fate and that of all his tribes depended on whether magic survived. Another day, he would have laughed at the paradox. Today, though, he had lost his city and most of his college. His mages and soldiers had died and those that remained were few and scared.

Never mind Tessaya, he had to get his devastated people through just one more day. And then the next.

"Gods, Ranyl, how I need you now."

But Ranyl, like so many, could not hear him.

Chapter 8

"Ilkar!"

Hirad sat bolt upright in his bed, the sweat pouring from him. He was soaked in it. Just like in the early days of his life on Calaius. But this was nothing to do with acclimatisation. His heart was pounding so hard his throat hurt and he was quivering all over. He rubbed his hands over his face and into his hair. He closed his eyes briefly but the images replayed and he couldn't control his breathing.

With a shiver playing down his back, he swung his legs from the bed and stood on the matting. He heard voices elsewhere in the house and craved their company. In two years he had learned enough elvish to get by. In fact it was a language he enjoyed and these days when Rebraal visited the village, the two of them spoke more in the elf's tongue than Hirad's.

He pulled on a shirt and loose trousers and walked out of what had once been Ilkar's room in his parents' house, heading for the veranda and what he hoped would be friendly faces. Outside in the cool but still humid air deep in the Calaian rain forest, Rebraal and Kild'aar, a distant aunt by some means Hirad couldn't quite understand, were sitting and talking. Drinks steamed gently on a table between them. A fire burned in the pit in front of the house, smoke spiralling into sky that was clouding for more rain.

It was the middle of the night. Out in the rain forest, the noise of life and death went on as it always did. The air smelled of rain and fresh vegetation. Hirad sat on one of the three other swept-back chairs on the veranda, feeling the weave shift to accommodate his broad shoulders.

"I'll get you some tea," said Kild'aar, levering herself out of her chair and walking slightly stiffly down the steps to the fire pit.

"Your shouting eventually woke you up too, did it?" said Rebraal, a smile touching his lips.

"I'm sorry," said Hirad.

Rebraal shook his head. "Tell me. If you want to."

"I've felt the same thing a few nights but not with this—uh—sorry Rebraal, I don't have the words." He switched into Balaian. "This intensity. It's like someone's been battering on the door and now finally they've broken it down."

"Ilkar?" asked Rebraal.

Hirad shrugged. "Well, yes. Daft I know. I still miss him, you know."

"What have you seen?"

"Oh, that's hard to say." Hirad pushed his hand through his hair, feeling the lank braids and the moisture left on his hands. "I know it's him but I can't quite make him out. His essence, I can feel that so clearly. Everything that made him. And I fill in the smile and those damned ears myself. But he's in trouble. That's why the dream is so bad. I got the feeling he was running but I don't know where. That something was close that scared him. And though I reached out, I couldn't help him. He was always just beyond my grasp and my vision.

"Huh, speaking it makes it sound lame. Not scary at all."

Kild'aar came back up the steps and handed him a mug of the herb tea that Ilkar had been so fond of. Deprived of coffee for more than a year now since his supply had run out, Hirad had developed a taste for the sweet aromatic teas of the elves. He'd had no choice really. The trade to Balaia had gone. No ships had come from the northern continent for three seasons now. Part of him worried about what that might mean. Most of him was glad they didn't trouble to make the journey. There was only one man on Balaia that Hirad missed and Blackthorne had never relied on trade with the elves so he would be unaffected. And Jevin, the last time he'd seen the elven skipper, had said he preferred not to sail north anymore. He didn't say why.

"Thank you," he said, once again speaking elvish. "I'm sorry I woke you."

Kild'aar waved away his apology and sat down, her eyes on Rebraal. "You haven't told him yet?"

"We hadn't got round to it," said Rebraal.

"Hadn't got round to what?" asked Hirad.

"You didn't wake us," said Rebraal. "Or at least, not me."

"So you were having a late night, so what?"

"So I've had the selfsame dream," said Rebraal.

"I beg your pardon?" Hirad felt cold despite the humidity of the night and clutched his mug tight between his hands.

"I have felt him too. He was your good friend. He was my brother."

"Yeah, I know, Rebraal, and we've laughed and cried about him a good few times these last couple of years but, you know. . . . He's dead, and there's nothing we can do about that."

"No, we can't. But that doesn't mean we can't help him."

Hirad felt a growing unease. Rebraal and Kild'aar were both staring at him too earnestly. He frowned.

"You've lost me completely." He knew his tone was a little sharp but he was tired and this was just riddles. "That's the trouble with dead people. It's too late to help them ever again."

"Hirad," said Kild'aar softly and leaned forward to cover his hands with hers where they were locked around his mug. "I know it hasn't always been easy for you here and that we, at least in the beginning, did not make it easy for you at all. But we have always respected why you wanted to come here. We know of your love for Ilkar and your desire to learn the ways that made him what he was.

"And you and your Raven will always be friends of the elves because of your actions in stopping the Elfsorrow. Rebraal calls you a brother and Auum, well, Auum let you run with the TaiGethen for a season, didn't he? And that is respect no human has ever had before."

"He still said I was slow and deaf and blind, though," said Hirad, smiling in spite of himself and the increasing feeling he was going to hear something he didn't want to.

"You will always be human," said Rebraal. "Some things not even Auum can teach you."

"Tell me about it," grumbled Hirad. "Never give me a jaqrui again. I think I scarred Duele for life."

"The point is this," said Kild'aar, stilling Rebraal's next retort with a sharp glance. "Though we trust you, there are those facts about us that you as a human should never know. Secrets that could be used against us. We have already seen what humans do with such knowledge."

"Not me, Kild'aar. Never me."

"I know, Hirad," said Kild'aar, releasing his hands so he could drink. "Even so, we are only telling you this because you have had the dream and that makes you closer to us than we could ever have thought possible. It makes you family."

"Telling me what?" Hirad took a long sip of the tea.

"The dead of an elven family are never truly lost," said Rebraal. "We can always hear them if they need us."

Hirad felt a thrill through his heart. "And can you talk to them?"

Kild'aar's smile extinguished his hope. "It isn't communication as you would understand it because the dead do not exist in any way you can conceive. But messages can still be passed. It is one of the purposes of the temple at Aryndeneth."

"The Al-Arynaar have been the keepers of this secret too," said Rebraal. "No other order can hear the dead. We learn it over years, decades. And even then it is difficult and uncertain."

"What do they ask you? Why would they need you?"

"That is a difficult question to answer," said Kild'aar. "Elves make life bonds of incredible depth and often the transition to death is difficult. The dead seem to have moments of clarity amongst so much else we cannot guess at. They seek support if they feel lost. News of loved ones. They impart knowledge they had no time to speak when they were alive. You must understand that any communication that comes through is broken and sometimes all but incoherent. The dead no longer have the rules that guide us."

"All right," said Hirad carefully, trying to take it all in. "But that doesn't explain one thing. How come I heard him tonight, if indeed I did?"

"Oh you heard him, all right," said Rebraal. "But you shouldn't have been able to and that is what is worrying us. I shouldn't have been able to do any more than sense him outside of Aryndeneth."

"So didn't you ask him what's going on?"

"I couldn't. It was like he was shouting for anyone to hear him, to help him. Anyone with a connection as strong as family. Hirad, other Al-Arynaar have had this same dream in the past days . . . this same contact I should say. But no one can communicate at the temple. Something is wrong in the world of the dead. Something is threatening them."

Hirad made to speak and then stopped, at a loss. He sat back in his chair. "What can threaten someone who is already dead?"

"We don't know," said Kild'aar, sharing a guilty glance with Rebraal. "Or at least, we aren't sure."

"Well we'd better find out and fast," said Hirad. "We've got to help him."

Hirad was half out of his chair before Rebraal's hand on his shoulder pushed him back down.

"That's why we're talking to you now. It might have been better in the light of day but since you are awake, now is the right time." Rebraal levered himself out of his chair, took all three mugs and jumped lightly down to the fire pit around which insects buzzed and died. "There are other elements to this which are too convenient to be coincidence."

"Like what?"

"The lack of trade from Balaia. I don't think you've thought why it's happened. Despite the war, it was beginning to pick up before we left to come back here two years ago. But it stopped abruptly. Merchants who travelled north didn't return. Elven vessels have reported seeing lights in the sky and felt a sense of wrong that no sailor will ignore. Ship's mages think they have felt the edges of Communion, but faint and desperate. That's why they won't land."

"Don't expect me to cry if they've managed to destroy Balaia. We did what we could. Everything they suffer they have brought on themselves."

"The Al-Arynaar who stayed to help Julatsa have not returned. We sent others north a year ago to find out why and they are gone too but we can't sense any of them among Shorth's children."

"Who?"

"Shorth's children is the name we give to the dead. He looks over them."

"I thought he was a figure of fear," said Hirad.

"Only to those who are our enemies," said Kild'aar. "A god of the dead is not necessarily vengeful on his own people. Ours is benevolent to those who serve our people well in life."

"I'm sorry for those you may have lost in Julatsa," said Hirad. "But it sounds to me like the college has fallen. Either to Dordover or Xetesk, it makes little difference."

But both Rebraal and Kild'aar were shaking their heads.

"Something else you're not telling me?"

The two elves exchanged glances. Rebraal motioned the elder to speak.

"In our mythology there is the belief that the dead face an enemy from whom they were sheltered in life. That death is a constant battle to achieve peace and sanctity of the soul. It is a belief shared with those on your continent Rebraal tells me, you call the Wesmen."

"I wouldn't put yourselves in the same arena as them. Hardly worthy," said Hirad.

"Do not scoff at what you do not understand," said Kild'aar sharply. "They have a link to Shorth's children, this is certain."

"Oh, come off it. That's all just primitive beliefs."

"At least they have beliefs!" snapped Kild'aar. "That is the problem with humans. You have denied the teachings of generations and lost your religion and now it is coming back to haunt you. But like with everything you people do, you don't think. And once again, you bring us trouble. This time to our dead."

"Gods burning, Kild'aar, calm down," said Hirad. "You're blaming me for things I have no control over. Just tell me how I can help, that's all I need to know."

"You need to know what all this is based on," said Kild'aar.

"No I don't," said Hirad. "Learning and me never went well together. Ilkar would tell you just to point me at the problem and tell me how to deal with it."

Rebraal chuckled. "He's right of course. But so is Kild'aar, Hirad. Look, this is what you need to know. You understand dimensions, you know the dragons have one and we have one. So do the dead, that is our belief, or else where do they go? No, don't answer that. I'm not suggesting we could ever go there, it is hidden. But there are creatures who travel space and feed off the very thing that all creatures alive and dead hold. Life force, soul, call it whatever you want. Such is our belief."

"You're talking about the demons," whispered Hirad, a chill stealing across him.

"If that is what you call them," said Kild'aar.

"We need Denser and Erienne," said Hirad. "They would know what to do."

"I think we will need the whole of The Raven. I have already taken the liberty of calling Thraun from the ClawBound patrols and messengers have been sent to Ysundeneth to find Darrick," said Rebraal. "I'm sorry, Hirad, but for such as yourself, there doesn't seem to be any peace. Not forever."

Hirad shrugged. "But can even we do anything? I don't understand, how can we help Ilkar?"

"We aren't sure," said Kild'aar. "And it will involve all of us. Humans, Wesmen and elves. But there is something about The Raven that burns brighter than life. Together, you can achieve that which as individuals you cannot. That none of us can. I can't explain it. But Rebraal and Auum have seen it and all who meet you can feel it. If we are right the task is immense, perhaps impossible, but we must attempt it."

"You aren't telling me anything I don't know already. What I don't know is what The Raven can do. Besides killing ourselves and standing by Ilkar, that is. So I'll tell you what I'll do. I'll travel to Herendeneth with Thraun and Darrick if they want to go. The Raven will talk and we will decide. That's our way."

"It is all we ask," said Kild'aar.

Hirad nodded. "You know, I've understood almost nothing of what you have said and I'm finding it hard to believe the rest. But I do know what I dreamed and if you say that means Ilkar is in trouble somehow, I will not rest until he is saved, whatever it takes. But first, I'm going to return to my bed, talk to Sha-Kaan. Perhaps he can explain it to me."

"The dragons would be a useful ally," said Rebraal.

"They call the demons 'Arakhe,' you know," said Hirad, getting up and placing his mug on the table between them. "What do you call them?"

"'Cursyrd,'" said Kild'aar. "The robbers of life."

"We should start first thing in the morning. Will Thraun be here?"

"Yes," said Rebraal. "Hirad. Thank you."

"I'm not doing this for any of us. Not for Balaia or Calaius. I'm doing it for Ilkar because he is Raven and he needs us." He laughed, surprising even himself. "You know it's incredible. What is it about that elf? Even dead, he can't keep out of bloody trouble."

Chapter 9

Thraun had heard the ClawBound communication and knew it concerned him. He had spent the last days running as a panther's shadow while she worked. Her partner had welcomed the wolf and together they had shown him so much of the ways of the forest and he had learned to love it again.

Two years and the only other man he had seen in that time had been Hirad. He missed the barbarian sometimes but in the rain forest, away from all the prejudices of man and the memories of the pack, he had learned to understand himself just as he slowly understood the ways of the ClawBound.

Nothing was quite as alive as the Calaian rain forest. Its sights, smells, joys and dangers. He had thrilled to hunt as a wolf and delighted in tracking as a man. He spoke the language of the panther, knew the signs of the Claw-Bound elves and spoke easily with Al-Arynaar and TaiGethen. He had never felt more at peace with himself in either form.

He knew why he had been accepted so easily where Hirad, for all his strengths, had struggled for three seasons at least. It was because he was not pure human and because he was looking for a new way to live and had an innate understanding of the ways of the forest. Hirad tried hard, but in the end he would always be making the best of what he had and yearning for the life he did not.

Still, Hirad had become an accomplished hunter and tracker and the elves respected him.

The communication had the overtones of sorrow laid on it because there were some of Tual's creatures who would be leaving the rain forest and none knew when they would return. He could not grasp the nuances but he was undoubtedly one of the subjects.

There had just been a prolonged downpour and the forest at night smelled fresh, clean and vibrant. Thraun stood and brushed water from his clothes. The panther lay beside him, her head resting on her front paws, her eyes fixed on him. The ClawBound elf was crouched a little further distant, but at the sound of the communication he had taken up the calls and had walked back to stand by his partner.

"It is me, isn't it?" said Thraun.

The elf nodded, his white-and-black-halved face impassive. He pointed away down the trails that led to Taanepol, where Hirad lived.

"Others too," he said, voice gruff and forced.

"Lead on," said Thraun.

He bent down and kissed the panther on her forehead. She growled, pleased. "We will run as brother and sister again another day."

The panther's ears pricked and she shot to her feet, looking north into the rain forest. Thraun heard a low call and the ClawBound relaxed. He became aware of sounds that he would not have picked up two years before, not as a man at any rate.

Auum, Duele and Evunn emerged from the vegetation. He greeted them each with the bear hug that had become his trademark.

"What's happening?" he asked.

"Shorth's children need us," said Auum. "And they need you too."

"Why?"

"Because Ilkar is among them and Hirad needs The Raven."

Thraun stopped in his tracks. The rain began again, pounding on the canopy above and searching toward the ground, spattering leaves and trunks, quietening the wildlife. Duele touched his arm. Thraun looked into the TaiGethen's face, saw the fading scar there from Hirad's accident with the jaqrui.

"You will understand," he said. "We will explain on the way. But now we must go."

"Tai," said Auum. "We move."

"Now release the power gently into your mind and channel it through your construct," said Cleress. "Feel how the elements stay around you, nipping at your fingers, but they can't release their energies because you have the control."

"It hurts," grated Erienne. "Gods, woman, it hurts."

"Hang on to it for a moment longer. Feel the pressure points and know you can eliminate any part of the elemental structure at any time for the effect you desire."

"The effect I want is not to have every muscle screaming at me."

"I think you might be exaggerating slightly but still, time to relax. Let it go but in control. See the power release harmlessly. Now stop. The shape you have, what will it do if you release hard and close off earth and stone as you do?"

"It'll rain won't it?"

"Find out. And don't worry, you won't do any harm."

Erienne drew a breath, looked across at the ancient, stooped elf bathed in beautiful warm sunlight under a cloudless sky and scowled.

"I wish you wouldn't make me do this," she said.

"Go on. I'll keep them off you." She picked up one of the sticks she'd been leaning on and waved it minutely.

"I feel safer already," said Erienne. She released the construct.

Elemental energy surged out of her mind and into the air. Broken from its shell, it fed on that around it, seeking equilibrium. As instructed, Erienne had shut off the energy from earth and stone, keeping it within her to bleed harmlessly back to its natural state.

What was left reacted immediately in the air above Herendeneth. Cloud boiled from nowhere, forming a dense black covering in moments. Mana light flashed within it, setting off the anticipated reaction. The deluge was brief but intense, drops the size of her thumb thundering into the ground, driving up spats of dirt and flattening leaves and grass to the earth.

Erienne laughed at the result and the relief in her body and clapped her hands. She looked down at the beautiful bed of flowers at her feet, soaking up the moisture.

"See that, Lyanna, see what Mummy can do!"

She knelt as she always did after they had finished a session and spoke words only Lyanna could hear.

"So much we owe to you, my darling," she said, moving specks of wet earth from yellow and blue petals. "So much we still have to learn. Remember I always love you and so does your father though I can hear him shouting even now. It's not at you. It's at me. Lie and rest." She trailed her fingers through the blooms covering the grave. "See what your beauty makes grow?"

She stood up. Cleress, bedraggled but smiling, was watching her, leaning heavily on her sticks. Behind her, Erienne could see Denser marching toward them, shaking his head.

"Here comes the complaint," said Erienne, wiping rain and a tear from her face and smoothing down her soaking hair.

Above her, the clouds dispersed as quickly as they had come and the sun got to work drying out the ground.

"Was that really necessary?" called Denser. "I had been reading. A little warning would have been nice."

"The pages will dry out quickly enough," said Cleress. "And we are done for the day. I need a rest before dinner."

"Wait a moment and I'll help you in," said Denser. He walked to Erienne and gave her a kiss. "Feel better for doing that?"

"Actually, yes," said Erienne. "Today was a breakthrough day."

"I can see where that would be useful. Deserts and such."

"As ever you miss the point," said Cleress, swapping a conspiratorial glance with Erienne. "You see, the secret of the One lies not in learning individual castings for individual effect but understanding the nature of the elements and the nature of your problem. Then, all you have to do is bring the two together. Erienne has all but grasped it, but for a few control exercises that need more work."

"Then what?" asked Denser.

"Then I can at last die and join my sisters," said Cleress. Her smile was brief and Erienne didn't like what was behind it. "I worry about them, you know. It is so long since I heard them. All there is now is a wailing. I do worry so."

"I'm not with you," said Erienne.

"No, dear, of course not." Cleress turned to begin the slow walk to the house. "Denser, if you would be so kind."

Erienne stood and watched them go, frowning. She wondered if Denser had been listening to the Al-Drechar. She knew he didn't always. He felt her to be edging into senility and it was true she rambled from time to time. What it was she dreamed she heard from her sisters probably fell into that category.

"But you don't really believe that, do you Erienne?" she said to herself.

Shaking her head, she knelt to tidy Lyanna's grave.

The Unknown pushed Diera's sodden hair from her face and kissed her lips. Caught in Erienne's downpour, they could do nothing else but laugh under the warm rain and try to hide the bread and cheese. Unsuccessfully. Some of it washed over the rock on which they were sitting and into the ocean. The Unknown had pushed the rest after it.

"I hope Jonas wasn't caught in that," said Diera.

"I doubt it," said The Unknown. "Anyway, he'll be as wet as us but by choice. He's still over at Sand Island swimming with Ark."

Ever the doubt was in Diera's eyes when she knew her little boy was with any of the ex-Protectors. Nothing The Unknown could do would completely convince her they were safe. She had seen them under the control of Xetesk and knew what they could do. Even now, two years on and with their masked, thralled lives and painful memories, she was unsure.

"Will he be safe?" she said.

"Ark's the best swimmer amongst them," said The Unknown.

"You know what I mean, Sol," she replied.

"Yes, which was why I answered a different question. You already know the answer to the other one. You ask it every time."

"He's my son," she said.

"Hey, I'm not criticising," said The Unknown.

"Come on, let's go down to the landing. Wait for them."

"You go." The Unknown helped Diera to her feet and crushed her to him. "Think I'll walk the estate. Have a think to myself."

Diera looked into his eyes. He held her gaze and tried to smile but it didn't convince her.

"You still miss it all, don't you?" she said.

"It's in my blood," he replied. "Balaia is my home. I'd so love to take you back one day, you and Jonas. Do what we set out to do."

He looked past her at the house and the lands surrounding it on the small southern island of Herendeneth. They had worked miracles in their time here the last two years. He and the five remaining ex-Protectors had rebuilt the house, turned some of the land into fertile crop land and brought more animals to farm from Calaius. But it wasn't his and he wanted that so badly. Something he could build and pass onto his family.

And of course, he wasn't the only one itching for change. The Protectors needed their own lives. Gods, Hirad and Darrick had only lasted a season here before getting bored to the point of madness. Only Denser and Erienne seemed content. But then, they had everything they wanted.

"And yes, I miss the loudmouth and I wonder what's happened to Tomas, Maris and Rhob in Korina. We didn't get the chance to say goodbye to them. But I know how much you love it here. It is so peaceful. And Jonas . . . he is the most beautiful child and I wouldn't sully his innocence for anything. But one day he'll be curious. He'll know this isn't it."

"So we'll go back. But only when it's safe," said Diera.

"And when will we know that, I wonder?"

"One day, Jevin and the *Calaian Sun* will sail into the channel and what you hear will tell you all you need to know. Perhaps we'll all go back then. What do you say?"

"I say I love the images you paint." He planted another kiss on her mouth and shoved her gently toward the path to the landing. "So you'll always know where to find me, won't you? Right here, looking for sails on the horizon."

Diera turned. "Never leave me again. Promise."

"Never. I promise."

Ry Darrick put his head in his hands and sighed long. "Gods, this is like pulling teeth," he muttered.

It was another ridiculously humid day though he'd been assured of fresher air on the coast. And last time he looked, Ysundeneth was still on the coast. It had been like this ten days straight now. He couldn't sleep, he had no appetite and it was grating on his nerves. And in the paddock in front of him, his apprentice was deliberately misunderstanding everything he was saying.

The young elf stood up and brushed himself down, turned to see the stallion standing irritably on the opposite side of the ring, its tail swishing. It snorted.

"What did I tell you just now?"

"Don't approach from the back?" he ventured.

"Right. So could you confirm by pointing which end is the front?"

The boy pointed. That was something else. No sense of irony. Clearly Ilkar had learned his over long years of exposure to Hirad.

"Correct, the end with the teeth and the rolling eyes. Now, I'll tell you once more, and go carefully this time. Approach steadily and calmly from the front and let him see you all the way. If you surprise him you'll end up flat on your back again if you try and mount him.

"Let him get used to you before you get a hold of the bridle and then move down his flank slowly. Make sure you keep in physical contact. Only then put your foot in the stirrup. Do it slowly and calmly and should he skitter, back off and try again. I'll tell you when to be more forceful, all right?"

"Yes, General," said the boy.

"Go on then, he won't bite." Actually, he might, thought Darrick.

Dear Gods drowning, would he ever be able to let the boy loose on a horse not already broken in? Stupid thing was, when he was up in the saddle, the boy was a natural, which wasn't something you could say for many elves.

And it had seemed like such a good idea at the time. He had brought half a dozen horses with him from Balaia when The Raven had left the continent, all courtesy of a very generous Baron Blackthorne. His idea had always been to breed them and introduce them to the elves after a short stop on Herendeneth. The elves knew precious little about horses and, if nothing else, learning to ride could be an expensive gift for rich children.

From a business point of view, it worked very well. Blackthorne's horses were good stock and he was anticipating a third generation. They should be the calmest yet, now he didn't have to rely on the old stallion. Great horse to ride. A bugger for passing on his bad temper, though.

He watched the boy approaching the horse. It eyed him warily but made no move away. Better. The lad held out his hands and the horse obliged, nuzzling them before giving him a playful butt in the chest. The boy hesitated.

"Keep going, lad," said Darrick. "You're doing fine."

He turned away at the sound of a cart rattling along the street behind him, pulled by mules. He waved at the owner, who nodded back. And that was all it took for it all to go wrong again. When he returned his attention to the paddock, the boy had his foot half in the stirrup and his hand clutched the loose rein tight.

"No," shouted Darrick. "You're dragging his head round. He won't . . ."

The lad tried to mount. The rest was inevitable. He gave a sharp tug on the rein, forgetting he was holding it, so much was he concentrating on the stirrup, his footing and the pommel where his other hand was planted. The stallion nickered and pulled back sharply. The boy didn't know which to let go of and in the end released the pommel not the rein and still tried to get up in the saddle.

The horse trotted a pace and unbalanced his would-be rider who fell flat on his back in the dirt with a shout of frustration.

"Give me strength," muttered Darrick.

"You look like a man who needs a change of career," said a voice he recognised very well indeed.

He swung round. Hirad was standing a couple of paces away. Darrick gave a shout of surprise and embraced him hard. "Gods, Hirad, it's good to see you," he said.

"Steady," said Hirad, pushing him back. "People will talk. All going well is it?"

"That depends on what you're really asking. I'm making money. I'm working with horses and other dumb animals." He spared the boy a glance. "Again! Bruising is good for the character. And don't think that about me. You'll thank me later."

Hirad was laughing. "Glad to see you've kept your cool."

"Hirad, I have to tell you something. I am so *bored*."

The barbarian's smile broadened. "So if I was to suggest something with rather more potential for excitement what would you think?"

"I'd think you were a blessing from the Gods," said Darrick. "So what is it?"

He'd been ignoring the other figures spread around the paddock fence while he spoke to Hirad but now he looked more closely.

"Isn't that—?"

"Rebraal, yes. And Auum. And Thraun's around here somewhere too."

"What's going on?" Darrick chewed his lip. Auum had sworn never to leave the forest again and his presence with his Tai was drawing attention. Hirad's smile had disappeared.

"We've got a problem. I'll explain on the way."

"The way where?"

"Herendeneth. Listen, Darrick, do what you need to do here and I'll see you on the docks at nightfall. There's a tide and Jevin is going to be on it."

Darrick stiffened. "Tell me what is going on before I get more irritable."

"You know how I said The Raven would never ride again? Seems I was lying."

Chapter 10

Dystran, Lord of the Mount of Xetesk, though the title rang hollow now, stared out at another dawn and shed a tear as he had almost every day for the past two years. It was going to be another beautiful day. That was one of the things the demons had not taken from them though they had done their best. The air was perpetually cold and the quiet made late spring a sham. No birds sang, dogs barked or children played. There was no sound outside at all but the keening of despair on the breeze.

Like every day, he wondered at the conditions on the outside where the demons ruled practically unopposed. How much worse it must be for those kept alive out there; though much of the time he wallowed so far down in his own desperation that the possibility others could be in a deeper plight was inconceivable.

So little news came in from the outside. Less and less as the seasons turned and resistance inexorably weakened. At first it had been relatively straightforward. They had unsealed the catacomb vents and been able to get people into the countryside. In the early days, the demons had only attacked a few population centres. Food and water in the wilds had been plentiful and survivors had been brought into the security of Xetesk's ColdRoom network. They'd even driven the demons back from the walls of the college at one stage and taken back some of the city.

But the situation hadn't been sustainable. The use of magic was like a beacon to any demon and he had lost mages in sudden overwhelming attacks across the mage lands. Mages he could ill afford to lose.

Slowly, they had retreated as numbers dwindled as a result of demon attack and, ever increasingly, illness and a breaking of the spirit that left no room for life. There was only so much a healing spell could do and regaining mana stamina was fraught with danger. Xetesk had had just three small areas of the catacombs the demons had still not found where a mage could sleep outside a ColdRoom, replenish and cast. And always under the eyes of guards ready to pull them the few inches back to relative sanctuary should they be discovered.

Now, the Xeteskian sphere of influence covered just the tower complex and the catacombs north. Everything else belonged to the demons. Scouting parties still searched for food and fuel but their sorties were the stuff of nightmares. Only the knowledge of starvation kept men venturing out under the rolling ColdRooms they had perfected when all they had in plentiful supply was time. But nothing could guarantee their safety. It was genuinely incredible what men and women could achieve when there really was no other option.

At least they had water. Wells had been dug in the catacombs. And that meant they could eke out what little food they had into thin stews as well as drink their fill. They could heat their food too. Stones fired with focused Orbs or FlamePalm were more than adequate but another drain on stretched mana reserves.

Dystran looked out for as long as he could at the flitting shapes of the demons about their business in Xetesk and beyond; and at the slash in the sky that was the most hated symbol of Balaia's almost total subjugation. From irritants the size of kittens to the tentacled monstrosities they had dubbed "enforcers," all had their purpose, all had their place. That fact of their organisation maddened him because it had become so clear that in their thousand-year association with demons, they had learned nothing about them. If only the reverse had also been true. If only.

But it was the people that he saw that depressed him. And it dragged at his soul when he caught one of them gazing up at the tower. Without spirit, without hope. Abandoned but still walking. And still building, growing, eating and sleeping. Still, he was convinced, breeding. They had to of course. There was that part of the human that denied even the most cataclysmic situation. And above that, there were the demons, seeing to it that all was done to their design.

It was the reason he came up here and shed tears every day and why all who survived looked out every day too. He had to remind himself why he still fought because in the base of the complex hope fled so easily. He knew what he was looking at down there. It was a farm.

Dystran turned from the window, weary despite the early hour. He caught sight of himself in a mirror and shuddered. Gaunt. Sunken eyes and cheeks. Skin flaking and blotched. Patchy beard and hair hacked short as pitiful defence against the lice. A quivering line for a mouth, lips pale and split. And he was one of the fitter ones. He had no choice. Soldiers and mages got the greater shares of food.

He signalled to the two soldiers who went everywhere with him.

"Let's go," he said. He spared a glance across at Ranyl's tower, shuttered and abandoned. "Gods be thanked that you didn't live to see this, old dog."

"My Lord?"

"Nothing."

They began the descent to the dome. Below them, teams of mages kept ColdRooms linked to provide best coverage of as wide an area as they could. He had seventy-eight mages, a hundred-plus soldiers and another two hundred-odd souls to protect. Pitiful.

Not far down, the sour smells of the last resistance of Xetesk hit him. Ventilation was not enough alone. They could not clean or scrub adequately, they had to bury their waste in catacomb tunnels but they could not lime it. Around four hundred people living and breathing for the most part in tight conditions because they felt there was safety in numbers. Gods burning, it was one of the few things they could cling on to.

There had to be something they'd all overlooked. Something that would give them the spark they needed to strike with purpose, not merely seek to exist another day. After two years it seemed faint hope.

A thought struck Dystran then. There had to be a reason why the demons seemed content to let them live like this. How long had it been since a concerted attack, a season or more, surely? It didn't make sense and it irked Dystran that it had never occurred to him to wonder why before now. The life force of a mage was so prized by demons. Their connection with mana made them burn bright. For a demon, comparing a mage to a nonmage was a fine Blackthorne red wine as compared with vinegar.

Yet every day, they must know they risked mages dying. It could be that they were not as numerous as he assumed but he wasn't sure that would make enough of a difference. Gods drowning, but they no longer even sacrificed city people in front of them to make them surrender.

Something in the demons' plans meant that keeping all the college cores where they were, helpless but alive, was the right way to go. It was a change in strategy from the constant attacks of seasons gone by. Now it was like they were waiting. But for what?

There had to be information and knowledge buried somewhere.

"Where are Suarav and Chandyr? Where's Sharyr?"

"All in the banqueting hall, my Lord." A sad irony at breakfast time.

"Good. Take me there."

It was time for another raid on the library.

Pheone took her shift like they all did. And every moment outside the college grounds was terrifying. It tore at her gut and tripped up her heartbeat. It gnawed at her belief and concentration. The knowledge of what she was doing was what kept her focused. It was the only thing that could.

She slipped out of the tunnel entrance and into the heart of the city. It was a tunnel they had dug without the aid of magic and because they would otherwise starve, so tight was the ring of demons around them. She had ordered another dug too. One day, the demons would find this one. They found everything eventually.

And to think that Julatsa should consider itself fortunate. When the demons had flooded Balaia, they had been given warning. A panicked Communion from a Dordovan mage had been picked up by Pheone's spectrum analysts. It had been cut off abruptly but had brought them precious hours to prepare. Mages had been called back into the college grounds. The grain store was cleared and the contents moved. City guardsmen were invited to leave their perimeters and beats. Livestock had been driven into the courtyard.

It was a time when Pheone had found her heart to be unyielding. They had assessed quickly how many souls they could shelter and had taken them from the streets. Whole families where they could. Smiths, builders and healers too. No sentimentality. It was only about survival.

They had plotted the ColdRoom coverage, ensuring wells and stores were well protected, and had withdrawn everyone they wanted behind the repaired college gates. The council had pleaded with her to let them in as panic had gripped the city riding on rumour and hearsay. The mayor had promised them the wealth of Julatsa for personal salvation. They had threatened to storm the gates but they didn't have the strength. Julatsa's mages were backed by Al-Arynaar swords, bows and magic.

She would forever recall the last words she spoke to the mayor before the gates were sealed with WardLocks.

"Your money means nothing as does your word. Much as the life of every elf and mage in this college meant nothing to you when Xetesk invaded. Where was your loyalty then? We asked for your help. You refused. Reap what you sow."

And thus she had condemned him to a life of servitude or, if he was lucky, a quick death. She felt no pity for him or his council of cowards. But for those innocents they could not take, she had wept hard. For them, the curse of magic had surely struck its final and most devastating blow and unleashed on them an enemy they could not combat.

Mages were their only hope but mages across Balaia were struggling merely to survive; those that were left. It was a cruel irony that Julatsa, once just hours from extinction was, a few days later given the information she had gleaned, surely the most powerful college.

Julatsa boasted almost one hundred and eighty mages, Al-Arynaar and current Julatsans, and almost two hundred of the elven warriors had also still been in the college when the demons attacked. They were still so strong in mind and body. Truly amazing people. So determined, so resolute. They kept the college going through the earliest and darkest days. They hunted, they fought and they survived. It simply did not occur to them that they might be beaten.

The demons were wary of them too, which was the one ray of real hope they could work on. Elven souls couldn't be taken by mere touch. Dila'heth said their god of the dead, Shorth, protected them.

Whatever it was, it meant that the elves chose to travel without Cold-Room spells when they foraged. And humans like Pheone simply had to trust them when it was their turn to provide mage backup. She knew how effective they were but their tactics still couldn't assuage her base fear.

There were six elves with her. Five warriors and one mage, all whispering through the silent street toward the immaculate and high-yielding farmland that had been created on the city's borders. At one time they had developed a conscience about stealing this food. But when the reprisals for doing so had ceased and it became clear that they were as good as being catered for, that guilt ebbed quickly away.

The paradox of course was that demons still guarded the farmland. They were happy to exact revenge for attempted theft if they could while apparently conceding the necessity for oversupply because theft was often successful. And for their part, the elves were happy to take them on if the need arose.

"We all have our demons," Dila'heth had said. "But you have named yours and they are real as well as being that dark part of the psyche we all harbour. Of course they have power over you. They are your nemesis. It is not so with the elves. Our association was never so close. Never myth made real.

"For you they are the descent. Everything your mothers and your priests warned you about. For us they are a powerful adversary but in the end just an alternate race. They have a place in our legends but that is because they threaten Shorth's children, not the living."

"You're saying the reason we're vulnerable is a difference in perspective?" she'd asked.

"State of mind and belief are powerful. The touch of a demon can kill you. It cannot kill us unless our will is broken. Shorth protects us but our souls are bonded into our faith and our race. It makes us strong. You are individuals so you are vulnerable.

"Humans have never really understood what binds a people. It is a shame for you that the demons do."

Creeping through gently waving stalks of spring crops, it was hard to disagree with her. The elves had an intuitive understanding of each other. They barely needed to speak or gesture. But she remained ultimately unconvinced of Dila's reasoning. She, like all elves, held her faith up as the reason for every circumstance. Pheone considered their greater resistance to a demon's touch was their innate link to mana.

Ahead of her, the elves had stopped moving. Lost in her thoughts, Pheone almost stumbled into the warrior in front of her. He turned and placed a finger on his lips, then pointed to his eyes and out across the fields to the livestock barns. Darkened for camouflage, shapes moved against the walls. Demons. Dila'heth had made it seem such a dramatic name but it was what they were. To humans at least.

The raiding party crouched low in the field, out of sight unless they were overflown.

"They are few," said Kineen, the leader of the group. "It is a chance."

"A chance for what?" whispered Pheone.

"To take breeding pairs," said Kineen. "We need more livestock."

Pheone paused, hearing the leaves wave about her head. Ahead, a cow lowed.

"Couldn't we have had this discussion before we left?" she asked.

"To what purpose? There could be no decision until now. We know you will support us."

"You want to steal livestock?" A nod. "And drive them back down the tunnel without killing them and without the demons finding the entrance?"

Kineen managed a brief smile. "The animals will not be conscious for the way back. We will deal with that. Four demons are circling the barn. We need to take them all together but we won't have much time between casting and more arriving. You will have to be quick."

Pheone blew out her cheeks. Her heart was crashing in her chest and sweat was beading at her hairline. She felt a shiver in her limbs. She only hoped that when the time came, she could muster up the concentration to cast.

"Just tell me what you want me to cast."

Another smile from Kineen. "Good. And Pheone. Run when we tell you and don't look back."

The five warriors fanned out into the field, keeping below the line of the crop. Pheone and the other mage, Afen'erei, moved in behind them. Neither prepared yet. The mana spectrum had to be kept quiet until the last possible moment. After a few yards, the two archers split off left, increasing their pace, hurrying for one end of the barn.

Pheone could just about make out the demons now. Four of them, a little smaller than man size with wings and tails. Their vein-run skin writhed. Every inch the archetypal figures of nightmare. It was the shape most had adopted on arrival in Julatsa. She presumed they found it easier to control their human flock that way.

"Hit them when they clear the barn to your right," said Afen'erei.

"Got you."

"IceWind and DeathHail are best. Something quick to cast."

Pheone nodded. She'd have preferred to crush them with a ForceCone but they couldn't risk the barn collapsing under the pressure.

The three sword elves were running now, feet silent over the ground. They broke cover at the instant the first arrows struck the demons, deflecting their attention. The fact that the shafts couldn't kill didn't stop wounds hurting and the demons wailed in pain, shaft after shaft thudding home. They had not gathered themselves to attack before the warriors were on them.

Swords swept from scabbards and the blows rained in. Pheone saw it all in a kind of detached awe. The relentless motion, the speed of the strike. All to a purpose. Swords bit into heads and arms, sliced through wing membrane. Feet thudded into gut, groin and temple. Disorientating, temporarily disabling. The demons had practically no reply. They lashed out with claws and tails or tried to bite. But the ferocity of the elves made mockery of their slight numerical advantage.

Only one made it into the air at all, to be brought down with arrows crippling critical wing muscle. The onslaught was quick but could it possibly be quick enough? Already, Pheone could hear the hoots of alarm that meant the cries of the attacked had been heard.

"Prepare now," said Afen. "No sense in delay. They are coming."

Pheone dragged herself into the mana spectrum. It was unadorned by any casting barring the mass of activity that signified the ColdRoom lattice. She brought together the shape for IceWind, a flowing sheet of interlaced mana strands, glowing yellow with captured energy, just waiting for release when it would tatter in the face of its targets.

Almost at once, the hoots became howls and the hunt was on for those casting magic. The warriors responded, driving demons out of the shadow of the barn and into a pool of moonlight.

"Break!" called Kineen. "Cast."

IceWind tore away from Pheone's fingers, mingling with the slivers of DeathHail cast by Afen'erei. The effect was at once hideous and incredibly satisfying. Where Afen's spell gouged strips of flesh from the demons, Pheone's IceWind ignited the loose mana so freed, feeding on it as a FlameOrb did on human flesh, gorging, consuming.

The demons screamed, their voices like those of infants in agony, tearing at Pheone's heart and dashing her concentration. The IceWind ceased but the damage had been done. Again, a solitary demon took to the air but it was little more than a mass of pure blue flame, bubbling a few feet up and crashing back to earth, wing beating feebly at the ground.

"Go!" shouted Kineen. His warriors and archers ran for the barn doors. "Pheone, retreat."

"No." She felt alive, vindicated. In two years, these were her first victims among the thousands that occupied her city and she found herself hungry for more. "I'll defend you."

"They can outrun you," said Afen. "But not us."

Pheone looked to her left. Shadows climbed thick into the sky. Far right, she heard the pounding of feet in scrub. It was no time for heroics.

"Don't get caught," she said, turning and running back into the field of spring crop, retracing her steps back into the city.

Behind her the yellow bloom of a spell lit the sky and a flat crack spoke of a FlameOrb detonating. More screams of dying children, this time further out of the city, away from the barn. Pheone smiled. A diversion.

The part-focused mana from the castings brought the demons to it, searching for the prized life force that only a mage possessed. Pheone ran harder, her ears playing games with her mind. She fancied she could hear a gravel-laden voice calling her name but it could have been the breeze through the crops. Wings beat close to her head though it could have been wind echo.

She was alone and unguarded in this demon-run city of the walking dead. She broke through the crops and into the streets, trying to keep her footfalls quiet and maintain her speed. But all she produced was a dry slapping that sounded like a herald of her passage.

Pheone slowed, ducked into heavy shadow and stopped, breathing hard. She heard no sounds of pursuit. The howling of enraged demons was distant but she knew she couldn't relax. She studied the silent buildings while she caught her breath. No one lived here any more. The demons had herded everyone they'd kept alive into the centre of the city, where they were penned and housed like animals.

A hand clamped across her mouth. She felt breath on her neck. She tried to struggle and scream but she was held tight. She let herself relax, made herself think. Kineen's face came into view and she all but wept. He released her.

"Bad place to stop," he said. "They are closer than you think."

"Gods burning, you almost frightened me to death," she managed, relieved and angry.

"Sorry," he said and set off toward the tunnel entrance and safety. "I couldn't risk you screaming."

She followed him, nodding. "What about the others?"

"They have taken other routes to split the pursuit. We have four lambs, four piglets. A good raid."

Pheone smiled, feeling safe though she ought not to. Only she was safe enough here, wasn't she? Here in a quiet empty back street the demons never travelled; as much as inside the college where they never attacked but just watched. No. Waited.

She caught up with Kineen. "Why don't they attack the college any more?"

"They fear us."

"Yes but that's not all of it, is it?"

Kineen glanced across at her. A few more turns and they were home. "It is why we fight them out here."

"What do you mean?"

"To keep that for which they wait as distant as we can."

Deep inside the crypts of Dordover, the last remaining bastion of college resistance huddled. Barely two dozen were left now. The onslaught had been relentless. They hadn't been able to replenish stamina outside the Cold-Rooms when the demons had found all their borders and they had too little strength to cure all the afflicted when disease had struck. Dysentery had stolen their best mages once it had taken their ability to heal themselves and now the demons were coming after what was left. They could sense the weakening. The ColdRooms were not secure, the casters were weak and the swordsmen barely had the muscle to raise their blades.

Vuldaroq, a shadow of the obese bulk he had been two years before, listened to the battering on the doors of the outer crypts. They had fled here the night before and had nothing with them. The Heart of the college was below them and they could no longer reach it.

He dragged himself to his feet and looked around the chill, lantern-lit chamber.

"They will be here soon," he said. "They must not take any of our souls."

A swordsman, Marn, turned to him. "The college must survive," he said. "Even if none live here until the demons are defeated. We cannot let our light fail."

Vuldaroq managed a smile. "That you still have hope makes you the strongest among us, my friend."

"Not for myself, my Lord Vuldaroq, but for you and the mages we still have." He gestured about him. "We have been talking, the nonmages I mean. If you all have the stamina left for one more casting, there is a chance you can escape."

Vuldaroq shook his head. He was tired. The bluster and arrogance he had carried were long since gone and he had developed an unflinching loyalty to those who had fought the demons so bravely though their efforts were ultimately to end in failure.

"We will take our lives here, leave them nothing to leech from us," he said. "It is as we agreed, Marn. We will die together."

"No," said Marn. "It is you they want, you they prize. We can get you out."

"How? We are trapped."

"Yes, my Lord, but not yet quite helpless."

Vuldaroq listened on and the spark of chance warmed his heart once more.

Chapter 11

"U nknown!"

Hirad's shout shattered the peace of Herendeneth, setting birds to flight and scattering the cattle in the yard behind the house. He pounded up the track from the landing, not even noticing the swaying trees to either side that flanked the path with such grace. All he could see was the man he hadn't laid eyes on for well over a year. It was a great sight.

The big man was dressed in light linens, his shaven head hidden from the sun under a tied-back cloth. The smile on his face was broad and his bulk almost blocked out his wife and child standing a little way behind him.

Hirad hurtled into his embrace, rocking him back a step. The two old friends spun each other around, the barbarian kissing him on the cheek before stepping back.

"Surprised?"

"I thought you'd gone elven native," said The Unknown. "It's wonderful to see you looking so well. Still off the wine?"

Hirad wrinkled his nose. "They have something almost as good. Made from some tree sap or other." He blew. "Very sweet, very powerful."

"So not wine at all then. Got some young stuff you should try."

"When on Calaius, Unknown . . ."

The Unknown shook his head. "Very funny. Seriously though, how have you been? There's a lightness about you, I'll say that."

"Life with Auum teaches you a few things."

"Hasn't quietened your voice though, I see," said Diera.

Hirad stepped around The Unknown, kissed Diera and ruffled Jonas's blond hair. The boy hid behind his mother's skirts.

"And a good morning to you, Lady Unknown," he said.

"It's good to see you, Hirad. It's been too long."

"Yeah," said Hirad, stepping back and taking them all in, feeling the guilt begin to nag at him like it always did when he saw them standing together, the perfect family. "Yeah it has."

"Come on up to the house, it's almost time for lunch anyway. Denser and Erienne are going to get a real surprise," said Diera.

"Yes, they are," said Hirad, unable to keep the light in his expression.

"So," said The Unknown, slapping him on the back. "You've got a year or more to fill me in on, man-elf. How long is Jevin staying for or is the *Calaian Sun* coming back to pick you up another time?"

"He'll be here a few days. As long as necessary, really," said Hirad. "Look, Unknown—"

But The Unknown wasn't listening to him. There were voices coming from around the corner in the path, still just out of sight.

"Who's that man, Mummy?" asked a small voice.

"That's Hirad, sweetheart, one of your father's . . ."

She trailed off, sensing the tension that had stolen through every muscle of The Unknown's body. Hirad looked briefly at her, saw the colour drain from her face and the tears already beginning to well up behind her eyes.

"Brought some friends with me, Unknown," he said, voice close to cracking. "I'm sorry, Diera, I'm so sorry."

And round the corner they came, their smiles and greetings dying on their lips as the scene unfolded before them. The Unknown spared Hirad a dangerous look and turned back to watch them approach, most of them people he hadn't ever thought to see again. Darrick, Thraun, Rebraal, Auum, Duele, Evunn.

"Hirad, what is going on?" he hissed.

"Think we'll be all needing that drink," said Hirad.

Whatever it was The Unknown said next, Hirad lost in the sound of Jonas beginning to cry and Diera shouting "no" over and over.

"There, see it?" Kayvel was pointing out over the southwest of Lystern.

Heryst was one of a dozen faces pressed against the highest window in the tower. The day was dull and drizzling, adding to the misery of the population of the enslaved city. He could barely concentrate on what he was supposed to be trying to see, his eyes as always drawn to the perpetual terrified drudgery that unfolded daily beneath him.

The demons had assembled the people they wanted to keep alive into buildings ringing the college and had cleared areas of the city in full view of the rebellious mages for crops and livestock. It was a reminder every heartbeat if one were needed of the Lysternans' failure to do any more than survive.

In two years, while they had expanded their domain within the college, nothing outside of it belonged to them. They had wells under their control but had to raid farms for food or fly high and fast to hunt or forage in distant areas still apparently ignored by the invaders. Those making the flights had at least brought back information about the wider state of Balaia and it made grim listening.

Those still living outside the control of demons lived in constant fear of being the next into the inexorably expanding net. In addition to the college cities, all major population centres bar one were in thrall. Korina, Gyernath and all the northern and eastern baronies were captured, leaving only Blackthorne as a bastion in the south. It was a testament to Baron Blackthorne's skill and farsightedness that he still remained free, if that term could really be applied to any of them. Only Blackthorne outside of the colleges had refused to victimise and drive away the mages in his town or employ when the Black Wings were at their height of influence. He was alive now because of that decision.

In the scattered villages, isolated farmsteads and hamlets, a subsistence life went on but there was precious little travel or trade. After all, the demons controlled every marketplace and port and had thrown an impenetrable ring around Blackthorne. Those living in these small communities would all have fled but there were no ships to anywhere. Some had tried to make it to Understone Pass but no news of their fate ever came back.

And everywhere the stories about what the demons were doing were the same. No one unable to father or bear children was left alive. The old, infirm and barren had been taken for their souls in the early seasons of the occupation. Those that were left were drilled into a workforce designed purely to keep them alive, let them breed and so perpetuate the supply of souls. And while the new generation were born and grew, the demons satiated themselves by draining life force slowly, using a horrifyingly exquisite touch to draw off only that which they needed.

Heryst had seen it from the windows of the college. He wondered why the enslaved hadn't given up, taken their own lives or their children's. He had witnessed in their faces the enduring shock and incomprehension. The eyes not dead but not alive either. The look of hope extinguished.

But somewhere inside them, most of them, the will to survive still lurked. It drove them to exist through the nights of terror, the knowledge of why they were being kept alive. The human spirit, never truly broken.

Heryst knew why that inner light still burned. It was because every day they could see the college. Still holding out. A torch to guide them through their bleakest moments, something to cling on to though they were helpless themselves. It meant an expectation was laid on Heryst and those few who worked to find an answer. It was why Heryst looked out every day to remind himself. They had to strike back. They had to. If only they had the means.

"My Lord?"

"Kayvel," said Heryst. "I'm sorry, miles away."

"Please, just for a moment, look away from the city." Kayvel placed a hand on his shoulder, all it did was remind him how thin he had become.

"Show me again."

"Look toward Xetesk, tell me what you see."

Heryst looked. Beneath the shale-grey cloud, there was a lightness in the southwest. It was faint but it was there. Sometimes stronger, sometimes fading. There seemed to be a pale blue hue to it but that could have been a trick of the distance.

"What is that?" he asked.

"You know how you've been asking why it is the demons don't try and attack us any more?" said Kayvel.

"Yes." Heryst shrugged and drew back from the window. "So what?"

Kayvel pointed. "Well, I think that's why."

Heryst regarded him coolly. "You're going to have to explain that."

"Naturally." Kayvel chuckled and scratched at his beard. They all had them these days. There were other things more important than putting the edge of a dagger to your chin every day. Until the lice struck. Then they shaved. "We know that what we possess as mages makes our souls prized by demons. That's surely why they targeted the colleges from the outset."

Heryst nodded, about to tell him to stop repeating the obvious when he realised Kayvel was speaking for the benefit of the whole room, which had fallen silent.

"But we saw them back off quite quickly when they knew they couldn't take us without great loss of life on their side. We know this has happened in Xetesk and Julatsa too but we don't know about Dordover. Worryingly quiet over there, if you ask me."

A murmur ran around the room. Heryst looked round. On the council table, the ColdRoom mages were lost in their casting. Two others sat next to them, monitoring the mana spectrum as best they could for any communication through the strands of mana that linked to the spell that kept them safe. How strong they had all been against all the odds. What character had been shown by so many. Heryst didn't know about anyone else but he knew he'd have gone under a long time ago without the spirit they had engendered here.

Kayvel continued. "So it seems clear they are waiting for something to happen before they can attack us with hope of success and without huge losses, right?"

"It's logical," said Heryst.

"They have been completely systematic in their approach to taking Balaia. It has been a textbook conquest."

"You sound as if you respect them for it."

"I think we must," said Kayvel. "Because the chaotic creatures we read about in our myths bear no relation to the organised race we witness every day. It's time to stop thinking about them as the evil in our mythology and start thinking about them as a capable, intelligent enemy playing perfectly to their strengths."

"Haven't we always done that?" asked a voice from the crowd that had closed in to listen.

"No, Renarn, I don't think we have," said Kayvel to the gaunt youth who had spoken. "It's so difficult to change the teachings of thousands of years. Don't forget that, with the exception of Xetesk and to a certain extent Julatsa, we have never viewed demons as anything other than a nightmare symbol. They really were the story told to keep children quiet at night. Trouble is, they are far more dangerous than that. They are a dimension-travelling race seeking domination of this dimension. And they are ninety per cent there already. Once Balaia falls completely, who will stand in their way?"

"Wesmen and elves, presumably," said Renarn.

"For how long?" asked Kayvel. "They have come to the colleges to take out the biggest single threat to them, that of magic. The other races they can defeat at their leisure because weapons can't kill them."

"The elves have magic," said Renarn.

Heryst went cold. "Not when the tower of Julatsa is destroyed."

"Right." Kayvel's smile was grim.

"All right." Heryst gestured for calm as consternation swept the room. "Come on, let's keep our focus. We're already deflected from the question, which is, what does that mist signify?" He pointed out of the window.

"It's mana," said Kayvel.

Heryst started. "I beg your pardon?"

"Think about it. What is the one thing stopping them from attacking us inside our ColdRoom constructs?"

"Mana of course."

"Yes. It is an integral part of their being. It's armour on one level but actually it's far more than that. Without it, they die. It's clear that there's enough mana in the atmosphere of Balaia to keep them alive, but not enough to overwhelm our castings and flood the ColdRooms." He indicated the window to the southwest. "That, I am certain, is the demons introducing mana to the air above Xetesk for just that purpose."

"But surely we'd feel it," said Renarn.

"No," said Heryst. "Not at all. We're inside a ColdRoom here, we won't feel anything. What about those that have flown outside?"

"Well, the spectrum is turbulent, or so I'm told. But that in itself isn't proof though I challenge you to tell me another reason why it should be so. There's something more. The temperature is dropping like it always does when mana is too concentrated. This is supposed to be late spring. It is unseasonably chilly."

Heryst sighed and walked back to the window. He looked out on the mist with greater suspicion. "Can it really be mana? I don't know. Don't we need to know more than anything exactly what it is the demons have planned for us? Mages and wider Balaia, I mean. Because extermination doesn't seem to be on the agenda, does it?"

"It would be incredibly useful to know," agreed Kayvel.

"Right," said Heryst, nodding. "Let's go and catch ourselves a demon and ask it, then."

It had taken The Unknown quite some time to calm Diera enough for her to take Jonas and walk the island. He didn't know how to feel. On one level he was furious with Hirad for threatening his idyll and the life he loved; just being with his family. But he knew that Hirad would not have come to Herendeneth this way unless he felt he had no choice. And indeed had he not been approached and whatever it was turned out to be Raven business, he would have been just as angry.

But he felt retired. Although he kept himself fit and sparred with Ark every day, the desire to fight had gone. He'd fought and won his battles and he'd earned the right to be here on this beautiful island, watching his son grow while his wife lay in his arms. It was almost everything he'd dreamed of though he would have preferred to have been on Balaia, and be landlord of the Rookery too.

So he'd kept a silence to let his emotions settle while he walked ahead of the party from the *Calaian Sun*. He took them to the kitchen of the house, away from the sights and sun of the island. Into a place where they could focus and talk. The only time he opened his mouth was to call Denser and Erienne to join them.

And now here they sat with drinks and food in front of them, waiting for Hirad to speak. At least he had the decency to look deeply apologetic.

"So, Hirad, perhaps you can explain why you've come here bringing who you have brought with you," said The Unknown. "And it had better be very bloody important."

"It's as important as it can get," said Hirad. "This is bigger than Dawn-thief, believe me."

The Unknown raised his eyebrows. He looked for some hint of exaggeration in Hirad's tone and found none. He felt his heart beat a little faster.

"So you have our attention." The Unknown gestured to his left. Both Denser and Erienne were impassive but their hands gripped a little tighter together.

"Look, we don't know everything at this stage but we believe that the demons have invaded Balaia and are threatening the spirit dimension and if they can beat Balaia they can take out the dragons too."

"Whoa, whoa!" said Denser, half laughing, his face a picture of scepticism. "Gods burning, Hirad, that's a statement and a half. Bloody hell, I don't believe there even *is* a spirit dimension."

"Then that is your weakness," said Auum.

Denser ignored him. "And what is this about demons? Come on, one thing at a time."

"You wanted to know if it was important. Why it was I came here with everyone. Now you know." Hirad sat back, his face set. The Unknown recognised it so well. That was why it worried him. Hirad wasn't given to exaggerating anything.

"It's all right, Hirad," he said. "One thing at a time. Demons in Balaia. Let's hear that first."

"I can't do it like that, Unknown. It's all linked together." He stopped and chewed his lip, taking a deep breath. "And I don't understand it all. What I do know is that if the elves think it's worth leaving Calaius for and worth coming to The Raven for then that's all I need to know. And I know that one of The Raven is in trouble and we never leave our people that way. Never."

"All right then, tell us whichever way you can," said Erienne. "Just know that this is so unexpected. We're happy here."

"And I was happy in Taanepol. Thraun was born again in the rain forest. Some things are bigger than our happiness."

"Gods, hasn't it always been the way?" breathed Denser.

"Yes it has," said Hirad and The Unknown felt his regret like a wave over the beach. "You have to understand this is the last thing I wanted."

"What's going on, Hirad?" asked The Unknown. "Just tell us the way you know."

Hirad relaxed and looked to Rebraal and Auum. Both nodded for him to speak. He took a drink and was silent for a little while, gathering his thoughts.

"This all sounds so ridiculous. A few days ago, I heard Ilkar. I was asleep but it wasn't just a dream. Wherever he is now, he's in trouble. All the dead are. Rebraal will tell you. It's because the demons are attacking them on a new front. They need to break down the resistance of the Spirits because if they do it makes all of Balaia and Calaius vulnerable to them. And if that happens, the dragons are under threat too. Don't ask me to explain it because I can't. But we can stop this, if we have help and if we do it now."

"Trouble is," said Denser. "Coming from you, it isn't ridiculous at all. Farfetched, yes. Ridiculous, no."

Hirad managed a smile. "Thanks, Denser."

"It doesn't mean we understand it, though," said Erienne. "Why does it mean Balaia's been invaded?"

"And how the hell have you heard Ilkar?" demanded The Unknown. "He's been dead more than two years."

"I just did, Unknown. And Rebraal has heard him too. It's too real to be just nightmares."

"Rebraal?" asked The Unknown.

The leader of the Al-Arynaar inclined his head. "Hirad speaks the truth as you know he does. There is so much humans don't understand about what exists outside their vision."

"We don't need patronising," said Denser. "Just the facts."

"There is a place that all the dead go, all the souls as you would call them," said Rebraal. "You deny it because it doesn't fit with your understanding of life and death but it exists nonetheless. It is a dimension as you understand them but the journey there is something only the soul can make, not the body. It is not a place you can ever visit though you can connect to it. Belief is everything. We know it. So do the Wesmen. It is time you knew it too.

"All the souls of the dead go there but most are silent because they don't know they can still communicate with the living. Ilkar knows as do all the elves who pass there. But right now, he shouts with a voice full of fear. The cursyrd are pressing the fabric of their realm."

"Why?" asked Denser.

Rebraal regarded him as if he was simple. "Because it contains countless millions of souls. It is everything the cursyrd want if only they could force a breach."

"Are you with this?" The Unknown asked of Darrick and Thraun.

The shapechanger nodded.

"We've been on board ship with them for three days," said Darrick. He shrugged. "I believe them."

"Which is fine," said Erienne. "But I don't get the connection with Balaia and I don't see that we can do anything to help. And I don't understand why Auum and the TaiGethen are here."

"Contact with our dead is a gift granted to us by Shorth," said Rebraal. "The Al-Arynaar and TaiGethen come to Aryndeneth to speak, to gain strength and to seek advice. It is written that they will defend us in death as we defend ourselves in life. We will not suffer the cursyrd to break that cycle."

Erienne smiled, disbelieving. "How will you stop them? This is a place you can't go to until you die. And then you will be in the same position as your dead. Helpless."

"They are not helpless," said Rebraal. "They fight. Every moment. To keep the enemy away from their borders."

"But you can't help them," said Erienne, frustration edging her voice.

"They aren't talking about joining the battle in the spirit dimension. We have to remove the threat further back along the chain," said Darrick.

"Great." The Unknown stood up and paced around the table. "This makes about as much sense as one of Hirad's battle plans. Look, I know you've all been on ship talking about this for days but it's coming across as gibberish, it really is. Ilkar's in trouble but he's dead. In fact everyone dead is in trouble and it's got something to do with a demon invasion of Balaia but the elves think they can sort it out by stopping some so far unnamed target in an unnamed place." The Unknown felt his patience thinning to breaking point.

"My wife is scared that I'm going to leave her and go off again with The Raven. I've told her it must be something critical or you wouldn't be here. What the hell am I going to tell her? 'My dead friend is sending dreams to my living friend and I need to sort it out?'" He thumped the table. "Someone start making sense or the lot of you can sod off back to whatever it was you were drinking on Calaius."

Rebraal gestured for him to sit down and waited until he had done so.

"Unknown, I'm sorry," he said. "But the fate of three dimensions hangs in the balance. One of them is ours, another is that of the dead and the other is the home of dragons. You can't stay here and hope it goes away because if you do, the cursyrd will eventually come here and you won't be able to stop them."

"So what can we do?"

"It's simple," said Hirad. "We have to kill the demons controlling it all."

"That's simple, is it?" said Denser.

"The way Sha-Kaan described it, yes. In theory." Hirad stopped and a slow smile spread across his face. "Do you want to come and talk to Sha-Kaan?"

CHAPTER 12

They all went in the end. Something about Hirad's manner meant that though the case had been introduced poorly, the notion that events worlds away would impact on them was never in doubt.

Darrick supported Cleress on her right side with the former Protector, Ark, on her left. She said little but there was a knowing look in her eyes. Like she had expected it all along.

Darrick left her to her thoughts. Walking apart from the rest of The Raven, he had the opportunity to assess them as he would have done his cavalry before a battle; searching for a weak spot. He knew he wouldn't find one but The Raven's demeanour was a constant source of fascination. They drew strength from each other. There was a power about them. You felt it on the inside and could see it from the outside. Like an aura. They moved so naturally around one another. The Unknown at their centre, Hirad next to him like always and the others grouped in close attendance. Darrick felt a surge of pride at being one of them.

The image was punctured by Jonas, who trotted along next to The Unknown, his tiny hand engulfed by his father's huge fist. And by Diera, who had forgiven Hirad to the extent that the pair strolled arm in arm. It was at Hirad's behest that so many would meet the dragon. And including Diera and Jonas in the group was a masterstroke. The pair had spent much time in the company of Sha-Kaan when he was marooned in Balaia and rested on Herendeneth. Diera would listen to him.

They were heading for the stone needle that dominated the island from its highest point. It was for no other reason than that Sha-Kaan had expressed a desire to see the island from the top.

They gathered in quiet anticipation, Hirad to the fore. He had told them what to expect but they all still took an unconscious pace back. A tall rectangle traced in the air in front of them. It drew itself slowly on three sides with the ground making up the fourth, and brightened from black to a blazing white. The doorway, half the size of a barn's, filled with swirling colours that moved sluggishly, like oil poured onto still water.

"Behind here would normally be a robing room and an antechamber before the main hall but I think the design has been changed," said Hirad.

The doorway dissolved, the intense edge light reducing to a warm orange glow and the slow-moving colours dimming to reveal a dimly lit interior. The scents of wood and oil carried on the breeze, sharp and pungent, but there was little sound from inside barring the crackle of fires. Heat flooded out, its humidity swamping the dry warmth of Herendeneth.

"Just like old times, eh, Unknown?" said Hirad.

"One old time only, Hirad," said The Unknown. "And the familiarity ends with my sense of impending doom."

"Better not keep him waiting."

"Hell, no," muttered Denser.

They moved inside, the relative gloom resolving itself into a short arched hallway, painted in dark green silhouettes of landscapes and dragons. Beautiful in their simplicity, sombre in their depiction.

At the end of the hallway, huge double doors stood ajar letting onto a vast space. Hirad led them in. The chamber was vaulted and stone clad, its sides scored and fluted horizontally. It reminded Darrick of a healer's sketch of a muscle. The walls were otherwise unadorned but fires burned in grates at ten-yard intervals in the one-hundred-yard-square space, filling it with an oppressive, moist heat. Sha-Kaan sat in the middle of the chamber, his head and neck resting on the ground, his body a mound behind him and his tail flipping idly about his hind legs.

Little Jonas broke free of The Unknown's grip and ran forward. He displayed no fear, toddling toward a creature that could swallow him whole. He stopped in front of the great dragon's jaws and half turned toward his mother as he pointed.

"Kaan!" he said.

"Yes, darling," said Diera, walking forward to join him.

The Raven hung back, watching the reunion from a respectful distance. Sha-Kaan moved his head slowly off the ground, speaking softly just above the boy's head.

"Hello, little man," he said, voice so tender in a beast so large. "You have grown. I had not expected to see you again. And I am sad that I must at this time."

Jonas didn't respond verbally, instead reaching up to rub the horned scales at the front of Sha-Kaan's muzzle. The dragon turned his attention to Diera.

"Your son is beautiful," he said, voice a bass rumble, his eyes a brilliant blue, shining with affection.

"Thank you," she said. "It is good to see you."

"But the reason why breaks your heart."

She nodded. Darrick saw her hands clench together.

"I don't understand why anything that happens on Balaia should affect my husband. He has earned the right to peace."

Sha-Kaan sighed. "I cannot argue against what you say. You married an exceptional man who is part of an exceptional group. And when the world is in trouble, it calls on such people and expects them to respond. It is the mark of their greatness that they choose to do so, though it is also your misfortune, is it not?"

"There must be someone else now."

"You must listen to what I have to say. I think you will agree that there is not."

Darrick saw her shoulders sag as she nodded her head and pulled Jonas to her. Sha-Kaan raised his head a little.

"Approach, all of you," he said. "I have no desire to shout."

Hirad chuckled and led them forward. "Your whisper would carry clear across the Southern Ocean, Great Kaan."

"It gladdens my heart to see you, Hirad Coldheart."

"And you, Sha. You're looking well."

"The air of Beshara and the streams of interdimensional space are kind to me." Sha-Kaan shifted. "How do you like my Klene?"

Hirad gave the chamber, where dragons came to rest and heal in inter-dimensional space, an appraising glance.

"It's a little plainer than your old one. Decorating not finished yet, or something?"

Darrick had to smile. Never in his most vivid dreams had he ever thought to witness a man debating wall coverings with a one-hundred-twenty-foot-long dragon. Next to him, The Unknown had also seen the humour in the moment.

"Effectiveness over aesthetics. The shape of the chamber and those grooves in the walls are efficient channels for the healing streams."

"Oh, right."

Sha-Kaan rattled phlegm in his throat, the sound echoing in the chamber and startling Jonas who clutched his mother tight.

"But in the fullness of time, we will hang the walls with tapestries, if it bothers you that much."

"Not for me to say, Sha-Kaan," said Hirad. "I just have to be at one end so you can use this thing, I don't necessarily have to look at it."

"I fear we are straying from the point," said Sha-Kaan, a hint of irritation in his voice. He looked beyond Hirad to those grouped in front of him. "I remember the days when I considered all humans except the Dragonene mages to be unworthy of the attention of dragons. Hirad Coldheart changed that assumption and you before me are examples of my folly.

"It makes it all the harder then to ask one more task of you. I am not sur-prised to see the elves represented by their best. You understand in a way humans do not the link between the living and the dead. Cleress, your presence honours me. Those who were Protectors, I am the happier to be able to gaze upon your faces. And The Raven. My friends. The fears that Hirad expressed to me are well founded. Our position is already desperate. Many will be involved in defence and attack; you will be the spearhead. And for that necessity, my heart is heavy with fear for you."

"You're selling it well so far," said Denser.

Sha-Kaan's head snapped round to regard the mage with slitted pupil narrowed.

"Would you rather I lied about the challenge ahead, frail human?" he asked. "Would you rather begin your journey one-eyed?"

"Not at all," said Denser. "But you have to understand that for most of us we had no inkling of any problem until Hirad put to shore. I'm still getting round the shock of it."

"Then let me explain what has happened." Sha-Kaan breathed heavily, the air rushing over their heads, sour and sharp. "Kaan birthings began a little more than two cycles ago, a little less than two years for you. It is a time when our efforts are focused solely on our brood and when the paths of inter-dimensional space are closed to us because the resonance set up by the brood at birth upsets our directional sense. It is the time when the Vestare repair and improve the Klenes.

"But you will understand that it is a time when we are most at risk from attack. The brood has fought in the skies every day of the birthings and the damage we sustain can only be salved by the ministrations of the Vestare. The fight has left us weak but the enemy broods of the Naik and the Skoor have not been able to break us and for that we give thanks. Now we are building our strength again. Our young are strong and, like Jonas, they grow fast and are confident, unafraid."

He paused, reflective. Darrick searched his face for expression but the mass of scales obscured anything but a tightening of the muscles around his eyes.

"Our joy has been tempered, though, by what we found when the Klenes were opened again and we tried to communicate with our Dragonene part-ners here on Balaia. Many were simply not there. And those that were, were in a state of such panic their minds were barely coherent. Worse, the Kaan have been attacked in their Klenes by the Arakhe, who are marauding in interdimensional space. They are strong and getting stronger and that only happens when they find a new home. That home is here."

Sha-Kaan's last words hung in the air, resonant and laden with ruin. Dar-rick felt a chill in his body despite the heat of the chamber. He'd heard all this once already but firsthand from Sha-Kaan made it so appallingly close.

"So the demons have invaded Balaia?" said Denser.

"Yes," replied Sha-Kaan. "And they will enslave every man, woman and child in this dimension. Then they will bleed them dry of their souls and when the land is spent, they will move on. They must be stopped."

"I still don't understand why this affects the dead," said The Unknown.

"Balaia is a key dimension for the demons and you must understand their nature. They are nomadic. They exist outside the boundaries we understand, taking dimensions where they can to increase their strength and, like I said, moving on when they are spent.

"But Balaia is different. They need it for the long term and that is why they have chosen enslavement rather than massacre. It marks a departure in their nature. A mode of organisation that is worrying to us all. Another reason they need Balaia is the links that both elves and Wesmen have with the spirit dimension. If they can break the will of either race, they believe they will have free access to the dead and all their myriad souls. I believe them to be right. As, I am sure, does Cleress. And the dead are under greater pressure than at any time in their fight against the Arakhe. From what the elves tell us, that much is clear. What do you say, Cleress?"

"It is a future I have seen, though it is uncertain," said Cleress. "There is still hope, therefore."

"So why didn't they attack Calaius or the Wesmen directly?" asked Erienne.

"For two reasons," said Sha-Kaan. "They have been waiting for a way in for millennia. Xetesk finally gave them that way in by meddling with powers they did not understand and causing a breach in the fabric of the Balaian dimensional shell. The souls of mages are prized and will give them great strength for battles to come. Second, they are attacking the colleges and the wider east of your country first because if they can remove magic, then none in this dimension have a weapon against them.

"The Brood Kaan, and through us every brood on Beshara, is at risk. The Arakhe are our enemy of eons. We cannot afford to grant them access to our home or they would overwhelm us as they will Balaia."

"They are that strong?" questioned The Unknown.

Sha-Kaan said nothing. Darrick watched him see everyone digesting the situation as best they could. Darrick couldn't see all their faces but those he could told him they believed. Gods, they had to.

"Xetesk has a great deal to answer for."

It was a heartbeat before Darrick realised who had said that.

"But no one blames you, Denser," said Hirad.

"Every Xeteskian mage is to blame, and I am one," he said. "We all swore the oath that brought us to Xeteskian magic, we all wanted to see the development of dimensional spells and we all gladly accepted the deal with the demons that brought us the increased mana flow."

"There will be a reckoning if there still is a Xetesk when the Arakhe are beaten," rumbled Sha-Kaan. "Your guilt is natural but Hirad is right. You cannot be to blame for that over which you have no control."

"It doesn't make me feel any better."

"Then use your anger," said Sha-Kaan. "Fight."

"But how?" Denser threw up his arms. "It sounds as if we are already too late."

"Not yet." Sha-Kaan shifted again, his claws grinding against the stone floor. Diera shushed Jonas who had become restless.

"Perhaps you should take him back outside," said The Unknown.

"I need to hear this," said Diera. "For me and for him. I have to be able to tell him what happened if you don't ever come back."

The Unknown looked pained. He drew a hand down her cheek. "I always come back. I promise you this will be no exception."

"You promised you would never leave again unless I was with you," said Diera though there was no accusation in her tone. "Why did I marry a Raven warrior, eh?"

"We cannot choose who we love," said Sha-Kaan. "In that if nothing else, we and you are the same."

Diera knelt by her boy. "Will you be good for me and your father? We need you to be quiet just a little longer while Sha-Kaan speaks."

"Then will he fly away again?" asked Jonas, his bright eyes on his mother. She shrugged.

"I expect so, darling. He can't stay in here all the time."

"How will he get out?"

"Well," said Diera. "He'll probably use the doors like we will."

Jonas's face held such an expression of doubt that Darrick had to fight back a laugh. In a voice that was meant to be a whisper, the boy said, "I don't think they're big enough, Mummy."

It broke the tension at least. All of them laughed hard, Hirad almost doubled over, leaning on The Unknown for support the big man was in no position to give. Sha-Kaan rumbled loud, the sound booming in the chamber, and Cleress had to wipe the tears from her eyes.

"Perceptive for such a nipper, isn't he?" said Hirad.

"You'd better believe it," said The Unknown. "Like father like son."

"He'll get stuck!" shouted Jonas, revelling in his new-found confidence and all the attention. "But we could pull him out."

"Calm down now, sweetheart," said Diera. "There's a good boy."

"But he will!" insisted Jonas. "He will."

He found himself confronted by Sha-Kaan's muzzle, canted to one side so he could be seen by one enormous eye.

"I do not have to use doors," the dragon said. "I will use the pathways of . . ." He paused. "I will use magic. One day I will show you. But not today."

Jonas sat down hard on his behind under the force of Sha-Kaan's breath. He was still smiling.

"All right now?" asked Diera. The boy nodded.

"Let us discuss what must be done," said Sha-Kaan. "Because the fight for Balaia will be difficult and, like the fight for the spirit dimension, will not be fought here, not by The Raven at least. And then I will prove to you all that Jonas was right. But while I cannot fit through the doors, I can poke out my head and look again on this beautiful island."

They ate outside that night. A breeze kept the air fresh and the tide was sending waves onto the southern coast, the sound comforting, bringing them all back to reality, at least for the time being.

They set up tables along the southern cliff edge so that they could see out across the expanse of ocean while the sun dipped down in the west, sending spectacular reds across the water. With a lamb gently turning on the spit and the young wine flowing, The Raven talked about everything but that which was to come. Around them, the elves and the former Protectors were relatively quiet but they listened intently, interjecting when they could.

When Jonas complained once too often, Diera took him to his bed. Hirad turned to The Unknown as soon as she was out of earshot.

"You could stay, Unknown," he said. "Look at her. Her heart is broken but she can still smile and laugh. But we're going to have to go and what then?"

The Unknown's eyes shined in the moonlight as he watched his wife walk away up to the house.

"You know I can't stay," he said. "But thank you for the offer, even though you didn't really mean it. I always said I would fight for the world in which my family could grow up in peace. I thought that here, and eventually back on Balaia, I had achieved that. But now it is clear that there is still one more enemy to be beaten and I will be there to do my part for Diera, for Jonas and for The Raven. This isn't going to be anything but personal for me and I think we'll all work better if we feel the same way."

"The Raven never work apart," added Thraun. "And what good would any of us feel if we didn't join the fight and that fight failed? We would die just as surely."

"Myriell once spoke to you, didn't she?" said Cleress. "About the One magic and why it must survive?"

Hirad turned his head to see the Al-Drechar looking at him and The Unknown, her eyes as strong as ever, burning with the barely suppressed energy of the One.

"She did," said Hirad. "After we'd beaten off the Dordovans from Herendeneth, if I recall correctly."

"You do," said The Unknown.

"But you probably don't remember what she said. She knew even then as we all did that there was a threat coming to Balaia and, we feared, to other dimensions. She told you that the One had to survive because it would be a potent weapon in the fight to come, whatever form it took. That time has arrived. The world will be grateful you kept your side of the bargain and that Erienne still lives."

"Thanks for keeping the pressure off me, Cleress," said Erienne.

"Ah, but you must understand what you can bring that no one else can," she said. "Yours is a magic that doesn't rely solely on mana for creation. It is one of the reasons the demons will want you gone. They will fear you as they will fear all The Raven because your belief, not just your power, makes you dangerous. Sha-Kaan sees it or he would not have involved you."

"But it's not as if I can create extra devastation at will and forever," protested Erienne. "I get tired too and if Sha-Kaan is right, there's one hell of a lot of demons out there."

"Think, child," said Cleress. "Remember what we learned so recently? How easy it is to strip one element from the target area? Mana is one element."

The silence around the table grew ever more knowing and, slowly, a smile spread across Erienne's face.

"We have a couple of days before the tides will be right," said Cleress. "You and I have a lot of work to do."

"Better pass me the meat and wine, then," said Erienne. "Looks like I'm going to need all the strength I can get."

CHAPTER 13

It was dawn when it happened. Damp and chilly with low, brooding cloud. An altogether fitting atmosphere for the state of Xetesk. Later, Dystran would see the fortune of the weather front but first sight had simply depressed him.

It was the day they had identified for the raid on the library. Dystran was contemplating the task ahead when shapes began dropping out of the cloud. At first he assumed them to be more demons. But the clarion calls, gale of noise and thrash of action from the streets told him instantly that they were anything but.

They were a way distant, probably a couple of miles and maybe more, and the demons were clamouring to get at them, whoever they were. Dystran took a quick look down into the occupied parts of the college. It was all but deserted. He took a deep breath and stepped out of the ColdRoom construct and onto his balcony, signalling his guards to flank him, ready to haul him back if any threat appeared.

Immediately, the feel of mana energised his body, a tonic for the weary like the sun on cold skin. He wasted no time in casting to augment his vision and reaching out to see what was approaching.

Men, flying. Mages. Pursued by demons who were bursting through the clouds around them and faced by more rising up from Xetesk. They flew hard, pushing the limits of ShadowWings, dodging, splitting, reforming. A battle where a single touch would be fatal. Where one side could not strike at all.

He concentrated harder, searching their faces, and his jaw dropped. At their head, a man who despite the weight that had fallen from him was immediately recognisable.

Dystran turned and ran from the tower, shouting for his mages, shouting for his library raiders. It was the diversion of his prayers and he was going to grab the opportunity with both hands.

Vuldaroq had no idea how any of them had maintained their concentration in the freezing air high above the clouds. They had started out exhausted, they had trimmed their wings for speed and they had pushed the limits from the word go.

But that was not all. The escape had been a nightmare scene of pulsing demon bodies; brave men facing them down, sacrificing themselves for their mages. It had been dark, dark corridors, shadowed halls and the stench of rotting flesh. It had been the pleading cries of the enslaved; the squeals of the newborn into horror and the briefest graze of a demon's finger that had chilled his soul. And ultimately, it had been the flight through the glass domes that roofed the chamber of light with the shrieking of demons just far enough adrift.

All leading to a day of pure torment. As quickly as they outpaced a demon pack, another would rise to block their path south and west. They could smell the mana from so far away. It meant they could not rest in each other's arms as they had planned and so cycle their effort.

How many times had they cowered behind clouds, dived at suicidal pace or spun dangerously close to each other risking collision? It was something of a miracle that they had lost only one of their scarce number. There was no time for reflection. There had not been time to mourn the fading scream.

And so they faced the final run. They'd dived from the clouds a little early but that didn't bother him. What did was whether Xetesk had seen them or not. It took only a few heartbeats to realise the demons had. Like a multi-hued cloud in the morning gloom, they lifted off, their alien calls taken up by their current pursuers who drove a little harder.

"Come on!" called Vuldaroq though he knew his words were lost in the battering wind on their faces.

He led the four remaining mages down sharply, off-balancing the pursuers who lost a little ground. Any chance was worth taking. Vuldaroq was surprised to feel a thrill pass through him. So close to death for so long but with relative sanctuary almost within reach, he had never felt more alive.

He breathed the feeling in deep, felt the energy revitalise his aching body and pushed more speed from his ShadowWings.

"Come on, Dystran, you bastard, now's the time."

Vuldaroq glanced back through his gossamer-thin wings, the protective film over his eyes adding to the slightly unfocused outlook. They were all still with him. The demons flitted in and out of his vision, blurred reds and blues, trying to steal a few feet to pressure the mistake. It was hard to tell how many there were. Ten or twelve at least.

But he considered them too far adrift if he and his could maintain their punishing pace just a little longer. To maximise their speed, the mages were all flying head first, arms pressed to their sides, legs straight and feet pointed backward. It left little room for communication but they had organised a few signals in quieter moments of the flight and Vuldaroq knew they would all be looking at him for their cues.

In front of them, the seven towers of Xetesk stood grim and gaunt against the dull sky. A few lights burned in Dystran's but the others appeared closed and dead. Much like the city. It was wreathed in an undulating dawn mist trapped within its walls and punctured only by the glimmer of a handful of fires.

The demons rising from the city had fanned into a wide net. Some were streaming toward them, others hanging back. There had to be two hundred at least, thronging the air above the silent buildings, flashing greens and deep blues.

Vuldaroq went hard at the line approaching them, saw it straighten to counter their expected direction. It was a surprisingly naïve move, but then the leader caste was not among this vanguard and without them there was little spatial awareness.

Dordover's Arch Mage flickered his fingers to draw his mages' attention. Then, he pointed up with his index fingers before splaying his hands. All he could do now was hope they had seen him and trust they would react when he did. Delay carried the severest of consequences.

Vuldaroq clung to his courage. He closed with the demons at high speed and sensed his few mages come onto his shoulders in a tight group. The demons mimicked them instantly, a good sign.

"Keep coming," he breathed. "That's it."

He was so close he could hear their calls when he angled upward at practically ninety degrees. The mana shape controlling the wings strained. Physical wings would surely have snapped. Vuldaroq felt the braking force across his whole body like he was going into reverse. If not for the demons racing beneath him and the undeniable forward motion driving him on, he would have believed it.

One quick look told him they'd all made it this far. Below him, the demons were braking and turning from all directions. Vuldaroq spread his arms, his body adopting a cruciform shape, falling forward in the air to arrow vertically down.

They all knew the sign. It was the last run and, of necessity, it was every man for himself. Mouthing good luck to any that were watching, he plunged groundward. He had about a mile of distance and a thousand feet of height to lose. No distance at all but surely the longest flight of his life.

"We're moving!" shouted Dystran. "Now!"

He pounded along the corridors from his tower and into the dome complex, seeing the torpid surprise register on dozens of faces.

"Up. Warriors to the doors. Mages, let's be thinking about focused Orbs. We're going outside. Library team, make ready."

His orders were carried on down into the catacombs. Puzzled expressions faced him. He paused.

"I do not have time to explain," he said. "Time to trust me. Allies are flying in from the northeast."

"Allies?" a warrior, standing, questioned.

Dystran grabbed the filthy blue kerchief tied at his neck and pulled. "Yes, allies. Anyone who isn't a demon is an ally now. Clear?"

"Yes, my Lord."

The sound of running feet came from all quarters and he waited for the gaunt, sick-looking figure of Commander Chandyr to appear before issuing orders.

"No time for whys. Dordovans in the sky heading this way. The demons have all but cleared the college to hunt them. I want eight mages out there giving covering fire as they come in. Another four will defend the flanks from demons still hidden inside the grounds. Twenty warriors as spotters, in and outside the doors. And the library team is going in now. We'll not get a better chance. Move."

"All right, you heard him!" Chandyr clapped his hands together. "Mage teams one and two, cover duty. Swords two and three, spotters. Sword four, you're on the doors as backup. Library raiders, to me. Gentlemen, it is time for some fun."

Dystran had to admit Chandyr was good. They moved for him, respected him. The Lord of the Mount himself, they just feared. He liked it that way.

Noise battered around the dome. Men shouting, weapons and armour clashing. Metal-shod boots ringing on stone and marble. Dystran swallowed on a dry throat. The great doors swung open onto the cool, misty dawn.

"Go!" shouted Chandyr. "Forming up flanks quickly. Focused Orbs for attack, I want an IceWind cover for area attack, ForceCones on defence. Ready for changes any time on Lord Dystran's word." His voice cleared the din easily. A commander's voice brought back to life by the promise of action. "Spotters, I only want to hear numbers and direction."

Soldiers and mages ran through the doors, across the marble apron and down the stairs in front of the tower complex. Out of the protection of the ColdRoom lattice.

Dystran followed them, buoyed by the flow of mana that coursed through him and the beautiful fresh air in his lungs. He pulled in the shape for a focused Orb, following three mages taking up a central position. A quick glance showed him the defence and spotters deploying. Behind him, Captain Suarav led the library raiding party left and out of sight. His last three archivists were with the scarred garrison commander under the eye of Sharyr. It was a gamble that couldn't afford to fail.

In the grey sky north of Xetesk, the desperate flight neared its conclusion. Tens, hundreds of demons thronged the sky, a net for the five shapes that darted, twisted, ducked and soared trying to dodge them. It was hard to see how any of them would get through.

"A path," muttered Dystran, then raised his voice. "Let's make them a path. Concentrate on the area dead ahead, where the lead flyer is coming in. Time it, my mages. The gaps we make will fill quickly."

Spells flew and the first demons perished in fire and ice, blasted aside to give Xetesk's erstwhile enemies a chance of life.

Blessed emptiness on the approach. The raiding team slipped left, passed the dome defence and trotted quickly and quietly around the base of the complex. The library doors stood open, hanging from their hinges. The timelock ward was no use now, broken when the timbers had been battered apart in the early days of the occupation.

In the bloom of spells across the spectrum, the augmentation they gave their sight to counteract the gloom inside the library went unnoticed. Sharyr led three archivists, Captain Suarav and a spotter soldier up the edge of the broad steps where the shadows remained deep enough and the mist clung to the stone.

Inside, he could make out the shapes of bookshelves and tables. Little seemed to have been seriously disturbed though the wind picked at the pages of a few volumes scattered on the carpeted floor.

There would be demons in here somewhere. An earlier abortive raid had reported what appeared to be a systematic search through every piece of work. They'd had two years to find what they wanted but still the searching went on. Sharyr wondered briefly what it was.

He checked the team. They nodded their readiness and he moved in, every footstep fraught with the potential of a protesting floorboard. He felt naked outside the protection of the ColdRoom yet energised by the connection with the mana spectrum. The crack of the first spell behind him told him he was not alone.

It was a curious mix of feelings. He'd grown accustomed to the aura of security the ColdRooms provided but always lurking was the pain of being shut off from the spectrum. This way round, he had the comfort of mana at his command. All he had to cope with was the dread that accompanied it. Death a mere touch away.

Suarav came to his right shoulder as they entered the library. Sharyr's augmented eyes picked out objects and edges in sharp, monochromatic relief. It showed him Suarav's face, lined with concentration, beaded in sweat despite the chill of the air. He felt a surge of respect for the man. Nominally, he and the other soldier were spotters. In reality, they were there to sacrifice themselves to save the mages should the need arise.

The grand three-floored building was silent but for the ruffling of loose pages. Light was edging through the stained glass windows leaving deep shadow untouched under stairwells and recesses.

Sharyr kept to the centre of the carpeted path, the team bunched behind him. Their eyes would be everywhere. Left and right past every aisle of shelves, up into the arches and upper floors, ahead into the heart of the library and down lest they kick a stray book or put boot to bare wood.

He could feel the tension soaring. Suarav repeatedly tightened and relaxed his sword grip. Sharyr had to fight hard to keep the ForceCone construct steady. The breeze outside threw unsettling eddies into the library, like the downwash of wings. Sharyr drew in a deep breath and moved further in.

The signs of the demons' search were everywhere. Bookcases had been moved, glass fronts smashed. Parchments, volumes and tied scrolls were heaped in piles on shelves, stacked on the floor or scattered into corners. The damage was worse than at first sight. Ripped pages sat in drifts on lower shelves. Ancient texts were torn, spines broken. The knowledge of ages discarded. Whatever it was they were looking for, the demons had gone about their work methodically.

Sharyr felt his heart fall. This organised demolition was going to make their job all the harder and they couldn't afford to be in here a moment longer than absolutely necessary. Looking about him, he wondered if they'd find anything useful at all.

At the base of the grand staircase that swept left up to the next floor, he took them from the central path and underneath the marble steps. The demonology section was just ahead. It was the first of three they'd identified. Sharyr checked them all again, saw the strained but determined faces. Outside, spells cracked and echoed in the quiet of early morning. Distantly, a demon screamed.

He turned back and there they were. Floating gently down from the upper floors. He wasn't sure how many. Ten at a quick count. He backed up under the stairwell. Suarav just in front of him, the others behind, all wanting to feel a wall at their backs. The demons were stark grey against the deeper background, shining slightly. They were all of one strain. Long faces containing huge oval eyes. Tiny mouths but rimmed with fangs. Distended skulls. Delicate feathery wings and long slender arms at the end of which spidery fingers writhed.

"Keep calm," said Sharyr. "Keep your concentration." He had lost his ForceCone construct and was desperately trying to reform the shape. "Don't show them fear. We can take them."

"You heard him," growled Suarav. "They've got to get past me first."

He stepped square in front of the mage team, indicating the conscript do the same. The man didn't move but for the quaking of his body. A whimper escaped his mouth.

"Stand aside, Captain," said Sharyr.

"They will not take you before me."

"You're standing in the line of our spells."

"Just tell me when to duck."

The demons watched the exchange intently. Sharyr, who hadn't taken his eyes from them, felt as if he were being examined. Studied. He became aware that he could hear the whirring of their wings at the edge of his consciousness.

"We don't want to have to cast," he said.

"The damage to the library would be considerable," replied one of the demons immediately, voice soft and seductive.

The conscript muttered again.

"Strength," snapped Suarav. "They don't know what to do."

The demons spread slightly, moving to cut off any escape back toward the main doors. There was a gap to the back of the library. It had been left quite deliberately. No escape there.

"They're going to get us," said the conscript.

"No they aren't, not if we stick together," said Suarav. "Keep your blade out front."

"Won't do any good. Just one touch."

Sharyr felt the soldier tense to run. They had little time. "Mages, what do you have? Speak quickly."

"Orbs."

"Orbs."

"Ice."

In concert, the demons opened their arms and glided in. "Your souls will replenish us."

"No!" The young soldier broke left and ran, colliding with one of the archivists and sprinting away into the shadows.

"Structure down."

"Re-form!" snapped Sharyr.

"Get back here!" roared Suarav.

"Forget him and duck," said Sharyr. Suarav dropped to his haunches. "Orbs now."

It was a single focused FlameOrb and it struck the centre of the pack. The glare was painful, the effect brutal and instant. The tight globe of flame singed wings and burned coarse hair. It ate demon flesh. Smoke roiled. The scream was terrible. Sharyr followed it with his ForceCone. He directed it at the left side of the group. Unprepared, the demons were flicked away, twigs in the gale. He drove them up and back, flattening their bodies against the marble balustrade opposite. He wouldn't kill them but it represented space and time.

"Ice, right!"

Hardly had he uttered the command than the spell washed out, sucking and tearing at demon bodies, driving freezing air through their mana protection. Gouging, flaying.

"Now run, left. Find that idiot and get searching. We've still got a job to do. I'll hold these here."

His men obeyed without question, scattering into the back of the library. "And be careful of what's down there!"

Sharyr took stock. He held four struggling demons in check. The others were dead or dying. The IceWind blast had covered shelves, texts and tables over a ten-yard area with a thick coating of frost. That wasn't what worried him. It was the fire taking hold where the Orbed demon lay. And as the first scream of pure terror rang out from the back of the library, he turned to warn them that time was running out even faster than they had first thought.

The four surviving mages flew in at a frightening pace. Left and right, spotter soldiers called out the locations of demons now turning their attentions to the Xeteskians in front of the tower complex. Focused Orbs scattered out in a wide arc. In the thinning mist, demons howled and the noise grew as more and more ignored their airborne quarry. And in the centre of the mage defence, deep blue ForceCones and IceWind kept open the slimmest corridor.

"Let's be moving back slowly!"

Chandyr's voice towered over the slowly rising panic. They had to get this just right or they'd lose more mages saving Dordovans than if they'd all stayed inside and let their erstwhile enemies die. Dystran eyed the sky again. Vuldaroq was at their head, the other three now in close attendance. They had abandoned any thoughts of evading the mass of demons closing around them and were flying headlong and headfirst straight at the doors of the complex. The timing was going to be tight.

"FlameWall preparation now," he barked to the mage at his side.

Both men formulated the rigid, single-sided structure into which was built the mechanism that caused the flames to decay slowly. It was a static spell. They could cast and forget. Right now that was more than merely a blessing.

From his left, Dystran heard a sudden surge in shouting. Demons were attacking hard on the flank, threatening to overwhelm the flimsy mage defence.

Chandyr's voice sounded softly in his ear. "It has to be now, my Lord."

Dystran nodded his understanding. "Ready," he said.

"Last spells and retreat!" shouted Chandyr. "Don't look back, get inside the ColdRooms. I want men ready if any of those bastards follow our friends in. Go!"

Heartbeats later, a volley of spells clattered into the mass of demons still a hundred yards distant but closing hard. To the left, the distance was not so great. Mist burned away, screams filled the sky and cold washed out over the college, IceWind finding its targets and flaying the skin from its victims. But there were so very many of them. They choked the sky and now the ground in front of the college. All the spells had done was buy them a few moments.

"Run!" Chandyr led the charge back to the doors, stopping by Dystran who had backed right to the edge of the ColdRoom.

Soldiers and mages rushed past. Demons closed in from left, right and above. The corridor down which the Dordovans flew narrowed, the quartet dropping to line astern to keep the demons crucial feet from them. The last mage didn't want to look back. A huge winged creature was slashing at his feet, missing them by hairs alone.

"Wait just a moment," said Dystran, feeling the anxiety of the mage next to him. Vuldaroq was fifty yards away. "Right, let's give them something to aim at."

The two mages cast, FlameWalls, parallel, forty feet high and a hundred long sprang up either side of the doors. Demons coming in from the flanks were forced to stop, those above veered away. Vuldaroq charged headlong.

"Oh Gods," muttered Dystran and stumbled back inside the complex, dragging Chandyr and the other mage with him. "We're going to have to break their fall. Get in front of the tower pillar. This is going to hurt."

He'd only got a few yards inside and turned before Vuldaroq flew into the doorway. The ColdRoom snapped off the flow of mana. His ShadowWings disappeared and he plunged the dozen or so feet to the ground and rolled out of control toward the uncompromising stone of Dystran's tower. Fortunately for him, he hit Dystran first and the two men sprawled to a stop.

Immediately after him, the surviving three flashed in, dropped and bounced, mages rushing to their aid. Behind them, those demons too enraged to pull away followed them in. Three of them, one huge, the size of a wagon, two smaller, man size, and all three keening in pain inside the ColdRoom that stripped them of the mana that gave them life.

The battle was brief but loud. Swords flashed in the torchlight. Chandyr shouted for concentration and caution. The demons flew raggedly, dropping quickly as their strength ebbed but determined to take any with them that they could. Right in Dystran's eyeline, one of his men moved too slowly. His blade missed the claw that dragged at him and he was helpless, his soul snagged and taken. He crumpled.

Chandyr's blade thudded into the back of the same creature, others joining him. They drove it to the ground, hacking and slashing. One blow took its head from its body and the whole of it shuddered and lay still.

Silence but for heavy breathing and quiet reassuring voices. The other two demons had fled through the open complex doors which were shut on the decaying FlameWalls. Dystran looked about him at the white-faced men sitting or leaning against walls. Many had their heads in their hands. He could see tears, though whether through relief or terror he couldn't say. The close friends of the man who had died surrounded him. There was the sound of a blade dropping from a tired grip.

"Well done, everyone," said Chandyr. "Well done."

Dystran turned his attention to the man lying in his arms. Vuldaroq. The last time he had seen Dordover's Arch Mage, he had been belligerent, obese and arrogant. The man he looked at now was a shadow. Gaunt and pale, the skin of his face and neck hanging loose as it must do over his entire body. Dystran felt the shake in Vuldaroq's muscles and saw the tears squeezing from his tight-shut eyes. He drew breath in ragged gasps. Blood ran from cuts on his face and hands, and already skin was discolouring where he had struck the ground hard.

Dystran knew he should hate the man but two years changed so much. The war had been over ever since the demons first appeared and the Wesmen had left the city. Since then, the scant communication between the colleges had been like finding long-lost friends. There had been no time for recrimination.

The Lord of the Mount of Xetesk sat up and dragged Vuldaroq to a seated position. The Dordovan was spent. He surely could not have flown for much longer. A quick glance told him that the others were in no better condition.

"Get me hot drink, food and blankets. I want beds made for these men to rest on," said Dystran. "We've saved them from the demons. Let's not lose them to exhaustion."

Vuldaroq's eyes flickered open. They were red and brimmed with tears.

"Thank you," he croaked, voice dry and cracked.

"That was quite some entrance," said Dystran. "What the hell happened?"

"Dordover is gone," said Vuldaroq, voice suddenly loud in the silence that fell in the dome as he spoke. "We're all that is left."

Dystran felt cold. The second great college of Balaia. Reduced to four mages. "How?"

"We were never strong enough and they grew stronger every day. It was sudden in the last few days. Like they'd gained power from somewhere." He coughed. It wracked his entire body and he shivered.

"Later," said Dystran. "Food and rest now. You're safe here for the time being."

But the words Vuldaroq had spoken backed up everything Dystran feared. He searched for Chandyr. The commander met his gaze levelly from across the dome.

"I need some good news," said Dystran. "Where's my library team?"

"They aren't back yet," said Chandyr. "Patience, my Lord."

"It's happening now," said Dystran. "We don't have time for patience."

The shadows of demons flitted in and out of Sharyr's peripheral vision. The whir of their wings was the only sound they made. He had to keep out of his mind the thought of their spindly fingers reaching for his soul while he searched feverishly among the shelves for anything that might give them a clue to the demons' tactics.

Smoke was filling the library from the fire that was fast consuming the accumulated knowledge of Xetesk. Whatever he and his team collected now could well be all that was ever salvaged.

Sharyr knew the demons had lost him temporarily after he'd pushed them through a skylight and dropped the ForceCone. But they hadn't lost Suarav. What a spirit the man had. He could hear the captain's taunts and shouts, trying to draw the soul stealers away from the two surviving archivists looking for Dystran's prayed-for panacea.

The conscript was gone. The sound of the man's cut-off scream would live with him forever. He smiled grimly at the thought that forever for him could be a very short time indeed.

Sharyr grabbed a demonology scroll and with a surge of excitement having seen the author's name, stuffed it into his cloak. Behind him, new flame flared high into the library and sent a billow of choking smoke across the lower hall. The shadow of a grasping demon was cast huge against a wall. He heard one of his archivists call a warning.

"Time's up!" roared Suarav. There was the sound of a sword thudding dully. A demon yelped and screeched. "Meeting point, now!"

Sharyr turned right, heading back toward the seat of the fire. Back toward the library doors. He heard the whir and saw a demon round the corner and float gently toward him along the aisle. He backed away.

"No escape," said the demon, advancing with hands outstretched. "We seek what you seek."

"It'll burn before you set eyes on it," said Sharyr. He backed off further and felt a chill, heard the whirring again, this time behind him. He was trapped.

"No escape," repeated the demon. It came on, fingers rippling.

Right was wall, left, bookcases. Sharyr's mind was made up. The rest went by in a blur.

"You will not have me," he whispered.

He could not cast, there was no time. Flames crackled menacingly in the centre of the library. Smoke irritated his eyes. The demons closed lazily. Sharyr had only one chance at what he intended to do. He threw himself shoulder first into the freestanding bookcases that were the left-hand border of the aisle. It was a long, solid structure with more shelves racked beyond it. About ten feet high and heavy with books. Mercifully, it was not bolted to the floor.

Sharyr felt it move and he started to climb, scrambling up the shelves, arms and legs scrabbling for purchase. His momentum carried him up while the bookcase tipped away from him. With his feet on the top shelf, the bookcase passed the point of no return. The thundering sound of books falling mixed with that of his breathing, his heartbeat, Suarav's shouts and the flames. The shelving creaked. He stood, riding the case. It gathered momentum and cannoned into the one across the next aisle.

"Oh shit," he muttered. There were six aisles before the wide gap of the centre aisle of the library.

He began to move again, running at an angle across the cases, jumping to the next, almost stumbling. He could feel the quickening movement beneath his feet. He kept himself going, his paces light. The clattering of the cases and the slipping of books reached a crescendo. Suarav was barking orders. He could see the heads of his friends bobbing as they sprinted down the centre aisle, demons in pursuit. He daren't guess how close his own pursuers were.

Sharyr took one last leap, caught the falling edge of a case and tumbled hard to the ground. He turned a diving forward roll, feeling a sharp crack in his collarbone. He sprawled and cried out, clutching at his clothing, desperate to keep the texts with him.

A strong hand gripped him under his good arm and hauled.

"By all the Gods burning, that was quite a performance," growled Suarav. "Now go, run hard left at the main doors as we'd planned. You know the way in."

Sharyr could feel the heat of the fire on his face. It was eating up at the walls. The pain in his right shoulder was terrible, nauseating.

"What about you?"

"I'll keep them back." Suarav leaned in. "Don't argue with me, boy. We always knew this could happen."

Sharyr nodded, turned and ran; the last thing he heard behind him was Suarav daring them to try and pass him.

CHAPTER 14

The Unknown made them all wait. The longboat was ready to take him and The Raven to join the others already aboard the *Calaian Sun* but he wasn't ready yet. There was never enough time for goodbye. Particularly when he had no desire to leave.

"I can't believe I'm doing this," he said, walking arm in arm with Diera through the woods to the left of the path that led to the landing beach. Jonas trotted along next to them, oblivious to the mood for the moment, lost in a nonsense game of his own devising.

"It's the price we have to pay because of who you are," said Diera, her words carrying no conviction.

A stiff warm breeze swayed the narrow trunks surrounding them. A few dead leaves fell.

"We've paid enough," he said.

"Apparently not."

The Unknown stopped and faced her, looking into her lovely face, the fear in her eyes clear behind her forced smile.

"One word and I'll stay," he said.

"What, and wonder how they are coping without you? We've been through this, Sol. There isn't a choice." She looked down at Jonas who had stopped his play to stare at them, a frown across his innocence. "There never is."

"I'm sorry." Every word was clumsy. None of it helped. He was trapped between his desire and his calling. Gods, he'd shunned the soldier's life to avoid exactly that. At least now he knew why. It hurt.

"What for?" She placed her hands on his chest, smoothed his shirt to either side. "I heard Sha-Kaan. I do trust him. This is the only way."

He was unsure who she was trying to convince.

"Come on," she said. "Or you'll miss the tide and we'll have to go through all this again."

He crushed her to him and felt her strength give and the sobs coming. Jonas clung onto his mother's leg, his expression collapsed into anxiety.

"Mummy?"

The Unknown swept him up and the three embraced long and hard.

"You're not coming back, are you?" said Diera, voice thick and half muffled by his chest. "Not this time."

The Unknown released her, keeping hold of Jonas. "I—"

"No time for dreams or lies," said Diera, stroking his face.

"I want to believe it," said The Unknown. "The Gods know it'll be the one thing that keeps me going."

"But your head says what?"

"That we're going against an enemy so powerful it has all but overrun the four colleges and controls Balaia. That in all probability, we will all die attempting to liberate our country. That what sort of husband and father would I be if I didn't at least try?"

Unexpectedly, Diera smiled, this time with warmth and humour. The Unknown smoothed away her tears.

"You know, when I was growing up, I dreamed I'd have a husband who was a true hero. Someone who I'd wave off to fight for me and welcome back time and again. I got my wish, didn't I? Almost."

"Looks like it," he said. "You should have chosen better."

"And be a demon slave or dead," she said. "I'll take the heartache."

"There is that."

"I can't wave you off. Not again."

The Unknown nodded. He unhooked Jonas's grip from his shoulder and brought the boy in front of him. Jonas regarded him quizzically.

"You look after your mother, won't you?"

Jonas's sombre nod dragged a chuckle from The Unknown's dry, sore throat where he'd been swallowing hard. He kissed the boy on his cheeks and handed him back to Diera.

"Goodbye, Sol," she said, tears falling anew. "I love you."

"And I love you. With every beat of my heart," he said. "Keep believing."

"I'll try."

He leaned in and kissed her on the mouth, a tender, lingering touch. Their tongues met briefly, firing passion, and pulled away. He stepped back, let his hand brush her cheek and then forced his legs to turn and carry him to the waiting longboat.

Sha-Kaan had stayed in the Klene a very long time. He had cursed the conspiracy of circumstances that had taken the eyes of the Kaan from the Balaian dimension. But he knew also that there was little the brood could realistically have done. The Xeteskians had dabbled once too often with the power of dimensional space and now they were all paying the penalty. Contact with Dragonene mages was sparse and difficult. Soon it would cease altogether. The demons grew stronger every day.

He was unused to the fear he felt at what he had to do. His brood urged him not to travel alone but he really had no choice. A flight of Kaan dragons would be seen as a threat and destroyed. Further, he still could not afford to take able dragons from the defence of his Broodlands while the newborn were so weak.

So it was that he flew high and alone for the Broodlands of the Naik, his fiercest enemies. He already knew he could rely on the Veret to support him. Longtime allies, they had foresight that the Naik had never displayed. His greatest fear was that the Naik would see this as an opportunity to destroy the Kaan, as indeed it was. But if they did, it would consign them to death also. The question was, could he persuade them of that fact?

One factor was of some comfort. Should he fail, the enemy would not be long following him to the dead lands.

No Kaan knew the exact location of the Naik Broodlands but they all knew in which part of Beshara they would encounter attack. Sha-Kaan prepared himself for the inevitable challenge. His flame ducts were full and lubricated should he need them. The Vestare had spent days massaging balms and oils into his scales and the old muscles at his wing roots to give him increased flexibility; and he practised in his mind what he would say to buy him life enough to at least face Yasal-Naik, their brood leader.

And once he was prepared, he pulsed a message to Hirad Coldheart that he was among enemies and dived through the high cloud, barking loud to announce his presence.

For a while, he saw nothing in the skies. Below him, a vast desert fled away to distant iron-grey mountains. The great ocean was far away to his right and behind him the lush plains of Teras were a distant memory. He saw them first as a cloud like a sandstorm brewing ahead and close to the ground. The cloud boiled upward, spiralling fast toward him, resolving itself into six rust-brown Naik dragons. All were young to his eyes, all desperate to reach him first, all charged with aggression and hate.

Sha-Kaan watched them come. He made sure he displayed no aggression himself. He circled slowly, his belly scales fully displayed, his neck straight and his wings deployed. Their formation worried him. It was by no means a holding pattern. It was an attack chevron.

He barked again, a sound of submission, but they still drove on unchanged, their calls a challenge to him and his brood. He held station a moment longer until it became plain their pace was going to take them straight through him. Barking his irritation, he beat his wings hard, propelling himself up and north of them, forcing them to break formation to intercept. One was ahead of the others. Sha-Kaan saw its mouth open.

He had not survived so many cycles without being a master of timing his dives. The Naik drove onward, sure of his quarry. Sha-Kaan saw the breath draw in and the neck swell around its flame ducts. Orange fire washed the space where he should have been but he had furled his wings and dropped like a stone, bringing his head round to pour flame over the young dragon's flank.

In the next instant, he spread his wings wide, braking his fall dramatically. He roared loud. The remaining dragons faltered in flight, watching their brother plummet groundward. Perhaps for the first time, they realised who it was they faced. This was no ordinary enemy. This was Sha-Kaan.

The five remaining fanned out around him where he hovered, again beating his wings gently, displaying his scales, hanging perpendicular to the ground thousands of feet below.

"Do you know nothing, or are you so full of anger you cannot read the signs of your visitors?" Sha's voice carried across the winds of heights. He saw them hesitating, caught between their awe of him and their knowledge that together they might just take him down and strike a decisive victory.

"You are alone, Old Kaan," taunted one. "Vulnerable."

"That I am," said Sha-Kaan. "And perhaps your minds should turn to wonder why that is? Had I come to challenge you, I would not have come alone."

"We are unsure that you are alone," said another.

Sha-Kaan looked long and slow at the skies all around them. The clouds he had come through were ten thousand feet above their heads. There was nowhere to hide.

"Then you should open your eyes, whelp. Now take me to Yasal-Naik, I must speak with him."

"We will not. It is a trick to gain access to our Broodlands."

Sha-Kaan sighed. "Then bring him to me."

"We do not take orders from the Kaan."

Sha-Kaan rumbled in his throat. "It is a request."

"State the reason."

"Because if he doesn't come and he doesn't listen to me, the Arakhe will soon destroy us all."

There was a pause while they digested his statement and no doubt spoke among themselves, pulsing thoughts and ideas.

"There is no evidence to support this. Yasal will not thank us for disturbing him but he will thank us for bringing back your carcass."

"And you will condemn your brood to extinction." Sha-Kaan beat his wings once and extended his neck before bringing it back to a respectful "S" shape. "I ask you to believe me. I am Sha-Kaan and I have travelled alone to speak to Yasal. Let him decide my fate. I will abide by whatever he decrees.

"The choice, my young Naik, is yours."

The Unknown didn't say much for a day. Hirad left him to it. The big warrior, limping a little more heavily, spent most of the time leaning on the aft rail, gazing back across the open water. He watched the Ornouth Archipelago diminishing toward the horizon. It was a beautiful sight with the sun still catching white sand or the azure shallow waters and throwing vibrant patterns onto the haze in the sky.

But Hirad knew he wasn't seeing that. All he could see were his wife and child disappearing beyond his reach and he had no real expectation of ever seeing them again.

It was dawn on the second day of their voyage back to Balaia. Hirad was on the wheel deck looking down on The Unknown's shaven head. Behind him, Jevin was guiding his novice helmsman. The elf's gentle voice little more than a murmur as he described the nuances of steering his sleek vessel.

Hirad felt a hand on his shoulder. Denser.

"Hey, big fella. Thinking too hard?"

Hirad turned briefly. "Look what I've done."

"He knows he's in the right place," said Denser. "Just give him time."

"I've torn him from his family. It's unforgivable."

"True but you can't think of it that way. Take it back as far as you like. Like I say, I'm more to blame. I'm a Xeteskian."

"No you aren't. You're Raven."

"I believed them for long enough."

The Unknown turned and stared up at them, his face stone.

"Neither of you are helping me with your feeble angst," he said. "I have my own mind. I exercised it. Now let it drop." He returned his gaze to the ocean.

"Where's Erienne?" asked Hirad after an uncomfortable pause.

"Resting. She and Cleress are still working on that casting."

"Will it work?"

"We'd better hope so," said Denser. "Or this is going to be a very short attempt to save the world."

Hirad chuckled but he didn't feel the humour, more Denser's unconscious adoption of Ilkar's turn of phrase. "It could be that anyway."

"How so?"

"Sha-Kaan pulsed me before dawn. He's trying to speak to the Naik."

"Ah," said Denser. He scratched at his neatly trimmed beard. "Tricky."

"Yeah. And if I don't hear from him again before we sight Balaia, we can assume he's dead." Hirad didn't believe the words as he spoke them.

"Do you think he was serious when he talked about how he felt the dragons had to help us?"

"Denser, he is not given to talking bollocks, unlike your good self."

"Just asking."

"Tell me something, Denser." It was The Unknown again. "How long can Erienne keep this casting going?"

"I've no idea. It'll be draining. All the One castings are."

"You two want to join me amidships? We need to think about tactics."

Hirad smiled and gestured Denser to precede him. This was The Unknown he wanted. Reluctant, maybe, but thinking. The three men sat on netted crates under the mainmast.

"You understand what I'm getting at," continued The Unknown. "It's all very well when we've evened the odds under Erienne's casting. What if she is unable to cast for any reason?"

"Well, we won't be able to take down a single demon," said Hirad.

"That's not strictly speaking true," said The Unknown. "What it will be is a question of keeping them distant enough for Denser to destroy with spells, right?"

"That's not something we can keep up indefinitely either," said Hirad.

"Correct, but we have to work on the premise that we won't have to. It's a contingency until we can find shelter or Erienne can cast herself." The Unknown must have seen the cynicism in Hirad's expression. "Put it this way, if we are in a situation where Denser is our only effective weapon, we're already dead."

"Thanks a heap," said Denser.

"You know what I mean," growled The Unknown. "We'll be working to buy time and space, right? I've had an idea we should work on."

"And there was I thinking you were back there mooning over your family," said Hirad.

The Unknown almost smiled. "Only ninety-nine per cent of the time. Go and get the others except Erienne. Auum and Rebraal too, we need them to act as demons."

Hirad pushed himself off the crates. "I hope this master tactic of yours protects us from a demon's touch. It only takes the one."

"Been thinking about that too," said The Unknown.

"Busy, this one per cent of your mind, isn't it?"

"Yes, Hirad, you should try it some time. Think about it. Rebraal says they are impervious because their religion gives them a single focus, a group belief. The Wesmen are apparently protected by the Spirits whom they worship and revere. The two are similar to my mind. It's about having something greater than yourself surrounding you. Something that binds you to the mass, gives you the strength of everyone who is like you."

"Fantastic. I'll convert to elvish immediately," said Hirad.

The Unknown's hand slapped him hard on the forearm. "No! Bloody hell, Hirad, you can be truly stupid sometimes. This should have occurred to you already. Remember when the demons got at Will in Sha-Kaan's Klene that time?"

"Yeah. I remember he died. So what?"

"Couldn't steal his soul though, could they? Will died because they chilled his life and he wasn't strong enough to resist. Why don't you think his soul went to the pit, eh?"

Hirad shrugged and looked at Denser who was smiling at him. "Something funny?"

"Only that I'm about to quote to you something you've quoted at me so many times I'm thinking of having it tattooed on my forehead."

"What? That he was Raven and that makes a difference?"

"Stole my thunder."

And even as he opened his mouth to object, Hirad could see The Unknown was right. He had felt it the moment they had sat together as The Raven in the Al-Drechar's house a few days before. You couldn't bottle it, it was just there. He could feel it now. Strength. Belief. Spirit.

"You know it," said Hirad.

The Unknown stood and stared him in the eye. "And I'll tell you something, Coldheart. I've already had my soul taken from me once. And nothing and nobody is going to part me from it again."

"We can do this, can't we?" said Hirad, believing for the first time.

"Course we can," said Denser, his face splitting into a grin. "We're The Raven!"

Their laughter echoed out across the open sea.

CHAPTER 15

Yasal-Naik circled Sha-Kaan very slowly, eyes following the Great Kaan as he spun on his tail, displaying his belly scales at all times. A gesture of respect, of peace and of submission. Sha-Kaan bit down hard on his pride, knowing that to gain audience with this most aggressive of brood fathers was more than he had genuinely believed he would achieve. To jeopardise that with a petulant display of superiority now would be truly calamitous folly. They both knew Sha-Kaan was the stronger dragon. This was not the time to demonstrate it.

The five young Naik circled nearby, keeping watch on the open skies, searching for the Kaan attack that would never come.

"You have killed one of my brood," said Yasal-Naik. "That alone is enough to see you taken from the skies with flames as your final companion."

"The whelp attacked me despite my attitude and bearing. I had no choice but to defend myself."

"And your intrusion into my skies is punishable equally severely."

"Then carry out your sentence, Yasal. My only regret is that I would not live to see you confront your blindness."

The Naik brood father continued to circle, aware of Sha-Kaan's discomfort.

"It is an action I can take at will, is it not?"

Sha-Kaan rumbled deep in his huge chest. "Then hear me, since you have nothing to lose. Know why it is I have come here alone to speak with you."

Yasal ceased his circling finally, clicking the back of his tongue. The rattling echoed in his cheeks. Sha-Kaan flicked his wings in acknowledgement, returning to horizontal flight.

"Let us fly, Great Kaan," said Yasal. "You have my attention."

"I am grateful to you." Sha-Kaan took up station beside Yasal and followed him in a lazy glide. "Your decision demonstrates maturity."

"From you that is a compliment," said Yasal. "But don't mistake maturity for conciliation. There is none."

"Just listen to me," said Sha-Kaan. "I am tired of your threats."

The two dragons' eyes met across the narrow gulf between them. Yasal's burned with an anger Sha-Kaan recognised in himself as a younger dragon.

"Speak."

"Yasal, I am not here to surrender, I am not here to challenge you. I have travelled alone as a demonstration of my veracity. You may always have hated the Kaan and despised me in particular. That is natural. All broods desire dominion and one day we will assuredly return to that state."

"'One day'? What is wrong with today?"

"Because today that battle is rendered pointless."

"One of my escort mentioned something similar. Explain."

"The Arakhe have taken Balaia," said Sha-Kaan.

"Surely a cause for celebration."

"You know what that means."

"Yes, Sha-Kaan. That your melde will soon be shattered, that the Kaan will dwindle. That I need not spill one more drop of Naik blood to beat you. Merely bide my time."

Sha-Kaan feathered his tongue in humour. "All these things are true. But can you fly a little further?"

"Where else do I need to travel? I will have achieved the Naik's destiny. I will rule Beshara unopposed."

"Idiot youngster," snapped Sha-Kaan. "Think."

"About what? You have promised me victory."

Sha-Kaan sampled Yasal-Naik's tone, smelled the odours of his body, faint in the wind. He was sure he was being toyed with but the Naik's bearing suggested interested neutrality.

"Should the Balaian dimension fall, the Arakhe will have everything they want. Doorways to this dimension, the dead, and thence to everywhere. Your melde, every brood's melde. You have heard the prophecies and the warnings. They are as much Naik lore as they are Kaan or Gost or Veret. They have to be stopped now."

"You have controlled your melde dimension poorly," said Yasal.

Sha-Kaan spat fire in sudden anger.

"Skies curse you, Yasal, I wonder why I haven't stayed at home to watch you die."

"Because, old Kaan, you need the strength of my brood; or at least to know that your lands are safe while you sort out the problems you say have afflicted your melde. You deny your lack of attention caused what you say we now face?"

"You know the birthing cycle of the Kaan. Your attacks over my skies were not random events, after all. You know what happens around the time of our birthings. So, it appears, do the Arakhe. What they did, to use a human phrase, was give mages enough rope to hang themselves with, then sat and waited until we were not guarding Balaia's fabric. Mages ripped the fabric and we were not there. The Arakhe were."

"You should have controlled your subjects more effectively."

Sha-Kaan let the comment ride for a while. He wasn't being goaded now. There was a gulf in the understanding between the two broods. It was as fundamental as their hatred for one another. After a long pause, he responded.

"That is why you will never be the dominant brood."

"How so?"

"Because you do not understand the relationship between your vitality and the independence of the minds in your melde dimension."

"You've lost me."

"I expect so."

"Dragons rule dimensional space. We take what we need," said Yasal.

"I agree with the latter statement. I take issue with the former purely because if you don't help me now, it will soon no longer be true."

"So you say."

"Kill me and find out for yourself," said Sha-Kaan.

It was a challenge but he knew Yasal could not afford to take him up on it. The Naik gave something approximating a laugh.

"You intrigue me, Great Kaan. And I respect the risk you have taken travelling here alone. Foolhardy but still. . . . Tell me exactly what it is you want the Naik to do. Agree a truce perhaps."

"You and every brood," said Sha-Kaan. "And I am afraid a truce on its own will not be enough. The invasion of Balaia is far more advanced than you realise."

"Accepted. State your plea."

Sha-Kaan told him and watched all that arrogance and humour fall from his scent, his eyes and his attitude on the glide. He saw genuine uncertainty and abrupt realisation. When he had finished speaking, Sha-Kaan waited as he knew he must. Yasal's wings were twitching slightly, the skin around his eyes pinched.

"Land with me," he said eventually. "I would take food and water. And so should you."

Hirad landed hard on his backside and laughter rang out across the deck again. He propped himself up on his elbows and looked round at Denser.

"Fancy a swim, Xetesk-man?"

"Sorry, Hirad," said Denser, plainly nothing of the kind.

"You should try having him as your practice demon," said the barbarian. "See how far you get."

In front of him, Auum reached out a hand. Hirad pulled himself to his feet.

"You saw my move," said Auum.

It was as close to a compliment as the TaiGethen leader ever came.

"Seeing is one thing, reacting is another," said Hirad, the elvish easy on his tongue.

"You are faster than the rest."

"That is small comfort."

"What's he saying?" asked Denser.

"That you should take a turn and he'd wipe that smile off your face," said Hirad.

"All right, enough," said The Unknown. "It doesn't matter that Auum is faster than any demon, he's found a flaw in the tactics. We've left a gap in the defence and it means we can't make the space between us big enough for Denser to cast."

"How much does that matter?" asked Hirad. "Assuming our souls really are safe."

"Just because a demon can't take your soul doesn't mean it can't rip your arms off while I'm helpless to cast," said Denser.

"Good point. So what do we do?" asked Hirad.

The Unknown looked at Darrick. "Any ideas?"

"I have," said Rebraal.

He along with Auum's Tai and four former Protectors had been playing the part of demons, unarmed but carrying thick wooden crate lids to deflect The Raven's blades—scabbarded though they were.

"And?"

"It has nothing to do with your tactics. The pushing roll is fine. The line defence is effective enough and tricky to pierce. The problem is there aren't enough of you to repel eight of us."

"There is more, though," said Darrick. "The nature of what you are trying to have us achieve leaves us vulnerable. We aren't going for killing thrusts, we're going for weighted blows to drive them back. Swords aren't balanced for that and our follow-throughs leave us exposed as Auum is so good at demonstrating."

The Unknown nodded. "Agreed, I was wondering about our weapons. Should be relatively easy to accommodate. Blackthorne should have maces enough for us. Rebraal's point, though, is more difficult, I fear."

"No it isn't," said Rebraal. "Some of us will have to come with you."

"That won't work," said Hirad. "We've already agreed we need you in Julatsa and Ark and his people in Xetesk. We have to have people in place to motivate and who know what is going on."

"And what is the point of that if you are overwhelmed by demons before you can achieve what you must?" Rebraal shrugged.

"You are only six," said Auum in halting, heavily accented Balaian. "Two mages, four warriors. It is too few."

The Raven looked at each other. Thraun inscrutable as always, The Unknown calmly weighing up all he was hearing, and Darrick nodding. Hirad knew the elves were right. And it wasn't as if The Raven hadn't fought with others countless times before. Gods burning, they'd spent ten years fighting in mercenary lines. But this felt different. It was admitting before they really began that they weren't up to the task. It left an unpleasant taste.

"We can't afford to be taken out," said Darrick.

"Thanks, General, I had worked that part out," said Hirad.

"I mean we have to be as prepared as we can be. Part of that is going in with the right numbers."

"Well let's take an army," said Hirad. "Do the job right."

"What's got into you all of a sudden?" The Unknown was frowning.

"Nothing." Hirad spat over the side of the ship.

"The problem is," continued Darrick carefully, "that we haven't sat and really thought this all through. The Unknown's tactics play here has demonstrated that we can't realistically hope to beat significant numbers of demons without Erienne to strip their protection from them. And we don't have the time to raise an army. And if we did, their souls would have no protection."

"We could ask the demons only to come at us in groups of eight or less," said Denser.

The Unknown spared Denser a brief bleak look before turning to Hirad. "Well?"

"You are our heart," added Thraun.

"But none of you think we can do this alone, do you?" said Hirad.

"That's about the size of it," said Darrick. "But ultimately, if you believe otherwise, we'll be with you."

"So, no pressure then," said Denser.

Hirad smiled thinly at him. "Funny." But bad taste or not, he couldn't blind himself to reality. He looked over at Rebraal. "What do you have in mind?"

"My heart says we should all go with you. I would consider it an honour to fight with you to save my brother's soul. But my people are in Julatsa. I lead the Al-Arynaar. What other choice do I have but to be with them?"

"Fine. So you're going to do exactly what we agreed all along."

"Hirad, what is wrong with you?" asked The Unknown. "This is impatient even for you. Just listen."

Hirad closed his mouth. He hadn't meant it to sound like it did. His mind felt unsettled. Like he was about to lose control. He nodded an apology. Rebraal acknowledged it.

"The same is true to a certain extent of Ark and his men. Some of them have to remain in Xetesk to organise what must be done. But you need more blades. Auum's Tai will come with you and, if they are agreeable, a pair of the Protectors."

"You're practically doubling our numbers," said Hirad.

"It isn't meant to be a slur on The Raven," said Rebraal. "But the fact is, not all who go will come back. We have to give ourselves the best chance. You're at the centre of this. The Raven, I mean. But even you need support and dragons can't give you that on the ground hand to hand. Without it, one mistake and the demons win. We can't take an army, as Darrick has said, or we leave Balaia defenceless. But we do have us."

"Spoken like Ilkar," said Hirad. "I know you're right. It's just hard to admit."

"None here would do The Raven disservice and you are still its core. While you burn, we can win. Don't let pride extinguish you."

Hirad breathed deep. He didn't have to look back at his friends to know what they were thinking.

"Right," he said. "We'll do it your way. Now I'm going to rest. I don't feel quite right."

Hirad walked as quickly as he was able to his cabin, his mind aflame. It made him nauseous and unsteady. For a moment he wondered if he was sea-sick but the ship was making serene progress and it was not an affliction to which he was prone. Entering his cabin, he splashed water on his face and towelled it dry before lying on his bunk and closing his eyes.

He felt detached from his body though he could still feel it; as if touching it from a distance. His mouth was dry and his forehead lined with sweat. He swallowed hard, his heart racing in his chest. He'd have cried out but he wasn't sure anyone would hear him.

The cabin was dim but behind his eyelids stark lights danced. Hirad felt himself slipping away from the creaking of ship's timbers, the call of orders across the deck and the screech of gulls far from shore. He didn't fight it, he had no defence. The last coherent thought he had was one of relief that he hadn't collapsed on deck. He didn't want anyone to worry.

There was a battering sound. It accompanied the lights that were so bright that Hirad couldn't see beyond them though he was aware something was out there. The battering was frenzied and constant, the work of countless rams and cudgels desperate to break in. He didn't pause to consider where. The tumult was accompanied by screaming. Faint at first but gaining in volume, getting closer.

He had heard the like before. It was the sound of a routed population driving headlong away from danger. It was disordered, panicked and terri-fied. He fancied he could see shadows behind the lights but it might just as easily have been a trick of his mind.

Pressure built behind his eyes. It grew quickly, in harmony with the screaming which dragged painfully in his head and the battering which dulled to a background clamour by comparison. Like the incoming tide it was inexorable and like rising flood waters it threatened to engulf him, drag him under.

Pain grew, blossomed across his consciousness. He thought he might have screamed but he couldn't hear the sound over those of the masses behind the light. But with the pain was the warmth of recognition. A touching of minds like the meeting of old friends.

Could it be Sha-Kaan? Hirad opened his mouth to bid him welcome but then the spirit passed through him on the crest of a scream and he was shovelled to wakefulness. He blinked at the half-light of the cabin, unsure whether to laugh or cry. He carried with him the tender feelings of the encounter; all the energy, life and love of his oldest friend. Yet beneath it, the fear of oblivion. Real, almost tangible, shouting from each of his muscles and the dulling thud in his head like a warning siren.

He sat up quickly, felt darkness threaten to close on him and a hand on his shoulder.

"Hey, not so fast," said Erienne. "Take your time."

Hirad focused on her slowly. "How long have you been here?"

"Ever since you shouted Ilkar's name the first time."

"I knew it!"

Hirad swung his feet out of the bunk and stood up, letting Erienne guide him.

"Where are you going?"

"On deck. Rebraal must have felt this."

"Felt what?"

Hirad moved past her and yanked open the door. "Ilkar. He moved straight through me. He was running. He was frightened."

"That's not . . ."

Hirad didn't stop to ease Erienne's confusion. He trotted along the short corridor to the aft steps and up out into the fresh smells and bright light of the deck. The sun washed over the timbers, the sails flapped idly in the light breeze and the scent of the sea filled his nostrils.

Rebraal was in a seated position, leaning against a crate and surrounded by The Raven and TaiGethen. The Unknown passed a cup to him and he drank. His face was pale in the light and his eyes darted here and there, settling on Hirad.

"You felt it too," said Hirad.

Rebraal nodded. "Through every fibre."

"What does it mean?"

"It means he is chased. It means the demons are breaking down the doors. It means they think they have found a way in." Rebraal paused and sighed. "It means we need the wind. I think the dead are running out of time."

Chapter 16

Dystran made sure the survivors had space, warm food and blankets. He had taken them into his tower and sat the three of them in his chambers. They were chilly like the day outside but the chairs were deeply upholstered and comfortable. Dystran had often sunk into one of them himself to try and imagine what life had been like before the demons came.

Already he had people looking at the texts they had brought back with them but he was more concerned with the condition of the raiders right now. They had lost one swordsman in the library, which still burned though it was clear the demons were trying to extinguish the blaze. Slaves had formed a bucket chain that snaked and split to six wells in and around the college.

One of his archivists had also perished, right at the moment he must have thought he was safe. It was ironic that the raiders' escape route back into the dome should be that first trodden by The Raven when they broke in. A time of life that seemed so distant now.

Suarav had survived by sheer force of will, holding off demons to give his mages enough time to get through the window and away into the ColdRoom lattice. But he was suffering for it now. He sat hunched in a blanket, staring down at his quivering hands. His fingers were blue and the twitching of his muscles meant he could barely hold his mug. Dystran pressed his hands around it and helped it to his lips.

Suarav's hands were so cold. Unnaturally so. His face bore the scars of a dozen demon's claws, his lips were cracked and pallid. The soldier had trouble taking the drink. Much of it dripped down his chin.

"Take your time," said Dystran. "You can relax now, you're safe."

"They couldn't take my soul," said Suarav. "They couldn't take it."

"No indeed." Dystran had been genuinely surprised by the fact.

"And do you know why?" Suarav's face cracked into a pained smile. The cuts on his face crinkled, spilling fresh blood. "Because not all of them can do it."

"What?" Dystran started and had to remind himself not to take his hands away from Suarav's.

"Some of the lesser castes clearly don't have the ability or I would not be here."

Suarav took another sip of his drink and coughed. A shudder ran the length of his body and he sighed, collapsing in a little on himself.

"All right, enough now," said Dystran. "Build your strength. Rest easy. We will guard you here."

"It's cold," said Suarav.

"Yes it is," said Dystran, though not cold enough to account for the captain's condition. "I'll get you another blanket. Maybe some gloves." He snapped his fingers at one of the guards. "See to it."

He pressed Suarav's hands to his mug once more and turned to Sharyr who sat on a small sofa with the other archivist, Brynel. Both men were lapsing into shock. Bodies trembling, eyes staring. Brynel swallowed repeatedly. He was going to need attention quickly. Sharyr was only marginally better. At least he raised a smile and was able to drink.

"You've done a marvellous thing," said Dystran.

"If the texts we took reveal anything." He tried to laugh but it came out a splutter.

"Even if they don't, it shows we are still fighting. That we still believe we can beat these bastards."

"Without him we'd all be gone." Sharyr nodded at Suarav. A glance told Dystran he'd closed his eyes, his breathing was laboured but at least it was even. "He was immense. He saved us all so many times." Abruptly, tears streamed down Sharyr's face and a heaving sob shook his body. "Sorry, sorry." Tea slopped over his hands and he dropped the mug which shattered in the empty fireplace, making him flinch violently.

"Shh," said Dystran. He placed a calming hand on his shoulder and stroked his upper arm. "Let it out. It's all right, you're safe now."

Sharyr clutched Dystran's robes. "They kept on coming and we were too frightened to cast. They clicked their jaws, they reached for us with those hands. They got so close. We just ran and he kept them away though they bit him and scratched his face. They wanted his soul but he was so strong and they couldn't get round him to get to us. But they taunted us, they taunted us and they reached out for our souls." He gripped harder. "I looked deep in their eyes and there was nothing there. Nothing. It's what we face if they take us. Emptiness."

Dystran gripped Sharyr's wrists and gently eased his hands away. "But they won't take us, will they? Because in this room, three men of incredible courage have given us a chance. You Sharyr, and Suarav and Brynel."

"They were so close," moaned Sharyr.

"And that is as close as they'll ever get. Think on it, Sharyr, and remember you're safe now. They can't get you in here. I promise."

At last, another smile from Sharyr. "Thank you, my Lord."

"No, my friend. It is Xetesk who should be thanking you. Rest. Rest, all of you."

Dystran stood up and spread his arms, embracing them all with the gesture. "Anything that you want that is within my current power, you may have. And consider yourselves stood down from any duties until further notice."

None of them were looking at him. He wasn't even sure any of them even heard him. He snapped his fingers at Chandyr and strode out to the first landing.

"Laid that on a bit thick, didn't you?" said the commander as soon as the door had shut behind them.

"What would you rather I do? Rush them back to the front?" Dystran moved away to the top of the stairs. "Did you stop to look at them?"

"Yeah, they look in some trouble."

"*Some trouble?* Bloody hell, Chandyr, I'm no healer but I'd say they were all dying, wouldn't you? Suarav is in desperate straits. Now you're out here to take orders, not discuss whether I'm patronising our survivors or not. I don't know what to do with any of them. Get our best up here and get me an answer. If that means getting them into the control zone in the catacombs so we can cast, then do it. Your men love Suarav and I need Sharyr able to help examine our new texts."

"And Brynel?"

"We need every mage, Commander." He indicated Chandyr go ahead of him. "I'm not prepared to lose any of those men in there. And that means you need to run faster than I do."

Dystran paused at the top of the spiral stair and watched his commander go. Halfway down he heard a hurried "Sir!" and then a second set of footsteps came closer as Chandyr's diminished. Dystran waited for the man to climb the stairs. It was a mage, Feiyn.

"My Lord," he said, breathing hard. He was weak from poor food and confinement and, like them all, dying by degrees.

"I'm presuming you aren't running up here merely to tone your legs."

"No, my Lord."

"Well, I'm on my way down. If you have breath, walk with me and tell me what it is that couldn't wait."

Dystran led the way down the stairs at a gentle pace.

"Vuldaroq has read one of the texts."

Dystran had to check himself before he spoke. "He could read our lore, could he?" he said instead.

"This is a general research paper. A theory based on a mapping of energies in interdimensional space."

"Ah. Sounds like the work of dear old Bynaar to me. He was the first man to postulate that mana flow could be ordered and driven without . . ." Dystran trailed off even as he heard the sharply indrawn breath behind him. "I don't recall asking for texts on that subject."

"It was inside another on demonology," explained Feiyn.

Dystran stopped. "What does it say?"

"Vuldaroq can explain it better. He asked if I'd come and get you."

"Right, let's hear what he has to say."

They found Vuldaroq sitting in the dome complex, his back to Dystran's tower, much as he had been since his dramatic arrival. There was still no colour in his face but his eyes had regained a little sparkle. He managed a smile as he looked up from his study to see Dystran approach.

"My Lord Vuldaroq, I understand you've been busy."

"Best that way," he said. Like those in Dystran's chambers, exertion and fear had left a tremble in his body and voice. But at least the shock hadn't set in. Not yet anyway.

"Care to enlighten me?"

"Your man Bynaar was an astute researcher. Arteche speaks highly of him in works we treasure . . . well, treasured."

Vuldaroq flourished the paper. It was a small but heavy-looking set of parchments, torn about its edges. Dystran estimated a dozen pages, no more.

"Go on."

"He was tracing shifts in mana density centuries ago. And in this paper he links it to the movement of demons from one space to another. I'm presuming the knowledge we have concerning your links with the demon dimension is sound."

Dystran coughed. "If our spies' assessments are accurate then, yes, you've done rather well."

"Normally, I'd be flattered," said Vuldaroq. "Now it all seems just a waste of effort." He cleared his throat. "Bynaar was the first to theorise that demons were a nomadic race, using up one home, then moving on by conquest."

"I am a scholar on the subject," said Dystran before he could stop himself.

"Then you will know that Bynaar has tracked demon progress across interdimensional space by measuring mana density and movement. Particularly noting the disappearance of mana clouds which he concludes is caused by those clouds entering the fabric of another dimension."

Dystran's smile was thin. "One cannot hope to assimilate every piece of knowledge."

"Assimilate this now. It's not a solution but it does answer the question of what the demons are doing."

"Which is?"

"Well, according to Bynaar, for demons, mana is an eminently movable element, one which they can attract to themselves. Which is how they move it of course. Establish demons at both ends of a path, so to speak, and send the mana along it—and the more they have, the stronger they get. It's almost a commodity to them, hence their obsession with getting into Balaia. We are mana-rich.

"Now I've cross-referenced that with your young mage, Feiyn here, who was kind enough to read a passage from the demonology text into which Bynaar's work was inserted. Would you be so kind as to repeat it, young man?"

Feiyn glanced at Dystran who nodded and shrugged simultaneously.

"It said that demons are forced into their nomadic existence because they consume the dimensions they inhabit. It says that when they have access to another dimension, that is when they destroy the last of what they have and move on. All of them."

"And they send the mana they have accumulated on ahead, to their vanguard," added Vuldaroq.

"So they aren't just passing through," said Dystran. "We aren't a territory." He'd known it all along when it came to it.

"No. I'm afraid we're home for them now," confirmed Vuldaroq.

"And the mana buildup?"

"You'll have to take readings," said Vuldaroq. "But for what it's worth, I'd bet the little I have that when it is complete, they will be strong enough to breach the ColdRooms. Or else why be so happy to leave us as we are— the stronger colleges, I mean. We can all feel the cold that the mana seems to bring—this chill is unseasonal and it's getting worse."

Dystran thought for a moment. Emotions clouded his mind. His immediate reaction was to dismiss the Dordovan's inferences simply because of who he was. But that attitude had to be consigned to history now if they weren't all to go before it. Vuldaroq had put a time limit on their future but the deadline was unknown. The course, difficult though it might be, was clear.

"Two things," he said. "One, we need to know when the density of mana in this dimension will give the demons the strength to overwhelm our defences. Second, we need a four-college strategy to see they never get there. And we need it fast."

Arabelle ducked a killing blow and backhanded her sword across the demon's chest. It howled and tumbled back. Four of her men closed in.

"Hold it, this time, hold it!"

Two were already dead, victims of the demon's soul-touch. Two others stood with her, one a mage, ready to cast if capture became an impossibility. They'd cornered the beast after days of surveillance from the upper windows of the tower had identified a pattern in its behaviour. They knew what it was doing: searching for their tunnel entrances, but it had become obsessed with a blind alley close to the northern wall of the college. This night, they were waiting for it.

The plan had been simple but they'd miscalculated its strength. Their first volley of blows hadn't weakened it enough and it had snatched its two victims too easily. Arabelle wasn't going to make the same mistake twice.

"Makkan, Terol, club it!"

The blows rained in on its body and head. The other two pounced on its arms, pinning them to the ground. The demon's fingers grasped and clutched, looking for a death-touch, but it couldn't angle its wrist enough. It was a tall demon, better than six feet in height. Its hairless body was a livid sky blue and the veins and muscles writhed below its skin. Underneath its back, its gossamer, mana-based wings beat uselessly at the ground. It howled and screamed, its toothless mouth snapping. They would not be alone for long.

Arabelle and her remaining two men closed in. They pinioned its legs, she moved to its head.

"Struggle all you like, you are coming with us. Now I can have my mage cast to subdue you or you can do it yourself."

The demon's small black eyes regarded her from a heavy brow, tongue licked the edges of its lipless mouth. It relaxed and quietened, holding her gaze.

"Don't ease your grip even one degree," she warned, not flinching from its stare. "That is exactly what it's waiting for."

The demon snarled. A sibilant hiss escaped its mouth. "You will still all be ours," it said.

"Maybe, but not yours, eh?" She turned to her team. "Right, on the double. Let's get inside."

The demon started to struggle again when they lifted it from the ground, contorting its body, shaking its limbs and arching its neck. But these were strong and determined men Arabelle had selected and they moved with purpose.

Pounding through the streets back toward the northern tunnel entrance they could hear the calls of demons to which their captive responded with a series of hoots and screeches. In the quiet of the night in Lystern, when the cries died to echoes, they were replaced by the swoosh of hundreds of wings. Arabelle was washed with a brief sense of futility. Here, they had captured one. Elsewhere in the city, there were thousands, and more arrived every day. She had to remind herself why it was she was out here.

Inside the tunnel, the passage was wide. Mages at its end laid trap wards before running after the kidnappers. They had to assume the demons would find this tunnel now. It had served its purpose. At least the wards would take some more of the beasts down with them.

In the centre of the ColdRoom constructs was a clear area measuring around fifty feet on a side. It was where the mages came to rest and replenish their mana stamina. The demon gasped as it was dragged into the ColdRoom lattice, exhaling only when they reached the centre of the great hall where the mana coursed freely. Arabelle ordered her team to set the demon down. Others ran from all parts of the hall, relieving the kidnap party and pinning the creature to the ground so tight it could barely move.

There was a pause for breath. The demon rotated its head, trying to take in whatever it could. Arabelle looked down on it, a smile creeping across her face.

"Got you," she said.

The demon hissed, its pointed tongue flicking out of its mouth. Abruptly, it settled, looking over her shoulder. Arabelle could hear footsteps. She turned round, her smile widening.

"Well done," said Heryst. "Well done indeed."

"We lost two," she said, deflating a little.

"I know, I know." Heryst squeezed her shoulder. "It was always a risk."

He turned his attention to the creature and knelt by its head. It tried to back away, sensing his aura, but only succeeded in writhing feebly under the weight of those pressing it down.

"You are aware who I am."

"Heryst," it said, almost spitting the name out.

"Good. Then you understand that whatever I say carries complete truth. You are caught and will answer our questions."

"No answers," it hissed.

"You will notice that at the moment, we are being very generous," continued Heryst, ignoring the creature. "You are lying in a place where the mana still flows. Do not mistake this as a sign of weakness. Where mana still flows, we can still cast and so we can hurt you very badly. Or, if we choose, we can take you into our ColdRooms to watch you die slowly. Do you believe me?"

The demon regarded him silently, breath rasping through its taut jaws. It nodded fractionally. "Then also believe that if you answer our questions and we judge you to be truthful, we will let you go."

The demon sputtered its contempt at the statement. Heryst cocked his head.

"It remains the truth. To take your life would be pointless. How many thousands of others are there to take your place? Nevertheless, it is your choice. But you will answer us."

"Nothing I tell you will help you, mage."

"Then there can be no harm in telling us the truth, can there?"

The demon smiled, bone ridges inside its mouth shining with saliva. "You will not know."

Heryst leaned in further and his tone surprised even Arabelle. "Oh yes, we will. Believe that also."

A hush fell in the great hall. Around the edges of the clear area, people crowded, not wishing to come too close to one of those that had caused such devastation and pain. Nearer, swordsmen kept watch for any incursion and mages stood ready to cast, should they be needed. Heryst circled the captured demon, Kayvel by his side.

"Now," he said. "This is where it begins. I will give you a choice. You can either answer my first question truthfully or I can ask my colleague here to demonstrate the pain that a tiny spell can wreak upon your body. Which is it to be?"

The demon hesitated a moment. "Ask."

"We know why you are here, we want to know why you have left the colleges alone."

"Not all colleges. Dordover is ours."

If Heryst was shaken, he didn't show it. "But we are still here. As are Julatsa and Xetesk. Why do you not press us?"

"We have no need. You are no threat."

"But surely one day you must move to attack us."

"When we are strong and you cannot repel us. We have time, you do not."

"Ah but do you, I wonder?" Heryst walked a slow circle around the demon which watched him every step of the way, face betraying its suspicion. "We have had some interesting intelligence from friends and it is backed up by knowledge we have uncovered here. We think you have miscalculated. We think your home is dying and you are forced here. We think you will never be able to overwhelm us because you cannot force enough mana here before your home is lost to you. We think you are fearful."

"Lies. We fear no one. Balaia will be ours."

"Will it, my enemy?" Heryst stood tall over the demon. "Is it not true that to complete your conquest you should have controlled our Hearts by now and you are not strong enough?"

"I have answered enough questions."

"Oh, I don't think so," said Heryst. "Tell me, it is true that you can never hope to beat Balaia's mages, isn't it?"

The demon was silent, as were all the occupants of the great hall. Arabelle considered Heryst's approach. His considerable embellishment of

Xetesk's message, received just before she had gone to catch the demon, had taken the creature unawares.

"Answer me. You need to consume the Hearts but you will never have the strength?"

"No more questions," spat the demon.

"Kayvel, explain to our captive that he doesn't have the option."

Kayvel's casting was quick and sure. FlamePalm. The middle-aged mage breathed in deep, a frown on his face, and brought his palm toward the demon's stomach. The creature tried to writhe away but was held too firmly. From the centre of Kayvel's hand, a green flame sprouted, firm and hot. He played it over the light blue skin. Immediately, smoke curled up, the flesh charred and a rank odour bit at the atmosphere. The demon screamed. Heryst raised a hand and Kayvel withdrew.

"If you keep quiet you make me do that again," said Heryst. "Answer my questions."

"You will be taken, mage," snarled the demon. "Nothing can stop that."

"Tell me why you wait, then? The real reason."

"I told you."

"Can you stop the mana flow?" Silence. "Kayvel, again."

More smoke, more stench and a murmur through the hall. More screams.

"Answer."

"No."

"No you won't or no the flow can't be stopped?"

"Please." The edges of the demon's wound might have been cauterised but it was deep and blood pulsed out over its belly.

Kayvel withdrew again.

"Well?" demanded Heryst.

"It cannot be stopped. Why should it? We are come and you will be taken as we please."

"Easy, eh?" said Heryst. "Now, when will you be strong enough to attack us? When have your masters said you will take us?"

"We have no orders."

"Liar."

The demon's eyes widened. Kayvel closed in.

"We attack when they say. No warning, we obey. Please."

"Liar," repeated Heryst. He nodded.

This time, Kayvel's hand played over the demon's chest and neck. Slowly, deliberately. Skin crisped, flesh bubbled. The creature whimpered, barely moving. Its eyes remained fixed on Heryst, the hatred almost tangible. The Lord Elder Mage did not flinch.

"Speak. My colleague can keep this up longer than you can live."

The acrid smell of burning demon flesh stung Arabelle's nostrils. She looked on at the torture, feeling nothing for the demon. Nothing at all.

"Truth. Please!"

"When you take the Hearts, will you destroy them?"

"No!" The demon quivered through its body. "Too valuable, too potent a source."

Heryst snapped his fingers. Kayvel withdrew his hand.

"Well, well," he said, catching Heryst's eye.

"Yes," agreed Heryst. "And so presumably you'll be keeping every mage alive too."

A gasping chuckle. "Your souls are most prized. We will enjoy you."

"A shame, then, that your masters are ignorant of reality."

There was a sheen of oily sweat covering the demon's body now. It was weakening quickly. The burns covering most of its torso were still bubbling and oozing. It regarded Heryst anew, forehead creasing slightly. A most human expression.

"Mages keep the Hearts beating," said Heryst. "No mages. No Hearts."

"Liar."

Arabelle wasn't sure but she thought the ghost of a smile crossed the creature's face.

"I cannot prove it, of course, but I have spoken nothing but truth to you so far. Perhaps you should have studied Julatsa's problems more closely."

"Your lies will not buy your life."

"Nor will yours save you, my enemy. Now. One last time. How long before you attack the colleges?"

"I do not know."

Heryst straightened. "A shame." He nodded at Kayvel. "And this time, only stop when it ceases breathing."

"No! No!" The demon's anguish echoed through the chamber, its eyes sought allies.

"Then answer me," snapped Heryst, raising his voice.

"Soon. It will be soon."

"Not good enough."

"All I know. Please."

Kayvel's palm rested flat on the creature's chest. It jerked violently, a gurgle dragging from its mouth.

"Tell me."

"You said you would let me go. Please."

"After you answered my questions. After. Speak. While you are still able."

The demon juddered, tried to speak but only succeeded in gargling deep in its throat. It mouthed the word "please" once more and tried to frame other words while its body melted away and Kayvel's hand sank lower. Smoke poured from its wounds, the stench worsened. The demon convulsed, spat black gore from its mouth and lay still, eyes milking over.

"Keep a hold," said Heryst to those pinning it down. "Don't relax."

Kayvel dismissed his spell. There was a muttering around the hall and an air of shock pervaded the chamber.

"Brutal, wasn't it?" said Heryst, addressing them all. "Cruel even. Speak if you feel the need."

There was a pause and a shuffling of feet.

"You didn't have to kill it," said one.

"Maybe it was telling the truth," said another.

A louder murmur accompanied this last utterance and heads nodded around the hall.

Heryst sucked his lip. He took a long slow stroll around the periphery of the clear area, taking in all those standing inside the ColdRooms.

"And is that what you think?" he asked, pointing at one. "And you? You? Hmm."

Heryst swung by Arabelle and she could see the set of his face and the disappointment in his eyes.

"Been comfortable in here, hasn't it?" he said. There was a ripple of laughter. "Funny, is it? In here where the demons can't pluck you like ripe fruit and you don't even have to admit what is happening outside. Any here think they are unfortunate? You have my permission to go and join those beyond these walls. You have become distanced, soft. Complacent. Weak.

"Perhaps I should send a few of you outside who haven't been, eh? Outside where there is nothing but fear and the certainty that one day they will come for you. Where you exist only to serve the invaders. Where every day you would gaze at the college and curse your misfortune while you wonder why we sit here and do nothing to help you. Where creatures like this wretch at my feet have your life or death literally in their hands.

"And you want me to show mercy? Damn you for your weakness. We cannot afford it. The day is coming when they will try and destroy us and I will do anything, anything to give us a chance.

"Never show these bastards mercy because believe me they will show us none."

He took them all in again.

"We are the lucky ones. But with that fortune comes the responsibility for the survival of our entire dimension. We have worked hard to earn what little we have today but it is clear we have been too slow. Soon we will have to fight and any of you who shirk from what you must do I will feed to the demons myself. You heard him. They want the Hearts. So we have to defend with all we have to stop them and give those with the strength the time to beat them.

"I hope you are scared. You should be. The fate of Balaia rests with each one of us. Now harden your hearts. Because if you do not, we are already lost."

Chapter 17

There was little hint of what had befallen Balaia when the *Calaian Sun* sailed easily into coastal waters and headed slowly up the Bay of Gyernath. It had been a voyage free of troubled waters, but approaching the southern coast of their homeland, The Raven had gathered often to see it growing on the horizon and wonder what they would find there.

Now, with the sun climbing high into a clear sky and a cool breeze speeding them up the bay, they assembled on the deck once more.

"You know, I've assumed Blackthorne has survived but we have no hard evidence," said The Unknown.

"We'll get some soon enough," said Hirad.

Each of them was scouring the shoreline at a mile distance, searching for any sign of demons. They shouldn't find any. Everything they knew about the race told them that they would stay close to centres of population. Much as any predator likes to stay close to its prey.

"Jevin's information states that Blackthorne is still alive and kicking," said Darrick.

"Yes, but it's old news. A season and more since he's been this way." The Unknown shook his head. "It worries me. Gods burning, he's not a college, his mage strength will be minimal. It's a miracle he survived at all but it's a situation with only one outcome, surely."

"That's why we're here, isn't it?" said Hirad. "To make sure there's another option."

"He will be useful to us if he is still alive. And not just because of the weapons he can provide us. Two years fighting demons on a knife-edge. There will be things he knows. Weak points," said Rebraal.

"I'm not sure demons really have weak points, magic excepted," said Denser.

"Everything has a weak point," said Auum quietly. "And I will find theirs."

"Fair enough," said Denser.

"Beautiful, isn't it?" said Erienne. "I've dreamed about this so often and here it is, just as I remembered."

"Apart from the occupation by demons," said Hirad.

"I don't mean that," said Erienne. "Can't you see it and feel it?" She shook her head seeing Hirad's blank expression. "You've no soul."

"That'll help," said Hirad. "Won't give the demons much to aim at."

"Gods, Hirad, you are an infuriating man." Erienne tried hard to keep the smile from her face. "This is our home. This is where we belong. Not on some island, no matter how warm it is and the memories it holds for us." She looked at Denser. "We can't let Balaia die. It's too beautiful and it's ours."

"Home," agreed Thraun. "Where the pack runs."

Hirad gazed across at the coastline. The gentle green rolling hills bordering the pebble-strewn shore. The dark mass of the Blackthorne Mountains rising up from the head of the bay. The call of seabirds. The smells of land and sea mixing in his nostrils.

"That's why I love you, Erienne," he said. "You make it real."

Erienne kissed his cheek and scratched the back of his neck. "Just as long as you're looking out for me, big man."

"Do you mind?" asked Denser. "You're making me seasick."

"All right," said The Unknown. "Nauseating it may be, correct it also is. We've been on board ship almost seven days. We've been through our drills, we've sharpened ourselves up as much as we can. The Gods know we aren't what we were ten or even two years ago but we're still more than a match for anyone we meet. Here is where it starts. We've come to get our country back and we don't know exactly what we will face, how strong they are and whether or not we can win. But we know who we are. Whatever we face, we have to believe, all right? Sorry, Hirad, I feel I've stolen your lines."

Hirad chuckled. "Delivery needs work but apart from that, not bad. So, how close are we going in?"

"Near as Jevin can get. They can't take the crew but they can bother us. Best we aren't in longboats for longer than necessary," said Darrick. "We've got extra mage support but we're hoping not to have to cast until we're very close for the run into the town."

"Gods burning, but it would help if he knew we were coming," said Hirad.

"He can," said Thraun.

"How? We've established we're not sending a mage in the air. It's too risky."

"They will be looking only for men, Hirad," said Thraun. "Not a lone wolf."

Ferouc flew lazily around the object of his orders feeling, as ever, peripheral to the organisation and deeply hurt by his exclusion. Below him, fires burned and humans moved in defiance of their rule. Free for a moment beneath their protection.

It confused him how they resisted still. He had done so much to weaken their resolve. Taking their food-production areas; enslaving or draining those that supported the population centre; probing ceaselessly at the barrier; keeping up a cacophony of noise during their resting hours; sacrificing slaves in front of them.

It hurt them but did not break them. Ferouc would admit privately to a certain frustration but he took solace in the knowledge that he was not alone. In every large gathering of humans barring the fallen college of Dordover, resistance remained, based around the barriers their mages could cast.

They were all that his cohorts feared. A casting that stripped the strength from their bodies and left them gasping and vulnerable should they breach it. And always, their warriors waited, cold metal sharpened to kill.

Ferouc had watched the humans around their dwelling for a long time now. He knew how they moved, where they went, why they performed any action and who it was they looked to for courage.

Their strength was based in the settlement's largest structure, over which their arrogant flags still flew. They also controlled a ring around it that accounted for perhaps a third of the area. The rest of the settlement, and the souls that dwelt there, belonged to Ferouc.

He had used these as he must, to drain the morale of his quarry and keep that of his cohorts high, bodies satiated. He had to work to weaken his enemies a little more every day even if he couldn't beat them yet. What irritated him most was that all the effects had been at best short-term. And the reason was clear enough.

One human was the difference. Tall, dark-haired and bearded. Eyes like crystal. His aura burned more brightly than any mage within. Blackthorne. He led with empathy linked to iron discipline and control. The latter Ferouc could respect and understand. The former was completely alien to him. Nevertheless, it gave them belief.

Ferouc flapped his wings lazily and fell into a glide above the settlement. The free below him paid him no heed. That had irked him but he understood it better now. Besides, he knew something Blackthorne didn't. Long-lived as their resistance had been, their time was finite. Their thrall and eventual destruction was an inevitability.

It had made him wonder why they didn't just wait. Use the souls they had and enjoy their new world. But he had been made to understand and it was why he had not been moved from this place. There had always been a contingency for dangerous resistance in the colleges. And that had been put into place. A no-risk approach to wearing them down. In the outlying settlements, the capital city, the major ports and regional capitals, there was no such allowance. The masters wanted these places under control before the final battle. There was just the chance that their strength would not be sufficient if they could not move forces from the regions to the college centres when they wanted to.

And one thing they could not afford was for there to be damage done to them in places that should be theirs by right. They had a dominant position now but when the time came that position would be at risk if they had not exerted the control they needed over all but the three remaining colleges.

The demon canted a wing and soared upward on a cool current of air. He breathed deeply, enjoying the sensation through his body. So much like home now. As it should be. He barely remembered the taste when he had first arrived, though he could recall the feelings of repulsion he had been forced to overcome.

A new scent caught in his receptors. Powerful. Desirable. He recognised it instantly as they all would. One of the true prizes in this dimension. Every thought he had harboured about his expulsion to the provincial settlement was washed away on a tide of pleasure and anticipation.

He soared higher, searching, calling to his cohorts. He felt an unconfined joy, his receptors ablaze with this most precious of auras. It was them. It was The Raven.

"Are you sure you want to do this?" asked Hirad the moment they hit the beach.

Auum's Tai, Rebraal and from the ship's company two elven mages, Vituul and Eilaan, had run to the first rise to scout the immediate terrain beyond the temporary wooden dock to which they had tied. The Raven had grouped around Thraun.

"It gives us a better chance," said Thraun, unbuttoning his shirt and handing it to Hirad.

The barbarian stuffed it into a pack along with his boots. Thraun's weapons were already strapped to The Unknown's back.

"I know. But I can't let you go without reminding you what happened last time."

Thraun met his gaze levelly, remembered pain flaring in his eyes.

"I will never forget why Will died. This is different. This is for speed, not stealth. You know that."

"You're sure?"

Thraun gripped Hirad's shoulders. "I'll be fine. Just bring my stuff and be there to call me back." He stripped off his breeches and handed them over. "Now get going and don't look back."

"Come on, Hirad," said The Unknown. "Let's get on with it."

Hirad nodded and The Raven formed up into a combat line adapted for the shapechanger's absence. The elves were to provide forward protection and warning, the Protectors remained on board ship, their souls being saved for the battles to come. Erienne and Denser were to prepare nothing unless they were attacked. It was two hours on foot to Blackthorne. A long time in a country occupied by demons.

It was a land Hirad had travelled so often but a land he hardly recognised now. The grass still grew in its multiple hues of green and yellow. The budding new trees swayed in the breeze and wild flowers decked the gently rolling land in glorious colours. But under his feet and to his senses it was alien. For a moment he couldn't place why, but slowly he began to understand.

None of the ambience of life was present. Where he had heard gulls on the open water, here the birds were silent. Only the breeze ruffled the undergrowth, while rodents kept themselves hidden. The distant echo of bleating or lowing was absent. And it was chill. Not right for the time of year and somehow malevolent. It was as if the seasons had become confused and let the vegetation burst into spring verdancy while the wildlife struggled to awaken from hibernation.

The answer came to him then and it fired his determination afresh. Balaia's soul was failing.

The Raven kept up a fast walk behind the all-seeing shield of the elves jogging ahead. Concealment was pointless, it wouldn't necessarily get them there safe since the demons didn't work just by sight. Speed just might.

Ahead of them, the land rolled up a slow incline bereft of anything but gorse, coarse shrub and loose shale. Blackthorne lay on the extremities of a flood plain that ran south to the southern ocean, dry itself because beneath the soil the foundation rock was porous, drawing water far underground. The town would be hidden until the last mile of travel but, even so, distant smoke smudged the otherwise perfect sky. The tiny circling black dots had to be demons.

Hirad shuddered. Behind him, something moved quickly through the undergrowth. Not breaking his stride, Hirad looked round. The dark, lithe shape of Thraun approached, loping easily in the bracken. His face was alert, his muzzle light striped and long, he sampled the air, tongue hanging between powerful jaws.

The wolf paced by Hirad, looking up into his eyes.

"I'll be there for you, Thraun," he said. "Just be careful."

Satisfied, Thraun ran away into the brush.

Thraun could taste the dying of the land. It pervaded his every sense, growing stronger with every pace that he left The Raven behind. The rotting assaulted his nose, the crushing of life he could feel on his tongue and see through his eyes. The prey wasn't there. No spoor, no trail. Gone into hiding or disappeared forever.

Thraun ran on, sampling what was left. The vegetation, unburdened by demon conquest, was alive and growing strong. Toward Blackthorne, the scent of wood smoke and human was on the air. It was gentle compared with the sick odour of the demons. They were the life after decay, the feeling after death and the dark that shattered the pack.

It was passed down through the generations. The fear. Thraun tried to shut it from his mind. He padded swiftly across the land, his wolven senses alert, that part of his brain that retained his humanity driving him toward his goal. His memories would dim quickly but the image of the human he needed was clear in his mind. Tall, strong. A leader with the scent of courage on him. Thraun would not mistake him.

At the periphery of his hearing, Thraun caught calls high in the morning sky. He hunkered down beneath a stand of gorse and scanned above. Demons. Flying west toward The Raven. He growled. They had smelled prey. Thraun felt an urge to protect The Raven, the pack. But his mind still retained the reason why he now lay so close to the human dwellings and it spurred him on more strongly.

He broke cover at a dead run, howling at the sky.

A mile from Blackthorne and the elves saw the demons' circling pattern change and come at them. Initially thirty, cascading from the heights and flying low to the ground. Rebraal barked out a warning.

"Time to put all those theories to the test," said Hirad. "You up for this, Erienne?"

"I guess we'll find out, won't we?" she replied, tension edging her voice.

"We'll protect you," said Hirad. "Just relax, you know you can do it."

"Easy for you to say," she replied through a half smile.

"Remember we have to keep moving forward," said The Unknown. "We can't afford to get bogged down here, not when we're so close."

The elves moved back into the prearranged fighting line. Auum and Duele flanked The Raven's left, Evunn and Rebraal right. They had dispensed with their classic uneven chevron formation this time. The line that approached the enemy was a shallow concave curve with The Unknown at its focal point. Behind the curve, the four mages ranged, elves flanking their Raven colleagues.

Erienne could barely control her heart rate. They were relying on her like never before. Without her, only mages could kill. It wouldn't be enough. The demons were coming in low and fast. She could hear the beat of wings and their harsh calls.

Fighting to concentrate on the move, she unstoppered the power of the One and felt it surge through her body and into her mind. The sensation was terrifying. In two years of Cleress's tutelage she had learned to control the well of power that surged around her body, but barely. And even now, the level of control her mind could exert when she released the energy to cast was minimal in the scale of One magic understanding.

Her sense of that which she contained was highly tuned. She understood very well the consequences of her failure to fully control it. What had been done could not be undone. The One was within her. She had no choice but to accept it.

She still considered the entity an enemy to be suppressed lest it should overwhelm her. Cleress had done little to disabuse her of that notion. Merely saying she would learn over time to work with what she had, not fight it for control.

But time had run out. And now the dam that Erienne had built in her mind to contain the power in her body was breached. She couldn't afford to fail.

The One flooded her senses, dimming her sight and hearing. The Unknown said something about being encircled but she didn't catch it before the full majesty of Balaia's energies was laid out before her. She staggered and almost fell, her feet and legs numb, but she was held up.

She saw the raw strong energy of the bedrock pulsing through the ground; the fluxing, capricious trails of the air thickened by wind and sun; the wisps from coarse grass; the complex auras of The Raven and elves around her; and everywhere, the scattered motes that were mana. Searching the sky, she found the demons. They resolved from a cloud of muddled elements into individual powerful forms. Lattices of life with none of the gentle modulation of man or elf, and meshed firm by hard mana.

It was just as Cleress had described and the theory of the spell, like any One casting, was simplicity itself. In the myriad streams of energy she could sense about her, natural linkages were everywhere, binding the elements together. She could see the arrays that gathered mana to the demons in the natural shield that made them invulnerable to anything but magic. All she had to do was disrupt the process and scatter the mana back to its natural random state.

Erienne paused for a beat, feeling the swell of the One through her body. She drew it to her, holding it tight inside while she built the construct. In her mind's eye, it formed. As with her Dordovan magic, she drew mana strands into the order she required, a fine-meshed net of pulsing deep brown magical energy. That was the easy part. Now she had to feed in exactly the right amount of One power to let the spell live. Cleress's words came back to her then and she fancied she could feel the presence of the ancient Al-Drechar in her mind once more though distance surely precluded that now as the frail elf's powers weakened.

You cannot calculate this. It is not a mana casting, just a mana construct. Mana alone will not power it, the One makes it live. You must believe, you must trust and you must feel. Be one with it, let it take you as far as you can. Always up to the point of no return but never further. Your mind will tell you. Trust your mind. Always trust your mind.

With the words running round her head, Erienne allowed the One power into the construct and held it there while it grew, clinging on with her mind. And all the time, the entity was whispering in her ear that she should feed in more, that to let go would be to win. This was her demon and she could not allow it free rein.

She could see the lines of elemental force all around her bend and reach toward her. The One sucked it in voraciously, using her body as a conduit while she kept iron control of her mind to stop from being washed away. The construct pulsed bright under the power flowing through her. A moan escaped her lips. The mesh glowed and then burst into a fine mist, every minuscule droplet still bound to every other.

She released the spell and it flooded out from her, covering everything around her, floating into the sky and across the ground, behind and in front. It washed past The Raven and it engulfed the demons moving to attack. She saw its result and knew they would not even know what had happened until the first blow was struck.

The mist soaked into them, penetrating deep into their skins where it simply dissolved the linkage that bound the mana to them. Immediately, Erienne could see the mana sloughing from the demons. Tiny particles glimmering in the mass of energy trails. Undetectable to everyone except her but, if she was right, absolutely deadly.

Dimly, she heard the thump of a sword point on the ground, rhythmic and sure.

Thraun was desperate to run faster. Demons were after him. Swooping low, raking at his back with claws and talons. Biting down on his body, slashing at him with sharpened tails. He wove this way and that, ran through thick vegetation, slewed through streams and leaped hedge and fence to enter the farm lands of Blackthorne.

His howling had brought them on as he had desired but their stench had gripped him and he was afraid. His heart was pounding and there was a shudder along his flanks that threatened the rhythm of his legs.

He dared not look around or up, instead he ploughed on. Men and women, their expressions cold, stared at him. Children with dark eyes pointed or ran. A few animals scattered but they need not have feared him. He was not hunting. He was hunted.

A demon's jaws snapped shut just above his head. He felt a deep chill and sudden pain flared in his ear. The beast climbed high into the sky. In front of him, another dived, arms outstretched, taloned hands grasping. He did not flinch but veered at the last instant as he would from a man holding a weapon. Behind him, the demon screeched its anger.

He was past the last people now and the dwellings he ran by were silent and empty. The streets were deserted and the smell of life was gone from the ground and weak in the air. But ahead he could hear shouting, rising in volume. The sound of weapons clashing and the vibration of feet on packed earth came to him too. He pushed harder and the demons behind him did the same.

Thraun felt a tap at his hind leg and almost lost his balance. He half sprawled but maintained his momentum while the reek of demon filled his head and dragged desperate barks from his throat. From either side of the road he ran, demons closed in. So many of them, crowding his way. He howled again and ran at them, eyes open, terror pulsing in his neck.

He darted this way and that, slewed almost to a standstill, jumped away, ran headlong. And ever more, those claws and teeth grabbed at him, looking to bring him down.

At the very last, one of the beasts clamped jaws on his back. Thraun tumbled, rolling in the dirt with the demon. The cold fired through his body. He convulsed but his speed carried him on. His vision clouded and he barked again, weaker this time.

The shouts were around him then, the ring of steel harsh and loud. He heard a squeal and the pressure on his back was lifted. He shivered and lay in the dirt while men ran past him to hold a position at the edge of a row of dwellings. One man shouted louder than the rest. His voice was close.

Thraun picked his head up to look round. He could feel the breath ragged in his throat and the cold of the bite ate at his flesh. A human squatted in front of him. Dark-haired, strong, and with the scent of a leader just as he had remembered.

The man looked at him, his frown turning to comprehension. He said something to Thraun but the wolf had no ear for what men said. The man stood, shouted. Other men ran. And then he knelt once again and rubbed warm hands across Thraun's heaving flanks.

He spoke once more but Thraun did not hear him. And deep, deep inside, his humanity prayed that he had done enough.

Chapter 18

The Raven lengthened their stride with the demons screaming in. The Unknown's sword thumped onto the ground, keeping time with their footfalls, chinking on shale. Beside him, Hirad readied himself, circling his arms, sword in his right hand, its weight feeling good for the fight. It had been too long.

"On my mark, Raven!" he shouted. "Denser, you have Erienne."

Fifty yards distant and the demons dispersed, scattering into the sky and making flanking moves. A core of eight came straight on. Immediately the elves responded, falling back to protect the mages.

"Looking, Raven. Mages, targets and hold."

Hirad's voice sounded above the calls of the demons and the rush of wings. He could see three coming directly for him, another trio just to the left moving hard at The Unknown.

Twenty-five yards and closing.

"Brace and hold. Let's take these bastards down."

Elven arrows streaked out. Hirad didn't see them strike but he heard the squeals of pain and surprise. He smiled. Deep blue and bright yellow flashes lit the sky. FlameOrb and Ice Wind scoured the air. Demons screeched. Hirad focused ahead. The Unknown's blade struck the ground twice more and the demons were on them.

Hirad knew the impact would be hard. He half crouched. Watching the trio closing. Their speed had tempered after they watched others pierced by arrows that should have had no effect. But still they were confident. Mottled green and with vein-etched wings they attacked, claws outstretched and jaws agape, calling their fury.

Left side was on him too early. Hirad ducked and struck, feeling his blade bite deep. Dark fluid gushed from the wound and the demon yelped and spiralled away. Centre and right were in concert and he was barely ready for them. One came in, reversing its body to aim its feet at his chest. The other cocked its hands to slash on impact. Hirad ignored it for the moment, concentrating on the other. He squatted and rolled, feeling the creature part his braids, and was up in the same movement, swiping at empty air. The other demon lashed out a claw, snagging his armour and half turning him round.

Both beasts climbed to turn back to the attack and it gave Hirad a moment to orient himself. He was facing The Raven now. The air seemed full of the deep-coloured shapes of demons. His ears rang from their calls. To his left, Auum and Duele wove death at great speed, their backs to Erienne and

Denser. Auum faced two. He lashed a roundhouse kick into the first's chest, sending it sprawling. He continued his spin, short blade flashing in the sunlight and carving into the second's neck. It howled and dropped, fluid sluicing into the dry earth.

Right by Hirad, Darrick and The Unknown fared well. The General fenced with a single assailant who was already bleeding from several cuts and weakening fast. The Unknown had one by the throat at arm's length and, with Hirad watching, drew back his blade and plunged it into the creature's stomach, casting the corpse aside.

Hirad's two demons rushed back to the attack, one from either side. He took a two-handed grip on his sword and waited, seeing both close from steep angles. They had reached the point of no return when he spun on his right leg and carved the air above his head, turning two revolutions. His blade cut into the face of one and took the arm from the other at the elbow. Both thundered into him, bowling him from his feet.

Half dazed, he struggled to strike again. One of the demons was on top of him. He could taste the rank stench and feel its blood running across his armour. He scrabbled backward, keeping hold of his sword, and tried to shovel the beast from his legs. From nowhere, a claw whipped into his face. He reacted fast but the nails dragged at his cheek. Cold pain fired into his head and he was knocked back against the ground. He felt faint for a moment, his vision dimming for a heartbeat. Fear flashed through his body and he grabbed at his chest as if that alone would keep his soul in place if the demons could really touch it.

He saw more spells detonate and heard the heavy thud of steel against flesh. A hand gripped his shoulder. The Unknown hauled him upright. At his feet, the bodies of two demons. One moved feebly, the other had been decapitated. Dark gore ran down The Unknown's sword. He shrugged.

"I think we frightened them off," he said.

Hirad breathed deep, feeling blood on his face. He wiped at it gingerly with a gloved hand. The demons were retreating, those that could. The ground was littered with their bodies. Twenty, perhaps more.

"We'd better get moving. Anyone else hurt?" he asked.

Shakes of heads greeted his question. He nodded. Erienne smiled at him, looking a little tired but satisfied.

"I'd call that a successful test," said Denser, hugging her to him.

"Just about," said The Unknown, leading them on toward Blackthorne. "What was that pirouette?"

"Something Auum taught me."

"I'd have preferred it if you'd just ducked and rolled."

Hirad smiled. "I'm still learning."

"Hmm." The Unknown pointed at his cheek. "You were lucky. If you hadn't turned your head, it would have had your eye. You feeling all right?"

"A little cold around the wound but otherwise fine." He chuckled, though his body trembled along its length. "Can't just grab our souls, can they?"

"Fortunately not."

They crested a rise and looked down the last mile to Blackthorne. The town was teeming with activity. Demons on the ground and in the sky hurried about tasks. Many were headed toward the castle where Blackthorne's flag still flew proudly. There was a gathering of people, clearly none were demon captives. They held weapons and the bark of orders carried across the quiet space to The Raven.

"Welcoming committee?" said Darrick.

"Reckon Thraun must have got through safely," said Hirad. "What next?"

The Unknown began trotting down the slope, the others following him. Left and right, the elves moved further ahead. "Let's not keep them waiting. I hardly think the demons are going to usher us in. Can you hang onto that wound until we're inside?"

"It's not so bad," said Hirad.

"Good. Erienne, ready for a repeat dose?"

"No problem."

"Let's go, Raven."

Wary now, demons flew high, tracking them all the way. Dead ahead, a formation was building above Blackthorne. It was large, over a hundred, and spread like a net over the town, covering their route in. The Raven were committed now but Hirad shared an anxious glance with The Unknown at the scale of the force laid out before them. Whatever it was that Blackthorne had planned, it needed to be effective.

The Raven ran on, having no option but to trust themselves and their friend on the other side of his ColdRoom protection. Hirad found himself trying to look everywhere at once. Left and right to check the elves, about and behind him to make sure The Raven were one, and ahead and above him to try and second-guess the next action of the demons.

But it was quickly clear that the demons were unsure. The slaughter of twenty-plus of their number by The Raven had undermined their sense of automatic domination and inside Blackthorne the Baron was making no secret of the fact that he was ready to strike out. It bought The Raven the time to make over half the distance to relative safety. It was a hiatus that couldn't last and duly, with The Raven and elves passing the outlying farm land, the demons moved.

"Watching, Raven," warned The Unknown. "Let's try and keep moving. Erienne, you're up."

The hoots and croaking cries of demons choked the air, echoing across the open space. Hirad felt a chill down his body and gripped his sword tighter. His cheek burned where he had been caught, a numbness spreading to his jaw. Moving in toward the outskirts of the town, the Raven line tightened appreciably. Auum and Duele fell in behind the mages, leaving Rebraal and Evunn scouting ahead, bows in hand.

"We're moving too fast," said Denser. "Erienne can't hold this pace and cast."

They slowed. Darrick dropped back to the other side of her, Hirad and The Unknown directly in front. From above, the cries of the demons intensified to a stunning crescendo. They packed and attacked.

"Dear Gods." Hirad almost froze. "We're in trouble."

"Holding positions, Raven. Spells at full spread!" shouted Darrick. "Let's give ourselves a chance."

They stopped again, needing the cohesion of a static formation to give them any chance at all. Hirad could hear Denser murmuring words of encouragement to Erienne.

"We can't afford that, Denser. Cast. They're on us."

"Can't afford for Erienne to fail either."

"We can't afford that for any of us. Please, Denser, not now."

"Got it," said the mage, an edge to his voice.

"Come on, Baron," whispered Hirad. "We need you."

He couldn't count how many demons were coming at them this time. It had to be twice the number of the first probing attack. Enough to overwhelm them if they weren't all right on their game.

From the direction of the castle came simultaneous deep orange and blue flares. The sound of a detonation and the cries of hundreds of men followed it. More spells struck out, tearing at the demons still hovering over Blackthorne. They were joined by those of the elves. DeathHail flayed across the clear blue sky, more IceWind surged behind it, catching the leading edge of the demon attack. But still they came on and Blackthorne's intervention was too late.

Sudden calm fell in the air, pressing on Hirad's ears. Behind him, Denser swore.

"Cover your eyes," he shouted. "Now!"

"Do it, Raven!" ordered Hirad.

He closed his eyes and put an arm across them. An instant later there was a flat crack. Searing light ripped across the sky. Hirad could see the glow through his squeezed-shut eyes as it flared through the flesh of his arm. Screams filled the air all around him.

"Safe!" called Denser.

Hirad looked up. The sky was a confusion of blinded demons. They crashed into one another, flew very high to escape the chaos or tried to land, tumbling. Some hovered where they were, their fists wiping at their faces. But most blundered on, trying to use other senses to reach their prey but distracted by the pain that would be pounding in their skulls.

Hirad and The Unknown glanced at each other, The Unknown nodded.

"Raven!" roared Hirad. "Raven with me!"

And they ran hard, all pretence at an organised fighting line gone. SunBurst was a spell rarely used and easily combated by area reverse castings. But when it worked, its effects were spectacular but, as they all knew, short-lived. The demons' sight would return and soon.

Auum's Tai and Rebraal took the lead, racing through Blackthorne's all but empty streets. In places, demons and humans alike clung to walls or sat with heads in hands, briefly united in their distress. Where they filled the road, the enemy were unceremoniously beaten aside.

Closing on the area of the town still under Blackthorne's control, Hirad had an idea. He sheathed his sword.

"Unknown!" He grabbed at the big man's arm as they ran. "We can save some. One each."

The Unknown nodded. "The others will follow the lead. Take the young, we can carry them."

Ahead, Blackthorne's men were beating a path clear for them among the disoriented demons who nonetheless tried to fight back. Spells roared out, engulfing hapless victims, and cudgels and clubs knocked sense from any who got too close. Hirad shot past an opening and saw a small boy, perhaps ten years old, yelling for his mother, his fists buried in his eyes. The barbarian slithered to a stop, darted back down the passage and grabbed him, throwing him over one shoulder, heedless of the knocks he'd take.

"Safer with me, boy," he said.

Panicked, the child began to beat on Hirad's back, his frenzied screaming reaching new volume. Hirad didn't have time to pause. He glanced right at the end of the opening and saw the demons regrouping and charging through the air.

"Time to go." He sprinted for safety. "Come on, Raven!"

Erienne and Denser had picked up a mother and baby between them and were chairing her to the line. The Unknown, typically, had one infant over either shoulder. In the midst of the crowd of demons milling in their path, Auum and the elves got to work.

They were a blur, kicks, punches and pulls driving the demons back and away. The mages killed with FlamePalm and close-focused IceWind. Ahead, the humans had retreated to the safety of the ColdRooms, edges marked by stones in the earth, and were beckoning them on. Darrick was furthest ahead, carrying something in his arms. The Unknown was behind him. Hirad dropped his pace to see Erienne and Denser to safety.

With the enraged screeches of the demons closing in on them at frightening speed, The Raven reached the relative sanctuary of Blackthorne's domain. Hirad carried on running for thirty paces until a familiar voice yelled at him to stop.

Lungs labouring, chest heaving and sweat running down his face and mixing uncomfortably in his cuts, he pulled up and turned round. Blackthorne was striding toward him, a broad smile on a face that couldn't quite believe what it was seeing. Hirad released the hysterical child into the arms of others and greeted the Baron with a long hug.

"Couldn't you have sent a note?" asked the Baron, stepping back. "I'd have cleaned up a bit."

"Well, we sent Thraun," said Hirad. "Clearly he got here."

Hirad looked around for the wolf, a little worried he wasn't immediately apparent.

"He did but he was hurt," said Blackthorne. "Don't worry, we're looking after him, but it was a demon bite. He should be dead."

Hirad chuckled. "Like me, eh?" He pointed at his cheek. "The Raven aren't that easy to kill."

"So I've noticed."

"Is he still a wolf?" asked Hirad.

Blackthorne nodded. "But he's calm enough. I'll take you to him."

"And at the same time you can tell me how you worked out from one wolf that we were coming. He's not exactly talkative like that."

Blackthorne put an arm around his shoulder and began to lead him back to the rest of The Raven who were standing or sitting in a group, drinks in hands, looking back at the demons clustered outside the ColdRooms.

"Later, Hirad. First of all, you should rest. We'll talk later over food and wine and you can tell me what by all the Gods falling you are doing here. But let me tell you this one thing. However much a wolf Thraun is, his eyes are still human. I recognised him straight away and where he goes, The Raven go."

"My Lord!" A young man ran toward them from the periphery.

"Luke," said Blackthorne. "Meet The Raven."

Luke stood confused for a moment before nodding at them all. "I'm glad you're here. Please excuse me, though." He paused and Hirad could see the conflict in his face. He was trying not to be overawed and mixed with it was the reason he stood in front of the Baron in the first place.

"Tell you what, Luke, join us at dinner. Now, what is it, you look flushed."

"It's him, my Lord. He wants to speak with you."

Baron Blackthorne nodded. "As expected but perhaps rather sooner than ideal." He took in The Raven. "You should come with me."

"To see who?"

"Head demon of hereabouts. We call him Fidget." He smiled enigmatically.

Erienne spoke for them all. "Why, and what is his real name?"

"Come and see."

Blackthorne strolled across the open space toward the periphery for all the world as if it was a lazy afternoon and he had not a care in the world. The Raven followed him, the elves in close attendance.

"I had this area cleared of buildings to give us a sight zone all around the castle. The demons own everything beyond it and they know where our Cold-Rooms start. We understand each other. We're still thinking of building a stockade, a physical barrier would be good for morale, but raw materials are hard to come by."

"It would make the place almost comfortable," said Hirad.

Blackthorne shot him a dark glance. "Never that, Hirad."

Mages and soldiers were grouped near an area of the perimeter, facing several dozen demons. They moved aside as Blackthorne and his retinue approached. Standing with wings furled in front of them was a demon of better than eight feet in height and jet black in colour but with veins pulsing blue across his skin. His face was human shaped but his features were anything but. He had a flat lipless slit that was his mouth, above which a single dark oval was presumably his nose. He appeared to have no ears at all and his eyes were huge, yellow orbs covering much of his forehead. His hands ended in long-boned fingers which clicked incessantly.

"Ugly bastard, isn't he?" said Hirad.

"I'm sure he feels the same way about you," said Denser.

"Does he really do that all the time?" asked Erienne.

"Hence the name," said Blackthorne. He strode up to the perimeter, standing only two paces from his enemy. "What do you want, Fidget?"

"I am Ferouc," stated the demon looking square at The Raven, fingers increasing their speed temporarily.

"Of course, how forgetful of me," said Blackthorne. "What do you want, Fidget?"

"You harbour that which we want and that which we own," said Ferouc, his voice whining, sibilant through lips unused to framing human words.

"You own nothing in this world. Theft does not denote ownership."

"Those behind you took six who are ours," said Ferouc. "They will be returned or others will suffer."

"Come in and get them," said Hirad.

"Quiet," snapped The Unknown.

"Brave out there, aren't you?" said Hirad, feeling his anger rising. He took a pace forward and began to unsheathe his sword. "Come on in, let's see how big you are."

Blackthorne waved him back. "As you will gather, we will do no such thing."

Ferouc looked past Blackthorne. "Raven," he hissed. "In my trap now."

"Is that how you see it?" Blackthorne raised his eyebrows and idly scratched at an ear. "We rather think that this is a place you are unable to breach. A place that strengthens every day."

Ferouc's laugh, if such it was, resembled the rumbling of phlegm. "We wait. We grow. You weaken. Your soul will be mine, Blackthorne."

"Is there anything more you wish to say?" asked Blackthorne. "I'm a busy man."

"Return the six to me. Give me The Raven. You will lose six of your fellows for each of those who stays in your shell."

Blackthorne shook his head. "The Raven do what they will and are not under my control. Something you would do well to remember. And of those in your thrall, to me they are already dead. Nothing you can do to them affects my heart."

Blackthorne turned smartly away and it wasn't until Ferouc couldn't see his eyes that they filled with tears.

CHAPTER 19

Tessaya had had a great deal of time to think since his retreat from Xetesk two years before. In rotation, he had released his warriors to return to the Heartlands on leave and he had allowed himself similar time. He had returned to a land where old tribal tensions had resurfaced in those that had been left behind. And his lack of a victory had done nothing to reaffirm his influence and standing.

Tribal conflict had robbed him of warriors and more than one attempt had been made on his life during his times away from the East. That these attempts had failed reminded him whom the Spirits had chosen to lead the Wesmen to dominion over Balaia.

And so he had been able to keep his counsel during the upheaval and wait for the blood to cool and the tempers of the enraged to ebb. It had not always been easy for his people to be branded cowards in the face of provocation. But he had their unflinching loyalty after so many years of provident rule and he rewarded it again. Once the tribal struggles had burned themselves to mere sparking embers, the Paleon remained the strongest tribe in the Heartlands.

Once again the tribal lords had been driven to kneel to him. Those who had backed the opposition to him had been banished to that place where the spirit would never find rest.

With the Heartlands at relative peace and with those he trusted most ruling the tribes he most feared, he could turn his mind once again to conquest of the East. And for the first time he wondered if it would be truly possible. Mages he could wear down. Mere men he could defeat by force of arms and courage. But he had no weapon against the demons.

Worse, if they defeated the eastern mages, they could eventually threaten him and his people. It was a curious paradox. On the one side, he had travelled back from the mage lands knowing that the rule of magic on Balaia was finally at an end. Yet on the other, he had confronted an adversary of which the Spirits themselves were scared. He had no reason to suspect that they would attempt to invade the Heartlands but there was trouble among the dead and he had no way to calm it.

Tessaya was sitting outside his farmhouse under a porch of woven thatch that kept away the heat of the sun as it climbed into early afternoon. It had been hot this late spring and they had been concerned about the survival of their main crop. It had been fortunate that hostilities among the tribes had concluded with enough time to see irrigation organised, the crops saved and starvation averted.

Around him, his small village was alive. A hundred farmsteads grouped in concentric circles with his at their hub. Young animals ran free in their paddocks, wheat, corn and potato crops burgeoned and swayed in the cooling breeze. Children laughed, men and women put their backs to their work.

From the small stone temple that was the spiritual centre of every Wesmen settlement, Tessaya watched his ancient Shaman, Arnoan, bustle toward him. Across the dirt road that separated their buildings he came. Tessaya called his wife and asked for more pressed fruit and spice juice. The old man would be out of breath at the rate he approached.

Arnoan was red in the face by the time he had crossed the short distance. Tessaya pulled up a chair for him and helped him up the few steps onto his porch.

"Sit, sit before you fall," he said.

Arnoan, dressed in the heavy cream robes of his office despite the weather, waved him back to his own seat.

"It is not me you have to be concerned about, Tessaya."

He was the only man whom Tessaya allowed to use his name without prefix, and then only in private.

"You have received wisdom, my Shaman?" He handed Arnoan the cup of juice his wife had poured. The Shaman gulped at it gratefully. The remaining wisps of his pure white hair blew about his head and the spotted skin on his face lightened visibly as he cooled. He regarded Tessaya with those sunken grey eyes that the Wesmen lord had long thought were years past death.

"How long ago was it? That the dragons came from the stain in the sky and you told me you had no need of spirits?"

Tessaya chuckled. "You have a long memory, old man."

"And I know how the world turns, Tessaya. And the problems you face are far more severe than any you have faced thus far."

Tessaya raised his eyebrows. "Really? How so?"

"Tell me. Do you truly believe in the strength of the Spirits?"

"They have influence over the hearts and minds of the Wesmen," he conceded. "They are wise and have helped us in difficult times past."

"And if they were no longer there, my Lord, what then?"

"Then we would have to seek our path in this world without the guidance of our dead," said Tessaya after a pause.

"No, Tessaya. Because there would be no path for us. The demons would take it from us."

Tessaya laughed but he felt a moment's anxiety. "They cannot touch us. The Easterners are weak and their souls are taken easily. Ours not so."

Arnoan leaned forward and gripped Tessaya's arm hard. "We only resist because the Spirits protect us, you know that."

"And they always will." Tessaya looked down at Arnoan's hand. The Shaman did not relax his hold.

"Should the demons defeat the East, they can strike west or south without opposition. They desire passage to the Spirit world from this one."

"How?"

"That I don't know but the Spirits believe they will find it here. And should they succeed we are all forfeit to them on a whim."

Tessaya shook his head. "This is madness. How can the demons threaten the dead? The heat has upset your reason."

"Perhaps it has, Tessaya." Arnoan let go his grip and fell back into his chair. The weave creaked. "After all, I am just an old man overdue to join them, am I not?"

"Maybe you are. I would not be tempted to think so if you made sense."

"I can do no more than issue the warning that I have been given. The contact is never transparent, Tessaya, you know that."

Tessaya threw up his hands. "But isn't it part of the Shaman's art to decipher the jumble they receive?"

"And it is a miracle we understand as much as we do."

"Tell me what it is you must."

"You must prepare, Lord Tessaya. A battle is coming and help will appear from an unbidden angle."

"Is that it?" Tessaya pushed a hand through his hair.

"The Spirits are in ferment, Tessaya. They fear the invaders and so should you. They have to be repelled. All I know is that you will not be alone in your struggle."

During the night that followed, Tessaya slept little. His mind was plagued by visions he could not begin to understand. He did not know whether it was the Spirits who talked to him or if it was his own mind churning over Arnoan's words. When morning came, he could not deny that the Shaman had shaken him, but he had no answers.

He went to the temple to pray before returning to the East and Xetesk.

It was a sight that no dragon had ever thought to see. Not Skoor, Veret, Gost, or Stara. And least of all Kaan or Naik. A sight that would have fired the breath of the ancients. But so it happened and word of mouth did so much more than their entreaties ever could.

Sha-Kaan and Yasal-Naik, flying wing to wing. Allied if not friends. Carrying a simple message. A plea.

The Great Kaan's feelings were mixed. The cessation of hostilities between the two mightiest broods of Beshara was a triumph but left him deeply dissatisfied in spirit. He knew Yasal would be feeling the same. Both would have preferred the other's capitulation and extinction. So it was with warring broods.

Yet linked to his deep-seated unease, Sha-Kaan could not shift the feeling that he had embarked on a task of soaring magnitude. A task that would secure, if it was successful, the survival of dragons. Which broods would prosper beyond that survival, he could not begin to guess.

"Does it not concern you, Sha-Kaan, that broods might pledge their support then not deliver it when the time came? It would leave such broods with an overwhelming advantage in Beshara."

Sha-Kaan regarded Yasal with his left eye. The pair were flying south across the great ocean, the aquatic Brood Veret their destination. For this meeting they had no need of escort and flew unaccompanied in the upper thermals.

"It is something I had assumed you would consider, Yasal," he said, not unkindly. "Indeed I would have been disappointed if you had not. But it is exactly that which we must counter in the minds of the brood leaders."

"Might they not also consider this an elaborate ruse on our part to gain dominion?"

"Yasal, if you still harbour such issues yourself, then speak them openly, not from behind another's mouth."

Yasal grumbled in his throat. "Not all of my brood believe you. None of them trust you even as far as I have chosen to do for now. How will you . . . we, answer them?"

Sha-Kaan sighed. "It is simple. I will lead by example and so will you. All but those who must remain in my Broodlands will fly with me. There will be no defence because there is no point. My brood will go first to the battle. If others choose not to follow but remain to destroy my home then they will be killing themselves for the briefest satisfaction. That is my belief and I back it with the lives of all those I rule. This is not a gamble. If we are not together, we will all perish."

Yasal-Naik said nothing but Sha-Kaan caught the change of scent on the breeze and saw the deferential tip of his wings.

"I need you by me, Yasal-Naik."

"I will be there, Great Kaan."

Below them, the bass-throated calls of the Veret floated up to them and they began their descent toward the ocean.

By the time The Raven were called to dinner, Blackthorne had regained his composure. They sat around one end of the grand banqueting table in the central hall of the castle to eat. The tapestries still depicted glorious deeds past; the arches still flew to balconied heights and the fires roared in nearby grates to ease the chill of evening. But in every other way, this was most unlike the celebration of a meeting of old friends.

They could not spare the candles for anything more than light by which to eat. The kitchen duty staff brought through the meagre platters themselves; and the quiet of the castle told them everything about the paucity of people Blackthorne had at his disposal.

In front of him, Hirad saw green vegetables, a sprinkling of chicken, and potatoes. Not exactly a Blackthorne feast of old but a step up from the broth he was assured they ate most other times. Still, they all had enough to satisfy them. And while they ate, they talked.

Blackthorne's eyes gleamed dark in the candlelight and his expression was set with a grim smile.

"This feast you enjoy is in honour of the return of The Raven," he said. "And the elves we are humbled to count among our friends. But for the life of me, I have absolutely no idea why it is you are here."

"News, advice and weapons," said Darrick.

"Yes, but really," replied Blackthorne. "Plenty of stories have surfaced as you might expect. We are led to believe you slaves to the demons; mastering the resistance; living with dragons; and hiding on Calaius. It is clearly none of these."

Hirad took a long sip of his vintage and quite exquisite Blackthorne red.

"Until recently, Baron, the latter was the most accurate," he said. "But I would like to correct the man who claimed we were hiding."

"I feel he would be in need of some of The Unknown's famous administrative guidance," said Denser.

A chuckle ran round the table. Even Blackthorne allowed a smile.

"Oh, I have no doubt that hiding was the very last thing you were doing." His face sobered. "What concerns me is why you are here now. Don't misunderstand me, your arrival has brought new hope to everyone here but, well, this was already a desperate situation you were well away from. Why put yourselves in it? Have events turned further for the worse?"

The Unknown told him everything they knew. For Hirad, every time he heard it, he doubted that little bit more that Balaia would survive. Blackthorne listened without interrupting a single time. But as the enormity of the crisis was revealed to him, he sagged visibly, scratched at his grey-flecked beard and chewed his lip.

A silence broken only by the unnaturally loud sounds of cutlery on crockery followed The Unknown's summary. When at last Blackthorne spoke, there was a weariness in his voice. It described so eloquently the slow crushing of his spirit since the demons had invaded.

"I'd always believed we were doing more than simply existing. For two seasons we even made ground. Tortuously slowly, but we made it. Took back some of those the demons had taken from us. Some even got to sleep in their own beds again." He paused, memories replaying. "But we paid every time. They killed our friends in revenge for everyone we took. Just as they will do tonight. And every time, we all die a little more but we can't let them see it.

"Strange, but we actually felt we were winning the fight. We wouldn't let ourselves see it, I suppose. How could we afford to? Not even when we reached the limits of our ColdRoom capability. Even when it became obvious that we couldn't help anyone still outside without losing as many as we saved.

"Still we waited, though. And worked and planned and thought. And hoped. Just that others were resisting. It had to be true or we'd have been overwhelmed. But after another season or more we heard nothing. We sent out brave souls who never returned. We risked our mages in linked Communion. But we had to carry on hoping. What other choice was there? For us, for our friends outside, slaves and prey to demons.

"Do you know how hard it is to lift the spirit of everyone you meet on the days that your own is beaten to nothing?"

Blackthorne stopped. He took a long, measured drain of his wine. His guests did not twitch a muscle. Barely even blinked. Beside him, Luke gazed at him transfixed with pure adoration. Blackthorne looked across at him and reached out to squeeze his shoulder. Luke dropped his gaze to the table.

"We have known such despair. Looking out at misery from our own prison. Waiting for the end in whatever guise it came. We go hungry. We are sick so often. The weakest we buried a long time ago. Women are barren, their men impotent. Eggs are laid sour. Livestock is diseased. Milk yield is almost nothing. We are dwindling slowly, though we try to pretend it isn't happening. All those bastards really have to do is wait for us to die but of course we're no good to them dead, are we?

"And then you come from a blue morning and for a moment, we are reborn. Feel the energy from our victory if you will! But the reality is that we lost four mages and seven soldiers bringing you in and now I've heard you I'm not sure whether you are here as our saviours or to read us our last letters before death."

His eyes glittered as they welled up.

"I want so much to believe you can save us. Can you really?" It ended as a hoarse whisper.

Hirad looked around the table. At Auum who would have understood only snatches but who reflected the mood in his eyes. At Thraun who took it all in without a flicker of emotion but who he knew would be replaying the run in here as a wolf and living the nightmare afresh. At Denser on whose shoulder Erienne rested her head, the two of them reflecting Blackthorne's pain as if it were their own. At Darrick whose eyes displayed fierce determination and the indomitable spirit that made him such a leader of men. The spirit that Blackthorne would never let fail while he was with his own people. And finally at The Unknown who understood the Baron perhaps better than any of them. He nodded at Hirad.

"Tell him," he said and the ghost of a smile touched his lips. "You know. In your own words."

Hirad knew exactly what he wanted to say. He wasn't exactly sure how it would come out but he was certain he'd get his meaning across.

"The only reason we are here is because men like you never give up on what you believe. You remind us of us. And that means we can win, but only because you're behind us, fighting all the way.

"Baron, outside of The Raven, you are the bravest man I know and we need you to help us. Every demon you kill makes our job more possible. Every demon you occupy here is one less that can strike north, and so you help the colleges to survive, and survive they must.

"Everything you have done has been right. You've got people who love you and will die for you. You and I know how valuable that is. And there will be others like you. There must be resistance in Korina and the Baronies. Baron Gresse is surely still alive—he'll be taking this as a personal insult. But everyone has to believe like The Raven do that these bastards can be destroyed. If you let go that hope for a moment, we are all lost.

"Look around this table, Baron. Do you see anyone who doubts that we will eventually triumph? This is our land. And no one is going to take it from us."

Blackthorne did look around. He searched all of their faces carefully. Hirad could see it in Blackthorne's face. This wasn't any sort of bravado. He absolutely *had* to know.

"When you say it, it all sounds so simple," he said.

"He does simple very well," said Denser.

There was a burst of laughter. Hirad pointed a finger at the Xeteskian.

"Now that was almost worthy of Ilkar."

"I'm honoured you think so."

"You should be."

The Unknown held up a hand for peace.

"All right," he said. "Down to business. Baron, we wouldn't be here if we didn't think we could turn this around. I've left my family behind and I will see them again."

"Of course," said Blackthorne. "Now, what is it you need from me?"

"Later, Darrick will need to visit the armoury for weaponry but right now, there are two things. First, you've fought and studied the demons for two years now. Anything you can tell us, no matter how insignificant, could help. Not necessarily now and not necessarily you. Throw it open to your warriors, mages, everyone. Anyone can approach any of us with information."

"No problem," said Blackthorne. "Luke, handle that for me, will you?"

Luke nodded. "Now?"

"Time is short," said The Unknown.

Blackthorne smiled at Luke's retreating figure. The young man was upright, confident and full of energy despite everything.

"I don't know what I'd do without him to run the place."

"He's why you can't ever give up," said Hirad.

"I know. Now, you said there were two things?"

"Yes. Well, clearly the demons feel they have us trapped. So we need a way out." The Unknown had the decency to look apologetic.

"Now there I can help you. As you know, our cellars are particularly extensive and we've extended them further." He allowed a smile. "Actually, we've built quite a network of tunnels to exit points beyond our ColdRooms, like I'm sure anyone else still holding out must have done. We rotate their use and close sections from time to time and as it happens have just completed another. You could be its first users. When do you want to leave?"

"Good question," said The Unknown. "Short answer is, soon. More helpfully, I think it rather depends on how we all feel tomorrow, Thraun in particular."

"I can run," said Thraun.

"We may need more than that, old son," said Hirad.

"Ideally, we'd like to leave tomorrow night. There's a favourable tide early the next morning and we should be on it," said The Unknown.

"It'll give us time to sort out a few things for you," said Darrick. "We've been working on some tactics I can adapt for you."

"Well, it'll give our warriors something to tell their grandchildren, won't it? Taught battle tactics by General Darrick of The Raven," said Blackthorne.

"And the more they listen, the more likely it is they'll actually be able to relate it," said Darrick. "I'll need them in squads of twenty or thirty or it'll get too ungainly."

"I'll see it's organised for you. Or rather, Luke will."

"There is one more thing," said The Unknown.

"Really. That makes three, doesn't it?" Blackthorne was smiling a little more easily now.

"He never was too good with numbers," explained Hirad.

"Gods drowning, hark at that," said Erienne, stirring herself from Denser's shoulder. She looked very tired. Her eyes were a little sunken but they still held their mischievous spark. "The barbarian looking down on another's numeracy."

"Isn't it time you turned in?" said Hirad. "I'm sure you and Cleress have much to talk about."

"I don't think she can hear me, Hirad," said Erienne, sobering. "I can't feel her in my mind."

Hirad frowned. "But I thought . . . ?"

"I was on Herendeneth for two years, Hirad. I wasn't tending the garden all that time. I learned things." Erienne's tone was testy, impatient. "I can hold it back without her now. It's hard but I can do it."

"What else?" he asked.

"The rest we'll just have to wait and see, won't we? You'll know if I do it wrong, that's for sure."

Hirad shook his head. "I don't understand."

"No, Hirad, you don't." Erienne rose and moved toward the doors of the hall, all eyes on her. "You don't know what it's like to go to sleep at night and wonder what state your mind will be in when you wake. You'll never have to experience the dread of using a magic you barely comprehend and that has the capacity to destroy you utterly. And you'll never once wonder, when you uncap the power, if the casting you make will help the people you love the most or instead kill them in an instant. That's me, Hirad. Me."

Hirad listened to her footsteps echoing away toward the stairs to their two small rooms; all that Blackthorne could spare.

"Sorry, Denser. I didn't mean . . ."

"It's all right," said the Xeteskian. "She's finding it difficult right now. When she gets used to Cleress not being there, I'm sure she'll be less moody."

"Sure?"

Denser looked squarely at him and sighed. "Actually, Hirad, I haven't got a clue. That's the most she's said about the One for ten days. I think you might even have done me a favour."

"We're all here for her, you know," said Hirad, feeling guilt grip his heart.

"She knows that. But sometimes I think she's so alone in her mind that not even we can be of any real use. That's hard."

"Here," said Blackthorne, pushing the decanter across the table. "Fill your glasses. I don't pretend to understand any of what I've just heard so I'm going to change the subject in as obvious a fashion as I can muster."

He waited for all their glasses to be charged then lifted his. The crystal caught the candlelight and the smooth red liquid within danced and sparkled.

"I'd rather Erienne were here but still, there's always tomorrow. To The Raven. To mankind across Balaia and to the endless support of the elven nation. May we all live to look back on this when we're old and infirm."

They drank. It didn't ease Hirad's sense of guilt about Erienne and what he had forced her to reveal but it did lighten the mood.

"So," said Blackthorne. "What was this third thing?"

"It's a difficult one," said The Unknown. "There's something we're going to need you to consider very carefully. It may never come to this but if it does, you'll receive a message, I promise you that."

"Go on."

"It's something you must do. You must make contingency for abandoning Blackthorne and for travelling north to Xetesk with everyone you can save."

Blackthorne's glass had paused midway to his lips. "Gods drowned, Unknown, why?"

"Because if we don't make it, it could be the only chance the rest of you have to give the demons one final bloody nose. Now, I know you say you've heard nothing from any other pockets of resistance. But not all of your scouts have failed to return, surely?"

Blackthorne smiled. "There are always methods of getting information. I'll tell you what I know."

CHAPTER 20

The Unknown Warrior watched the three Protectors jog away up the western side of the Bay of Gyernath, the elven mage Vituul with them. Ahead of the group was a journey nominally the lesser of two evils. They would have to avoid contact with Wesmen and take one of the mountain passes to the north of Understone Pass to bring them within a few hours of the walls of Xetesk.

Ule, Ryn and Qex had made their goodbyes to their brothers Ark and Kas, and to Sol the one to whom they all looked now they were free. For his part, The Unknown felt as they did, that it was unlikely that they would all stand together again. By the time The Raven reached Xetesk, he couldn't conceive that they would all have survived.

"We can't afford one error," said The Unknown when the longboat had put in to the bay to head back to the *Calaian Sun*. "If Blackthorne's information is anywhere near accurate, Balaia is in a far more desperate position than we feared."

"They will not fail us," said Ark.

"Dammit but we're so thin on the ground." The Unknown scratched his shaven head. "I wish there was some other way."

"Don't think that way," said Darrick, who had accompanied them to issue final orders and check they understood exactly what they were to relay to Dystran, assuming the Lord of the Mount still lived. "We've passed the point of no return. We can't afford to worry at the corners of what has been decided. A change now could be catastrophic. And even if they don't make it to Xetesk, we have to be confident we'll make it, though vital preparation time will have been lost."

"You're right, I know," said The Unknown. "But there's no contingency. No backup."

"Like there was when you went to cast Dawnthief, you mean, or when the Noonshade rip was closed?" Darrick's tight brown curls blew about his head in the offshore breeze.

The Unknown raised an eyebrow. "Funny, but it seemed different then. For all the risk we faced, I didn't give any serious thought to failure."

"And you do now?"

"Yes," he confessed. "For some reason, the stakes seem higher for Balaia. Stupid, I know, but they do. After all, destruction or domination have always been the cost of failure."

"But not for the scattered dimensions too," said Darrick. "Not for the dead, not even for the dragons. And it's more personal to you, Unknown. You have a family beyond The Raven and that changes everything."

The Unknown shook his head. "There's more to it than that. Look, I'm worrying about elves and Protectors when it's us that concerns me most. When push comes to shove, it's us that has to win this for everyone. I know we'll be helped but we're in the centre of it again. I don't know if you were watching our skirmish with the demons but we were rusty. The fact is, General, we're getting too old for this. One fight and a sprint and we're all nursing pulls and aches except Hirad. And he almost got himself killed trying something he shouldn't."

Darrick was nodding. "I noticed. Well, we can do some fitness work on board ship as well as practice with those maces Blackthorne gave us."

"It won't be enough."

"Every little helps. And believe me, we'll get fit quickly once we're in action."

"That assumes we live long enough," said The Unknown.

Darrick opened his mouth to reply but paused and frowned. "Don't take this the wrong way, but this does not sound like you."

"No, I don't suppose it does. But then I've never been about to take on an enemy I'd be worried about losing to if I was accompanied by an army. Gods drowning, Darrick, there are about ten of us. What chance do we really have?"

"On our own, none. That's why we're calling on dragons to help us and the rest of Balaia to fight. It's why Erienne is training so hard. Unknown, you can't afford to think like this."

"Why do you think I'm airing this when only you, the Protectors and our oarsmen can hear me? And they can't understand a word I'm saying."

"You're worried what Hirad will think if he knows you're like this?"

"Course I am," snapped The Unknown. "Look. This is going to be really difficult. Like nothing we've ever done before. And I felt lethargic fighting those demons. Really slow." The Unknown shook his head again. "I've done nothing but half-hearted sparring with Ark for two years, what else do I expect? The point is, I want you to watch us, all of us. You have the eye of the professional soldier still, it's not something you ever lose. I want you to tell me anything that is awry with how we do things. Hirad will take it from me better than you and we can't afford to fall out. Watch Erienne especially. I don't like the way she reacted last night. She's not handling the pressure so well and we've barely begun." He sighed and looked at Darrick, saw the understanding in the General's eyes. "If she falls apart . . ."

"She has The Raven behind her," said Darrick.

"One day, even that isn't going to be enough."

"Hey, well let's make sure it isn't this time, eh?"

The Unknown relaxed a little. "Yeah, let's do that."

Baron Blackthorne strolled up to the periphery of the ColdRoom shielding and barked for Ferouc. He was used to delay and this time was no exception. He stood calm and quiet until the demon master was in front of him.

The dawn had been chill and the early morning sun was doing little to warm the land. It left Blackthorne almost glad he had no vines in the ground. In these conditions, they would have withered anyway. He lamented the loss of the vineyards and the object of his blame floated before him, his membranous wings rippling to keep him airborne. He was a comfortable shade of deep blue, his skin still. Not for long.

Blackthorne had gathered all his commanders with him to gauge Ferouc's reaction. It was a gamble but, as Hirad had said on more than one occasion, this was a time for gambles.

"It's a fine morning isn't it?" said Blackthorne, adjusting his coat against the cold breeze.

"Every day the air you breathe makes us stronger," replied Ferouc. "Your time to strut about your meagre kingdom is short."

"Ah, but is it? You've not tasted real frustration barring your abject failure to take my town, have you? How does it feel to know a damaging reverse?"

Ferouc looked nonplussed. "I am not aware that I had experienced one."

Blackthorne made an extravagance of turning round to smile at those gathered behind him, taking in the protective steel of those closest to him.

"Well, well, well." He couldn't suppress a heartfelt chuckle of genuine surprise and pleasure. "This is better than I could possibly have hoped."

Consternation flickered briefly across Ferouc's features, characterised by a shifting of veins and a modulating of his pigment. "I fail to see any cause for amusement in your position."

"Our position? No, my jailer, you misunderstand as so often. We are laughing at you." Blackthorne cleared his throat. "I would have thought you could sense their absence much as you sensed their arrival. But what's really amusing is that you clearly never had any inkling at all that they'd left. You haven't even mounted a pursuit, have you, Fidget?"

Ferouc snarled, his colour paling dramatically. Veins writhed under his skin and the muscles across his chest rippled violently. His fingers clacked together.

"You are lying."

"No, I am not. The Raven have gone. Spirited away from beneath your noses, Fidget. That's why you can't sense them. And you can't, can you?" Blackthorne paused. "But if you don't believe me, search for yourself. I'll guarantee you safe passage around my town. It'll be uncomfortable for you but I expect you'll live. Long enough to report back to your masters that you have lost something you so very badly wanted."

Ferouc opened his mouth and emitted a high-pitched shriek. He tore into the air. Blackthorne followed his path which crisscrossed the town. He would pause occasionally, dart to the edges of the lattice, sniff and back away. But largely it was a frenzied movement, desperate. When he landed again, his rage was almost too intense for him to speak. His skin was a pulsing, roiling bright blue.

"Where have you hidden them?" he managed.

"My dear Fidget," said Blackthorne calmly and quietly. "I assure you they are gone from here. My, it's as if you were scared of them being outside your control."

And there it was. Just what Blackthorne had been hoping to see. A flicker across Ferouc's eyes and a trembling through his body. Fear. The first time any of them had seen it but unmistakable nevertheless.

"You will pay dearly for this."

"Really? Going to kill more of the already dead, are you? Please. There is nothing you can do to hurt us further. But we have released The Raven and there is much they can do to hurt you. The world is turning, Fidget, and you have been found wanting."

With a second shriek, Ferouc was gone, high into the sky, calling his cohorts to him.

"See that?" Blackthorne pointed at the fast-receding figure. "That is why we must fight on. Fidget knows as well as we do what The Raven represent. We've been divided and kept weak. The Raven can unite us and they fear that more than anything.

"Now, I think you should prepare those under your command. I imagine things might get a little warm around here."

For fifteen days, the *Calaian Sun* sailed the southern, eastern and finally northern coasts of Balaia. The view from the starboard rail was endlessly striking and beguiling. Untamed landscapes, stark cliffs and glorious expanses of white sand studded the coastline with the promise of much more beyond.

Not that The Raven saw a great deal of it between dawn and dusk. Darrick put them through a punishing regime of exercise as tough as that to which Lysternan cavalry recruits had been exposed in years gone by.

He had them spar for hours with their new maces; relay race with weighted barrels; and climb the mainmast rigging using just their hands. He had them swim laps around the ship when the wind was light; he cut lengths of rope for skipping and pressed longboat oars into service as group exercise poles. It wasn't with a view to bringing great gains in their speed and endurance but for them to test themselves, feel the state of their bodies and give them just a little more sharpness.

And unlike in years gone by, he participated in every exercise, putting himself through extra rounds if he felt he was below standard. And while he drove them as hard as he could, he watched them, fascinated. They grumbled as he knew they had to but every task was undertaken with enormous energy, spirit and determination. They fed off each other. If the battles to come could be won by sheer will alone, they would be unstoppable.

Individually, though, he had his concerns about them. Besides himself, Hirad had remained very fit. His time with Auum and Rebraal had dictated that. But that couldn't hide the fact that he was not a long way from forty years old and just not as fast as he used to be.

The Unknown Warrior's problem wasn't so much his forty-two years but the long-term degradation of his left hip following his hideous injury on the docks at Arlen over three years before. It stiffened quickly in the chill water and relay running had him limping from early on. That and the inevitable softening gained from two years' easy living on Herendeneth. It was the difference between farming fit and fighting fit and it could prove fatal.

Thraun looked and acted no different. Quiet, withdrawn at times and without an ounce of excess bodyweight. Life on Calaius had clearly suited him.

But Denser and Erienne worried him the most. Their contentment at being back where they truly belonged, in the bosom of The Raven, was undermined by their awareness of the situation. It wasn't that they were unwilling; they would quickly become as fit and capable as ever if allowed the time. It was that he could see in their eyes that they simply weren't *ready*. Not for the task ahead, not to put their lives at risk as a daily habit and not to accept the responsibility that had been thrust upon them.

And Erienne was clearly struggling to make sense of what she was required to do. It drew her attention away, took her edge.

Darrick knew he could rely utterly on the elves. And the Protectors still maintained their aura of confidence, inscrutable even without their masks. No, the problems all lay at the heart of the operation, with The Raven themselves.

He spoke to The Unknown Warrior every evening and the big man listened. He spoke candidly about his hip, but like all of The Raven was far more concerned about his friends than himself.

"Everyone needs to understand the reality of their situation and limitations," Darrick had said one evening. "And that includes you just as it includes me."

"I'll be all right."

"That's exactly the problem, Unknown. Until you accept that you're not twenty-one anymore, you'll be taking too much risk."

"You think I don't know that?" said The Unknown Warrior.

"Judging by what I see out there under exercise, no," replied Darrick. "Don't get me wrong. We're an extraordinary team. The weapon skills are still there, the belief is undimmed and the will is staggering. But it's been two years since Julatsa and our stamina is not what it was. That's why we struggled after the short fight the other day. We aren't used to that exertion and it showed. The trouble is, you all still act like you fight every day. You don't conserve because you've never had to.

"You asked me to do this, Unknown. Now listen to what I'm saying. You're the one who has to relate this to the rest of The Raven. And you-know-who isn't going to like it."

"Thanks for reminding me."

"We haven't got time for tact," said Darrick.

"Hirad's never thought so."

"Then he should respect what you tell him."

"You know, Darrick, that is no help whatsoever."

The *Calaian Sun* dropped anchor in the quiet waters of Triverne Inlet on a chill but sunlit morning. All eyes scanned the eastern shore, searching for signs of demon activity. They found none, keen elven sight revealing only late spring growth in a peaceful landscape.

From the shore, Hirad watched the ship take sail and turn for the open sea once more. Jevin took vital messages home with him for the TaiGethen and Al-Arynaar. Should The Raven fail and Balaia's colleges fall to the demons, the elves would have to prepare for invasion.

Hirad turned to them, assembled on the sandy beach.

"This is it, then," he said. "I still think we should be coming with you to Julatsa."

Rebraal shook his head. "You know what was discussed. The cursyrd want you. You'll endanger us all in there." He smiled. "Besides, we're quicker without you. See you at the lake."

"Don't be late." Hirad hugged Ilkar's brother and clasped hands with each of the TaiGethen then finally, Eilaan. "Remember why we're doing this."

The elves ran away toward Julatsa and were soon lost to sight. Hirad felt exposed without them.

"Come on, Raven," he said. "We can make the lake by tomorrow nightfall if we sail through the night."

The Raven returned to the longboat which had been fitted with a single mast for their journey along the River Tri. With packs already stowed under the gunwales and benches, they were under way quickly. The atmosphere, as it had been outside Blackthorne, was oppressive. Only the sound of the breeze rustling reeds and grass came over the gentle burble of the water against the timbers of the hull. Balaia was dying meekly.

Despite being unlikely to encounter any demons in countryside bare of all but scattered farms and hamlets, they kept very quiet throughout the trip, resting as much as possible. Thraun in wolven form scouted ahead periodically, giving them extra security.

The Unknown took his time to watch The Raven during this curiously peaceful interlude. Despite his own concerns and those raised more recently by Darrick, he felt happier with the tightness he saw around him now. Two years apart had dulled them without question but their time aboard ship had rekindled their spirit of togetherness. But what they had to guard against was overconfidence in the fight. Looking across at Hirad, it was not a conversation he was looking forward to having. He'd save it for Triverne Lake. Now was not the time.

"We all feeling all right?" he asked.

Darrick raised a thumb from his position on the tiller. Erienne and Denser, sitting together and talking in whispers, both nodded. Thraun's eyes were sparkling after a recent run in the undergrowth and Hirad grunted assent.

"Hard to believe we're headed for the toughest days of our lives, isn't it?" said the barbarian. "This is all very pleasant."

"Don't lose focus," said The Unknown.

"Hardly."

"Denser, Erienne, a question for you." The Unknown waited for them to look back to him. "This information that Blackthorne got from Lystern about the sanctity of the Hearts. What do you think? We're relying on it, after all."

Erienne shook her head. "Not really my area," she said, a smile on her lips. "Demons are more Denser's thing. He used to own one after all."

Denser jabbed a finger into her side. "Technically correct. I suppose whether it's likely or not, I trust information from Heryst and Lystern. Actually, despite my wife's denial, we've been talking about this a fair bit and it makes good sense. Look at it this way.

"Best intelligence suggests that the demons are here to stay, to milk the life force of this dimension for as long as they can, not just rape it and move on. That means they need to keep people alive and mages particularly. Not just because of their souls but because they hold the key to mana. Demons are mana creatures, why would they destroy that which they need to live? The answer is, they wouldn't. Not if they plan to stay. We know they're flooding mana into Balaia, that's why it's getting so cold. And in future years, the Hearts will keep it from dissipating, give them a base from which to rule."

"But we know something they don't, don't we?" said Darrick.

"You're talking about the Julatsa experience, I presume," said Denser.

"Absolutely. Which raises an interesting question. Should we not be considering burying all the Hearts if colleges have to be deserted?"

"No no no no no," said Erienne quickly. "For one, we can't assume the mages are there that know how to bury the Hearts. But much more than that, burying the Heart takes what little strength we have for a long battle. The Hearts are useful to the demons but hardly critical to their success, I'd say. But the other part of your point the survivors will be forced to employ if the demons break us finally. We do know that Hearts die without mages to sustain the mana flow but will the demons believe us?"

"Well, we'll never have to find out, will we?" said Hirad. "Because either we'll have beaten them or we'll all be dead."

The Raven reached the stunning setting of Triverne Lake deep into evening. The fading light reflected off the lake's surface, picking out the extraordinary beauty of the landscape. Triverne Lake lay at the base of the Blackthorne Mountains. The lake waters, touched by magic, were sheltered, giving perfect conditions for the vibrant green vegetation that bordered them on three sides. Only the eastern shore was open. In the half-light, little of the colour of the vegetation that burgeoned among the trees was visible. But the sense was there of a spectacular matting that clung far up into the foothills before the cooler air running off the mountains let only hardier scrub, moss and heather grow plentiful. Last time he was here, Hirad remembered the calls of thousands of birds. This time it was quiet and as the longboat nudged the shore, it was clear that the beauty was tarnished.

Thraun trotted over the open ground toward them as they climbed out of the boat. Hirad brought his clothes and left them in a pile on the shore. The wolf trotted up to them and sniffed them closely, a contented growling in his throat. The rest of The Raven walked away up the short beach to give him a little privacy.

"There's been fighting here," said Darrick.

The Unknown nodded. "Indeed there has."

The ground underfoot was broken and scuffed deeply. Grass lay flattened and dead, the earth was cut and scored, scattered with loose clods. Far to the right, haphazard stones thrust twenty feet into the air, remnants of an Earth-Hammer casting. And everywhere were the dark stains of blood and the blackened scorches of spell impact.

"Strange, eh?" said Hirad.

Darrick agreed. "You'd have expected some scraps at least but this place has been cleaned."

"Thorough, these demons, aren't they?"

"So sure it was them?" said The Unknown.

"Spell battle at the birthplace of magic," said Darrick. "And recently, too. Hirad's right, I'd say."

"How recent do you think?" asked The Unknown.

Darrick shrugged. "Hard to say. Looks fresh. Forty days maximum? I'm guessing though."

"Where's an elf tracker when you need one, eh?" said Hirad. "Hey Thraun, what do you think?"

The shapechanger was pulling on his shirt as he trotted over from the longboat. Hirad watched him kneel and touch the ground. He crumbled earth in his palm and rubbed grass between his fingers. He breathed deeply over the bloodstains and scorch marks. And finally he sat back on his haunches and gazed all around him.

"The air is still bad," he said. "And the blood is human. Less than twenty days since a man walked here." He turned toward them. "But who?"

"Now that is an extremely good question," said Denser, coming to the shoulders of the warriors. "After all, Blackthorne is sure every free mage is in one or other of the colleges."

"Looks like he was wrong," said Hirad.

"How many involved in the fight, do you think, General?" asked The Unknown.

"Given the combat area, upward of fifty swords and magic," he replied. "The Gods only know how many demons."

"Hmm," The Unknown sighed. "This isn't good. I think we can forget any ideas of a fire tonight. We should take the longboat across the lake and sleep under tree cover. Tomorrow, let's see if we can't piece together what happened in the light of day. Any objections? Good, then let's get to it and remember, there have been demons here. They'll know this place now and the mana flow around here. We're not safe."

Hirad found himself quite happy at the prospect of sleeping under the trees. He hoped it would remind him of the rain forest, a place he would very much rather have been.

Chapter 21

"Southeast quadrant!" yelled Blackthorne. "New attack. Luke, commit the reserve."

Blackthorne was already running to the northern incursion. Flags in the castle towers signalled Luke's shouted order, flashing green and white in Blackthorne's periphery. He ran down the central stairway and through the arched hallway, leaping down the wide castle steps and on through the courtyard gates. Shouts came from all around him. Men, women, children. Running, screaming, calling out alarms or orders.

Above him the ColdRoom lattice held firm, but circling around it incessantly were demons. Soul stealers all, with their leathered or gossamer wings, their long taloned fingers and bald skulls on which the skin writhed in tune with their excitement. They were every hue he had ever seen, from the deepest blue to the most vivid of red or yellow. Their shrieks echoed around the buildings and their threats chilled his heart.

Beneath the lattice, spotters stood on every vantage point, watching the skies. They could come in anywhere. Usually it was in groups but occasionally they had taken to trying to snatch a vulnerable individual alone. It was a nervous time but they were holding.

Blackthorne called a guard to him and barrelled through the tight streets in front of the castle. He could hear the sounds of the battle on the northern periphery of the ColdRooms where he had stood six days before with The Raven. He had thought at the time that Ferouc would not take kindly to their escape. He had been right.

Entering the cleared ground, Blackthorne assessed the situation. Not thirty yards from him, thirty of his men had formed a tight square, shields and maces a barrier against a concerted attack by a greater number of demons. Circling just above and outside the lattice other enemies waited, and on the ground more squads of swordsmen darted into the backs of the demons, striking hard and running away before they could be overwhelmed.

It was exactly as Darrick had taught them and Blackthorne grinned fiercely. The demons were attracted to the largest spread of life energy and had left themselves open to the counter. Satisfied though he was with their defence, these attacks marked a change in Ferouc's attitude. But more than that, they told of the swiftly increasing strength of the invaders. While still vulnerable within the ColdRoom lattice, they were no longer merely sitting targets. Their power lasted long enough for them to make meaningful incursions and the length of time they could fight within the mana-free environment was growing.

Next to Blackthorne, his mage looked on in concern. The young woman's face was thin from lack of food and the worry lines etched deep on her pale features.

"What it is, Kayla?"

"They're different somehow," she said. "I can see a mana signature encasing them. It's like they're coming in on bubbles of mana energy which isn't dissipating like it should."

"That explains a lot." It was as Ferouc had said in earlier conversations. Mana density was growing. He didn't really need Kayla's confirmation. It was getting very cold now.

A burst of noise from the southeast told of the reserve engaging the demon attack there. Blackthorne wiped a gauntleted hand across his mouth and tightened grip on shield and sword.

"Kayla, back to cover. Three of you go with her. The rest, with me. Time for some fun."

Blackthorne ran in, feeling the cold air fill his lungs, blowing away the cobwebs from his mind and body. Ahead of him, the demons were upping their frenzy. More fell from the sky to join those attacking the square. Beyond the thrashing limbs and beating wings of the blue, black and green soul stealers he could see the faces of his men. Scared for their lives but determined. They focused on what Darrick had taught them. Heavy body blows to weaken. Drive them back, don't break ranks. Shields up and to the fore. Don't blink, don't flinch.

A tall, wiry demon staggered backward from a mace blow to the chest, its flailing hand missing its target by a hair's breadth. Blackthorne scythed his sword through its back, slicing its left wing from its body. Dark blood sprayed and the creature screeched and tried to turn. Blackthorne backed up one pace. The demon's skin writhed. Veins pulsed and its colour snapped to a startling blue. Unbalanced by the loss of its wing, it couldn't face up to attack and Blackthorne drove his sword deep into its gut and heaved it up and out. It dropped.

"Back!" he yelled to his guard. "Looking up!"

Four of them dropped from above. Claws in front, wings swept back and tails streaking behind them. As he had been taught, Blackthorne held his shield above his head and peered round it, waiting for the beasts to strike. He and his men bunched close.

"Steady," he said. "Waiting." The demons were on them. "Crouch!"

They dropped to their haunches, feeling the clatter of demons on their shields and the swish of claws. Next to him, one of his guard crumpled, talon marks deep in his face, his soul taken. Blackthorne bellowed fury and surged upright, bringing his other four men with him. The demons flittered away but the killer not far enough. Blackthorne smashed his shield into its face and whipped his sword through its chest, practically dividing it in two. Like its victim, it didn't have time to scream.

Around him, his guards beat back the others, leaving Blackthorne a run back toward the square which was holding firm. Sword squads ran in from three sides and he joined them. Demons were cut down, blades opening up their backs, the cuts as easy as scything corn.

"Hold, they're weakening," he called. "Let's hear you!"

A roar greeted his shout and he punched the air with his sword, backing off a pace again, collecting his guards and looking up. Around the periphery, the activity was lessening. Ferouc was up there, flitting from side to side, his pigment close to white in his unfettered rage.

"Got you this time you bastard!" Blackthorne laughed upward.

And it was true. The sword squads came in again. More demons perished, more alien blood spattered his ground. With one ear-splitting shriek, Ferouc called the attack off. Blackthorne saw winged figures climbing back into the sky from three locations and heard cheers sound around his town.

He nodded and breathed out heavily. A quick count around him told him he'd lost eight men, but the price for the demons had been much heavier. Even so, it was an attrition rate with only one outcome. He turned to a guardsman.

"Find me Luke. They'll be back and they won't be so easy next time."

Blackthorne strode back toward the castle. He could see Ferouc's game plan. It was as obvious as day followed night. Weaken them enough, then go after the lattice mages. He wasn't sure if the demons really knew where they were but he would have to increase the guard on them. Either that or pull them further underground. It was an option but doing so reduced the ceiling above the town.

He and Luke had much to discuss.

Dystran and Vuldaroq stood side by side and watched the demons drift slowly across the ColdRoom shield above Xetesk. There were hundreds of them, if not thousands, like a carpet across the sky. So many that the light of day was dimmed and lanterns were lit inside. It was a new departure for them and a new class of demon. Unlike the classic terror shapes of myth, legend and now hideous reality, these had already been dubbed "gliders" when they first appeared in the sky two days before. Since then, their number had multiplied dramatically and he had received reports of flights of gliders heading north toward Julatsa and northeast to Lystern.

They were a strange-looking demon and that was among a race of unusual creatures. Flat, coloured and textured not unlike a beaten and tenderised steak. Thousands of fine hairs covered their undersides, which also housed eyes and mouth. These hairs rippled and swayed as the creatures moved, undulating their bodies gently. They had little in the way of limbs. Vestigial arms either side of their head section and no legs at all.

That they weren't soul stealers had become apparent very early on, not to mention a huge relief. The gliders were present in numbers enough to really threaten them but instead they had crawled over the lattice, directed by the tentacled masters who hovered nearby, eyes on everything.

"You know what they're doing, don't you?" said Vuldaroq.

Dystran looked across at the man at his side. He had discovered a respect for his former enemy during the few days of their enforced close contact. The Dordovan Arch Mage had worked tirelessly with Suarav and Sharyr, helping them in the aftermath of their ordeal in the library and bringing them, if not out of their shock, then at least to a place where they could begin to deal with it. Neither had taken up his duties to the full and the other survivor, Brynel, was still in the makeshift infirmary, the chill deep in his body.

"Enlighten me," he said.

"Watch the way they move across the shield. It looks random when you first look but there is an order to it. I've counted greater densities in some areas that then disperse and allow other even more concentrated groups to form in the same place. Like they're confirming what they think they've discovered. It's actually very logical."

"You haven't done a lot else but stare at them, I take it."

Vuldaroq shrugged. "There is so much time for your mind to play tricks on you and undermine you. Best to keep busy."

"What are they tracking?"

"The mana trails feeding the ColdRooms, I think."

Dystran pulled his cloak tight around him, a chill gust whistling through the open doors of the tower complex in whose shadow they stood.

"That's a worrying thought."

"I suppose it rather depends why they're doing it," said Vuldaroq.

"Much as I'd like to, I can't believe it would be out of curiosity," said Dystran.

"No, but there is more than one possibility." Vuldaroq had never had much of a sense of humour but these last two years had removed whatever vestiges remained.

"They shouldn't be able to detect the trails, you know," said Dystran as the thought occurred. "They would dissipate instantly on contact with the edge of the construct."

"Well, I think they can and you only have to see where it is they're hovering for longer periods and where their density increases. It's always above the mana-feed trails." He shook his head. "They're getting stronger."

"Agreed," said Dystran. "Mana density is rising fast out there now. So, you think they're coming in?"

"Yes, and it won't be too long. The most likely reason for tracking the feed trails is to target the casting mages. But they could be doing something as simple as probing the linkages. After all, where the overlap is less, we are more vulnerable."

"But you don't think so."

"No. If I was them, I'd be wanting to fly straight down the trails as far as I could and take out our only real defensive weapon. It's blindingly obvious."

Dystran blew out his cheeks. "And now they think they're strong enough to do it."

"We're moving into another phase, young Lord. Best we're prepared."

They assembled on the plains of Teras over the course of three days. The burnished red Naik; aquamarine Veret; golden-scaled Kaan; dark green Gost; bronze Skoor and pale brown Stara. And these representatives of the largest broods were joined by those of another seventeen. All the colours of the brood spectrum were represented in the largest single gathering of dragons ever seen.

It was a scene that would never be repeated. Sha-Kaan and Yasal-Naik sat on a small rise in front of the mass of scale and furled wing. Both chose upright, respectful stances, their necks in "S" shapes and belly scales revealed. Both dragons wore the scars of their recent work. The Skoor had attacked them. Yasal bore a long burn along the top of his head and down the first third of his neck. Sha-Kaan's displayed belly was scorched black and painful. Six Skoor had died before the reluctant emissaries had forced their leader to hear them. Six they could ill afford to lose.

Immediately before Sha and Yasal, the brood fathers were gathered. It was an uncomfortable grouping. Old animosities were barely hidden, postures were hostile. Some would not rest within scent of others. But these dragons had at least agreed to carry the message to their broods gathered behind them. They would relay by thought pulse what could not be heard across the crowded plain.

Sha-Kaan gazed out over Teras and felt enormous pride in his achievement mixed with a deep anxiety. Here lay the greatest risk. Here they had to prove to all assembled that what they proposed was the only way to save them all. The only way to preserve their right to hate, attack and attempt to eradicate each other. To preserve the dragon's way of life.

Spread out before him, at the edges of his vision in every direction, some two thousand dragons weighed each other up. So far, minor flaring and disagreement had been easily calmed. Kaan, Naik and Veret diplomats moved among the gathering.

But this would decide it. If they couldn't mass and debate in relative peace on the plains, what hope of constructing a robust attack on the Arakhe to give The Raven the time and backing they needed?

Sha-Kaan scanned the extraordinary assembly. Far away to his right, dragons were squaring up. Wings were deployed, bellies clashing. He pulsed to his brood to quell the disturbance. Elsewhere, the rasp of breath and the rustle of wings furling set the ambience. From the north, another flight of Gost approached. He waited for them to land, drinking in the veneration that dominated most of those present.

Not all of them knew why they were here but every dragon knew it was momentous. It couldn't be otherwise.

"It is time," said Yasal-Naik. "We cannot hold the peace any longer without giving them something."

"I will speak for us both if you will allow it."

Yasal turned an eye to him that spoke everything about the respect in which he was held and about the Naik dragon's aspiration to his position.

"They will listen to you," he said.

Sha-Kaan rose up on his hind legs. He unfurled his wings and beat them three times. His tail flashed as it made the whip shape for attention and he barked long and loud, a huge gout of flame scorching the air above him. Across the plains, the gathering calmed and quietened. In front of him, the brood fathers prepared to relay his words. Sha-Kaan felt a wash of reverence cross him and he all but choked on his first words. We may hate you, it said, but we are here for you, Great Kaan.

"You know me," he began, voice booming across the hush. "I am Sha-Kaan. I stand here wing furled with my sworn enemy, Yasal-Naik. Always we have shared hatred but always we have had respect. And today we stand before you as one. Allied as you all must be."

There was a rustle through the assembly, spreading out to the periphery as the pulsed thoughts reached every dragon and the reaction came back.

"Today we face the greatest ever threat to our home dimension. To counter that threat, we must become one brood with one mind. There are those of you who do not know your role, why you are here. I will tell you why. The Arakhe have invaded the melde dimension of the Kaan."

Noise erupted across the plain. Hoots and barks shattered the calm. Flame gouted into the sky on a battering tide of sound. Sha-Kaan drew

CHAPTER 22

Auum looked across at the borders of Julatsa from the deep cover of dense heather and the dark of night. So much for the complete overrunning of Balaia by the demons. They had seen very little activity in the outlands and though the air was cold with the flood of mana, the demons were certainly content to concentrate on the major population centres. And this was after two years of invasion.

Of course, it could be that they had swept up any outlying villages and towns and driven the people into the cities. It was no concern of Auum's. All he knew was that he had to get the five of them into the college unseen. He had to nudge from his mind the disbelief that he was here and trying to get into the college for a second time. On his return to the rain forests of Calaius, he had sworn never to leave his shores again. And again it was humans who had caused him to travel north. Enough.

"Thoughts," he said.

"Baron Blackthorne is certain all the colleges operate tunnel systems to keep their supply lines open, such as they are," said Rebraal. "One thing we do know is that they won't be hidden magically."

Auum nodded. "Then we can search using the old ways. An unexpected pleasure. Eilaan. Prepare nothing. Just follow. Rebraal, be with him. Tai, we move."

Julatsa was a quiet city. Barring the circle of light and life that signified the college itself, precious little illumination punctured the darkness. Away to the south of the city, some lights burned from windows in what looked like long, low warehouse structures, and ahead of them lanterns bobbed on poles, lighting a group of people on their journey back into the city. Above them, demons hovered, watching. None of the slaves made any noise whatever.

They were returning to the city from the farmed fields that stretched left and right in a ring that disappeared around the city and presumably encircled it.

"Look for the signs of passage. Elven not human," whispered Auum. "Spread five paces and sweep."

The TaiGethen leader brought his people quickly to the edge of the fields. The crops were whole and hearty, apparently untroubled by the air temperature. Thick stalks of corn jostled in the breeze. Root crops grew well in ordered banked rows, their leaves strong and broad.

Auum paused, listening to the ebb and flow of the wind. He could hear the diminishing echoes of demon calls and sporadic cries from young, scared mouths. Dying away slowly. Like Balaia.

breath at the scale of the tumult but kept his bearing proud while he waited for it to subside. He had to wait some time for the last echoes to fade.

"Indeed a cause for celebration." He felt the wave of mirth. "Normally. But they will not stop there. We all know their nature. Total conquest of Balaia will grant them access to the dead through the races of the elves and Wesmen. And to Beshara through the surviving Dragonene."

Sha-Kaan paused to sample the rapt attention. He and Yasal shared a glance and the younger Naik indicated he continue.

"Our task is simple. There are those who seek travel to the dimension of the Arakhe to stop the invasion. They cannot fail. One of them is my Dragonene. When he arrives, we will have our beacon. We will attack in support of these Balaians. We must keep them alive because they can go where we cannot."

Sha-Kaan spoke through the roars of disapproval.

"You are here because your brood fathers believe that this threat is genuine. But there will be those of you who do not. To you I say, fly to my Broodlands. Destroy them. I shall not raise a wing to stop you. But neither will I lead you to the Arakhe. And when they come here, as surely they will do, I will be deaf to your pleas and entreaties.

"This threat is real. Dragons will perish in repulsing it. Fight together to save us or fight each other to a swift oblivion for us all. The choice is yours."

He waved his Tai on toward a low barn set between two corn fields, aiming to skirt it to its far side and approach the college from the north. To his right, he could just make out Duele's progress through the stalks. Behind him, Rebraal and Eilaan kept as quiet as they were able. Left, Evunn had paused. Signalling stop, Auum joined him in the deep shadow cast by the barn.

Evunn pointed at three tiny holes in one of the timbers. They sat below a timber split and splintered by arrow strikes. Only a rain forest elf would have understood their significance.

"Hope or expectation?" whispered Evunn.

"Good habits," replied Auum. "And Yniss brought you here to find them." He touched Evunn's shoulder. "We have direction."

A sharp wave of the hand and the elves moved off again, a little faster now. Entering the first streets of Julatsa, silence fell abruptly, the wind broken by a high stone courtyard wall. Auum paused briefly, cupped a hand to his ear and put a finger across his mouth for the benefit of the Al-Arynaar. Here, the merest sound could be heard streets away.

Twenty yards ahead, Evunn had found another marker, this time mere grazes on the wooden wall of a dark empty house. Further into the city, the lights of the college burned unnaturally bright, casting a halo over the surrounding buildings.

Auum indicated he turn into a side alley away from the wan wash of light. They continued on, veering right, further north of the college. Elves had been busy everywhere. The tiny marks were visible on buildings and brazier stands, on windows and the bark of trees.

They were taken in a lazy curve that would end near the college and, Auum presumed, a tunnel entrance. He resisted the temptation to run, hard though it was. Not just the muted stench of human civilisation insulted his senses but the insidious evil of the cursyrd that pervaded everything, even the air he breathed.

Leading them through a network of tight-packed houses, Auum picked up a faint scratching sound ahead and left. He held up his hand. Behind him movement ceased and the silence closed around him. Even he could not discern without looking that any others stood behind him. He angled his palm left and held out his index finger. Moments later, he felt Duele's breath on his neck.

The scratching echoed faintly in the cramped space. The passages they travelled were narrow enough in places that their shoulders all but grazed the damp, moss-covered stone and timber either side. In hunter's stance, Auum paced deliberately toward the opening in the left. His weight was slightly forward, short blade in hand, his feet probing the ground ahead each pace.

In this city of shadows and silence, it might have been a rat but his instincts told him otherwise. The sound was too ordered. He edged his head slowly around the opening. Crouched facing the right-hand wall, the cursyrd was dragging a piece of flint repeatedly over the same foot-long section of stone wall. It was completely rapt in its task, oblivious to the world around it.

Auum frowned. One reason for its action came immediately to mind. It would have to be stopped. Auum reached back and touched Duele, never taking his eyes from the slim, wingless creature he guessed would be about his height if it stood up straight. It had a small head on wiry shoulders and a covering of fine hair. Little apparent muscle and a solid dark hue were strange makeup for the cursyrd; surely a lesser creature in their hierarchy.

Duele could see the cursyrd now. Auum pointed to himself then at the target. He tapped his leg, indicated the target again and finally Duele. The Tai nodded his understanding.

In the next instant, Auum had sprung, landing square on the cursyrd, driving it flat to the ground face down, one of his hands clamped across its mouth. A beat later and Duele had pinned its legs down. It tried to bite, shout and scratch. Its body rippled strength despite its slender frame and a kaleidoscope of colour chased across its writhing skin. Auum held it until he felt the thrashing pass its peak. He put his lips by one of the flat slits it had for ears and spoke pure elven.

"You know my race. You know my calling. You cannot take me," he whispered. The cursyrd subsided immediately. "Struggle is pain." All that heaved now were its lungs. "Good. Do not test me." Auum half turned his head. "Duele, release and watch."

The creature was pulled upright, Auum's hand still over its mouth, his short sword at its eye. They both knew the weapon wouldn't kill it. But the pain would bite so deep.

"Move."

Auum drove the restrained cursyrd forward, following the arc marked out for them. They turned again and again, deep into the heart of Julatsa's slums where the stench was unquenched by time. Duele had taken the lead and when he stopped to read a more detailed mark, Auum knew they were close.

The TaiGethen paced away and round a right turn into a dank dead end. It was bare but for weeds, grass and the detritus of humans long gone. The opening was marked by a delicate pattern in cracked mud that was obscured by grass about halfway down the passage. He knelt and plucked it open, speaking softly into the hole he uncovered.

It was as wide as a man but made by elves. The demons would never find it unless led straight to it. Auum nodded for Duele to continue and the five elves and their demon captive entered the college of Julatsa.

The warrior and mage guard in the tunnel clearly couldn't quite believe what they were seeing. The leaders of the TaiGethen and Al-Arynaar dropping unannounced into their laps and accompanied by a captive demon. Auum had no time for explanations.

"We need a large open room. Defensible. Now."

One of the warrior guard led them down the tunnel into the college proper. They brushed aside elven questions and the fears of men. The demon, cowed and scared but very alert, was held now by just its arms.

The tunnel ended inside a cellar beneath the library. Their guide took them through the sparse bookshelves and across the short distance to the single lecture theatre. Already, word was spreading and elf and human alike were being drawn in.

Auum spared one glance up into the sky at the cursyrd circling there and pushed his captive inside. He hurried it to the centre of the stage.

"Rebraal, guard the door," he said. "Evunn, stand ready and watch." He released the cursyrd which backed away confused, deep reds and blues chasing each other across its skin. Auum's smile was bleak. He turned to Duele.

"Fight it."

Ule backed a little further into the cave. He looked down at Vituul, spent and shivering; and across to his brothers, bloodied, frozen, but unbowed. Both stood to his left, mace and axe in hands, waiting.

"They are coming back."

Minute nods greeted his words, a tightening of grips on weapons, a shifting of stance.

"When the time comes, you know what to do."

The three former Protectors stepped forward to the cave entrance where the gap was at its narrowest. They looked out over the last foothills of the Blackthornes. To their right, Understone, the Pass and a sizeable encampment of Wesmen. To their left, the forward Wesmen positions and the city of Xetesk. Their destination. A day's walk but impossibly distant.

Ule wasn't sure how the demons had detected them as they descended from the peaks into the deep grey and black mass of the range. Perhaps a lone scout. Perhaps the elf mage's aura was too bright. It hardly mattered now.

Upward of fifty demons were flying at them. Most were soul stealers and all were of the warrior strain popularly termed "reavers." They were tall and well muscled with powerful wings, trademark hairless bodies and writhing veins. The band had repulsed three attacks on their descent, with spells accounting for dozens of the enemy, but still the demons came and Vituul had no more to give. His face bore the terror of the fight and the wounds that iced his blood and sapped his will to a point where he could no longer protect his soul.

Ule had time to appreciate the irony of the position in which he and his brothers found themselves. So long in thrall and so relatively short a time released. Had they never been freed they would be in the halls of Xetesk even now. He breathed in the air, felt it over his face. He experienced a moment of pure release, almost joy. He smiled.

The demons flooded the cave mouth but paused just out of weapon range.

"Ule," said one, a pulsing deep green creature with huge eyes in an otherwise largely featureless face. "Return your soul. It belongs to us."

Ule stared at the demon. He felt calm, at peace. As did his brothers.

"There is no hope," said the demon. "You cannot resist us."

"You will not taste our souls again," Ule said. "While we live, we will fight you. And in death, we will escape you."

"You cannot harm us."

"Wrong. We cannot kill you. Know pain."

The Protectors' speed was startling. Ule's mace came from his right side and blurred upward catching the demon on its chin. The force of the blow echoed in the confined space and catapulted the squealing creature end over end into those massed behind it, wings flapping uselessly.

Ryn and Qex drove into the enemy simultaneously. Ryn flat-bladed his axe into the side of one's head, sending it tumbling sideways, scattering others back and forward. Qex slammed his mace into the midriff of his target and scythed left to right with his axe, biting deep into the demon's forehead. It fell back, screeching.

The wound did not bleed but instead healed over almost immediately, leaving a livid blue line where it had scored most deeply. And then the demons bunched and charged. Ule faced a blistering assault of claw, tooth and tail. He worked feverishly to keep them at bay. The mace was a potent weapon thudding time and again into head, chest and gut. And with it came the axe; flat-bladed to block strikes, edge-on to inflict pain.

But inexorably, the press grew and deepened. Claws raked his face. Tails threatened to trip him and fangs bore ever closer. He could feel the desperation beginning to creep into his brothers as he could the chill of the demons' touch through his body. Every time they struck, he felt himself weaken. But he would not let it show.

He dragged the spikes of his mace across the throat of his nearest enemy, deriving strength from its strangled yowl. He followed it up with a carving swing into its waist. It was a blow that would have severed a human. But here it cut just so deep, forcing the creature back.

To his left, his brothers suffered. Qex had been on his knees more than once and Ryn's face was a lattice of cuts, bleeding and blue from the cold. They didn't have very long.

"Once more my brothers!" he shouted, his voice bouncing off the cave walls.

He launched a ferocious attack, summoning everything he had left. He battered at the press of demons, seeing his mace buried in face and arm, his axe chop claw from hand, only for it to regrow. He took what pleasure he could from the cries of pain and the anger of his enemies that they had not cowed their prey. And nor would they.

"Duck."

It was a moment before he realised it was Vituul who had spoken, so unlike him was the voice. But there was no mistaking the intent in the word.

"Brothers, drop!"

And they did, together as always.

The IceWind scoured over their heads and swept into the defenceless demons. And now the screams were of agony and death. Flesh boiled away, wings froze and shattered and eyes glazed. Veins stood out proud and still, the supercooled mana penetrating skin and stopping flow in an instant. The entire front rank of the demons died before Ule could blink and the rest scattered back into the air, howling their anger and fear.

Ule turned to look at Vituul. The elf slumped back onto his side, his breath laboured and his eyes sunken deep into his skull.

"You were spent," he said.

"I am now," said Vituul between gasps. He managed a smile. "That really was the last."

"I didn't think you had it in you."

"Neither did I." Elf and Protector eyes locked. "We cannot take another round."

Ule nodded. "I know."

He swung back to his brothers. Both were leaning on their weapons, exhausted, all but finished. Out in the light, the demons had gathered once more and were approaching cautiously.

"Ule," said Vituul, dragging his attention around. "Just make it quick."

"It is something I am very good at," he replied.

Vituul chuckled. "Glad to hear it."

"My brothers," said Ule. "Prepare. They shall not take our souls."

Each man drew a dagger from his belt, letting his other weapons clatter to the floor of the cave.

"Vituul," said Ule. "You understand we will die as one. Your journey must begin sooner." He knelt by the elf and wiped the tear from the mage's eye. "Your courage will be remembered among the Protectors. Even in death, we will not forget you."

The strike was quick and sure.

Ule stood and embraced his brothers. Daggers rested against throats. "Release is ours, my brothers. We are one."

"We are one."

The crowd watching the fight grew steadily. Auum could sense them and at times even hear low words but he didn't ever take his eyes from the scene being played out in front of him.

At first, the cursyrd had been reluctant. It had felt the weakening effects of the ColdRoom construct but slowly had come to terms with it. What it had found more difficult were the probings and lightning strikes of Duele.

The elf tried to goad the cursyrd into retaliation and aggression but for an irritating length of time it merely squealed and backed off, rolling itself into a ball or standing with its hands covering its face. But when Duele jabbed a straight-fingered blow in its throat, its temper snapped and it struck back.

Duele stood his ground while the creature attempted to land blows with its clawed hands, whiplike tail and long fangs. The fluid movements of the TaiGethen left no room for the cursyrd which found its best efforts countered easily. Duele blocked, ducked, jumped and counterstruck with the speed that had made him so formidable even among the elven elite. Time and again, the cursyrd would lash in left and right with its claws and attempt a bite only to find itself dumped on its backside by foot sweep or the heel of a palm in its chest.

As the weight of Duele's blows and the cumulative effects of the Cold-Room casting took their toll, the cursyrd became at once weaker and further enraged. It knew it would not get out of the college alive and became ever more desperate to inflict damage where it could.

Three times it tried to break away to attack those watching it but Duele was too fast and its screeches of frustration grew louder. But well before it became too weak to defend itself, Auum had seen what he wanted to. The cursyrd didn't once raise its arms over its head to strike, only ever to defend blows to the head, and even then it preferred to duck and move or use its tail.

He moved into its compass.

"Duele, rest now."

Auum paced forward, assessing the cursyrd's attention. It switched to him right away, a frown on its face. Its skin modulated from a livid green to a deep, menacing blue. It was breathing hard.

The TaiGethen circled it for a moment, seeing the track of its eyes and the movement of its feet unchanged from its combat with Duele. It was disciplined at least. But it was lagging slightly, tired and bruised. Auum struck.

He ducked inside a flailing right arm, grabbing its wrist with his left hand and holding the arm high and away from its body. He continued his movement forward, raised his right elbow and smashed it into the cursyrd's exposed armpit. The creature jerked once and collapsed.

Auum stepped back and nodded. "Everything has its weakness," he said. "Everything. Tai, we pray."

CHAPTER 23

Pheone kept her distance while the TaiGethen prayed. Around her, all the elves had heads bowed, listening to the words Auum spoke and murmuring in response. By Auum's feet, the demon lay unmoving. Pheone couldn't tell whether it was dead or just stunned. But like all present she had been beguiled by the dance Duele had led the demon and shocked by the sudden violence meted out by Auum.

The import of what she was seeing trickled slowly into her mind. Not the fight with the demon or the fact that Auum had rendered it unconscious or even killed it with a single blow that hadn't broken its skin. The fact he was here at all, with his Tai and Rebraal. Why now? Why ever, come to that. It didn't take a seer to tell her that it wouldn't be good news.

The Tai cell finished their prayers and rose to their feet. Auum gave the demon a cursory glance and said something in elvish. Two Al-Arynaar warriors picked up the body and carried it out of the lecture theatre. Auum watched them go before walking to Pheone. Julatsa's High Mage found herself more than a little nervous. Auum had an air about him that combined total authority with a controlled menace. A heady blend.

He and Rebraal held a brief conversation and the latter, at last, gave her his attention.

"We apologise for the abrupt entrance and this little display," he said, gesturing at the stage. "Auum had to work while the cursyrd was strong."

"Did he kill it?" Pheone heard herself say despite the dozens of more pressing questions she had.

"Not quite. Warriors will complete the job. The body must be pierced."

"So what did he prove?"

"That they have a vulnerable spot we can exploit."

Pheone half smiled. "Come on, let's go somewhere more convivial. I think there's some soup on the go."

She led them out of the lecture theatre and across the dark courtyard to the refectory, trying to marshal her thoughts. The shapes of demons flitted around the periphery of her vision, watching everything. Once seated opposite the two elves, soup and herb tea at hand, she felt a little more in control.

"I do admire your confidence, Rebraal, but don't you feel that it was already weak and Auum caught it with a lucky blow?"

Auum regarded her through the steam from his tea, his expression unreadable.

"The TaiGethen examine every move a prey makes. They chart their strengths, learn their failings. We strike only when prepared. Only humans have a god of fortune; and he has turned against you."

Pheone felt she should apologise but stopped herself. Instead, she drained a spoonful of soup before speaking.

"It's been two years and it seems like ten," she said. "What are you doing here? I'm pleased to see you but I don't think five are going to make a whole lot of difference. Not even if two of them are you two."

"Nevertheless, we are here to organise the last chance for humans," said Rebraal. "The last chance for all of us."

Pheone almost laughed but the fear in Rebraal's eyes stopped her. She didn't think she'd ever seen an elf afraid before; not like this.

"It's really that bad?"

"What do your reports tell you?"

"That we've reached an impasse," she said. "The demons barely press us. They know they can't force a way in with the numbers they have. We think the balance will shift."

She saw Rebraal's eyes widen.

"Do you have no contact with other colleges?"

"Precious little," she said. "Why? Surely when the demons know they can get no further they'll withdraw. Or we'll force them back."

"Pheone, the cursyrd *are* home," he said. "You haven't heard from Xetesk in the last days, you're sure?"

"Certain," she replied.

Rebraal and Auum exchanged a look. "That explains your confusion and the lack of any preparation," said Rebraal. "Vituul and the Protectors must have fallen."

"What is this all about?"

"You will be aware of the increase in mana density, yes?"

"Of course." She shrugged. "Comfort for demons."

Rebraal shook his head. "You misunderstand. The cursyrd are flooding Balaia with mana from their dimension because they are abandoning it. Soon the density will be enough to overwhelm your castings and the demons will truly rule Balaia. Then they will strike west and south and neither we, and certainly not the Wesmen, have the ability to resist them for long."

"Unless we stop them, right?"

"Pheone, before I tell you what we must do, you must understand this. We believe Xetesk remains the focal point of their attack, Lystern to be under increasing pressure, and that Dordover has fallen."

"What?" Pheone felt her heart race and a sick feeling cross her gut. "Dordover?"

"We can't be certain but Baron Blackthorne, who still resists, reports that his last spies saw no light in the tower. But the Heart still beats because it feeds the demons mana strength. But what has happened to Dordover will happen everywhere unless there is unification. The colleges are the last free outposts of any real substance. If they are picked off one by one we are all lost. Elves, men, Wesmen, dragons and the dead."

"The what?" Pheone's nervousness allowed a smile to creep onto her face.

"Don't mock what you cannot understand," snapped Rebraal.

"I'm sorry," said Pheone quickly. "It just all sounds so farfetched."

"Have you not talked to the Al-Arynaar?" asked Auum. "Humans are so blind. You do not even know when you are dying."

"The cursyrd are on the verge of dominating this, and through it, every dimension we hold dear. We must unite to defeat them and it must be now. The fight will not take place here, it will take place in Xetesk. That is why we are here and that is why you must prepare to leave Julatsa."

Pheone was so surprised that she replayed Rebraal's words to make sure she'd heard him correctly.

"You want us to do what?"

He had known constant fear. And beside that fear there was a pulse that he could sense and it was growing stronger. Malevolent in intent. He distanced himself from it like they all did. It confused his senses, threatened to overwhelm them.

And he experienced utter clarity too. Clarity of thought and memory brought him joy, comfort and a pure sense of belonging. These times were as common as they were craved.

He was aware of meeting others, of their presence and support. Whoever they had been they were immense in character and clear of purpose. And like him, they retained the link to those they had left, though he wasn't sure, like them, if his communication was truly understood.

All his senses were changed, were more complex than mere sight, touch or smell. He had no words to describe them but he understood and used them as if he had been born with them. He could describe without seeing, listen without hearing and speak, if speak it was.

He believed he communicated on his new sensory level without the need for words though he still considered it speech. It produced images, soundless yet they contained the meaning he needed.

When he had arrived here, with its warmth and comfort, with its beauty and calm, and with its threatened borders and fear, it hadn't been the way it was now. How long ago that was, he couldn't say. There was no conception of time passing, though surely the knowledge of change indicated such.

Now, though the link provided his most clear sense of the life he had left, it was no longer the only way. He had become aware that he could sense those for whom he felt enduring love without the need for the link buried in his ancestral homeland. But he couldn't always feel them and he didn't know if he was felt by them.

He felt a growing worry. The sense of threat to their existence was building and he, like all of them, had travelled away from the developing pulse to minimise its effect. But in travelling, he had lost the link and his ability to feel his loved ones. He was certain that distance dulled feeling. Others felt it too and it worried them. The threat was forcing them from the link quite deliberately and it was weakening them, denying them joy and comfort.

He craved the sense of touch and he knew what he must do to try and regain it. Others would follow if they understood his reasoning. He had to approach the pulse, approach the burgeoning fear. He wanted to know if those he loved felt it too and if they could remove it and leave him with the peace and calm that was his by right.

He began to seek the direction of travel, a curious reminiscence flowing over him. The familiarity of purpose and of knowing he would soon be where he knew he truly belonged. He brought the words to his mind and the images washed through him. Had he lips he would have spoken the words. As it was, he felt exhilaration power his soul.

He reached out to them, sought them and pushed away the fear.

Them. The Raven. And within them, one mind and soul was for him so much brighter than the rest.

Hirad's head felt full and it kept him from his sleep. It had been coming on through the evening and he'd bitten his lip several times during the talking they'd done to avoid sparking a dispute. He knew it was something the others couldn't feel or understand. So he'd taken himself to sleep away from them, volunteering to take the last watch before dawn.

He tried to examine the way he felt. It was nothing like the touch of Sha-Kaan, which was warm; a gentle probing that sought permission to enter his mind. What he was experiencing now was more akin to an attack. Like someone was hammering on a door, demanding entrance. Everything was muffled but the pressure grew until he developed a thumping pain in his head.

Denser had offered a casting to give him relief from the pain but he didn't want that because he thought he knew what was causing it. Because as he lay and studied the weight inside his skull, he filtered feelings from the morass. He felt love, strength and the longing for contact, lost in time. And he felt fear too and that was reminiscent of that night in Taanepol.

But unlike that awakening, which had a dreamlike quality to it full of half-remembered images and snatches of sound, this was a solid block of emotional force. And closer than the dream. Hirad closed his eyes and tried to probe the block but he had no real idea how to. All he knew was that the more he relaxed, the more certain he became that his first impressions had been right.

"Ilkar?" he spoke out loud but softly. "It is you isn't it? Gods burning, I don't know how but it is. I can feel you, Ilks, but I can't understand you. I don't know how to respond. I'm not a mage, my mind isn't trained. But if you're sending a message keep on." He chuckled. "But perhaps you could speak a little quieter, I'm not enjoying the hammering."

He paused. His words had had no effect. He took a deep breath and tried to concentrate on the seat of the pain in the back of his skull.

"Ilkar, please. If you can hear this, back off a little. I can't understand you, it's just coming over as pain and noise in my mind. Ilkar?"

And abruptly, the feelings were gone. Hirad sat bolt upright and closed his eyes against the yawing of his mind and the blackening of his vision as the blood rushed away. There were tears standing in his eyes.

There was something else too. Just like Rebraal had said he'd understood back in Taanepol.

It was a desperate cry for help.

"I have to put this to the council," said Pheone.

"We have no time," snapped Rebraal, his palm smacking on the table top. "You have a hundred and eighty mages here, almost two hundred Al-Arynaar warriors. You represent the strongest force on Balaia, don't you understand? Without you, the pressure on Xetesk will become intolerable. And we can't afford that to happen."

"Well why the bloody hell aren't they coming here then if we're so damned great?" shouted Pheone, losing her cool. She was already tired and hungry and now these elves were putting her under enormous pressure. Damn, why was she the only one of the council awake?

"Because they won't make it and we need the information we know they hold. We have to make preparations now and leave in a day. Every moment is critical."

"Hold it again," she said, drawing breath and waving a palm at Rebraal. "What information?"

Rebraal smiled. "I haven't been able to tell you everything yet. You're quite a forceful character, you know. Probably what my brother loved about you."

"Among other things," said Pheone, relaxing a little. "Go on."

"We can't beat them simply by fighting them here. Our job on Balaia, and more critically, in Xetesk, is to drain them of resource, force them to bring more demons here than they want to. Keep them at bay to give the time to strike them in their own dimension; cut off the mana flood and stop the invasion at a stroke."

"And you think Xetesk has the knowledge to get people there?"

"We know they do," said Rebraal. "Sha-Kaan is certain that the development of their dimensional spells, together with the link they've always had with demons for mana channelling, means they will be able to open a gateway to the demon dimension that we can use."

"And who're the lucky ones getting the job of going through it?"

Rebraal gestured to his left. "Auum, his Tai, some Protectors, a little mage support and The Raven."

Pheone shook her head. She'd heard it all now and wasn't the least bit surprised to find The Raven cropping up. "Even after all their time away, why did I half expect you to say it would be them?"

"Perhaps because Ilkar is one of those under threat."

"Ilkar?"

"I told you, the dead are vulnerable. The demons crave their souls and they are helpless."

"Gods drowning, this is all too much to take in," she said. She rubbed a hand across her forehead. "Look, it'll be dawn in a few hours and I'm exhausted. Let's go through it again with the council, discuss it with the Al-Arynaar and we'll go if everyone agrees it is the right thing."

Rebraal shook his head.

"What?" demanded Pheone. "Look, I'm not saying I don't believe everything you have told me and I want to do everything I can to save Ilkar's soul if he is in danger as you say. And I want Balaia to be free. I just won't get driven at one solution when there may be others to consider."

"The decision is made," said Rebraal.

"Not yet it isn't."

"Listen to him," said Auum in a voice barely above a whisper but that sent a chill down her back. He leant forward. "You do not see what is before your face. Rebraal commands the Al-Arynaar. He will issue orders at dawn. They will accompany him. You can stay if you so choose."

Rebraal held up his hands both to stop Auum saying any more and Pheone retorting.

"I didn't want to fall back on that but Auum is right. But we do need your help. Your college is the one allied most closely to elves. We would not be suggesting this if we thought there was any other way to save it long-term. I want you to agree to this willingly. But if you won't, I will take my warriors and mages anyway and you will be taken."

"I'll be deserting all those people out there beyond the ColdRooms. Abandoning them." Her voice was quiet now, defeated. They had left her no alternative.

"Sleep on it."

"Sleep? Fat chance."

"And then talk to your council, tell them what must be done. We will be leaving at first light the day after tomorrow." Rebraal covered her hands with his. "I believe you will be saving more lives this way than if you hold out here for another decade. The Raven believe it too."

"Oh, Rebraal, I wish I could, I really do."

Chapter 24

Sha-Kaan had dispersed the broods across the plains of Teras in the hopes of maintaining peace while keeping the gathering close enough to react when the time came. Now, with Hirad and The Raven hidden above Triverne Lake and less than two days from Xetesk, he had called them together once more.

It would not be enough, he had reasoned, to simply shift to the home of the Arakhe and fight independently of one another. For this time only, they had to fight together; a single force with a solitary purpose to give The Raven support while they fought those who controlled the gateway and mana flow into Balaia.

He was reminded of the days of the uncontained rip in the skies that had joined Balaia and his home, Beshara. How different the conditions were this time. Then, warring broods had threatened the Kaan defence of the rip as it widened uncontrolled. The Raven had developed a way to close it before it became of a scale that would invite invasion of Balaia from enemy broods.

This time the gateway was managed and controlled by the Arakhe. Its origin somewhere in their dying dimension and its outlet, by all calculation, somewhere in the sky above Xetesk. And all brought about by Xeteskian foolhardiness. This time, the dragons could not afford to do battle over it because it could be the end of them all. And again, The Raven would have to succeed. As Hirad Coldheart would put it, be there at the sharp end.

As much as the sprawl of thousands of dragons on the plain had been impressive, the sight that he could see all around him now was simply awe inspiring. Skoor, Naik, Veret, Kaan, Stara, Gost and the lesser broods, flying in their familial formations, providing honour guard for those gliding lazily at the centre of them all. Sha-Kaan had called the leaders of all the broods to this summit in the skies but even he was distracted by the sight of light dancing on a rainbow of scale colours. He basked in the sounds that echoed across the clear blue sky and delighted in the complexities as each brood tried to outdo its rivals.

"None have been idle during our short isolation," rumbled Sha-Kaan.

"We all tired of waiting for your call," said Caval-Skoor.

"I trust you have news of our ultimate destination," said Koln-Stara. "I am not alone in having those within my brood for whom this delay has bred suspicion."

"And have any of you experienced attacks on your Broodlands?" Sha-Kaan waited. "Perhaps that is because you and your broods have all had time to reflect on what I and Yasal had to say. Don't forget that was a principal reason for you to scatter across the plains."

"Some of us are waiting for our scouts to return from our lands," said Caval. "I for one do not know if my Broodlands are safe. I am too distant from them to hear the calls of the attacked if such there are."

"But do you really believe your lands are under threat?" asked Yasal-Naik. "Surely the presence of every brood here is evidence enough that we are, for now at least, of one mind and purpose."

"I have not counted the head of every dragon," said Koln. "None of us knows if members of any other brood are absent from here."

"You are accusing us of something, Great Stara?" Eram-Gost's voice was sharp.

"I accuse no one of anything. My knowledge is incomplete."

Sha-Kaan felt the tension rise among the circling dragons, instantly transmitted to the cohorts surrounding them. The displays of skill ceased. Ranks closed and distance was sought. All around them, broods massed and waited. How easy it was. How fragile the peace. High above them, Kaan and Naik dragons maintained their mixed flight and kept a watching brief.

"My broods, please," said Sha-Kaan. "We have no cause for mistrust." He let his words filter through the tension. "Almost two thousand dragons are circling in this small area of Beshara. There are two ways this can go. It is either the greatest opportunity in our long and bloody history, or it is the greatest disaster to afflict us and all our melde dimensions. Remember: if the Arakhe reach us, all those on whom you depend will be vulnerable to them. I say again, we cannot afford to fail."

He flew into the centre of the ring of Beshara's most powerful dragons and altered his attitude, hanging vertically in the air and rotating slowly, displaying his belly scales to them all.

"Which is it to be?"

There was a long moment when Sha-Kaan wondered for the first time whether he had constructed a monumental folly. But with increasing pace, one by one, each of the brood leaders mirrored his attitude. He let feelings of warmth and comradeship pulse away from him and he barked a huge gout of flame into the air.

"Then let us get to work."

Auum considered this the time of greatest risk. The moment they had detected the change in activity within the college, the cursyrd had swarmed the periphery of the ColdRoom shell. A strain had appeared that he hadn't seen before. Flat and largely featureless but for a coating of fine hairs on their underside. At one stage they had covered the shell, blocking out the dawn light. He had watched them while they crawled and had summoned an Al-Arynaar mage to him. An elven female he knew and respected.

"They are seekers," Dila'heth had said in answer to his question. "At least that's what we call them. We have seen a few but nothing like this density. They are searching for the trails in the mana."

"Good," Auum had said. "So they waste their time. Tomorrow, the location of our casters will be obvious even to the blind."

"Well, I will give thanks to Yniss for anything that stops them trying to disrupt us."

"Nevertheless, we must be prepared."

And so while Rebraal, with his greater command of Balaian and his god-given patience, had the unenviable task of placating reluctant humans, Auum marshalled the defence. Guard on casting mages was trebled. Watchers studded the college walls and the roofs of all buildings. Mages waited under-cover in groups with Al-Arynaar warriors, ready to react to incursion. And everyone in the college carried arms, tasked to move as ordered.

From his vantage point Auum scanned the shell for indications that an attack was imminent. He could see groupings of the quick, powerful soul-stealing reavers cruising the shell. He presumed they were looking for weak points. It was a futile exercise. What worried him more were the occasional overflights of the senior strain; the huge Arakhe which floated on beds of ten-tacles but had the bodies of grotesque men. These were the masters over Julatsa. Their decisions would bring attack or maintain the examinations.

Down in the tower courtyard, Rebraal had emerged from the lecture the-atre and was heading for the main gates, surrounded by humans. Auum couldn't hear them but their body language suggested anger and a heated exchange. He turned to Duele and Evunn.

"The humans are being difficult," he said. "I will see what I can do. You know what needs to be done here." He sighed and felt a surge of irritation. "Yniss preserve us, but these people would argue themselves to guilt if pro-nounced innocent."

Auum ran quickly down the stairs by the main gatehouse, leaping the last few steps and landing on the cobbles right in front of Rebraal and the group of six unhappy humans. Pheone was not among them. Auum had their attention.

"We have problems?" he asked Rebraal in elvish.

"They do not agree with us," said Rebraal. "They haven't seen and heard what we have. They do not believe in a threat to other dimensions."

"It makes no difference to what must be done."

"It makes a difference to us," said one of the humans in passable elvish. Auum nodded minute respect. "We have had two years with your people," he explained. "And much time on our hands."

"Name?"

"Geren."

"Geren, your efforts are appreciated but your objections are damaging."

"We feel there are other ways."

"There are no other ways. You will leave Julatsa tomorrow or become a slave of the cursyrd." Auum turned for the stairs once more but Geren's raised voice stopped him.

"How dare you come in here and lay down what will or will not be done? This is our college and only we, the council, will decide when or if we leave it. Do you understand?"

"Rebraal?" Auum dropped into an older dialect. He didn't turn back.

"I have been hearing this for an hour and more," said Rebraal, taking his lead. "They are belligerent and their ears are closed to my explanations."

"Then it is time to stop being polite. You have done all you can."

"Auum, we need the human mages' help. Their expertise in the castings that shield us is much greater than ours."

"And you will get it." Now he swung back to Geren, his expression bleak and his mind cleared. He saw the man step back a pace as he should.

"Your threats will mean nothing," he said, his voice holding a slight quaver.

"I threaten nothing," said Auum. "This college stands only because the Al-Arynaar, ClawBound and TaiGethen died to preserve it. It maintains its independence because the Al-Arynaar have supported you for the last two years. Rebraal, the leader of the Al-Arynaar, has explained to you why we must all leave and travel to Xetesk. And this is the respect you show those who have saved your lives?"

"Your sacrifices for the college will never be forgotten and our respect for you all is undimmed. But what you ask is not in the best interests of Julatsa and the wider city, I'm sorry," said Geren.

Auum's hand clamped around Geren's throat and he drove the man backward into his companions, all of whom appeared too scared to speak up in his support.

"Do you think for one moment we wish to be here? We have no choice because humans have let the cursyrd into our dimension. We are here because we too will die from your folly if we do not put a stop to the threat. Do not make the mistake of thinking that I care if you live or die, human. We will take our people and what we want and we will travel to Xetesk where your race and ours has its best chance of survival. Rebraal says we need your help, so help us. Make the choice to live."

He thrust Geren away. The mage looked at him with undisguised hatred.

"All of you, go and do what I ask, please," said Rebraal. "I'm sorry it had to come to that."

Auum took his arm and led him away from them. "Enough. Forget them. We have the strength without them should they refuse to come."

"We have a responsibility to save them too."

"You have spent too much time listening to Hirad and your brother's spirit." Auum allowed himself a small smile. "Now. Carts and horses. Do we have enough?"

"Barely," said Rebraal. "We're fortunate that Pheone demanded Julatsa keep its breeding pairs alive. Consequently, we have some young and strong animals capable of pulling carts though fertility is as bad here as it was in Blackthorne. How they would fare under attack, we won't know until we try. Carts are a more pressing problem."

"Firewood?"

"Enough have gone that way but even those that remain are in disrepair. There isn't a wheelwright in the college. Carpenters are doing what they can and we're searching the stables and college buildings for traces and tack. We should have enough workable gear to carry casting mages and the bulk of provisions but any other mages might have to travel unprotected."

Auum nodded. "I will instruct the warriors to that end."

"Will they attack, do you think?" Rebraal gestured above his head at the demons circling and watching there.

"Unlikely," he said. "They know we are planning something but they also know the price they pay for attacking this college. What would you do?"

"I would wait until I was certain what was happening. When we drive through the gates, that would be the time."

"Yes, my friend, it would. We will be at our most restricted and vulnerable. Our warriors will have to fight hard."

"Tual will guide our hands."

"And Shorth will see our enemies to torment." The two elves clasped arms. "We will do this."

"Yniss will watch over us all."

With night full, Auum had been proved right and the demons hadn't attacked. But there were signs that they were massing, expecting a breakout. Roadblocks were plainly visible on all approach roads to the college. Demons flew a grid over the area immediately surrounding the college walls. Others hovered above the college, looking, watching. Waiting.

Auum and Rebraal had conducted a series of briefings with the Al-

Arynaar mages and warriors in the lecture theatre, discussing tactics for the first move out of the gates and what was expected of them on the anticipated three-day journey south to Xetesk. For some of that time, the TaiGethen cell would be absent, heading for Triverne Lake to collect The Raven.

Finally, Rebraal was standing with Pheone before the college council and the surviving humans in the college. There were one hundred and seven of them all told. Thirty-four mages and the rest college guard and those who had been invited inside the walls before the demons attacked. All were scared, all resentful. But all resigned to what was going to happen.

"Much has been demanded of you all in the last day and there has been little time for politeness. Much more will be demanded of you in the days to come. Most of you have questioned the decision that was taken without your consent. There is no debate. Now is the time to trust me. Trust Auum."

He waited for a murmur of conversation to settle.

"You have heard all you need to about the conditions outside this college and the plight in which we find ourselves. Now is the time to believe that you can make a difference. That by this journey and the subsequent defence at Xetesk you can play your part in the salvation of man- and elvenkind."

He held up his hands at the ripple of comment.

"You think that overdramatic? How quickly you have become accustomed to the way you now live, if that is the case. When was the last time you made significant advance or saved a soul from beyond the shell of the ColdRooms? Do not doubt that the cursyrd, the demons, are in control of your country. They mean to stay here and consume you. You have become prey, and like all other natural predators they pluck you as they need you. Do you truly believe that by staying in this cocoon you will defeat them?"

Again he waited, this time greeted with an uncomfortable shifting. He nodded.

"Those of you who know me and who have got to know the Al-Arynaar during your confinement here will no doubt have gathered that elves do not necessarily hold humans in high regard."

A chuckle ran around the chamber.

"But neither are we frivolous with your lives. Many of us have lifelong friends among you and we appreciate your strengths as well as lamenting your weaknesses. My own brother chose to live and die among humans. For me, there is no greater measure of the potential of your race. And for that reason alone, I would see you thrive, and us with you. That is why you must accept that the course we now take is all that remains open to us. The evidence you will see with your own eyes beyond these walls.

"The journey we will undertake at dawn tomorrow will be dangerous.

But I want to give you this assurance. Elves know your vulnerability to the demons' touch. We do not expect of you heroics and sacrifice. That is to come in Xetesk and all of you need to live to see the walls of the dark college. We will take on the burden of defending the caravan while you rest as you can and watch as you need. For the mages, we need you to be the bedrock of our moving ColdRoom construct and so you will travel for much of the time in the wagons we have repaired.

"For the rest of you, we need those who can drive wagons and who know horses to volunteer for that duty. We are not knowledgeable about these animals." He smiled. "It seems even we have weaknesses."

More laughter, a little easier this time. He held up his hands.

"I won't keep you from your rest much longer and I urge you to sleep for as long as you can because this caravan will only stop to rest horses, not humans. Two final things. You will naturally feel that the caravan leaves you more vulnerable than the college. It does not. Only the ColdRooms keep you from being taken by the demons at will. This structure will still be around you. Walls are no certain defence against demons, only spells.

"And last, wherever you stand, walk, cast or rest, there will be an elf watching over you. An elf who will stand against the demon that comes for you and who will protect you. In this we are stronger and you need not fear otherwise. We will never desert you.

"We leave at first light tomorrow. Be ready."

Rebraal started at the unexpected sound he heard. They were clapping him.

Hirad had his back to a tree, knees pulled up to his chest and his arms around them, hands locked in front. His sword leant sheathed against the trunk. Around him, an early leaf fall was testament to the cold that the demons had brought to Balaia. They had risked a fire to cook by when the night closed in but it was long dead now and in these hours before dawn the world was frosty and quiet. Hirad felt exhausted. His sleep had been broken first by Sha-Kaan and subsequently by the force he assumed was Ilkar, still trying without success to contact him.

And now he was awake on the dawn watch and looking over his sleeping friends, the two Protectors, Kas and Ark, and the quiet but determined elf, Eilaan. None of them slept undisturbed. Thraun chased the demons of his past, his body twitching and his mouth moving, murmuring. And Erienne, he knew, was occasionally found by Cleress despite the huge distance and the ageing elf's condition. Right now, she was somewhere to the left, having woken suddenly.

He had asked her to call his name regularly but she hadn't. In the end, she wasn't gone long and he felt her hand on his shoulder as she eased herself down to sit beside him.

"So I'm not the only one hearing voices tonight, eh?" said Hirad softly.

Erienne linked her arm through his and laid her head on his shoulder.

"She didn't say much. She doesn't have the strength, poor woman."

"Does she help you?"

"What can she really do? She speaks the right words when I can hear them but I'm not skilled enough to reply over this distance so it's all rather one-way." She picked her head up. "Look, Hirad, sorry about Blackthorne, the way I behaved I mean."

"Erienne, you never have anything to apologise to me or to any of us for. All I care about is that you're feeling more comfortable now."

"I'm not sure I am, that's the trouble. It isn't the One magic itself, because in theory I can perform the castings. But this isn't like casting an IceWind or putting up a HardShield. Failing in those is one thing, failing to strip the mana shell from demons would be fatal for all of us. It weighs on me."

Hirad thought to reply immediately but some words from The Unknown replayed in his mind and he paused before saying something different.

"We can't help you with your power, I know that and I won't pretend to understand the pressures it places you under. But remember how hard we've worked on fighting assuming your casting isn't there to aid us. Keep that with you because it means we can survive if you're having a problem. You are the most potent weapon we possess but you aren't the only one. We're all still here."

Erienne chuckled. "How do you do that?"

"Do what?"

"Say something patronising and belittling and make it sound like comfort and support."

"Because that's what it is supposed to be."

"And there's my answer." She pulled at his arm with hers. "Tell me about your voices. Are you really sure it's Ilkar? I mean, that's farfetched even for you."

Hirad shrugged. "Oh, I don't know. I've sat here tonight wondering if it's all because I so want to believe he's still here in some way that I've created the whole thing."

"And what did you conclude?"

"That it's all too coincidental. This has happened only since the demons began to flood mana into Balaia, if Blackthorne's timings are right. But more than all that, it just *feels* like him. I can't explain it. I've heard no words. It's all just fuzz and mist. But you know when you can smell someone on the clothes they've worn? It's like that, only inside my head. I just wish I could make it clearer."

Erienne moved so that she faced him and laid her forearms on his knees.

"Go with it," she said. "Try not to fight it or force it. Let it drive you on. If that's what means you fight harder, then use it."

"I'll try."

"But it's hard, isn't it? Having something inside you that you want but can't use. I know a little about that."

"I guess you do." Hirad smiled. "Now if you'll take my advice, you'll get your head down. Auum could be back any time from tomorrow and then this little oasis of calm is gone forever and it's fight and fear all the way."

"But just one more time. Then we can go back to being bored."

"Do you really believe that?"

"What do you think?" Erienne leant in and kissed his cheek. "Good-night, Hirad."

CHAPTER 25

The cursyrd were waiting for them before the first wagon was hitched to its nervous horse. Since they'd begun loading the fifteen wagons, some little more than makeshift covered trailers, in the dead of night the enemy had been preparing. Auum knew they would. For him, it had always been a question of superior tactics come first light.

But for the humans and those Al-Arynaar who hadn't listened to everything said at the briefing, the sight had to be truly terrifying. Reavers swarmed the shell, anticipating the moment it was dispersed. They thronged the area in front of the main gate, emitting a staggering kaleidoscope of colours. They hovered above every roadblock, herding slaves into the road as human barricades. And from their mouths came a cacophony of sound that echoed against the buildings of the college and high into the air, sending shivers through the bravest soul.

"I want runners either side of each horse!" shouted Rebraal. "Drivers let's mount up and assemble in the courtyard. Free mages, to your wagons. And watch those borders. Move!"

Auum's breath clouded in the cold air, mixing with that of around one hundred and eighty mages and two hundred and twenty Al-Arynaar warriors, college guard and the free Julatsans. He turned a full circle. Blinkered horses were goaded from the stables and out into the arena. Two to a wagon, they were skittish and either side of their heads elves stood and whispered soothing words, stroking cheeks and necks.

In front of the first clutch of five wagons, thirty Al-Arynaar mages gathered with fifty warriors. They were the vanguard, tasked to clear the path for the first wagons and if they could, blast a hole through the mass of cursyrd gathered beyond the gates. In each of the wagons, which would go through the gates two abreast, six human mages and six warriors, human and elven. For them, the task was to set up the forward ColdRoom shell immediately once they left the protection of the college. The wagons would be flanked by elven warriors and mages, some of whom were already perched atop the wagons themselves against attack from the sky.

Behind this first wave would come two others made up almost identically. The few spare horses were tethered to wagons in the second wave. Again they were blinkered and near them would run elves ready to cut them free should they threaten to bolt.

They had done everything they could. Auum was as satisfied as he could be. He and the Tai would bring up the rear because there they perceived lay the greatest immediate risk of losing mages. Right now, heavily guarded in cellars in the college, the ColdRoom casters still held the barrier strong. They would have to be moved.

He understood it was the nature of the casting that three mages were needed for each one to maintain its core strength. Under normal circumstances, if any of this could be considered normal, mages coming to take over the casting would feed into the same construct, thereby maintaining a seamless shell. Moving all three would inevitably lead to the spell collapsing.

They approached the moment of greatest danger. In five locations around the college, ColdRoom trios were waiting to move. In order, they would disperse their spells and run to their designated wagon, flanked by Al-Arynaar. For three of the trios, the problem wasn't too great. Their exits were clean, the wagons parked close and they could disperse their castings without risk to any but themselves. When those parts of the college were cleared, they could be moved and the cursyrd could take the territory.

For the remaining two, the situation was entirely different. Their castings covered the courtyard and main gates. And because those mages in wagons inside the courtyard were unable to cast until they could touch the mana and form new constructs, there would be a time, short but telling, when there was no cover. Everyone was aware of it and so were the cursyrd. It was what they were waiting for.

Auum waited. Three times he was given the signal that areas of the college were clear and three times ColdRooms were dispersed and their casters ran hard to wagons beneath the remaining shell. First went the refectory and lecture theatre area; second, the Heart and library; third, the personal chambers, rooms and offices. The cursyrd didn't attempt to chase the casters. They didn't have to. A better chance was coming.

Three wagons lined up, making their part of the third wave. Two remained empty, surrounded by Al-Arynaar. They were placed centrally in the courtyard away from obvious casting points. Dila'heth was of the opinion that the cursyrd knew where the casters were located but anything that threw them off the scent for any time at all was crucial.

Cursyrd flowed into the parts of the college so recently vacated. The ColdRoom constructs now grounded right at the edges of the courtyard itself and they clustered around, taunting, promising death. The reavers strutted around their new domain, displaying colours from deep green through purples and blues to jet black. Hundreds of a tiny dark grey strain flittered overhead, chittering. These were no real danger alone but their claws would be sharp and their touch cold. Enough could overwhelm man or elf. And way overhead, the master strain hovered on their tentacles, directing their minions. In all, the Julatsan escapees had to be outnumbered at least ten to one right here.

"Rebraal!" called Auum. "Prepare them!"

The cacophony from the demons rose to a deafening level. Al-Arynaar and TaiGethen switched to sign language to make themselves understood. Words were whispered into the ears of wagon drivers, horses and the few human swordsmen who refused to be placed in wagons for the escape.

Auum heard a demon calling Rebraal's name. He swung round and strode to the border of the shell. There it stood, taller than he, wings furled at its back, long face glaring in, a smile on its lipless mouth, its colour shifting grey to green.

"Rebraal," it cried in a poor impersonation of Auum's pronunciation. "You will be first. Your soul will be mine. Step to me, come closer."

It beckoned at Rebraal who surely could not hear it, its arms piercing the ColdRoom shell as it did so. Auum faced it until it focused on him.

"And you, elf, will not stop us," it hissed. "Come, surrender to me. Let us touch and you will know—"

Auum's hands flashed out and he caught the demon's wrists, dragging it inside the shell. It squealed and broke free but stumbled. Auum pounced on its chest, swept a short sword from its scabbard and pinioned one arm to the dirt. It screamed.

"Be careful what you wish for," he said.

The dagger in his other hand stabbed deep into the pit of its arm. Its eyes widened in fear. It spasmed and lay still. Auum retrieved both his weapons and swung back to the shell's edge, moving fluidly to his feet.

"Shorth will take you all."

He backed away a few paces, Duele and Evunn at his shoulders.

"We are prepared," said Duele.

"Then we will pray."

The Tai dropped to its knees. Auum led the short prayer that was taken up by every elf in the courtyard. With one voice they spoke, their ancient words stilling even the calls and shrill of the cursyrd.

"With our breath, Yniss, we are yours. With our bodies, Tual, we are yours. With our souls, Shorth, we are yours. Guide us, keep us and bless us as we do your work. Let it be so."

Auum brought the Tai to its feet.

"Tai, we move."

The TaiGethen cell jogged back to the centre of the courtyard in between the two wagons waiting for their casting trios. The cursyrd found their voices once more. Howls, shrieks, calls and cries battering on the ears, etching on the mind, scratching at courage and fortitude. Auum commended his life to Yniss a final time and nodded at Rebraal.

The gates of Julatsa were hauled open. The vanguard of Al-Arynaar warriors, led by Rebraal, drove out of the gates. Behind them, Pheone led the mages beginning to prepare the moment they were beyond the shell. The first wagons started to roll. Horses stamped and snorted, moved forward under protest. In the stables and in the gatehouse guard room, mages cut off the last of the ColdRooms and hell descended on the college.

Cursyrd poured down from the sky and rushed in from the periphery. In the centre of the courtyard, mages inside the second- and third-wave wagons began to cast, as did their colleagues in the rolling first wave. ColdRooms took care and time to prepare, so outside, Al-Arynaar mages and warriors had to buy them the space they needed.

Auum signed and shouted as he moved to the second-wave wagons. "Hold the horses! Mages, casting at will. Warriors, drive space, protect your mage groups."

IceWind and ForceCones drove into the air, battering cursyrd aside or melting the flesh from their bodies. In front of the mage groups, warriors hacked, slashed and bludgeoned, forcing a ground perimeter. The tiny strike demons dropped like rain from the sky, digging their claws into skull, shoulder and back. As fast as one was torn away and thrown into space, another two struck down, scratching and biting, weakening their targets with the frost in their touch.

"Strike the weak point!" roared Auum. "Send them to Shorth!"

He rocked back on his left leg and lashed in a kick to the head of a soul stealer racing hard at one of the wagons. The creature fell flat on its back, bounced back to its feet and advanced on the TaiGethen leader, spitting bile and hatred. Auum moved fast, dagger in his right hand, left hand free. He delivered a blistering multiple strike, thundering blows into the creature's midriff and chest, stabbing high into its throat and upper body, looking for the killing stab.

But the creature was quick enough to keep its vulnerable area clear though it couldn't land a single blow. Others joined it, flanking Auum. He backed up a step. Took in the five that faced him, the dozens of the strike-strain flying at him, and smiled. Around him, he could hear the desperate cries of Al-Arynaar being overwhelmed. He heard the shriek of cursyrd caught in the howl of IceWind; the sickening crunches of the creatures crushed beneath ForceCones. And above it all, the whine and buzz of the winged enemy as they attacked in storms.

Quite deliberately, he shut out everything else but his targets. He took a pace forward, feeling the first strike-strain home in. His smile was undimmed. Shapes moved to his left and his right, closing at extraordinary speed. He, like the cursyrd, was never alone.

Rebraal led the Al-Arynaar through the gate and into the open space beyond the walls. Cursyrd thronged the path ahead and the sky immediately above them. Their attack was instant. Soul stealers and the strike-strain flooded toward them.

"Keep formation, keep driving!" he called into the teeth of the enemy gale.

The two sides collided head-on. Rebraal struck hard straight ahead, battering a reaver aside. He used a shortened mace in his left hand, a short sword in his right. The creature stumbled backward and Rebraal drove on. The diminutive strike-strain lashed in like hail, each one smaller than his head but full of claws and fury. They swarmed over the front ranks of the Al-Arynaar, biting and scratching. Rebraal felt the chill of the wounds they inflicted and the blood run freely from his neck and arms.

Head-butting the reaver ahead of him, he made a heartbeat of space and used it to sheathe his sword. With a hand free, he ripped at the strike-strain clawing at his body, hurling them aside, urging his people to do the same. Spells roared into the air. DeathHail and IceWind froze the sky right above his head. Cursyrd screamed and fell from the air, skin boiling from the Wind or tattered and torn from the Hail.

In front of him, the cursyrd fell back. He saw them bunching on the flanks and running down left and right.

"Front rank keep driving, second fall back, guard the mages. Keep those wagons moving!"

He had turned to sign as well as shout and swung back only to catch the claw of a reaver clear across his face. The blow raked his cheek, freezing the side of his face. He felt his muscles tighten then weaken. Al-Arynaar piled in front of him, carving into the attackers and forcing them back. Rebraal felt dizzy, his vision blurred. Arms grabbed him, pulled him back into the mass, behind the front rank of mages.

Strike-strain were everywhere, disrupting the concentration of his casters. He had to do something. Not enough spells were coming out, and in the sky the cursyrd were massing to dive again. He wiped the blood from his face and blinked to clear his vision. There was a roaring in his ears. He shook his head. The sound of weapons thudding into cursyrd reached him. A few spells crackled into the sky.

He focused hard. Strike-strain landed on the top of his head. He snatched one away from him and hurled it to the side. Time to act.

"Keep the mages clear to concentrate. Let's go."

Warriors moved through the mage teams, grabbing strike-strain from them. Around their flanks, reavers were being kept away on the ground. More Al-Arynaar moved to attack those that came from above. All was confusion. Their line was completely compromised.

"We need that ColdRoom," he muttered, dragging a strike-strain from the back of a mage, ignoring the chilling scrapes down his own neck. At least they were still moving forward.

Warriors worked feverishly in the morass. Blades glinted in the early light. The buzz of the strike-strain grew more intense. A ForceCone struck into the air, bludgeoning a path and a little respite. Behind him, he heard a squeal. He turned.

The lead wagon was under concerted attack. The elves guarding the terrified driver were both standing and weaving their blades in intricate defence patterns. Strike-strain were being batted aside, reavers hovered menacingly overhead, looking for the way in.

Rebraal began to move back through the fight. He hitched his mace and took out a dagger. Strike-strain flittered before his eyes and he carved the air in front of him, trying to keep them away.

"Keep that wagon coming," he yelled at the elves walking by the horses.

The animals were beside themselves with fear. Under their blinkers, eyes were white. Every pace they took, they skittered to the left or right and the anguished snorts touched his heart. No doubt those behind, two abreast in the street, were faring no better.

Rebraal was scant paces from the wagon when the cursyrd made a critical breakthrough. Three reavers plummeted from the sky and thumped onto the canvas roof, feet cannoning into the elves positioned there, sending them flying. While one began to tear at the flimsy covering, the other two ran forward.

"Behind!" roared Rebraal, pointing.

But the driver's guards couldn't hear him. The first they knew was when one of the creatures landed square on the driver and clutched his face. The poor man had no time even to scream before his soul was gone. The reaver exalted, lashing out left and right, catching both guards in the chest and flattening them against the wagon frame. The other leapt straight onto one horse's back and bit down into its neck.

The animal reared and screamed. It sought escape and, without a driver to control it, plunged away left across the cobbles, the other only too willing to follow its lead. Strike-strain and reavers gave chase. On the wagon's roof, cursyrd had torn up the canvas and were dropping inside. On the kicker board, the elves fought with the reaver in the driver's position. Others made to pursue.

"No!" shouted Rebraal. "Keep discipline. You can't help them. Keep moving forward. Drive on, Al-Arynaar!"

They listened to him as they always would. And in the midst of the disaster, an opportunity opened up. Carried away with their success, a large number of cursyrd were pursuing the wagon. The pressure lifted just enough, the enemy were distracted. Rebraal seized the moment with both hands. Amidst the howls of anger from high above as the master strain saw what was unfolding, Rebraal led his warriors and mages in a renewed assault.

Strike-strain were grabbed from mages, who were left free to cast. Warriors reformed at the head of the wave and drove hard at the reavers massed in front of the first barricade. Moments later, spells blazed into the sky and head-on once more. Demons were melted by IceWind, flung high and wide by ForceCones, ripped to shreds by DeathHail. Strike-strain burned under the focused power of FlamePalm. FlameOrbs arced into the sky. To the left, a FireWall roared into life.

Rebraal, at the head of the wave once more, ignored the blood running down his face and the deep cold that had frozen his cheek. At a call from the mage teams, the warrior rank paused and ducked. Spells flashed over their heads, scattering reavers from their path. Warriors ran left and right, pressing home their brief advantage, battering a path for the wagons to follow and opening up the route to the barricade.

In front of piles of wood, stone and rubble, cursyrd had herded dozens of Julatsans. The white-faced humans stared from black and sunken eyes and through lank hair. They made no move when the cursyrd were driven from the path of the Al-Arynaar and oncoming wagons. The pace wasn't fast, ColdRoom casting would be impossible otherwise, but it was inexorable. And Rebraal was not going to stop for anyone.

"Move!" he bellowed. "Move!"

His dagger lashed into the face of a reaver that landed in front of him. He kicked out straight and caught it in the stomach. It grunted, fell back a step and was engulfed in Al-Arynaar.

"Move!"

But they didn't. They were beaten, terrified and unable to think for themselves. They were caught between two horrors, their cursyrd masters and the oncoming elven forces. Neither was going to give.

"Prepare the Cones," said Rebraal.

There was no dissent behind him. The elves advanced at a trot, the mages now with clear sight of the barricade, both material and human. Rebraal waved his arms again.

"Please! Get away. Get away!"

Nothing. And in that moment, he wondered whether they actually welcomed the end that approached them. None pleaded, none cried for rescue. Not a tear was being spilled. They merely stood and waited.

"We are ready," came a voice from behind his left shoulder.

Rebraal fell back behind the mage line.

"Cast," he ordered.

The barricade had been erected at the head of the road that led south through the city. Tall buildings reared up either side. It was a perfect focus for ForceCones and their effect was as dramatic as it was terrible.

The invisible rams of mana energy slammed into the unprotected humans, and their cursyrd shepherds. Man and cursyrd were plucked from the ground and flung backward into the barricade. Blood splattered the walls left and right, bodies smeared against the buildings. The barricade exploded backward. Elven casters kept up the pressure, driving the rubble and timber left and right. Rebraal heard the agony of men whose bodies were crushed flat, and the squealing of metal on stone. Shattered, the elements of the barricade bounced and spun down the street. Cursyrd shrieked in fury. He watched one man try to rise and begin to run but another Cone tossed him full face into a building across the street, no more than a doll in a gale.

"I'm sorry," muttered Rebraal. "May Shorth speed you to your rest." He had no time for anything else. Too much rubble littered the ground. "Focus on the cobbles. Clear the street or we'll lose wheels going down there."

Left and right, Al-Arynaar were closing back in to guard their mages as they entered the street. Cursyrd ran and flew at rooftop height. Their masters had gathered their attention once more and they came again from above and behind. Rebraal ran back down the line.

"Single file. Wagons single file."

They were rolling now. More wagons were coming from the gate. The sounds of fighting from within the walls echoed up to the sky where cursyrd massed from all points of the compass. Rebraal smiled grimly. They had made one small advance but the journey had only just begun. He prayed the ColdRooms would not be long in casting. He wasn't sure how much any of them really had left.

CHAPTER 26

Auum saw it all with utter clarity. He and his Tai moved as one, acted as a single entity, a boiling of controlled action in a sea of confusion. They targeted the reavers. Easy prey for the cell. Strike-strain clawed and buzzed around them and were knocked away as an afterthought. The real threat to the human mages, the wagon drivers and horses lay in the tall strong soul stealers who stalked and dived in the throng of the courtyard.

Duele and Evunn pirouetted together and downed a muscular deep blue creature. It barely had a chance to breathe before Auum pinned it down by its chest. Duele snatched an arm outward, Evunn backhanded a dagger into the nerve ganglion revealed and the cursyrd died.

Auum rose to his feet. To his left, an Al-Arynaar had become detached from his warrior group. Cloaked in strike-strain, he became confused and disoriented. Quickly, three reavers were on him, lashing in claws, biting and gouging. One clutched him under the chin as he weakened and drained his broken soul.

It would be happening everywhere. Cursyrd flooded the courtyard, dropping from the sky; the strike-strain like malevolent hail, their reaver brethren sails on the breeze. Duele and Evunn came to his shoulders. They watched a change in the cursyrd tactics as the second-wave wagons started to roll. Combat against the Al-Arynaar on the ground and on wagon was both difficult and, should their weakness be exploited, deadly and now they were concentrating solely on the horses, trying to take out the escape's prime motive force.

Barking out orders and signing the alarm, the Tai cell raced into the centre of the courtyard. They were already too late to save one wagon. The driver was swarming in strike-strain, the flanking elves were under attack from twice their number of reavers, and the horses were being cut to pieces.

"Leave it," said Auum. "Left and right. I'll take centre. Tai, we move."

The trio split, heading for three separate wagons in the third wave. Al-Arynaar were keeping the cursyrd away on the ground but more fell from the sky. Auum dodged individual battles, increasing his speed dramatically. Dagger in hand, he took off, arrowing feet first into a reaver just landed on the back of a terrified horse. He caught the creature in the side of the head and the two of them hurtled to the ground, the cursyrd disorientated. Auum took a forward roll on landing, coming smoothly to his feet and spinning on his heel, balance perfect.

The soul stealer was struggling to get its legs under it. Auum pounced, stamping a foot into the creature's neck, wrenching one of its arms up and driving his dagger deep into its nerve centre. He turned and ran back to the wagon, leaping onto the kicker board and straight-punching another which tumbled to the dirt.

Next to him, the driver was screaming in panic, covered in strike-strain. Auum grabbed the man's face.

"Calm," he said. "Drive. I will protect you."

Slowly, the man focused on him and managed to nod.

"Drive," repeated Auum.

The TaiGethen swivelled and made quick assessment. On the roof of the wagon, Al-Arynaar were holding off the reavers while on the ground warriors and mages kept their perimeter around it. On the roof of an adjacent wagon, Duele danced. Auum could have watched him all day. Feet planted on roof struts or blurring through the air to strike. Arms laid out for balance, block and punch.

To the right, Evunn, like Auum, was standing by his driver. An Al-Arynaar stood on each horse's back. All three wagons began to move. Across the ground, the bodies of cursyrd and Al-Arynaar were scattered; more of the latter than the former had fallen in the hand-to-hand combats but losses on both sides were climbing. Skirmishes raged across the open space. Warriors drove space for wagons to move into. Spells fired across the ground and into the air. Mages using FlamePalm ran in all directions, burning strike-strain, wounding reavers. Under the eaves of the stables and behind a solid rank of elven warriors, mages cast hard and fast. Cursyrd were being washed from the sky and flung far from the combat. The air stank of blood and burned flesh but still they came on.

Auum nodded at the Al-Arynaar warrior beside him on the kicker board.

"Clear the driver. I will watch."

A soul stealer landed heavily on the back of one horse which reared and threatened to bolt, kept in its traces only by the weight of the other which skittered. The driver, with strike-strain being pulled from his back and face, fought for control. Auum jumped lightly onto the animal's rump, his left foot already coming round to clatter into the upper back of the cursyrd. He planted the foot and struck with both fists, tipping the creature onto the ground.

Beyond the walls the ground shook and the sound of tumbling stone echoed across the city. Auum heard screams. Still on the horse, he crouched and turned to the driver. The Al-Arynaar stood by him, working to keep him clear of strike-strain.

"Faster," he said. "We move."

The wagon picked up pace, the flanking Al-Arynaar being forced to break into a trot to keep up. A movement caught Auum's eye, high and to the right. Reavers, eight or more, diving hard for the wagon. Not even he could keep them all away. He leaped back onto the kicker board.

"Above," he said to the Al-Arynaar. "Trouble."

The reavers came in steeply, claws first, shrieking fury. Auum stepped up onto the roof with the two Al-Arynaar. It was temporarily clear of enemy. The gatehouse was approaching.

"Faster," he ordered. "Gallop."

He heard the reins snap. The horses took off, happy to be let go, jerking the wagon behind them. Auum knew the mages beneath would lose the spell but others would still be casting. Above, the reavers adjusted their direction, knowing they wouldn't reach the horses before they reached brief cover. Three of them pulled away, flying over the gatehouse to meet them on their exit. The others ploughed on for wagon and driver. These would strike in time.

A shiver ran across the college. Nothing could be seen, but the sense of power rushing into the air was undeniable. Cursyrd howled and screamed. Hoots of alarm bounced across the courtyard. A concerted roar from the masters above rent the air. Auum smiled. It was mirthless. He dropped his dagger and had two short swords in his hands in a heartbeat.

Above, the reavers came on but they had slowed dramatically, deep inside what had suddenly become a dome of pain. They couldn't brake in time. Three, wings swept back, tried to change their attitude to feet first. It made no difference to Auum.

"Take them," he said.

He sidestepped the first and drove both his swords deep into its back. Dark gore sprayed into the air but the thrusts were not fatal. The mana shells surrounding the cursyrd were stronger now, making them dangerous even within ColdRoom castings. Auum dragged the blades clear, ducked a claw from another reaver and whipped one blade across its throat, stabbing the other into its eye.

"Our turn now," he spat at the creature as it died.

Across the courtyard, cursyrd broke off their attacks and fled back into the air. Denied mana, Al-Arynaar mages took swords from belts and formed up by the wagons once more. Strike-strain died in their tens and dozens, snared by the same claws that so recently had been hooks to drag through the flesh of men. Reavers not quick enough to flit up to safety were hauled to the ground and hacked to pieces, their skins boiling through bright colours, their veins spewing their life onto the cobbles.

The Julatsan wagon train drove out of the college and south through the city at an easy trot. Within the eleven surviving wagons, human and elven mages with their Al-Arynaar warrior guard searched for space among the baskets and barrels of provisions and water. The ColdRoom shell held steady, covering the train front to back and spilling over into adjacent buildings, keeping the cursyrd at bay for now. Auum moved back to sit by the driver, nodding his respect at the man who, though bloodied and shivering, held the reins steady, determination in every muscle.

But the sky outside the shell was thick with cursyrd, tracking them as they fled to open ground. And what worried Auum was that with the mana density clearly growing stronger, it wouldn't be long before the enemy could fight effectively inside the shell.

The fate of man and elf hung by the slenderest of threads.

It was dawn in Lystern but the light was dim and the few lanterns they could afford to use burned bright in the gloom. Faces were pressed to every window of the grand council chamber, though that was a misnomer now. The periphery of their ColdRoom castings was scant yards outside the filthy stained glass and across its surface, for the third day running, the flattened seeker demons crawled, searching for the telltale threads of mana they could use to direct their attacks.

In two days, they had lost two casting teams to lightning raids from the winged reavers and had been forced to withdraw into an ever-tightening space. They had too few mages to cycle their strength should they lose any more teams and their warriors were exhausted, trebling their day and night guard on this most precious of resources.

Heryst had no desire to look. Others would tell him if the seekers found what they were looking for. A slight discoloration in their pale underbellies would give them away. He had done all he could, moving the casting teams time and again. But their available area was small enough that it surely only put off the inevitable.

It had all been so sudden. The demons had seemingly become so much stronger. They had known the mana density was increasing but nothing had indicated this ability to strike so quickly and effectively at the heart of his defence. The last message he had received from Blackthorne told him that the wily Baron was under similar pressure and that they were considering running north to Xetesk where apparently the last vestiges of Balaian resistance were gathering.

He had no idea if that was true. So what if The Raven were back on the scene? So what if elves still fought in the open? He had heard nothing from any other college in over fifty days. For all he knew, his was the last that still stood free. Free. He almost laughed at the word. He had been right. They had grown complacent in their sanctuary. Lazy. They hadn't seen the signs. The growing numbers of demons, the sudden appearance of these seekers early one morning three days ago. They hadn't pieced it together.

And here they sat as a result with only the tower still to call their own. They had lost, temporarily it was to be prayed, access to all their tunnels and all but one well. If they couldn't regain some space quickly, the next problem he would be facing was starvation. It was a factor that had escaped none of his dwindling band of survivors.

"My Lord?"

Heryst took his head from his hands and looked up into Kayvel's sick pallor. His old friend was dying by degrees. Gods drowning, they all were but something had infected this brave old man in the last days and he was fading so fast.

"Sit, Kayvel. Gods man, you should be resting."

Heryst pulled out the chair next to him and Kayvel sank gratefully into it and rested his elbows on the table. In the centre of the table, guards completely obscured the casting trio who held death away from them all.

"We need a plan," said Kayvel gently. "They need to hear your voice, your strength."

"Do they believe I really have any?" said Heryst, feeling the spear of doubt that had become all too familiar.

"Never let them hear you say that. You are their leader. They love and respect you. Don't ever forget that."

Heryst nodded. "I know," he said. "But it's so hard sometimes. Just look at what I have brought them to."

He gestured around the council chamber, knowing what they saw was reflected in every room of the tower they called their own. Dirt, dust and rubbish covered the floors. The stale air was heavy with the smell of lantern oil and sickness. Every man, woman and child carried lice, was clothed in little more than rags and had the lank hair, dark expression and stoop that signified imminent defeat. He knew he looked the same. They had a mirror in one of the latrines but he didn't think anyone looked in it anymore.

"Yes," said Kayvel. "It is dirty, it is squalid, it is diseased, and soon we will all succumb one way or another. But out there is the only alternative. Do you really have to ask which any of these people would prefer?"

"But am I not just prolonging their deaths? Kayvel, you are a realist. You know what is happening to you. If what you have is infectious, well . . ."

Kayvel nodded. "And we have had to face it since the first day. But nothing will kill them faster than a lack of faith and belief."

Heryst sighed. "What can I tell them? They aren't blind and we are failing. What? That they should hang on and hope for salvation? That eventually the demons will get bored and drift away? What can I tell them?"

He felt helpless. He'd have cried but his tear ducts were, like his mouth, dry. How could he give them hope when he had none?

"You have to give them a purpose and that purpose cannot be simply to hold on until they are overwhelmed. Until four days ago, we thought we were secure enough and we were wrong. Look at the fear. Taste it. Do something about it."

Heryst looked into Kayvel's face. He saw the fading light in his friend's eyes and knew he had to give the dying man something to take with him.

"You think we should try and leave, don't you?"

"Staying here can have but one conclusion, Heryst."

"Dammit." Heryst rubbed his hands over his face. "I can't make them do this, you know. Gods burning, not all of them are fit enough to travel."

"Talk to them," said Kayvel, his tone gently chiding. "Your silence is damaging."

"Yes. Yes, I know," said Heryst through a breath. "Thank you."

"I'll stay here with any that can't travel. None of us will be taken."

Heryst jolted at Kayvel's words. "I wouldn't leave you."

"Don't be daft, my Lord." Kayvel smiled. "I'm too ill to run. At least let me die with dignity because die is what I undoubtedly will do." He paused. "Anyway, this could all be hypothetical. We don't know if anyone will want to leave."

"Well, let's find out, shall we?"

Everyone that could be spared from watching, guarding or casting was assembled in the growing light of the grand council chamber now that the seekers were beginning to melt away. While the light was welcome, what it meant was that the seekers had probably found what they were looking for. Heryst didn't necessarily have much time before the next attack came in.

He took a look around the gathering. He knew every name, he knew all their family histories. He knew their strengths and their weaknesses and he knew their desire to live. He was looking at about a hundred people. All of whom looked back at him, desperate for answers. That wasn't exactly what he was going to be giving them.

"I'm not going to patronise you and I'm not going to pretend things are any less desperate than you already know them to be." Heryst smiled gently. "And things are extremely desperate."

A dry chuckle ran around the chamber.

"Kayvel and I have been talking and we are faced with a choice. Long ago, I stopped being the man who told you what to do and we have tried to do everything by consensus. This is why I am going to put this choice to you now. The demons are getting stronger and we are weakening though we are far from beaten. I look at all the faces assembled here and I see the will to survive burning bright. The question is, how will we best achieve our survival?

"And so to the choice. It is stark. We can stay here. Defend more stoutly and pray for release because it is clear we will not beat them with the numbers and resources we have. Or we can leave. Head north for Xetesk where the rumour is that the last free Balaians are gathering to fight. But I must stress it is only a rumour. We have no confirmation from the dark college, they are silent.

"You know what we face should we stay here. Making a run for it might seem attractive and indeed we will be in the open air, we will have access to fresh water and vegetables, perhaps even wild animals."

He paused while the smiles spread through the gathering.

"But we will also be vulnerable. There will be no walls to guard us, only the ColdRoom shell. And to maintain casting on the move will be difficult. We are going to have to steal our own wagons and horses before we start.

"Now, again, before you decide for yourselves, think on this. If we strike out, we strike out into the unknown and we might be overwhelmed quickly. Here, we know how long we can hold out, health willing. And there will be those of us who will be unable to travel." He held up his hands. "Please. Hear me out. Those of you know who you are. You could not survive the trip and you would be a burden on the rest. It is harsh but we must face the full reality.

"Among those who would not travel is Kayvel." Heryst had to pause, fearing his voice would crack. The sick mage gripped his hand tight. "It breaks my heart but he knows his condition and he still believes the fit should leave. He will be with those who have to remain behind. He knows what it means and he will not let any be taken by the demons.

"Think on it, and we will talk at nightfall. Thank you. Thank you all for everything you have done so far and everything that you still have to do. We will prevail. We will survive. Balaia will rise from the ashes of this invasion."

The babble of conversation that broke out was doused quickly by a screech from below. The demons were attacking again.

CHAPTER 27

Lord Tessaya was in the forward positions overlooking Xetesk when the demon master approached. Not for the first time, the creature came to speak to the Wesmen. Always feeding them their forthcoming doom unless they joined the fight to bring the colleges down.

Tessaya recalled the offer that had been made the day before. Something to do with the sanctity of the western lands should the Wesmen complete the job the demons had begun in Julatsa. The Wesmen Lord had spies in the field near each college and was not as blind as the demons liked to think he was.

He had his chair brought up for him. It was horse hide, padded and stretched across a hardwood frame. High backed, it was stitched with the Paleon crest. He settled into it and accepted a mug of herb infusion. He cupped his hands around it gratefully, the warmth combating a little of the freezing midday air. His furs were gathered about his shoulders and he had let his beard and hair grow thick, covering much of his battle-scarred face.

Settling into his chair, his lieutenants around him and every warrior tasked to show nothing but strength and belief, he waited for the demon to issue across the ground. He watched its tentacles rippling beneath its torso and was pleased to see its colour brighten to a midblue, its temper already frayed by Tessaya's lack of respect for its authority.

Closer to, he could see its brow was pinched in hard on its hairless head. Its nostril slits were flared and its long-fingered hands were clasped together in front of its writhing chest. It came to a halt about ten feet from him. It towered better than twenty feet above him, a fetid smell drifting on the light breeze. An imposing figure but impotent to do him harm.

"You push my patience to its limit, Wesman," it said.

"Let us at least use the names we know we have," said Tessaya, taking a sip of his drink. "Unless, Drenoul, you wish me to call you 'demon.' Can I offer you a beverage?"

"I would rather chew my own body than accept the filth you drink," replied Drenoul. "Enough, I have a great deal to do. I will hear your answer to my proposal."

"A moment," said Tessaya, raising a finger. He beckoned one of his lieutenants close. "Speak softly and make as if you are responding to my questions. I think this demon needs to understand its place in the eyes of Wesmen."

"Indeed, my Lord," said the warrior. "One thing that might interest you is that we have received a scout from the college of Lystern recently."

"Really?"

"He reports the college is on the verge of breaking."

"Ah, something of a shame. I would hate to see the enemy forces able to divert north to join the Xetesk battleground. Is there any indication as to their ability to hang on for any length of time?"

The warrior shrugged. "They like all mages have proved themselves tenacious. It is inconceivable that they will simply roll over."

"We will talk more later," said Tessaya. He turned back to Drenoul. "My apologies, I was reminding myself of the detail of your offer."

Drenoul breathed out in a snarl. Its fingers unclasped and grasped at the air in front of it. Its colour lightened a shade further.

"As I understand it," said Tessaya, "you felt that we would best serve you by attacking Julatsa and its attendant elven defence under your local commander's direction. The reward for this was a promise that you would not seek to enslave my peoples."

"That is an accurate summation."

"What I nor my ruling cadre can understand is why you would make this offer. You have consistently told me over the last two years that we could not hope to stand against you once the colleges had fallen and magic destroyed. Yet here you are plainly unable to complete your task and apparently needing my assistance. You'll understand my scepticism and my reluctance to trust a race for whom utter dominion has long appeared to be the only conceivable goal."

Drenoul was quiet for some time, forcing its colour back to a more palatable deep blue.

"We would concede some surprise at the length of college resistance," it said eventually. "And we want a swift resolution to allow us to take rightful control over the mage lands and the entirety of eastern Balaia. Those who aid us will be treated as allies in the years to come. Those who stand by or oppose us will be enslaved. There is your choice."

Tessaya smiled, knowing it a patronising gesture. "Or perhaps the reality is that without us you do not have the strength to beat the colleges and never will have. Perhaps you have lost more of your minions than you expected and your forces, finite as they must be, are actually being stretched."

Drenoul flashed bright sky-blue. "And perhaps you need a personal demonstration of our strength, Tessaya. The loss of Wesmen Spirits might serve to remind you of your tenuous hold on your own life."

Tessaya fought the urge to stand, and instead leaned back further into his chair. "But you cannot afford to, can you, Drenoul? Is it not true that should you send a force capable of taking some of my warriors, you would compromise your siege of Xetesk, or of Lystern or Julatsa, and allow them to strike out?

"You do not frighten me, Drenoul. Nor do you frighten any of those I command. I am aware we cannot kill you or any of your race but neither can you break us with a touch or a cut. My warriors are strong and they are numerous. We can keep you back at will. We have Understone Pass at our backs. We are a problem you wish you didn't have to face. As are the elves. Easterners are weak, their spirits are vulnerable. And in two years you have failed to break them. What makes you think you will ever be able to break us?"

Drenoul made a move forward and immediately eight warriors drew their weapons and responded. Drenoul stopped, his colour now a thin, pale blue verging on white.

"Your words will not save you when we march on your helpless lands, Tessaya. They will ring hollow in your ears. The offer is withdrawn."

Drenoul floated high into the sky, turned and flew quickly back toward Julatsa.

Tessaya pushed himself from his chair. "Withdrawn? Rejected, I would suggest." He looked for the lieutenant again. "They don't need us to help them fight in Julatsa, I am certain of it. But they want us out of the way. Every scout that returns from the north, I want reporting immediately to me."

"Yes, my Lord."

Tessaya began to walk back toward the fires at the centre of the camp.

"Something is about to happen. Something critical. I can feel it."

Dystran and Vuldaroq were studying one of the more arcane and complex texts stolen from the library when the change in atmosphere happened. It was quite sudden, like the sun burning through thin cloud to warm the earth. They were in Dystran's chambers, surrounded by guards and with their few script-scholars nearby. These latter four were working on language which had defeated both the senior mages.

It took Dystran a while to work out what it was that had alerted his subconscious and caused him to look up and through his closed balcony windows.

"What has just happened?" he asked, pushing his chair back.

"You were struggling to decipher this word and wondered where it was they went, whoever they were, and if there are any of them left," said Vuldaroq, a half smile on his thin face.

Dystran glanced sideways at Vuldaroq as he got up. How strange the fortunes of Balaia had revealed themselves to be. Vuldaroq was a man that Dystran would gladly have seen swinging from a tree in the college courtyard before the demons had invaded. But without losing any of his trademark bite, the head of the Dordovan college had revealed himself to be a man of depth and strength as well as possessing a sharp analytical mind. It had taken him some time to throw off the memories of his flight from Dordover but he and his few mages had proved a tonic in the college of their erstwhile enemies.

If only they could break down the terminology contained in the texts Sharyr had brought back. Something important was eluding him and it was based around an allusion to a people called the Charanacks. They held knowledge, so the text maintained, that had been the basis of the first deal struck between demon and Xeteskian mage well over a millennium ago. Dystran was frustrated. He'd have loved to know who they were. They would almost certainly be worth talking to.

"I don't mean that," said Dystran. He walked to the balcony doors and opened them, standing inside while his guards gathered about him. "Just listen."

Everyone in the chamber did so. Dystran saw a frown cross Vuldaroq's face.

"Quiet," he said.

"Silence more like," said Dystran.

He indicated his guards accompany him and he walked out into the fresh air of his balcony. Every day since the gliders had finished their search of the mana trails that identified the positions of their ColdRoom casters, demon activity had been incessant.

They had suffered a number of quick attacks from the reavers that they had been lucky to repel without losing any of their mages and only three swordsmen. And when the attacks weren't coming in, the creatures swarmed the shell, probing and teasing. They kept up a barrage of sound, hoping to distract their targets, and further away, any who cared to look would see enslaved Xeteskians being herded from one area of the city to another. There seemed no discernible purpose to this barring the sapping of morale.

But now the shell was deserted. Dystran couldn't see a single demon flying above the college or walking the outer walls. Further afield, he could see no slaves in the streets, no clusters of demons hovering over them as they worked. He could hear no cries of the exhausted, terrified and dying. There was no smoke from cook fires. Nothing.

Far in the distance, he could see the shapes of demons clustered in the air to the north. Confident, he walked the circle of his balcony. Away to the south, the fires of the Wesmen signified their confusing and continuing presence. Dystran wished they'd join one side or the other. Or indeed return to the Heartlands. Occasionally he had seen demons hovering near to the Wesmen. Attacking, talking or simply watching, he couldn't tell. There were none there now. In the distant east there were more demons. West toward the Blackthornes too. Dark patches in the sky at the edges of the city and beyond.

Dystran completed his circuit and looked up into the sky above the college. In the blue, the vibrating white slash hung. If he tuned in to the mana spectrum he knew he'd be able to see the pure mana flooding into Balaia, strengthening the demons with every passing heartbeat. And occasionally, more demons would travel from wherever it was their homeland lay across interdimensional space, swarming into the sky before dispersing about whatever tasks they had been summoned to perform.

There was a crowd at the balcony doors.

"A trap, do you think?" asked Vuldaroq.

Dystran shook his head. "It isn't their style, is it? I just don't understand it."

"We should take advantage," said Chandyr, who never left Dystran's side. "Bring some of our people into the college."

"No," said Dystran.

"My Lord—"

"No," he repeated. "Think, Chandyr."

"I am," said the commander, bristling. "We have a chance to save some of our own."

Dystran ushered them all back inside. He shared the urge to do exactly what Chandyr desired but he knew it was folly. "Whether it is a trap or not is immaterial. For one thing, I don't think you will find any Xeteskians within a mile of the college. Wherever those demons are hovering, that is where our people are, believe me. But even should you bring them in, it is impractical. We can barely feed and water ourselves, let alone any more mouths."

Chandyr relaxed a little and inclined his head. "I know you're right, it's just . . ." He gestured out toward the city.

"I understand," said Dystran. "There is no one in this room, in this college, who does not want to save every man, woman and child in our city. But we have to liberate them when we can truly help them. That isn't now but we will do it.

"But you're right, we must take advantage. So don't stand there. Take the fastest runners you have and let's get something more from the library, assuming it didn't all burn. And Chandyr, we don't trust these bastards, right? So make sure some of your sprinters can cast, won't you?"

The Raven had enjoyed a peculiar rest. They, plus Kas, Ark and Eilaan, had camped on the idyllic shores of Triverne Lake for three days and four nights. They had seen no sign of demons. They had seen no sign of anything barring forest creatures, in truth. Curious. They'd sparred and trained, talked and rested but it all had a surreal quality. None of them could ever ignore the fact of what was to come.

If they'd been in a storm before then surely this was its eye.

Understanding Rebraal and Auum's likely timescale for evacuating Julatsa, they ate a quiet breakfast on yet another cold and clear morning before heading back for the longboat to row themselves to the main shore of the lake. No one spoke the whole way across the placid water either. Hirad had wanted to break the ice but had seen the look in The Unknown's eyes and kept himself quiet.

He shook his head. He found it absurd that in this one longboat the future of Balaia and at least three dimensions rested. To him, it felt like a funeral procession. Prophetic perhaps. Hirad left them all to it for the row but couldn't keep himself quiet when they'd reached the eastern shore, hidden the boat and moved to shelter.

"Brooding doesn't suit you, Unknown. Thinking about the family?"

"Not this time, Hirad." The Unknown shook his head.

"So? I'm not going to guess just to amuse you. Tell me."

The Unknown smiled briefly and looked across at Hirad to gauge his expression. Hirad mugged at him, stretching his eyes.

"This is serious. Think about what we're about to attempt. Think about the weight we carry, the lives of those reliant on us. Like never before, this is no game. We need to watch ourselves, Hirad," he said. Hirad didn't reply. "We need to watch what we do, how much we take on ourselves and how much we rely on those around us. Not overstretch."

"Right."

"Hirad, we are not sharp. How can we be? It'll take time even to get close and that means we cannot rely on each other the way we could."

"I'm not with you."

"I can't say it much plainer, Coldheart. What we were five years ago is a memory. What we were two years ago is probably unattainable. If we fight on those memories, we won't survive."

Hirad frowned. "We knew we weren't enough on our own. That's why we've brought a crowd with us."

"You aren't listening to me." The Unknown took a quick glance behind him and hushed his voice. "I'm just asking you to wise up and understand that The Raven we all remember isn't the one walking here. It's got nothing to do with belief in ourselves. But we've sat around for two years. You know what that does and Darrick has seen its effects in our stamina, in our speed and teamwork. It's a matter of degrees but it's critical."

"Unknown, in case it escaped your attention, I spent my time running with the TaiGethen and Thraun with the ClawBound. I am faster than I have ever been."

"Fine!" The Unknown slapped his hands against his thighs. "But I am not and nor is Darrick, Denser or Erienne. Nor are Ark and Kas come to that. Remember your little spin move outside Blackthorne? It almost got you killed. I was only just in time."

"But you were there." Hirad felt confused and a familiar anger grabbed at him. "So what's the problem?"

"The problem, Hirad, is that you cannot rely on us as you did. And that means that for now at least, you have to slow down. Stay in line and in touch."

"If you think I'm going to ignore an opening to kill because you think you're too old and slow you're wrong. I fight my way. Like I always have. And you yours. And we look out for each other. Like always."

The Unknown stopped and faced Hirad, his eyes hard, face reddening slightly. "Why do you always have to be such a stubborn bastard? I'm trying to help you stay alive here."

Hirad could sense The Raven bunching around them. He thought to walk away but stayed. "No you aren't. You're trying to clip my wings. Undermine my belief in you all and I can't understand why you'd do that. Where we're going, we'll need every advantage we've got and what I've learned from Auum is a big one."

"And stopping any of us dying is another," growled The Unknown.

"All I know is, we survive because we don't compromise. Because we do things our way. We're The Raven, Unknown."

"Think it had slipped my mind? Gods drowning, it's because we're The Raven you need to understand this. Face reality. We're too old to be doing this but there is literally no one else. And we have to stay alive. We have to."

"It's a tactic I like to employ myself," snapped Hirad. "Don't you stand there and tell me you can't watch my back. Don't ever say that."

"When did I say that, Coldheart? What I recall telling you was that if you persist in trying fancy elven moves I'm not ready for, I might not be fast enough to save you if you get in trouble. Big difference. My hip is weak. You have to be aware."

The Unknown was standing very close now and shouting into his face. Hirad could feel his heart beat and hear their voices echoing from the bleak faces of the Blackthorne range foothills. Hirad should have backed away, he knew he should.

"You're always there. That's why I have the courage to fight."

"And what if I'm not, eh?" The Unknown's eyes searched his face. "It'll be too late to realise I might have been right when you're lying in a sludge of your own intestines."

"You're giving up, Unknown. You're giving up."

The Unknown grabbed Hirad's face and pulled him close enough to kiss. "No, dammit, I'm being real because if I ever let you down I could never live with myself. What are you being?"

Hirad stepped back a pace, The Unknown's admission rattling through him, shuddering his every nerve. He had no answer to it, how could he? The Unknown had begun by trying to advise him and had ended baring his soul.

Hirad became acutely aware of the silence that surrounded them, punctuated by the swirls of wind across hillside and lake. He stared into The Unknown's eyes, still at a total loss.

"This is it for us," said The Unknown. "I so want us all to live."

"Movement," said Kas abruptly.

Hirad bit down on his response, on his shock and confusion at what The Unknown was saying. Instead, he and the big man gave themselves room and drew their swords. Thraun and Darrick moved easily alongside them while Denser and Erienne took station behind, already preparing to cast.

"Direction," said The Unknown.

"Due north, moving against the low ridge," said Kas. He, Ark and Eilaan were slightly detached from The Raven but working as an individual unit as they had trained.

"Running?" asked Darrick.

"Yes," replied Kas.

"Good," said Darrick. "Probably not demons, then."

"Let's hope you're right," said Hirad.

The Raven moved north along the lake front. Presently, they could see shapes moving against the horizon. Three of them, quick stepped and sure. Auum's Tai. It wasn't long before Hirad could see Auum's expression, one of irritation and exasperation.

Hirad smiled and put up his sword, waiting for them to approach.

Auum, Duele and Evunn ran up to them, barely breathing hard.

"This is your idea of concealment," Auum said to Hirad.

"We've only just rowed over here."

Auum tugged at his ear.

"And you are fortunate there are no others to hear you," he said. "Gyal's tears, but humans are noisy when they argue." He appraised them all. "You can all travel now."

It was not a question. The Unknown inclined his head.

"We've said what needs to be said right now."

"Keep it so," said Auum. "Threat closes."

He turned to his Tai and spoke quickly. Duele and Evunn jogged away. When he switched his attention back, his face held familiar contempt.

"We move," he said. "The caravan is in trouble as it approaches Xetesk. Rebraal feels your presence will aid belief. I am at a loss why."

Denser grabbed Hirad's arm.

"Just don't say it," he said. "We already know."

CHAPTER 28

Baron Blackthorne stood in his banqueting hall and battered the demon about the head again and again. Gore splattered across the filthy stone flags, oozing into cracks and puddling under the creature's body. And with every blow, Blackthorne roared his defiance.

"You . . . will . . . never . . . take my castle. You . . . will . . . never . . . take me."

He felt a touch on his free arm and swung round, ready to hack at another enemy. He raised his dripping blade but halted his strike when he saw it was Luke.

"It's over," said Luke, holding his gaze. "It's dead. The demons have withdrawn."

Blackthorne became aware of the heaving of his chest and the heat in his face. His eyes would be blazing and wild, he knew. He took a few moments to calm himself, laying his sword on a table and smoothing down his hair. He nodded.

"I'm all right," he said. "Thank you, Luke."

But he could see that Luke wasn't. The young man's face was crossed with cuts that bled freely. His leather armour was torn and his right hand was covered in a makeshift bandage, already stained dark and dripping. He was shivering violently and leaning heavily on his long-handled mace.

"Gods falling, Luke, you need attention," he said. "Come, lean on me. I'll take you to the infirmary."

"There won't be room," said Luke. "But I'll lean on you gratefully. Show you what we have left."

Blackthorne turned to walk back through the banqueting hall and stopped in his tracks. Ten days since he had hosted The Raven here and felt such hope. Now it had been reduced to a battlefield and almost all of that hope had been extinguished.

The main table was strewn with demon and human bodies. One end of it had collapsed under the weight of the fighting, spilling dishes and candelabra onto the floor. And that was only the half of it. Across the length of the two-hundred-foot room, those who could still walk moved among the bodies of those who could not, trying to help where, how and if they could. A quick count told Blackthorne that at least forty of his people lay dead, dying or incapacitated. Should that weight of numbers be replicated throughout the ColdRoom shell . . .

"How much do we have left?"

Luke's face was grim through the sheen of blood.

"The castle, the stable block, the back courtyard, the inner courtyard and the equipment sheds. That's about it."

"Oh dear Gods." Blackthorne shook his head. "How many have we lost?"

"I don't know," said Luke. "We'll do a count later but it's bad. We've a core of mages for the ColdRooms but there's no way we can see off another attack of that magnitude."

"We might have to find a way."

Blackthorne, with Luke leaning on him heavily, headed for the main doors of the hall. On his way, he caught the eye of a warrior looking up from a dead companion.

"He put himself in front of me," the soldier explained. "The demon tore at his heart. Should be me."

"But it isn't, Sergeant," said Blackthorne gently. "And everyone, living or dead, is a hero today. If we weren't, they would have overrun us. Pay him back; never give in."

The sergeant nodded. Blackthorne could see the man shivering. His eyes were unfocused as if there was nothing behind them. He was absolutely terrified, traumatised by the experience. Blackthorne reached out and helped him up. At least he was steady on his feet.

"There is nothing you can do for him. The duty watch will take him with the others, if there's anything left of them that is. Why don't you fetch my sword from the table over there and help me with Luke?"

Blackthorne took a last gaze around the banqueting hall. It was a charnel house. It stank. At the far end, teams were being organised to clear the bodies out to the courtyard where they would be buried. They couldn't afford the wood for pyres, nor the water to wash away the blood. Not until they'd ascertained what supply they had left.

He became aware of the filth on his own body; demon as well as human. And also the increasing weight Luke was putting on him.

"Hey, boy, not feeling so good?"

"I've felt better," agreed Luke.

The soldier hurried back across the floor.

"Take his other side," ordered Blackthorne. "I take it the barracks are out of bounds."

"Yes, my Lord," said Luke.

"Then you will rest in my quarters."

"No. There is so much to do."

"Yes, there is. And I and the good sergeant here will organise it. When I have the numbers, I will bring them to you. No buts, Luke, I need your mind and right now it's not all there, is it?"

Blackthorne all but crumbled faced with Luke's look of gratitude. The young man slumped against him.

"Dammit," he said. "Come on, let's get moving."

He and the sergeant hurried Luke from the hall. The situation in the corridors they travelled was little better than that they'd just left. Bodies, not enough still moving, littered walkways, stairs and chambers. They passed the infirmary, a hive of activity and bursting at the seams, on the way to his rooms.

"Attention, my chambers. Now." He barked, not waiting for a response.

They bundled Luke up the stairs and all but threw him on Blackthorne's wrought iron, curtained bed. It was dim in the bedchamber. The fire was cold, no candles were lit and the windows were shuttered and nailed. Demons marauded outside.

The sergeant wrung out the cloth in Blackthorne's basin and folded it for a compress.

"He's not got a fever, man!" snapped the Baron. "Bank and light the fire. Quickly."

Blackthorne pulled the covers to Luke's neck and sat on the bed. He used the cloth to clean away the worst of the blood, feeling Luke's icy skin.

"Hang on, lad. Hang on. It'll pass."

"Not going anywhere," said Luke faintly.

"Good."

There was a tentative knock on the door. He shouted them in, two healers.

"Don't let him die. We need him. I need him."

Blackthorne ran from his chambers. He had to know what he still controlled, what forces were still under his command. At every turn, the prognosis became less palatable and it forced him to consider three questions. Why had they suddenly become so very much stronger; why had they pulled back if they were really as strong as they appeared; and when would they be back to deal the fatal blow?

Until that afternoon, his ColdRoom shell had covered about a third of the area of his town; and they had held it comfortably. He was now having to come to terms with the fact that he was a prisoner in his own castle. Luke had not been exaggerating and Blackthorne was thankful that enough order remained for a watchful defence perimeter to be in place. He owed Darrick particularly and his determination that they set up multiple overlapping defensive cells. He'd probably never have the opportunity to thank him personally.

Blackthorne took a longer look in the infirmary the second time around. The once calm and quiet whitewashed chamber was awash with noise and blood. It echoed to the cries of the injured and fading, the exhortations of healers and the squeal of metal on stone as cots were dragged from examination to treatment and, if the incumbent was fortunate, recovery. Every inch of floor space was covered with his warriors, mages and ordinary townspeople. They lay on makeshift pillows, were propped against walls and pillars and cradled in the arms of loved ones.

He paused to offer comfort to those he could and promise resources to the healers if he could muster any. Hot water and clean cloth were in desperately short supply.

Clattering down to the kitchens, he found some cause for hope. Deep in the bowels of the castle, with their chimneys grilled and venting smoke into the foundations and caves, they had escaped the attack. Food was being prepared, water was boiling and a bucket chain was in operation from the trio of wells. Blackthorne nodded approval at the level of guards in this room that now found itself the hub of operations.

He shook hands, patted backs and spoke encouragement. It was crucial he was visible. Gods, half the castle probably didn't know if he was dead or alive. He toured quickly; checked the stable block, assessed the condition of horses and mages, the courtyard where guards still walked but where anxiety had replaced confidence and where twos had replaced threes and fours, and the periphery of the shell. He felt its closeness and tried to count the demons.

They were still there but they had suffered huge losses. Blackthorne and his people had given them a real bloody nose but at great cost. Surely, the demons, even if they were temporarily depleted which he doubted, could simply reinforce. His numbers were severely diminished and they knew it. Yet there were no taunts, no displays and no shows of strength or intent. The town was quiet. So quiet that they were barely even being watched.

Later, having completed his tour of the grounds, gardens and buildings still in his gift, he went back to his chambers and sat with Luke. The boy's eyes bored into the ceiling while he spoke.

"What would your assessment be . . . it could be worse? That about covers it. We have the mage strength to cycle our casters. We have the secure area for mana replenishment and we have access to food and water; the latter indefinitely, the former for another forty days at least.

"It would have been fewer but I'm afraid our losses have been steep. We might have a shell over the castle but realistically, we can't defend much more than the kitchens, stables, ground chambers and banqueting hall. We should really relocate the infirmary too. If we do that, I feel we can hold out until there is no food in our bellies. We're still strong, we have our belief. But we can't break out though. We don't have the people anymore. At least, I don't think so.

"Your opinion would have been so valuable. Your insight and organisation too. And most of all, your optimism. I'm sorry I left you, Luke. I'll grieve when I am alone."

Blackthorne reached over and closed Luke's eyes. He turned to look properly at the bodies of the healers and the sergeant he had brought up here only to die.

"I am moved almost to tears, but I cannot cry. Was that speech for me or for him? He with the glorious soul that so sates me now."

"His name was Luke and it was for us all," said Blackthorne, standing.

"And do you believe it? Truly?" Ferouc moved from the shadows, wings furled at his back, his colour a resonant, relaxed deep green. "Or have I finally convinced you that this futile struggle is at an end?"

"It's funny, you know. Had you come to me as I walked outside instead of this," Blackthorne indicated the broken shutter, "I might have had half a mind to agree with you. But you have just killed the wrong man and now I will fight you to the very last. Do you find that funny, Fidget? What drives men on?"

Ferouc's colour flared briefly bright. Its fingers clacked together.

"Beware your insults, Baron Blackthorne. You are unarmed."

"And you are within my shield. Weak. Vulnerable." Blackthorne moved toward the demon. "Want to find out who would prevail?"

"Just one lingering touch, human."

"Do you really believe I would succumb that easily?" Blackthorne found he had no fear of the creature. Powerful though it was, he could feel only a brooding anger and determination. It gave him true courage and a line to every like-minded man and woman across Balaia. It was the perfect defence. "I am Baron Blackthorne. No one dominates me. No one takes from me what I am."

Ferouc's hands clasped together and in its throat, it forced a dry rasp.

"It is a shame for Balaia that not all humans are so strong. Even so, you can be defeated. Broken."

Blackthorne saw the reavers float in through the twisted shutter. Three of them.

"We have won, Baron Blackthorne. Our strength is too much for you even inside your shell now. But believe me, surrender is painless."

Blackthorne snatched the dagger from his pocket sheath, backhanded it across the throat of the nearest creature. The demon crashed backward, dying quickly, and Blackthorne moved into the space and to the door. He felt small gratification at the genuine surprise on Ferouc's face and the lightening of its colour.

"Every Baron has enemies, Fidget, and none ever walk unarmed," he said. "We will prevail. The Raven and the elves will beat you and you will die never having taken my castle or tasted my soul."

He took the stairs down three at a time, bellowing for his guards.

The furious barks split the Besharan sky. Immediately, the choreographed grace of the mock attack pattern dissolved. Broods pulsed and called their dragons together. Sha-Kaan watched helplessly while across the arena the structure broke up. Gost climbed high and circled. Stara bunched and gave themselves space in their homeland direction. Skoor sank into a cloud layer, taking on a defensive pattern.

Smaller broods scattered to the winds and the orb. Dragons bumped and barged. Flames lit up the fading day. Several dragons could be seen spiralling from the sky, trailing smoke. Tension flared, sudden anger drove the mood. Naik and Kaan dragons flew into the gap, appealing for calm.

From the south, Sha-Kaan watched the clutch of Brood Koli approach. None could fail to feel the fury that they pulsed into the psyche. And all knew instantly at whom it was directed. Space widened around the Skoor, who protested innocence and defiance in equal measure. Sha-Kaan requested Yasal follow him and he soared away to join the gathering of both their broods.

"There must be no conflict whatever the crime," he pulsed. "Surround the Skoor. Yasal, please, with me to the Koli."

"Of course," said Yasal.

The forces of the Naik and Kaan flew onto the cloud bank where the Skoor waited. The psyche was packed with disgust, betrayal and anger, and tinged with a little conciliation.

Sha-Kaan felt a burgeoning sense of inevitability. Tension and grievance had taken longer to surface than he had anticipated. His naïvety had been in beginning to think they'd escape without serious trouble. Flying toward the onrushing Koli, just seven of them, Sha could see flights of dragons from almost every brood detach and fly for their Broodlands. He had been tempted to do the same.

"Slow," he pulsed to the Koli. "Slow."

They ignored him, powering on and adjusting to fly by the two emissaries for peace. Yasal angled away too, Sha letting him go and continuing on his trajectory to bring him into formation with them rather than bar their passage.

"Falon-Koli, you will stop and you will talk. You cannot reach them."

"Do not try and stop me, Sha-Kaan," pulsed Falon. "This is not your concern."

"Every conflict is my concern at this time," said Sha, letting irritation enter his tone. "We work for all our futures."

"I have no future!" roared Falon. "The Skoor have attacked our Brood-lands. We are destroyed. We are all that is left."

Another pulse flooded Sha.

"We trusted you, Sha-Kaan, and we have been betrayed. You fight for your future. All we have left is revenge."

"No," said Yasal, his pulse angry. "You must not attack. You must not risk all that we are building."

"You build nothing," spat Falon-Koli. "Alliance based on lies and rumours. Where is your threat, Sha-Kaan? I will tell you. It is the Skoor. And they have used you to destroy us. We will die but we will exact revenge. It is all we have."

"One more time. Slow. Please."

Sha-Kaan was cruising in a high arc above them now. Closing fast. Yasal bored up from below on intercept.

"Stop us and feel our flame."

At a signal, the seven Koli split. Sha-Kaan bellowed his frustration. He pulsed his brood as Yasal would be doing. Skoor scattered from their cloud base. One hundred and seventy-five of them; completely overwhelming for the Koli.

"Flame take you, Caval-Skoor," he pulsed. "What have you done?"

"What we had to," came the calm reply. "And now the task will be completed and you will have my attention."

Caval had broadcast to all that might hear. A flood of enraged responses filled the psyche. They would not fly with the Skoor; they had put aside their disputes; they would side with the Koli to drive the Skoor from the skies.

Naik and Kaan dragons begged for calm while they aligned themselves for defence. Sha-Kaan, his heart thundering in the centre of his body, felt the hope drain from him. He roared again, blasting flame into the empty sky. Koli and Skoor closed on one another, calls of hate, taunts of death sounding loud. Broods across the sky formed into attack and defence formations. Stara and Gost packed together. The smaller broods gathered, some already flew in the slipstream of the few Koli. The first flames struck, the first jaws clamped on.

"Yasal, break away. Don't put yourself into this. Kaan, to the heights."

The Broods Kaan and Naik spiralled upward. Sha-Kaan heard the screeches of burned dragons and he closed his eyes.

"Please," he pulsed to any that would listen. "Pull away. Tanis-Veret, Koln-Stara, Eram-Gost. All of you who would save our dimension pull away. Join us in the heights."

But the deafening roars of battle below tolled at him that they were lost.

CHAPTER 29

The Raven had been aware the elven-led Julatsan force was approaching long before they could see it. Auum had brought them slightly south of Triverne Lake to a hidden position overlooking the route of the wagons.

It was largely a psychological cover point. True, the crag formation gave them a sight and attack barrier from everywhere but head-on; but The Raven had a signature that the demons craved and they would sense it long before they needed their eyes. The risk was a calculated one. Denser considered the density of mage souls would be enough to deflect their attention for long enough to allow a clear run in.

For some time, they had been watching the demons tracking the train, swarming and swooping to attack in their hundreds. Spells had flared and bludgeoned in response. The low roar of order, combat and movement had been a constant companion. But only now was the picture complete.

Coming into view on the crest of a long, shallow rise, the first wagons were picked out in late-afternoon silhouette. They were no more than a mile away. Hirad could see elves shadowing each wagon as well as those that rode canvas roofs and running plates.

Demons clustered in the sky above and battled inside the ColdRoom shell as the train made its ponderous progress toward Xetesk, pace governed by the fragile concentration of the casters within the wagons. The mages without whom the allies would be overwhelmed.

Yellow light washed out from just behind the crest of the hill. Demons screeched and scattered. Some fell, spiralling helplessly, others dived on the casters.

"How are they doing that?" asked Hirad.

"Rebraal must have spaced the ColdRooms," said Erienne. "Created mana-rich areas."

"Fascinating," said Denser. "If you consider that mana is channelled over the outsides of the shells, it'll create areas of real density if the spacing is right."

Hirad looked across at him. "We really must talk about it some more. I'd so love to learn."

"You are such a heathen, Coldheart," said Denser. "It's a very clever idea. Nothing you'd ever dream up."

"Risky, isn't it?" said Darrick.

"Only if they hang around once they've cast," said Erienne.

Hirad watched the fighting inside the shell and couldn't help but smile.

From this distance it was impossible to identify facial features but it hardly mattered. A demon attack went in. A swarm of tiny demons Auum identified as strike-strain, and that Hirad recognised only too well, were backed by the man-size reavers.

The strike-strain were there to cause confusion where they could and they plunged straight for the wagon drivers. And there they met the defence. The elves, deliberate, graceful and always on the offensive. And their human companions, those that had survived this far, frenzied, panicked and forever on the back foot. That was why Rebraal needed The Raven. To give the humans focus and belief.

"How many wagons set out?" he asked.

"Fifteen," said Auum.

"Dear Gods burning," said Hirad.

The end of the train was in sight. Eight wagons remained.

"They'll be here in less than half an hour," said Denser.

"Know that for a fact, do you?" said Hirad.

"Educated guess."

"Hardly matters. We need to get in there and get involved. We've done enough hanging around. We've—"

"Hirad, are you all right?" Erienne's hand was on his neck.

"I—"

The full force of the rage hit him then. He knew he was falling but he was helpless to save himself. His body was suffused with the strength of Sha-Kaan's fury and he had no option but to let it wash him away.

"Sha-Kaan," he managed. "I can't—"

The Great Kaan was close to losing control. The frustrations and anger thudded around Hirad's skull, rendering him helpless. He was dimly aware of his friends speaking to him, touching him, but he had no way of responding. He gathered the vestiges of his consciousness to him and did the only thing he could.

"Sha-Kaan, stop. You're killing me."

Abruptly, the hammering of emotion within him ceased but did not allow him to return to consciousness.

"Skies take them, they are destroying all our hopes." Sha-Kaan's words flooded his senses. Hirad felt his despair and impotence.

"Who?" he asked into the void.

Sha-Kaan sighed, a sonorous exhalation laced with sorrow. "It would take so long to explain. Since you're unexpectedly at rest, I will grant you this. See through my eyes. Feel what I feel."

Hirad experienced an acute sensation of falling. He felt the ground disappear and a sense of vastness take its place. Cold air channelled across his body and every nerve and fibre was suffused with ancient pain and longing.

He heard the beat of wings, felt their resistance against the air, their driving power. His nostrils caught the harsh scents of wood and oil, the smell of wrecked, burned flesh. He could taste something acrid and sour in his mouth. His mind reeled under the weight of emotion pressing from every direction. And finally, he opened his eyes and drank in the skies of Beshara.

What he saw chilled his bones. Beneath him, as Sha-Kaan's head swept around to give him the panorama, the sky was a mixture of flashing scales, blinding yellow flame and dark smoke, torn by the winds of the upper skies. The battering roar of mouths disgorging fire swept up to him on a tide of fury so intense it shuddered him.

Hirad couldn't begin to count the dragons intent on destruction below. He recalled the sight he had seen in these same skies at the time of the Noonshade rip but it was a mere skirmish compared to this.

"Almost a thousand dragons chase a petty squabble and damage us all such that we may never recover," toned Sha-Kaan. "And outside our dimension, the Arakhe will be sensing it all. Fire this intense and the temptation of dragons to switch out of the battle and move into interdimensional space to escape could open the door to them."

The noise from below was truly extraordinary. A flight of Skoor, twenty strong and glittering sand-yellow, curved in a tight arc and drove through the left flank of their enemies where they pressured fellow Skoor. Massed in a roughly spherical formation, they tore into their targets. Flame scoured every point of the compass around them. Forward, the lead dragons collided with those in their path.

It was a devastating tactic and one being mimicked across the fight. Dragons bellowed and squealed, their wings, bellies and backs scorched and bubbling. Smoke trails crisscrossed. Fangs ripped into necks. Dragons by the dozen fell from the sky. Yet still the Skoor were losing the battle. Outnumbered five to one, their moves couldn't hope to counter the enemy strength forever. But their pride kept them fighting. The attrition rate was awful.

"On a day when we should have been working to secure all our futures, one brood has been rendered extinct and others will be so depleted they cannot hope to survive."

Hirad felt the ocean-deep grief as if it were his own.

"In our pride we used to think it was other species so blind that they would fight each other over nothing though their mutual extinction was the only sure result. And yet we are worse. Our failure could extinguish so many lives because we have chosen to touch them without offering them the choice to refuse us.

"Tell me you are close to Xetesk."

"Less than a day, Great Kaan. But there's one hell of a fight coming to get in there. The demons aren't exactly going to usher us in, are they?"

Sha-Kaan paused. Below, the centre of the fight exploded in appalling flame, engulfing fifty, a hundred even. "When is the fight?"

"It's already begun. Julatsans and the Al-Arynaar are under attack as they approach Xetesk. We're joining them and we'll all enter the city early tomorrow morning."

"I will bring the Kaan to you."

"No," said Hirad. "We shouldn't declare our hand and announce all our allies. Save your strength, save as many as you can and be ready when I call."

Sha-Kaan rumbled. "You could fail at the gates."

"We won't fail," said Hirad. "We're—"

"Don't," said Sha-Kaan. "Don't say it." Embryonic humour flared, gone in a wing beat. "Time to go, Hirad Coldheart. I must pick through the ashes and rebuild what I can."

"Good luck."

"Skies keep you, my friend."

Hirad opened his eyes, pain already a fading pulse in his head. Above him, a ring of anxious faces. Thraun's cracked a smile.

"Sha-Kaan?" he said and held out a hand.

Hirad grasped it and pulled himself up.

"Yes," he nodded. "More trouble, I'm afraid. Look, we need to get a move on when we get into Xetesk. I'll tell you on the way but it seems to me that every day we delay, fewer dragons will be alive to shield us."

The cacophony surrounding the wagon train was so complete Rebraal could barely make himself heard. The demon attacks were incessant now and since the disastrous loss of two ColdRoom mage teams the previous night, the pressure on the Al-Arynaar warriors was acute. The humans were panicked now, losing their heads and then their souls when their discipline failed. Five of the eight wagons had elven drivers now and so few humans actually remained that Rebraal contemplated placing them all in wagons. Through his irritation at their failings, though, he couldn't help but be impressed by the sheer doggedness that they showed. And every time their numbers fell, they still found time to joke. The Al-Arynaar couldn't understand laughter in such dire circumstance but Rebraal had seen it all before with The Raven.

Right now, though, he was more concerned with the horses. All of them were tired and the accumulated stress was evident in trembling limbs and eyes that spoke of their confusion. His elves still spoke soothing words to them but eventually that would not be enough.

Above him, the demons were massing again. He didn't have much time. Rebraal ran down the line of surviving wagons. His limp was becoming more pronounced. The cloth tight around his thigh could do only so much. The claws of the cursyrd had raked deep during the last attack and of course he hadn't been able to rest and so the blood still flowed. The wound felt frozen, his muscle damaged, but he could not afford to stop. Not until Auum and The Raven reached them.

But where were they?

The wagon train was passing to the southeast of Triverne Lake now. Before long, they could expect concerted attack from the Xetesk cursyrd, adding to the legions that had dogged them from Julatsa.

Two days of constant noise, repeated attacks and movement broken only to change horses was taking quick toll. They were all tired: the mages in the wagons with paper-thin concentration; the warriors running beside them with muscles burning and fatigued; attack mages with barely time to cast the simplest spell in the mana holes before the cursyrd were upon them.

In every face he passed, human or elven, he saw exhaustion growing. In humans, he saw belief wavering. He shouted encouragement, clenched his fists and demanded strength. He invoked Yniss and Tual. He muttered under his breath for Shorth to be ready to accept them all.

Over five hundred had left Julatsa, man and elf. They had lost over a hundred and the survivors needed fresh hope. The Raven would provide it. The Raven never joined the losing side.

He reached the head of the column. Elves drove the leading pair of wagons now. Tired horses flagged but he was loath to stop. He glanced up for the thousandth time. The sky was darkening with cursyrd, their voices clamoured ever louder.

"Ready!" he called.

The word was passed down the line. Elves rode wagons, clustered by their sides, defended mages running close to mana holes. All felt their hearts quicken.

"Dila'heth!"

The lead elven mage answered him. She was out of sight on the other side of the wagon. He jogged round to her where she talked with Pheone. The Julatsan leader was still strong, hanging onto the threads of human courage.

"Gyal's tears, Rebraal, you should be resting."

Rebraal grinned fiercely. "You know I can't."

"Where are they?" asked Dila. She like him was shouting to make herself heard above the din of the cursyrd above.

"Close," he said. "They have to be." He caught Pheone's eye. "They'll be here."

She smiled. "I'm sure."

"Where's your position?" asked Dila.

"I'll be with the second pair of wagons. Keep the horses straight. Try that move outside the shell if you get the chance. Anything to disrupt them."

She nodded. "They are so many. And think of the hundreds we have already killed."

"No, don't think that way. Think only that Xetesk will be in sight before dark and that we will be inside before noon tomorrow. They'll be expecting us."

"I hope so."

"Yniss watches over us."

"He needs to do more than that."

"I hear you, Dila. Run strong."

He turned to Pheone. "Get on the wagon."

"No," she replied. "I need to be seen."

"You need to live," said Rebraal. "There are greater fights to come. Please. I don't want to have to put you on there myself."

Pheone bit her lip but nodded. "I guess you're right."

Rebraal inclined his head and jogged away back toward the second pair of wagons. He could barely see the horses for the elven escort. The human drivers though, he could, and they were terrified, eyes up not ahead. He breasted through the flanking guards, shouting his confidence and hearing it reflected back. He leapt onto the kicking board of the left-hand cart.

"We go forward, not upward," he said, his hand on the shoulder of the driver.

"Yeah, but death comes from upward not forward," growled the middle-aged man, Brynn. He had a face latticed by the cuts of the strike-strain, a bandaged head and a belligerent belief in his right to survive. Rebraal liked him. He was Hirad, ten years hence.

"Let me watch the sky, Brynn. Just keep these animals in a straight line."

"They know better than to deviate with me behind them," said Brynn, face softening by a degree. "Ride with me this time, eh? See what it's like from up here."

"I intend to," said Rebraal.

And the sky fell in.

Strike-strain poured into the back of the line, reavers to the front. It was a tactic they had worked before, attempting to drive the train at different speeds front and back, creating a chaotic middle ground.

"Keep your form!" called Rebraal into the din, his words carried up and down the line. "Hold your pace! Hold your pace!"

Like the locusts that plagued the southern dry plains of Calaius, the strike-strain flooded the rear wagons. For a few moments, Rebraal watched the clamouring cloud descend. Blades flickered in the sudden half-light. An IceWind howled a tear in the enemy and the wagons were obscured from view.

But Rebraal had problems of his own. A large number of reavers, well into three figures, was rushing at the front wagons from both flanks, from ahead and, inevitably, from above. Taunting and laughing, they dove into the ColdRoom shell whose effects clearly lessened by the day.

"Keep those horses forward. Blinkers tight!"

The lead wave swooped over the front wagons and drove on headlong.

"Yniss preserve us," muttered Rebraal.

His sword in his right hand, his left squeezed Brynn's shoulder and they were engulfed.

"Brace!" he yelled.

The cursyrd struck the wagon, more of them than he could quickly count. He placed his body in front of Brynn, turning his back to the impact and feeling claws rake his armour and teeth graze the top of his head.

"Still here," said Brynn.

In front of them, the horses bucked and Brynn struggled to control them, demanding calm. Al-Arynaar carved the air around them, beating back the reavers intent on ripping out their eyes and throats.

Rebraal straightened, sword whipping out in a wide arc. He felt it catch the wing of a cursyrd which squealed and twisted upward, colour flaring a bright red. He took in the quick view. The roof of the wagon was threatened. The cursyrd's charge had taken three elves from their precarious canvas perch to a fight in the dust and grass behind. Two remained. Rebraal glanced across Brynn.

"Gheneer, keep him safe."

The Al-Arynaar nodded, not breaking from the fight. Rebraal jumped onto the canvas, felt for a strut and balanced instantly, the wagon bucking beneath him. The Al-Arynaar with him fought hard and fast. A sword sliced high into the chest of a cursyrd. A kick to the stomach saw it from the wagon. Another lost an arm to a downward slash and took off, wailing and cursing.

Rebraal took in three, two others flying to join one with its claws already rending canvas. The Al-Arynaar leader took a pace to the next strut and smashed his left foot into its head. The creature somersaulted backward, wings flailing to break its fall and propel it back into the air. The other two flew on, back-beating their wings, wary of the elf barring their way. Rebraal stood over the tear, sword in two hands, waiting.

They came in left and right. Rebraal smiled and feinted left, ducking low. He jabbed upward, his sword driving deep between the cursyrd's legs. It screeched, dark gore pouring from the wound. Rebraal twisted the blade and dragged it clear, surging upright and in the same moment beating his right foot into the midriff of the second creature. Off balance, it couldn't drag its arms back quickly enough to stop the elf's blade puncturing its chest.

Keeping himself moving, Rebraal headed down the wagon toward the rear. The remaining two Al-Arynaar were heavily engaged, strike-strain adding to their problems. He pulled a reaver back by the neck, his sword grating against its spine on the way through its body. He threw the corpse aside. The elf in front of him nodded his thanks, backhanded his blade into the face of another enemy and turned for the next.

Reavers filled the air above them. Al-Arynaar were climbing back up the sides of the wagon. Rebraal looked into the body of the carriage, saw the upturned faces of the guards and the bowed heads of mages. So far, the shell remained protected and intact. But with the air full of cursyrd and The Raven nowhere to be seen, they would have to fight well to keep it that way.

Chapter 30

Dystran had felt it like they all had. The demons' extraordinary withdrawal to gather at the periphery of Xetesk the day before had allowed them not just to relieve the library of a mass of texts but to go among the people and reassure them of their intentions; bring in fresh food from the farms within the city; gain information about the demons and their ways; and most importantly, bask in the mana stream in the open air and sample the spectrum.

But they had been reluctant to move too far out. Over two years of imprisonment had taken their toll and each mage and soldier could see danger and death in every shadow and corner they passed.

The Lord of the Mount stood on the walls of his college above the main gates and looked out over the city. He could see demons in the sky way to the south where the spectrum was in complete turmoil. The Julatsans were coming.

"What do you think it means?" asked Prexys, one of the surviving members of the Circle Seven.

"Opportunity or desperation. Probably both." Dystran smiled, luxuriating in the fresh air. "But I still can't work out why they have left us so alone."

"Perhaps they are under more pressure out there than they expected."

"I can't see it," said Dystran. "There are so many of them. But even those coming out of the tear are heading straight out there. Whatever the size of force that's heading this way, they certainly don't want it arriving."

Prexys shook his head. "Julatsa. What must have happened to drive them out?"

"Be a shame not to find out, wouldn't it?" said Dystran. He turned to Chandyr and Vuldaroq. "Gentlemen, are we not honour-bound to help our people under duress? Tell me, Chandyr, do you think they are heading this way?"

"There's no doubt about it but they are in a great deal of trouble. I've had mages in the sky over the college and they can see the dust cloud but it's almost covered by a cloud of demons. I don't recommend we leave here to help them but we can plan to smooth their progress through the city."

"Wards, waymarks and mage defender trios, those we can spare," said Dystran. "But do not compromise the defence of the college, that would be foolhardy in the extreme."

"I'll see to it."

"Good. I want sight of your plans so be quick. We have limited time."

He turned to Vuldaroq. "Meanwhile, I think you and I would be well used looking at a few more texts. There has to be more we can discover."

"I concur," said Vuldaroq.

"Good. Then let's be about our business. And Chandyr?"

"My Lord Dystran."

"Arrange a delegation to visit the Wesmen, would you? I'll prepare a message. I think it's time we invited Tessaya to the party."

"Slow that wagon!" Rebraal straight-punched a cursyrd on his way to the back of the canvas, seeing one of the third wagon pair closing too fast, driver smothered in strike-strain. "Al-Arynaar to the rear."

He swore under his breath. Behind him, Brynn called a warning. Swinging round, he saw the right-hand lead wagon veer sharply away, chased hard by a pack of some twenty reavers. It was the resting wagon, it had to be. No mage could have retained a ColdRoom structure at that pace. And Pheone was inside it. A cloud of strike-strain swooped overhead and plunged onto the roof, claws jabbing into the already damaged covers. Still standing, three Al-Arynaar laid about them with blade and knife, trying for Auum's trademark killing blow, but they'd surely soon be overwhelmed.

"Guard the casting wagon!" he yelled, kicking out at a lone strike-strain, catching it in the gut. "Dammit." He tugged the sleeve of an elf. "Hold this roof."

Rebraal dropped down next to Brynn. "Straight on. Don't flinch."

Brynn's face ran with blood. To his left, Gheneer kept two reavers at bay. Rebraal snatched a strike-strain from Brynn's back and crushed it under his foot.

"Don't be too long," growled the human.

Rebraal jumped to the packed earth and sprinted away toward the stricken wagon. Around him, a storm of noise and chaos was breaking. The wagon-pair captains roared orders. Al-Arynaar warriors tore into their attackers and amongst the thud of weapons, he could pick out the screams of those whom the cursyrd overwhelmed.

Ignoring the fighting that closed in around him, Rebraal focused on the wagon. The reavers had caught it and were engaged on its roof, at its rear and were tearing at its sides. Above, a ForceCone launched from one of the mana holes, battered brief respite into the horde of strike-strain that threatened the driver and his guards before it dissipated quickly within the shell.

Closing on the wagon, Rebraal saw an Al-Arynaar blade sweep into the neck of a winged soul stealer. The creature's grip on the roof strut was lost and it tumbled to the earth, bouncing and rolling. Rebraal hurdled its bright blue dying body. He increased his speed and leapt at the wagon's tail board. Pain lanced into his back from his injured leg as he landed. He grabbed hold of the rocking carriage and drove his blade into the back of a cursyrd, hurling it backward and out of the entrance to the wagon.

Inside the light-shot gloom, the fight raged. Strike-strain and reavers battled with Al-Arynaar and desperate human mages. At least one lay dead among the cursyrd bodies and blood gleamed wet on tattered canvas. Pheone was still standing, covered by Al-Arynaar.

"We have them," came a voice. "Go forward."

Rebraal nodded and hauled himself up onto the roof. Three warriors fought there, beating back the reavers storming in from all sides and above. Rebraal couldn't stop to help them. Running from strut to strut, he struck out at any that came into his path with blade, foot and fist. He felt bone crack and wing tear. Colours flashed in front of his face; dark gore and elven blood mixed underfoot, dripping onto the combatants below.

Carving his blade through the spine of a tall, thin cursyrd, he made the front of the wagon and looked down to the bench and kicking plate below.

"Yniss protect us."

A dead Al-Arynaar sprawled half off the right seat. The driver was still alive, his screams muffled by the strike-strain covering his head. A reaver was poised above him and Rebraal was going to be too late to save him. In front, Al-Arynaar warriors tried desperately to control the panicked horses under constant bombardment from around them.

The reaver plunged its hands up to the wrists into the driver's exposed back, delivering appalling pain in the moment before its theft.

"No!" shouted Rebraal.

He thudded down beside the startled cursyrd and snatched a strike-strain from the air, jamming it onto the point of his sword. The reaver's eyes met his, hands still buried in its victim's shattered rib cage. Its colour, a smug deep brown, swam to a bright purple. It knew what was coming and that it could do nothing about it.

Rebraal closed his posture, spun on his uninjured left leg, unwound and took the cursyrd's head from its shoulders, seeing the dead strike-strain fly from the point of his sword moments before impact.

"Shorth bring you eternal pain."

Rebraal had to act fast. The wagon was heading out of the ColdRoom protection, such as it was. Uttering a quick prayer, he shovelled human and cursyrd bodies from the kicking plate, first taking the reins from the dead elf's hands. He straightened, knocked a strike-strain aside and breathed hard. He had never driven horses before.

Behind him, demons surged onto the wagon and his warriors fought for all their lives. Ahead, elves ran hard, keeping up with the horses, distracted by cursyrd buzzing around their heads and harried by reavers. One slip would be fatal.

"What do I do?" he shouted.

"Slow them!" came the reply. "Turn them left."

"And we are all Tual's children," he breathed. "That much is obvious."

He had seen the humans drive. The sure hand, the confident voice of order. He did what he felt Brynn would do. He pulled hard on the reins.

Far too hard.

The horses half reared in their traces and bolted afresh, the sweat flying from their flanks under the chafing leather. On the roof behind him, elves rebalanced but cursyrd suffered. Wings beat, claws scrabbled. Blood was spilled quickly.

In Rebraal's hands, the horses were an unstoppable force, driving head-long toward certain doom. As they had for two days, cursyrd swarmed outside the shell, waiting for such a moment.

"Stop!" He snapped the reins. The horses merely hastened. "Gyal's tears, no."

He stared around the sides of the wagon. In the air directly above, more cursyrd bayed and called, whipping the horses' panic.

Rebraal knew he was helpless but he would not abandon his cargo. He urged the animals to stop. He dragged the reins more softly, pulling left, but they were lost to control. His ears were filled with the protestations of axle and timber, the desperation from within and the calm destruction of cursyrd foolish enough to attack the roof. Dust filled the air around him, clogging his lungs. The horses ploughed on across broken ground. It was a toss-up whether they'd be driven through the edge of the shell aboard the wagon, such was its shaking.

Rebraal consigned his soul to Yniss. Inside the shell, the cursyrd attack was faltering. Outside it, excitement grew. He had watched this from afar three times. Now it was his turn. Again he pressured the reins. Again, nothing.

"Clear!" he shouted down to those Al-Arynaar sprinting alongside the runaway horses. "Clear!"

They ignored him and he felt proud to die with them.

A detonation sounded beyond the shell. A curious momentary silence followed. Cursyrd bunched then scattered like birds dogged by a predator. A deep green light washed across the space, scattering on impact with the Cold-Room shell. For the first time, Rebraal heard fear in his enemies' cries. The attack faltered. Reavers took to the air. Strike-strain bunched and flew high. And where the green light touched them, the cursyrd melted.

Wings dripped away, bodies sloughed flesh. They fell in their dozens, wailing and agonised. And through the gap they had made, came The Raven, Auum's Tai and the Protectors. Rebraal shouted his relief though in truth he wasn't sure they would save him. The cursyrd were regrouping quickly, determined not to let their prize escape them, and yet more gathered in the sky above The Raven, wanting to claim the greatest prize of all.

Resigned to his position as passenger and spectator and content to keep the strike-strain away, Rebraal watched the extraordinary approach. Thraun, Darrick, Hirad and The Unknown formed a forward line, maces battering the cursyrd in front of them. Immediately behind strode Denser, his dark cloak flowing behind him. From his fingers, a ForceCone claimed space in the air above them.

And finally, the ace in the pack. Erienne, with a guard that brought laughter from Rebraal's lips. She was flanked by the two Protectors, Kas and Ark, at whose flanks ran Duele and Evunn. They moved as blurs, keeping the space around the One mage's head clear. Almost anonymous, Auum and Eilaan swept behind and the whole advanced with total belief, total control.

Again the glorious green light surged across the field and again the cursyrd panicked and broke. But this time Erienne stumbled and half fell, pushing her hands out toward her husband. Immediately, the formation changed. Evunn and Duele ran ahead of the Raven line. Ark scooped Erienne into his arms, passing her immediately to Thraun, and took up station behind with Kas and Auum. Denser and Eilaan's next ForceCones were directed ahead. And they ran straight for the shell and into the path of the runaway wagon.

Sensing an opportunity, the demons regrouped in the air above the shell. The wagon was suddenly free of concerted attack but the horses showed no inclination to slow. Rebraal turned.

"Al-Arynaar mages to the roof. Now!"

The wagon approached the edge of the shell. The Raven ran on. Rebraal could see The Unknown pointing. Cursyrd flocked in the air. A group of reavers circled behind. A hundred yards from relative safety and it could prove too far.

Rebraal snapped the reins. "Get on!" he shouted.

The horses had no intention of doing otherwise. Spooked out of any vestige of good sense, they drove on toward the waiting pack who had parted to allow the wagon a way through. Ahead, Hirad and Darrick broke formation and angled toward the bouncing, bucking cart. Rebraal heard the sounds of elves across the roof of the wagon. He turned his head.

"ForceCones," he said. "The moment we break the shell."

But facing forward again, he wondered what he could realistically achieve. Perhaps a little confusion. It would have to be enough.

Hirad had never run so fast. Trying to remember all that Auum had taught him on his sprint technique, he forged on. Darrick ran beside him, an athlete born to the land. The two raced. And while they did, the fortunes of many were in the balance.

Auum had identified the runaway wagon and the helpless Rebraal holding its reins. While The Raven approached, it had been a curiosity. Now it was a chance at life.

"Coldheart, you are old and slow," chided Darrick.

"General, you owe me a drink for every failure. This will be one."

"I'll be proud to buy it."

"And I to drink it."

Hirad could feel the breath scorching into his lungs, mixing with the taste of spell residue and demon stench. They were above him and the General now, gathering to dive. And before them, reavers turned into their path to begin attack runs.

The two men hefted their maces, feeling the weight on tired arms. Behind them, Denser unleashed another spell, freezing the air. Demons tumbled from the sky.

"Here they come," said Darrick.

"Rebraal needs to drive that wagon faster," said Hirad through gasps.

"Hirad, he isn't driving it at all."

"Roll!"

The pair dropped to the ground, rolled once and regained their feet. Claws slashed the air above them. Wings beat a downdraught across them. Hirad spun and thumped his mace into the back of the nearest enemy. Darrick's blow crushed wing bones in another. It would slow them but no more.

Strike-strain rained down on them as they ran on. Hirad felt claws scratch at his head and neck, teeth nip into his legs through heavy cloth. He ignored the frost that each break in his skin fed into his body, striking out left at a reaver cruising in to the attack. The blow caught it in the face but it came on, knocking him from his feet. He tumbled and rolled. A tail sliced across his back, cutting into his skin, leaving ice behind.

Not stopping, he scrambled back to his feet. Darrick was ahead of him now, mace cracking strike-strain aside, the feeling of metal on flesh heavy and satisfying. Ahead, the wagon ploughed on. Hirad could see its roof and sides busy with elves and its wheels bouncing on the uneven ground as it rushed toward them. The periphery of the shell moved too, its speed governed by that of the wagons bearing the casting mages and mercifully under greater control. Its edge could be estimated by the demons clustering outside of it and Rebraal was all but through it.

Hirad caught Darrick in time to bludgeon away a clutch of strike-strain poised to attack the General's head. Reavers were coming in again too, but this time it was spells that stopped them. Rebraal's wagon plunged out of the ColdRoom shell. Back in the world of mana, his mages cast quickly and efficiently. ForceCones drove rents through the demon clouds, scattering them through the air. Immediately, they were attacked from the rear, the Al-Arynaar fighting hard to keep them away.

"Confident?" shouted Hirad.

"Never not so," replied Darrick.

They were twenty yards from the wagon and running straight for it. Maces were stowed in belt loops, strike-strain were free to snipe at them.

"Good luck."

Darrick timed his run to perfection. He angled into the galloping horses, caught the rein harness of the right-hand beast and swung up onto its back. Two paces later, Hirad leapt for the kicking board, impacting heavily on the frame of the wagon. Ignoring the flare of pain in his ribs, he turned to Rebraal, grinning and taking the reins from him.

"Bloody elves. Never did understand horses." He looked ahead. "All right, General, let's get this thing pointed the right way!"

He felt a blade whistle above his head. A reaver tumbled away, flaring a ghastly yellow.

"Thanks."

Rebraal shrugged and sought his next target.

Darrick, flanked by elves, was calming the horses. Commands mixed with soft words in one's ears brought it back to its senses and it began to slow, bringing the other with it, suddenly aware of its peril and needing direction. Hirad provided it, turning them right toward The Raven and snapping the reins to maintain impetus.

His friends were in trouble. Strike-strain in their hundreds had gathered above them and reavers approached from all quarters. The Tai cell fought with grace and control at the head of the running pack, never seeming to break stride. The Unknown and the two Protectors were a power block, delivering shuddering strikes that battered a path clear. Thraun ran alongside Denser and Eilaan in their wake. The two mages clearly held ForceCones above their heads, sweeping them around and behind, denying the demons access to Thraun's vital cargo.

"We need more spells keeping the sky clear," said Hirad. "Darrick, get your arse up here. It's going to get interesting."

Rebraal called out the order. Al-Arynaar mages on the roof of the wagon turned their attention to The Raven. Two followed Denser's example, deploying ForceCones ahead of the horses, using them as battering rams. Hirad waited for Darrick to step nimbly up the horse's back before snapping the reins again, encouraging more speed from the tiring animals.

The two groups closed quickly, demons getting caught between them. Elven ForceCones drove the creatures left, right, up and forward. Hirad saw the danger.

"Move those Cones!" he shouted, gesturing with his arm as he did so. "Above head height."

Rebraal confirmed the order and The Raven could run in under temporary cover. Hirad threw the reins at Darrick.

"Your turn, General. We need Erienne inside at the earliest."

With that, he thumped to the ground and ran toward The Raven, the ice from his demon cuts stiffening his muscles, the sweat streaming from his forehead and the blood rushing in his veins. And at the periphery of it all, he kept at bay the fear that they all harboured. That these hordes were always within an ace of snuffing them out forever. That one slip would end it all.

He roared to clear his head and dragged his mace out to smash it into the back of the first reaver he encountered. It felt good. It felt very good.

"Unknown, get ready," yelled Hirad, voice carrying over the narrow press of demons separating them.

He saw The Unknown nod and thunder his mace into the skull of a reaver. The creature shrieked and fell backward, shaking its head, its skin a blazing bright blue. Beside him Ark and Kas, operating with mace and axe, upped their pace. Demons flew from their path. Strike-strain carrying clear over Hirad's head, reavers crumpling and falling, trampled as they tried to rise, shaking off the shock of the blows.

Auum's Tai had dropped behind Thraun and the mages now and were operating with dreadful efficiency. Not for them the path-making power of the mace. Instead, feet and hands denied the demons the rear of the Raven line and, where they fell, they'd find a TaiGethen pounce to deliver the short-sword stab under the arm.

Hirad slapped his mace into the demon pack once more. He could hear the rattling of the carriage and feel the thud of hoof underfoot.

"Break them, break them!" ordered Darrick.

The wagon slewed hard right, dirt and grass flying up from under its wheels. Denser shifted the focus of his ForceCone, driving a wedge through the demons, dismissing the spell before it could threaten either Hirad or their transport. The barbarian battered his way toward Thraun, mace in both hands now. He felt a claw swipe across the top of his head and the blood began to run. He staggered and straightened, took two more paces and was knocked clean from his feet. Pain scorched into his side, winding him. Demons closed around him, their calls and shouts mixing with those of The Raven.

Rolling onto his back, he saw sky above him and the wings of demons closing in. He carried on rolling, a claw missing his face by a hair. A weapon whispered across his body. He heard a thud and a cry of frustration. A fist grabbed his collar and hauled him upright.

"Get on board, Coldheart," said The Unknown.

Thraun had reached the back of the cart. Kas and Ark flanked him still, their weapons keeping the baying demon pack at bay. IceWind, bleak yellow and Julatsan, swept out from the roof of the wagon. The TaiGethen sprinted past him and vaulted to the wagon's roof to join the fight. Denser and Eilaan paced backward, the latter's ForceCone still under control, still keeping the enemy back from the sky above.

"The roof, Unknown. We need to get there."

"Not you," said The Unknown. "In the back. You're hurt. I'll take the bench with Darrick."

"Hurt?"

"Yes."

The Unknown's mace struck again. He ducked a flailing tail, dragging Hirad with him into the lee of the wagon. He pushed the barbarian to the tailgate and thrust him at Ark.

"Don't let him go."

Hirad frowned. His head was swimming a little but otherwise he was fine. He smiled up at Ark but the Protector's face was impassive.

"Get aboard," he said.

Hirad thought to disagree but he took one more pace and staggered, legs suddenly lacking strength. He glanced down and saw the blood from his side staining his leather. He began to shiver.

His last certainty was hearing The Unknown shout for Darrick to get the wagon going. But after Ark had picked him up and he thought he'd heard Rebraal order more ForceCones, everything else was a chill blur.

Chapter 31

Sharyr and Brynel knelt to prepare the ward. They were far from the gates of the college and could hear the sounds of demons whose attentions were mercifully still diverted elsewhere. Next to them stood Suarav. He was the only man they would have trusted to look over them. It was a curious strength they had gained from their ordeal in the library. None of them had truly recovered from it. They all still shivered intermittently and felt the chill of demon touch and proximity.

Yet it had instilled in them a fierce fatalism and brought the three of them together in a bond of mutual respect and belief. It was something that would be put to severe test in the hours to come.

"Attach it to the corner there," whispered Sharyr.

Brynel nodded. The ward structure was simple and designed for a closely directed effect. Positioned on the junction of streets running away to the broken north gate, to the cloth market, and the college itself, it was a key focus of Chandyr's plan to help the Julatsans into Xetesk. Another key part of that plan was the three of them.

Sharyr watched his charge meld the ward into the building. When it was fixed he fed in exclusions to its activation to ensure no stray human or elven approach caused disaster. It was a quick process.

"All right," he said, standing and helping Brynel up. "That's our lot."

"Well done," said Suarav.

The three men looked at each other in the gloom of the street. The quiet was eerie and suffocating. Each knew what the others would be feeling. The desire to run back to the college. The dread at what they had volunteered to do. The pride at their own strength and the trust that had been bestowed upon them.

While other trios, some classic mage-defender structure, completed the ward lattice to Chandyr's design, they would be leaving Xetesk to contact the approaching allies. No one had to tell them the risk they were taking. No one had to remind them of their chances of success. They already knew that Chandyr had a contingency for their failure. It wasn't supposed to discomfort them, it was simple reality.

"Do you need to rest?" asked the gruff guard captain.

Both mages shook their heads.

"We should go," said Sharyr.

"Just remember to follow my lead and keep yourself moving. To stop is to die," said Suarav.

Sharyr chuckled. "Only that?"

"Strength," said Suarav.

"Let's go," said Brynel. "It's cold standing here."

Denser looked down at his wife and a tear dropped from his cheek onto hers. It was the deep of night. The demons were attacking again. He could hear their calls echoing across the wagon train as it rolled inexorably on toward the gates of Xetesk. Feet skipped across the roof struts overhead and he could see the stress in the canvas in the half-light that permeated the wagon.

Rebraal had said the night would be the worst and so it was. Because the demons, indefatigable, lit up the sky with the colours of their bodies. They set up a stunning array of lights, at once terrifying and undeniably beautiful. Shifting patterns across the rainbow of colour, bright washes and gentle tones that were quite extraordinary, almost mesmerising. But they denied man, elf and horse any rest. Their calls gnawed at the nerves. And periodically, they would swoop into attack. Not with the intention of destroying the convoy, but in the knowledge that with the dawn would come new fear.

Denser tried to put it from his mind while he considered the folly of what The Raven would soon be attempting. Next to Erienne, Hirad lay sleeping fitfully, his many scratches and wounds bound and treated and his body shivering. He was strong. He would come back. But Erienne was a different case. Denser tried to believe that she was as strong willed and determined as the woman he had met all those years before. But tragedy had dogged her and the pressure to be what she did not want to be was tearing up her soul.

Her façade cracked often yet still she tried to achieve what The Raven desired and what Balaia and all its linked dimensions needed. Out there in the fields as they had run toward the ColdRoom shell and the security it represented, Erienne had attempted something new, something awesome.

Denser understood what it was. She had created a structure that expanded on encountering the air and had evacuated the space it covered of any vestige of mana. But this super-ColdRoom wasn't the end. She had then stripped an element from demons that they could not survive an instant without. Something that bound their flesh. It would be like taking water from a human body. Whatever it was she had seen in their makeup, she had used to devastating effect. But as with all the castings of the One, there was risk in the new idea.

And the second time she had cast, she had let too much of the power flood her body. Her collapse had been her body's defence mechanism against a complete disaster for her and for Balaia. They had been lucky. The storms

Erienne would unleash if out of control would make those that Lyanna had triggered seem like puffs of breeze.

But when would she awake from this latest trauma? And when she did, what would she be like? He could only hope that somewhere in her mind, Cleress was with her.

"Why did you try it, love?" he asked, stroking her warm cheek, wiping away his tear. "There's nothing you need to prove to us. Nothing."

Around him in the wagon, resting Al-Arynaar mages and humans including Pheone kept their thoughts to themselves, respecting his need for whatever privacy of mind he could eke out. A strong hand rested on his shoulder.

"Deep inside, she knows even that. But she cannot deny that part of her that desires to experiment. To find her limits."

Denser turned his head to look at Thraun. The big blond shapechanger was seated behind them, sword across his knees. He would not leave her side while she was helpless. He never would. Thraun had known her longer than any of them. He'd seen her twins grow and had buried them alongside her first husband. Theirs was a bond that comforted Denser. Something he knew would never fail.

"What makes you say that?"

A smile touched Thraun's lips. "A shapechanger drives his body when he is not a human. He desires to push it further than he ever could his human frame. It is something he never truly controls but in that lack there is such life and excitement. It is to be feared as it is to be loved."

The wagon bounced across a rut in the ground. Above there was a shifting of feet and the multiple impact of weapons. Bodies hit the ground, death cries fading to nothing.

"You know, you might be right but I think there's more to it," said Denser. "The One is Erienne's only link to Lyanna. When she lets it thrive it's like life."

Thraun shrugged. "Yes. It is why I have to live part of my life with the pack. It is a link to something I cannot deny."

"Do you remember any of the years you spent as a wolf after the Noonshade rip?"

Thraun's face darkened. "No. It is at best like scent on the breeze. Fleeting reminiscence, soon dispersed. I'd rather it was that way."

Erienne shifted in her sleep and Denser caressed her brow. "It's all right, love. You're safe."

Denser hated himself for saying it but it was the only way he could feel any worth at all. He glanced up at Thraun but the shapechanger wasn't looking at them. He was sniffing the air, sword clutched in his hands and his muscles tensed.

"Thraun?"

The shapechanger's eyes glinted yellow in the swimming lights reflected from the demons' bodies as they flew outside. "Threat," he said.

He stepped over Erienne and Denser and stood at the covered rear of the wagon, silent and unmoving. Denser could see him balancing with the shifts of the axles and could hear The Unknown shouting instructions from where he was riding with Darrick at the front.

There was an impact on the wagon's tail board. Thraun stiffened, crouched very slightly. The canvas rippled. Thraun's right hand shot out through the opening and dragged a reaver in by the throat. He held it down by his knee and growled, sword cocked and ready.

The demon screwed its head round, its body flaring yellow, bathing the wagon with an alien light. Both Hirad and Erienne moaned. There was a concerted movement toward the front of the carriage.

"Shapechanger," grated the demon, voice strangled through Thraun's grip.

"And the reason you will never take what you want so badly," he replied.

He jerked the creature further into the wagon. It spat and struggled, wings beating against the canvas, arms clutching Thraun's wrist. Thraun merely tightened his grip.

"Look," he said. "Look at what you are so close to but can never touch."

His sword drove through the demon's chest. Within the ColdRoom shell, there was no defence against that. The creature convulsed and died. Gore drained onto the floor timbers. Thraun flung the body from the wagon and thrust his head out into the open air.

"Any more of you come right in."

Denser had never seen him this animated. The big warrior withdrew and retook his seat.

"Glad you're on my side," said Denser.

"Always," said Thraun.

"What's got into you?"

Thraun's eyes bored into his. "I have watched her these years, only leaving her side when I thought her to be safe. I have seen her grow in strength even as her heart broke. She can save us all. It is best that they know it." He gestured outside.

"You're baiting a trap," said Denser.

"And The Raven are its jaws."

Hiela was unused to resistance. But the incompetence of the aggressor strains over an insultingly long time had forced his early appearance in Balaia. It had not been in his plans for this time. The orderly transfer of mana energy from their home of the last generations needed careful marshalling and he was particularly schooled in the linkage between their land and Balaia.

Hiela, of course, was the designated Shroud Master. He had overseen the capture of so many souls from the Balaian mages when their petty squabbles had forced them to come to him for protection. He understood how they thought. How anything was better than that which they had just faced.

He still remembered how the Julatsans had capped and dismissed the shroud around their college almost at the moment he had forced a breach that would have made all that had happened since an irrelevance. Balaia had been so weak at the time. One rabble had been fighting the other and breaking the spirit of the whole. How easy it would have been to invade at that moment.

But dragons had become embroiled in the dispute. And so had this group of humans and elves that so went against all their teaching about the weakness of the spirit of those from Balaia's northern continent. This Raven. To find they were still a thorn in the side of conquest and dominion had hastened his departure.

And so, rather than sit basking in the warmth of the mana flow and see to the needs of the masters who maintained the gap and focused the stream, he was here. In the heat of the Balaian dimension. Smelling their foul air and hearing the pathetic excuses as to why the land they had identified was not yet sanctified for habitation. Why so many humans, elves and damned Wesmen ran free to cause them trouble rather than build, breed and die at their pleasure.

Hiela hovered outside the walls of the city known as Xetesk. He was aware of the activity within its boundaries. Of the lift the withdrawal of forces from its people had given them. It bothered him very little. He had overflown the city before agreeing to the order to defend the borders and had found them broken. Even those still nominally at liberty within their spells were cracked and their wills close to collapse. He could hasten that inevitability by the destruction of those who came to their aid. Hence the arrangement of his forces as a welcome. Latterly, though, this tactic had been somewhat complicated.

"They are within, you are sure?" he demanded.

"Yes, Master Hiela," said the messenger. "All of them."

"I see."

He turned to his advisers. Incompetents all but with more knowledge of the developing situation at present.

"Tell me, any of you, why this force should be so keen on driving to the heart of a college which we have so effectively sealed from the outside?"

Hiela regarded them, waiting for one to speak. He scratched at the beard he still preferred to sport. It was a legacy of his grudging respect of the Julatsan mages of old. Men and elves of some strength and spirit. Those who would have been a challenge to break.

"It is their way," said one. "They group together for strength in times of duress, believing their best hope for survival lies in their numbers."

"Hmm." Hiela nodded. "But there is more, isn't there? The Raven are with them now. These are not men who come merely to extend their life-spans. These are men who expect victory and travel only to the places where they believe that chance exists."

Silence.

"Idiots. Isn't that why you crave their souls? Isn't that why they fascinate you yet more than a mage or an elf? Within them is that life force that is so exquisite it burns us not to be able to touch it. Do you believe such as these would join a hopeless defence?"

"But even for them there is nothing to be done," said another. "We will prevail. It is a question of time."

"Even at the time of our burgeoning strength there lies risk," said Hiela, letting his colour drift to a brighter blue. "You swallow too much of what you are told by the masters. They have not dealt with these people before. I have. And this is not a futile gesture. There will be a purpose."

"But surely there is only one . . ."

Hiela snapped around in his position, floating in their midst, to stare hard at the long-fingered cerebral that had uttered the words. He let the import sink in.

"Yes," he said. "And can you think of another reason why the Julatsans would leave their college—the one place where we had doubts about our ability to dominate—and travel to the heart of dimensional research and understanding of our race? And why do the Wesmen still watch? Why are they so close?"

There was a wind blowing across the open lands. It brought a welcome chill though the assembled company barely acknowledged it. Hiela turned a slow rotation in the air, making sure they all heard him.

"Out there, travelling toward us, are those who are capable of beating us, should they receive the help they need. We can suppose that this is why they are travelling to Xetesk. And you can suppose this is why we are ranged here. Because they shall not make the walls of the college. And they shall not ask for what they need, let alone find it.

"This is no longer a battle to defeat the will and farm the souls of those who approach. This is an order to destroy. We have all we need here. Never mind the sweetness of its taste, let us kill that which we can live without. We must focus on this and this alone. What is the state of our conflicts to the south and the college of Lystern?"

"The resistance is weakening in both places but it still holds. These are determined men," said Drenoul, master of the Xeteskian battle front.

"So they are but that must end. I know your commanders will want the prized souls of those within but we need their strength of numbers here to keep the Wesmen from causing us delay while we face Julatsa and Xetesk combined. Order them to extinguish that which will not be cowed and travel here with all haste.

"It is time to deploy the destructors."

"Surely they will be too weak yet. The mana density is not high enough," said Drenoul.

"But not for long and they are many," said Hiela. "Summon the karron."

The malevolence was causing panic throughout. The others were packed far away from the pulse of pure hate that was spreading. Like a battering on the door to their world. And it was getting louder and stronger. He had struggled with the concept of there being a force wanting to harm them. But then he had travelled to a place where the sense of evil intent and salacious desire washed over him in a wave.

While searching for The Raven he had seen in a moment of clarity that the threat was genuine and that they in their countless number were helpless against it. Those who could have heard him in his homeland were gone from there but one had resurfaced near The Raven. It would be his brother, he was sure. It was logical, if logic held sway here, that they were aware of the threat and were battling it.

But did they really know the extent of it? And did they know where to travel? He knew. And now here he was, unsure how to proceed. He had the battering pulse filling his mind and soul. He had The Raven, bright lights surrounding one that dazzled. And he had the sense of the destination. It was a place of enormous power that ebbed slowly as if that power was being drained. He could feel it pass him like a wind through his being and tracing it back had found its source in an otherwise cold and dead land.

The Raven had to go to there and nowhere else in that land. He needed a way to contact them that was not the loose meeting of subconscious minds that he had managed so far. So often, Hirad had almost grasped him but each time the fluidity of dreams had snatched away what he was trying to say.

He concluded that he had to get closer, if closer was possible. Before him, indeed all around him, the battering was weakening the Spirits within. The anxiety had spread through all of them and communication was laced with terror and the knowledge that they had no defence against those wanting to break through. There would come a moment when the door would fall and the panic would overflow and communication would be impossible. But until that time, he had to believe in his own safety and in the strength of the Spirits that wished him success.

He forced himself to concentrate. There was a point between The Raven, the place where they had to go and the door through which they must pass. It was a place of great risk, where the boundaries between worlds were weak and the malevolence waited its chance. But it was the only place he was sure he could make a difference.

Letting the light of his friends suffuse him and protect him, he journeyed on.

CHAPTER 32

"**Y**ou are in no fit state to be standing here," said The Unknown.

"You can say what you like, Unknown, but I don't think what we're looking at leaves us any choice, do you? You need me here."

"Gods, just let him do it," said Denser. "At least if he dies we won't have to listen to this sort of bleating anymore."

"Thank you, Denser," said Hirad.

"You are not helping," said The Unknown.

"I can't believe you're surprised he's here."

"I'm not surprised, I'm questioning the wisdom of his decision."

"You think wisdom ever applies to anything Hirad does?"

"All right, Xetesk-man, I thought you were on my side."

"He is, Hirad," said The Unknown. "We all are. If you must do something foolish, why don't you do it in the wagon where you can protect Erienne at the same time?"

"Thraun has got that covered."

"You are so stubborn."

Auum shook his head and scratched at his forehead. He would never understand how they had survived this long. Always arguing. He finished applying the green and black paints to Duele's face before leading them all in prayer. Throughout, he could hear The Raven bickering like children over a broken doll.

He brought his Tai back to their feet and they walked to the front of the stationary wagon train. It was dawn and it was cold, very cold. The breath clouded in front of his face and the chill breeze whipped it away. The wagons had been halted when the cursyrd had ceased their attacks an hour or so before first light. They had retreated as far as the edge of the shell and most of them were grouped on the ground. Very few still remained in the air and none encroached on the periphery.

The temptation had been to continue on but both Darrick and Rebraal had advised the stop. It was inconceivable that they would not be attacked severely on their way into Xetesk, which now lay just three miles ahead, and any chance to rest horses and mages had to be taken.

It was a decision that looked at best overcautious as light had strengthened. It could turn out to be a huge mistake. Beyond those gathered before them, other cursyrd were moving up. These were not reavers and they were not strike-strain. They were a strain none of them had seen before in this conflict.

Auum watched them approach. There were hundreds of them. Squat wingless figures with rolling gaits. They were covered in a dense, dark, fine hair. Each one had eyes to the front and sides of its head and no discernible mouth or nose. But what they did have was arms that ended in what for all the world looked like spiked clubs or hammers.

The assembled company had fallen silent while these things advanced toward the shell. Other cursyrd made way and a screeching filled the air. Auum couldn't make out what it meant but it was more a sound of anger than of anticipation.

"Gods drowning, but they're ugly bastards. What are they?" asked Hirad.

"Karron," said Auum, the word leaving a harsh taste in his mouth. "Destructors."

"This isn't going to be any fun at all," said Hirad.

"I don't understand this," said Denser. "I mean, these look capable of causing us a real problem. Why haven't they thrown them at us before?"

"Because before, they wanted our souls," said Rebraal. "Now I fear they just want us dead."

"That's comforting," said Hirad.

"Thoughts?" asked The Unknown.

"They're slow but powerful," said Darrick. "If I'm not mistaken, we'll be harried as we have come to expect by the winged strains and these will look to break us from the front."

"Can't we just drive round them?" asked Hirad.

Darrick shook his head. "If they got into our flanks they could fragment the train. Far better we take them head-on, at least we can marshal forces in the right direction."

"I don't think it'll be enough," said The Unknown. "They're strong enough to stop us moving forward and that's something we cannot afford. We have to break that line or we'll be surrounded and picked off."

"I've got an idea," said Darrick. "But it's a big risk."

"Let's hear it," said The Unknown.

Darrick looked around him. "Is Pheone here? I need to know our casting strength."

"Will it make a difference?" asked Hirad. "We're inside a ColdRoom here."

Darrick smiled. "Yes it will. And you know the thing with ColdRooms is you can let them go all of a sudden. If you want to."

Auum nodded his head. He understood what Darrick was about to suggest. It would be, how would Hirad say it? Interesting.

Tessaya, Lord of the Paleon tribes, stretched his mouth in a prodigious yawn. He had slept well the last night and welcomed the cold of the new day. He wrapped his furs about his shoulders and strode from his tent. Around him, the activity was frenetic. Weapons were being sharpened, fires heated water and broth, warriors ran in all directions taking messages, striking camp and loading pallets. Others foraged for what food they could sweep up easily before the move.

Patience, Tessaya had always said, would pay off and today was that day. Because yesterday he had received the most extraordinary visit of his life. A deputation from Xetesk, in effect inviting him into the heart of the college. He had felt it churlish to refuse, and now two thousand warriors made ready to advance.

The demons had left them alone these past three days and his scouts had reported them massing to the north. They had also reported an approaching dust cloud that was overflown by the enemy and under apparently constant attack. Clearly, others were heading for the college too.

This had been confirmed by the Xeteskians and it was proposed that the Wesmen help these runners into Xetesk and then join the final battle for the freedom of Balaia. He had been given a blank slate to demand whatever he wanted from the Easterners in return for his aid. Short of the end of magic of course. That, he conceded, was unlikely but the deal he had struck would make the Wesmen the dominant power across the whole of the country. The Xeteskians would have seen that. He would have to tread carefully.

Tessaya walked quickly down to the forward positions, trailed by his aides. There he found Arnoan, the ancient Shaman apparently lost in thought. Communing perhaps. Still, it was a reverie easily broken.

"Am I being lured into a trap, do you think?"

"I consider that to be very unlikely," said Arnoan, focusing on him with a frown. "The Xeteskians have nothing to gain by so doing barring a hastening of their own demise. I am merely saddened it has taken them so long to see that the Wesmen are their best chance of salvation."

"And you believe us so to be?"

"I do, my Lord."

"But let us not fool ourselves," said Tessaya. "The Xeteskians have only come to us because the demons allowed them the time to do so. Consider also that the demons themselves may have orchestrated this whole event."

"Again, unlikely," said Arnoan. "After all, we are not even being watched, which I find very curious. They will only know of our decision to move when we are under way."

Tessaya chuckled and slapped Arnoan on the back. The Shaman staggered and coughed. "Perhaps their grasp of battle tactics is as poor as yours, my friend."

"Let us hope so, Tessaya, let us hope so."

Behind him Tessaya could hear the strains of songs rolling down the slope toward him. They filled his heart with strength and pride. The standards were raised and stood together.

The Wesmen were marching once more.

It had become their only hope of reaching the Julatsans and it was a terrible choice to have to make. They had cowered in renewed terror when the new strain had appeared from the rip and descended to the ground to march away into Xetesk and out toward the Julatsans. They had an aura about them that sucked the will and brought a dead shiver to the limbs.

Sharyr would have welcomed death then but in their hiding place they had been ignored and had been able to watch the gathering of demon forces. It had become obvious then that their plan of running in while the demons were engaged in battle was unworkable. Most of the demons were covering the ground around the periphery of the ColdRoom shell surrounding the wagon train. The only way in was by air.

"I will remain here and see you safe and then return to Xetesk," said Suarav, the words dragging reluctantly from his mouth.

"No," said Brynel immediately. "We are stronger with you. You must come with us."

Sharyr agreed. "Without you, I do not believe I have the strength."

Suarav gripped an arm of both of them. "My friends, you can do this. You have to. And besides, I cannot fly."

"We can carry your weight between us," said Sharyr. "We won't leave you. How much chance do you really think you have of getting back into the college?"

Suarav closed his eyes and Sharyr knew he had touched the reason for the soldier's fear. Alone and travelling back through the streets of Xetesk. One swordsman. It would be suicide.

"But split up, you have a better chance of one of you reaching the Julatsans."

"The difference is slight. The journey is quick but fraught. I'd rather the confidence of you with us than the extra mobility," said Brynel.

Suarav sighed. "Can it really be done?"

"Oh yes," said Brynel. "ShadowWings do not tangle. They aren't corporeal. You hang onto our belts and we fly. Low and fast."

"One thing more," said Sharyr. "When we pierce the ColdRoom, the Wings will disperse very quickly. It'll be a rough landing."

"I'll bear it in mind." Suarav sighed again and shook his head. "You know, I'm too old for this sort of thing."

"You're never too old to fly," said Sharyr.

"All right, let's do it. But if I fall, do not come back for me. I outrank you and that is an order."

Both mages nodded. Brynel turned to Sharyr. "Ready to cast?"

"Ready. Captain, take your grip now. As soon as we begin to cast, the demons will be aware of us. We're going to have to leave quickly."

The two mages stood side by side. Suarav knelt between them. His hands gripped the front of their belts, his arms between their legs.

"Cast now," said Suarav.

The spectrum responded to them and the demons began to howl.

The instructions had been snapped out quickly and Darrick just had to trust that they would be understood. If it worked, they'd break the demon line, he was sure of that. If not, they would be in desperate trouble and praying for a miracle from inside the walls of Xetesk.

Forty Al-Arynaar mages now stood in front of the two lead wagons. They were guarded by an equal number of warriors, leaving the rest to continue normal duties back down the train. The front of the shell was fifty yards ahead of them and it was crowded with karron, reaver and strike-strain. Around the flanks and behind, winged demons waited for their orders to attack, most resting on the ground as they had been since before dawn.

In the traces, the horses were as fresh as they could be. Darrick had handed the reins to another human driver, a man named Brynn whom Rebraal recommended as the ideal man to hold the front line. Darrick went with the elf's decision. Brynn was a man covered in scratches and bandages but clearly unbowed despite the shiver in his body.

Now Darrick stood with The Raven, minus Erienne and Thraun, and the TaiGethen, just behind the line of mages. Hirad had won his battle as they all knew he would and had taken his place at The Unknown's right-hand side. He was plainly discomforted but Darrick for one would rather a half-fit Hirad in the line than no Hirad at all. And it was equally plain on The Unknown's face that, despite his protestations, he felt precisely the same.

Time was almost upon them. There were still karron moving up to the edge of the shell, sorting themselves into dense lines. And overhead, two masters floated. One with the tentacled underbody, the other a rather plain-looking blue demon, small but clearly important, given its position. Pheone moved in front of her charges, Dila'heth near her. They knew what they had to do. Each one had casting instructions and direction. That they would fail was inconceivable.

A movement caught Darrick's eye to the right beyond the shell's periphery. At first he thought it demons flying in to join the attack but the movement was erratic and had the air of a chase. He brought it to Auum's attention. There was growing consternation among the demons as they too became aware of it. The level of noise, building steadily, had an angry edge to it. Strike-strain left the shell to intercept.

"It is humans," said Auum. "Three. Two carrying the other one."

"Coming this way?"

"Yes," he said.

Darrick raised his eyebrows. Something had to trigger the attack. He had expected it to be the demon masters. Perhaps it would be this random event. What he couldn't afford was for the Al-Arynaar to be distracted.

"Eyes front!" he ordered. "Check your targets."

Rebraal translated his words and focus was restored. The same could not be said of the demons and there was just a small chance that this would work in their favour. It was a chance that did not come off. The trio of flyers, skimming the tree line, dipping and rising suddenly to shake off a growing tail of pursuers, closed on the shell. High above, the masters raced to the back of their main force. The noise rose to a deafening volume and the karron came to shambling readiness.

"Ready!" called Darrick. "Remember your roles. Do not deviate, do not falter. Dila'heth, cast when ready." He turned to a flagman. "Now. Signal the disperse."

Up on the roof of the lead wagons, flags were waved. Inside the right-hand one, the casting mages dispersed the ColdRoom structure. Demons howled, sensing victory, and from above they poured down to attack. Immediately the flags were seen, the wagons behind began rolling forward, bringing the remaining ColdRooms closer.

"Come on, come on," muttered Darrick.

The front line of Al-Arynaar was motionless, lost in casting. The General looked anxiously up to the heavens. The sky was full of demon bodies, clamouring for their souls, gibbering their desire. The karron upped their pace, trotting over the packed ground, arms pumping, the weapons that replaced their hands glistening. They were followed by packs of reavers and flanked by clouds of strike-strain. This was going to be close.

As one, the elven mages raised their heads. Pheone snapped out an order and the spell barrage was unleashed. ForceCones jabbed into the air, scattering the onrushing winged demons which squealed their displeasure. They were the lucky ones for now. Immediately following the Cone deployment, bright yellow light flashed across the early morning sky. FlameOrbs arced out. At least fifty wheel-sized globes fizzed through the damp air. Steam trailed in their wake.

The karron could see them coming and warning cries echoed out but they could do nothing to protect themselves. Harsh magical fire burst across and through the demon lines. Karron directly beneath the Orbs exploded under their impact. Gobbets of flame splattered far and wide, eating into defenceless flesh. The detonation of spells sent fire hurtling into the sky, trapping three reavers not fast enough to move. Black smoke belched from bodies and trailed behind those falling from the sky.

On the ground, blinded and agonised karron collided with one another as the ordered advance became a chaotic rout. The air stank of charred hair and flesh, it reverberated to the screams of those caught in the holocaust. And the elves had only just begun.

Now, Dila'heth's voice sounded once more and IceWind delivered appalling damage to the still-advancing flanks. Flesh sloughed from bodies, eyes were frozen and voices were stilled in throats. Karron fell shattering to the ground, dark bodies scorched blue and hairless by the cold. Strike-strain fell like fruit from a tree in a gale, cracking on the ground. A terrible wailing was taken up across the battlefield. It was demon rage and it struck at the heart.

Darrick turned his head. The second wagon pair was moving into range, and would fill the space in between the lead pair, bringing with it the respite of a replacement ColdRoom.

"Advance!" he roared.

Dila'heth and Pheone brought their mages back from the mana spectrum and they split left and right, running back along the sides of the train. The Al-Arynaar and Raven moved forward toward the demon lines and the Cold-Room covered them once more.

It had been a devastating blow and Darrick was tempted to let the mages strike again. But stamina was finite and the Gods alone knew when they would next be able to replenish. Looking forward through the clearing smoke, he could see the rents they had torn in the demon force. But even now it was beginning to re-form and if they were to break through and reach Xetesk, it had to be now.

CHAPTER 33

I *can't do it, Cleress, I can't.*

Oh my child of course you can. You are a most able student.

Don't bloody patronise me. Want me to start calling you "old woman"? You weren't there. You weren't in my mind. That casting should have worked exactly the way of the first. The fact that it didn't means I cannot be trusted to do this right every time and if I don't, my friends will die.

If you don't try they will die anyway.

Erienne had a sensation of movement but nothing more. Her awareness was otherwise limited to the roar of the One magic force surging around her mind and body and the attempted calming of the frail and distant Al-Drechar elf. Erienne was not dead and therefore The Raven must have made it to the Julatsan carriages. She was, she presumed, aboard one of them. And if she concentrated very hard, she felt a comforting strength nearby. She knew who it would be.

And you think my giving them false hope will make it better?

Don't be stupid, Erienne. Yours is not a false hope. The power you oversee can be the difference. All you have to do is understand where you went wrong. Explain what happened.

Erienne bit back her retort. It would have made her precisely the school-girl she had been about to deny.

I didn't go wrong, Cleress, I didn't. I had worked out the gauge of the casting so well and it worked exactly as I had planned. You would have been proud. I mapped the mana trails, plotted the link lines to the demons and removed the linkage that held their blood vessels together. It was perfect. But when I did it again in just the same way, there was some form of surge within me and although the casting began, I had to shut down but I wasn't ever in complete control of that decision. It was like my body sensed the danger before my mind did. What happened? Why can't I repeat? I have to be able to repeat, it's all we have.

Erienne felt her anxiety rising and the One power bore down on her. As ever she fought the entity, imagining it was a spider whose legs she had to pry from her mind to stop them crushing her. Abruptly, the pressure eased and Cleress's presence pushed the power aside.

Calm, Erienne. It knows your fear and it feeds off it. Remember what we showed you.

It's so hard, Cleress. I'm so tired.

I know. But listen to me. You pose so many questions yet the answers are there before you. I am proud of the casting you made. It shows true understanding of the potential of the One and demonstrated your control over the entity.

But—

Please, let me finish. You are the one who always felt the entity had more sentience than it actually possesses in reality. It was we who explained to you that it is your mind that gives it this virtual life. What you imagine, it can become. That is why you need to control your mind so closely when you release the power.

You're saying I caused the problem with the second casting?

We have all of us done the same. You crossed a waypoint in your understanding though I know it feels like failure to you at the moment. What you realise is that it is as we have always said. Casting with the One is essentially very simple but it is the feeding of power that is the complex part of the equation. I would stake my life that all you did the second time around was relax just that iota, as if you couldn't quite believe how easy it was.

Erienne thought to reply but Cleress wasn't finished.

Think before you respond. Recall what went through your mind as you prepared the second casting and saw how easily it all slotted into place. Examine your process. If at any moment you felt that it was too easy, that would have been enough. That would have relaxed the muscles of your mind to let the wrong gauge of power out. The One became what you imagined, just that little bit slack. And in a One casting, that can spell disaster.

She was right. She was absolutely dead right.

So what should I do? Next time there may not be a sanctuary.

You do nothing but believe in yourself, as I'm sure your friends have been telling you all along. The good part of this is that your body is now so attuned to the power flow within you that if it detects a flaw, it will close off. And it won't always leave you unconscious, either.

I'm just so scared of failing.

Then don't. You are equipped with all you need to know. You do trust me, don't you, Erienne?

Yes.

Good. Then trust what I say. Believe what I say. You must not doubt yourself. Focus on all the castings you have made that have been perfect. They far outweigh those which were not. Remember the tautness of your concentration.

It all sounds so straightforward when you say it, Cleress. But when I open my eyes, what will I find, I wonder?

Remember you are everything you think you can be. You are the One mage.

I am when you are with me.

Cleress laughed but it was a tired sound. *You don't need my strength. You have a surfeit of your own.*

If only I knew where to find it.

You know where it lies, child.

And you must be tired, old woman.

I am. So if you will excuse me I will rest. Bring yourself round. Gain from the contact of The Raven. You are each other's best chance.

Thank you, Cleress.

Sharyr knew he was screaming but he had no desire to stop. He thought perhaps Brynel and Suarav were doing the same and if they weren't, they ought to be. They were moving as one, he leading, shouting commands between his screams and keeping them simple. One thing he couldn't afford was for he and Brynel to pull in opposite directions. It would leave Suarav a dead man.

"Left!"

And they flew left, feeling the wind as a pack of strike-strain missed them to the right. They turned back in toward the shell. The sky lit up with a Julatsan barrage. Sharyr exulted. What a sight.

"Straight in. Trim those wings, Brynel."

The mages adjusted their wings for raw speed and immediately began to lose height, Suarav's weight dragging them down. Sharyr heard Suarav shout in shock as the speed struck them. This was a final approach. They wouldn't get another chance. In front of them, the wagons had started to move but there were those who had detached and were heading toward the edge of the shell where they were aiming to break through.

Their way was blocked by strike-strain and reavers, floating in the air ahead of them. Sharyr looked briefly below. They were no more than twenty feet in the air now and still sinking. They had nowhere to go.

"Hold course, Brynel. Close your eyes and let's pray."

He felt a strange exhilaration. This was the defining moment of his life. For once he had been in control of his own destiny, and had chosen this path. He recalled being browbeaten by Dystran, he recalled his protestations and how he could never hope to have his voice heard. Not this time. So he didn't pray. He bellowed his rebellion.

"Hang on, Suarav. Enjoy the ride."

They collided with the strike-strain. Sharyr felt the small creatures buffeting him. He put his head down and let it happen. Bodies hurtled into his head, midriff and legs. He felt the drag on his waist when Suarav was struck and just one huge impact that could only be a reaver.

And then he was falling.

He opened his eyes. They were inside the shell and the Wings had dispersed on the instant. The ground rushed toward them. They were travelling so fast. Too fast surely. Then they were all bouncing over the ground. Every impact was a new pain. He felt hard earth on his backside and the sharpness of wood or rock in his gut. He tasted dirt in his mouth and cried out when his shoulder jerked uncomfortably under him as he slid to a stop.

"Oh dear Gods, I'm still alive." And he began to laugh.

Hands were about him and he could see faces. Voices questioned him, heavily accented. They were elves of the Al-Arynaar. He had heard about them.

"Are you hurt? Can you stand? We have to move now."

He didn't know the answers. He moved to stand and pain lanced through his back. He winced. The arms helped him slowly to his feet. He looked about him. Suarav was still on the ground but shaking his head, and moving freely. Brynel was smiling and gasping at the same time, a difficult combination.

Sharyr became aware of the sounds in the shell. The calls of demons and the cries of men and elves. The rattle of wagons, the hoofbeats and the fighting in every quarter.

"The cursyrd attack. We must move."

"Yes," he said. "Yes."

They started to move. Demons flew down on their heads. Tiny strike-strain nipping at their scalps and ears. He flapped his arms ineffectually. The elves hurried them along.

"They cannot really hurt you," said the elf running beside him. "Why are you here?"

"I need to speak to the man . . . the elf in charge. You need to know about the streets of Xetesk."

"I will take you to Rebraal."

Sharyr had never heard of him but the reverence in the elf's voice was enough.

"He sounds perfect."

The elf didn't answer him.

Behind them the wagons were rolling under attack from the skies above. Auum led his Tai through scorched grass and smouldering flesh. The cursyrd line had broken but it was re-forming quickly. They, the Al-Arynaar and The Raven had to keep the cursyrd on the back foot. If the karron should reform in any great numbers, the mages' work would be undone.

Working within the compass of the ColdRoom shell, Auum tore into the attack, operating with twin short swords. Duele and Evunn were on either flank.

"Target the karron. Tai, we strike."

The karron were identically formed, unlike their reaver brethren. The fine hair he had seen from a distance was in fact a writhing, coarse sensory mat. The eyes were small and dim, perhaps only able to tell the difference between light and dark. The squat creature's raw power lay in its trunk and arms. And these latter swung with surprising swiftness, defying its lumbering gait.

Auum ducked a swinging spike limb and lashed his blades into karron legs. He stepped smartly aside, a hammer thumping the ground where he had been standing. He pulled back, reassessing the creature's speed. It came at him, arms punching and swinging. A bludgeoning tactic but directionless. Auum swayed left, took a pace and lashed in a kick to the side of its head. It grunted and shook its head to clear its senses but Auum was already upon it. He stepped inside its arms and buried both blades in its face.

The karron wailed and collapsed forward. Auum dropped and rolled backward, bouncing back onto his feet. Beside him, Duele and Evunn tackled three that worked in unison.

"Feel the dance, my brothers," said Auum.

Behind him The Raven crashed into the fight. Auum dodged another battering attack and struck out, carving his blades into the club arm and seeing grey gore spurt out of the deep wounds. He moved to deal the killing strike but Hirad got there first. The barbarian's sword sunk deep into the karron's midriff, driving it backward.

"Let's keep these bastards going our way!" shouted Hirad.

He dragged his sword clear, grinned at Auum and ran to join The Unknown Warrior. Auum cleared his throat and stepped in to aid his Tai. He breathed deep and achieved the pure state. The karron could not move fast enough to threaten him. He looked into their small eyes, buried deep under heavy brows, and watched the movement of the mat of hair. The limbs followed the sensing of its targets but it could not hope to lay a blow on the TaiGethen.

Auum needed quick kills. He rolled under the arms of his target and hammered his blades into its chest. He stepped right, jumping high and thudding both feet into the face of the next, landing on its stomach as it crashed onto its back. He tore out its throat with a double slash. A club fist whistled toward him. Still too slow. He jumped over it, turned in the air and straight-kicked the assailant. He dropped low, swept its legs from beneath it and jammed his blades high under its left arm. It spasmed and lay still.

He rose to his feet. Duele and Evunn were next to him. The Al-Arynaar and The Raven were deep in the fighting, driving a wedge for the wagons that trundled along behind. Auum felt a burning inside him and realised it was pure pleasure. It was not an emotion he associated with consigning his enemies to Shorth but he was prepared to enjoy it.

He smiled.

"Tai," he said. "As one. We move."

You could only stand and admire. It all but cost Hirad his life. He had dragged his sword through the ribs of one of the ugly haired demons and watched the creature bleed to death at his feet when he felt a moment of space. It was then he had seen Auum's Tai go to work and had known that for all that he had learned in their company back on Calaius, he would never come close to their ability.

He almost felt sorry for the demons they faced. After all, he couldn't follow every move they made himself. And they were so much in concert that it left no room for inroads into their attack or defence despite the fact that reavers had joined the fight against them.

Auum led them in a ferocious assault dead ahead of the wagons' path. His swords glittered in the early morning sun. Each strike left a trail of blood in its wake. The clumsy karron tried to batter at him but he drove on relentlessly, his blades biting into neck, chest and under the arms where he could deal the fastest death blow. And his accuracy was matched by the mesmeric moves of his Tai in his defence.

Each elf carried a single short sword at his outer flank which he used to slice into karron flesh at every opportunity. But the main focus was inside and up. Every strike by a karron was parried or countered. Every dive by a reaver met with a kick or a fist, sweeping high over Auum's head. Demons shrieked in frustration or spun away half senseless. The Tai's focus never wavered. Their understanding of each other was total. It was what The Raven had striven for all their years of fighting. They thought they had achieved it. They weren't even close.

It was a dance that the Tai wove and those who didn't know the steps had no chance of survival.

Hirad staggered under the force of a blow to his stomach. He looked down to see a severed hammer limb strike the ground.

"Gods' sake Hirad, watch yourself." The Unknown backhanded his blade into the face of the same karron and limped a pace to his next target. "Fight or leave."

Hirad broke his reverie. The Raven were fighting close to the Tai. The karron were quick but not quick enough. Denser, blade in hand, was watching their backs from attacks by reavers. The Unknown and Darrick ploughed a furrow straight ahead. Furious with himself, Hirad dived back into the action. A club fist came at him. He blocked it away with his blade, feeling the strength of the strike. Quickly, he switched his blade to his left hand and lashed out at the creature's head, bursting one of the eyes on the side of its skull. It howled and fell back. Hirad pounced after it, slicing through the tendons at the back of its legs. It collapsed and he finished it through the chest.

"That's more like it," said The Unknown.

"You know it," said Hirad.

He stretched to deflect a blow aimed at the big man and felt the stitching on his hip give way and blood flow. The pain pounded through him and he swayed. The karron's next strike battered into The Unknown's defence, knocking him into Darrick who stumbled sideways, just avoiding the arm of another enemy.

Hirad dragged himself forward and punctured the karron's side. Grey splashed onto his armour.

"Don't even think about it."

The Unknown had recovered and unleashed a huge strike left to right, decapitating the karron. The line was almost broken. Reavers flew down to bolster it but the strike-strain were flitting away. Hirad felt a new energy and ran forward, trying to ignore the tear on his hip.

A shout from behind slowed him and he looked back. The wagons were with them now. The Al-Arynaar flanking the cart horses moved with purpose, using their numbers as a battering ram, and the Julatsan wagon train burst through the demon line and aimed for the sundered north gate of Xetesk.

CHAPTER 34

The demons had come back in force and they'd brought some new friends with them. His teams falling back into the sanctuary of the college had reported the karron disappearing into all quarters of the city. It was too late to tell the Julatsans but they, it seemed, were making good headway.

Dystran stood on the balcony of his tower as he had so often during the past two years and experienced another new hope. That both Wesmen and Julatsans would be flooding his courtyard before noon. Gods, how alien it was but how natural it felt to wish it.

Looking north, he could see the cloud of dust that signalled the Julatsan approach to the city. South, another showed the Wesmen advance. The latter's was under minimal pressure. The demons clearly didn't consider them a threat. Dystran prayed fervently that Tessaya would demonstrate to them otherwise.

Everything was set in the college. Every man, woman and child knew their task when the order was given. Dystran couldn't cloak the excitement he felt. Something had run through the college when it was sure that the Julatsans were coming this way. It gave them all new life and new hope for whatever spurious reasons. This didn't feel like resistance; more like rebellion.

Where would it go wrong, that was the question. He couldn't fault the ward grid. It was something of which Septern himself would have been proud. All it needed was activation and it was he that would take that task. Chandyr's strike and fall-back plans were sound, he knew that. The commander was a skilful tactician and had studied General Darrick for many years.

But he couldn't shake the nagging feeling that the demons were still a step ahead. What was it they had missed? There had to be something. There was always something.

Hirad's wound had been rebound but he had conceded he should travel on the kicking plate of Erienne's wagon, driven once more by Darrick. Thraun still rode inside. The rest of The Raven were out front and just behind the Al-Arynaar line, keeping the path clear.

The success of Darrick's tactic seemed to have confused and demoralised the demons. Half-hearted regroupings of karron had been battered mercilessly aside by the TaiGethen-led elven force. The lumbering demons appeared badly hampered fighting inside the ColdRoom shell.

It had been left to the reavers and strike-strain to continue their sniping attacks. And while they scored small victories, they couldn't slow the advancing wagon train which was crossing the old battlefields in front of the north gate. It was a curious atmosphere dominating the demon forces. Hirad likened it to defeat and he told Darrick so.

"Don't believe it. They'll look to pin us down in some narrow street in the city," said Darrick.

"Well, we have surprises for them in there too, don't we?" said Hirad.

"And it's all main street," said Denser, hauling himself up to the bench. "We can drive two abreast all the way to the college."

"Simple enough," said Hirad.

The General shook his head. "I doubt that very much."

It was less than a mile to the college from the north gate. Hirad had travelled in Xetesk enough to know that even the widest of its streets felt tight. Tall and ancient buildings loomed over the equally aged cobbles and stone pathways, blotting out half the sky. Every street in Xetesk had the potential for ambush. The recently arrived Xeteskians needed to be right about their ward work.

They had seen flights of demons heading back toward Xetesk, giving credence to Darrick's observation. The General's initial delight at the outcome of his snap tactic had quickly given way to introspection and now he wore a troubled expression.

"Come on, Darrick," said Hirad. "We've broken them. What's the problem?"

"You know it was too easy, don't you?" he replied.

"I know we gave them a good hiding."

Darrick shook his head a second time. "They were inept in the extreme and I don't buy it. They planned to fail."

"Hardly. From where I stand they didn't expect us to drop the ColdRoom and we took them down."

"Maybe they didn't but after that, that's what worries me. They didn't attempt a concerted reformation, they didn't bring up reserves from the rear of the shell. They practically stood there and let us slaughter them. How many did we lose? Five? Ten?"

"I think you worry too much," said Hirad.

"Do I?" Darrick turned his head to stare at the barbarian. "Think it's plain sailing from here on in, don't you?"

Hirad raised his eyebrows. "So long as Xetesk lends the hand it has promised. I mean, look at the enemy. They aren't up for this, none of them."

"Right. And that's what most of the elves think to look at them. Don't let your guard slip for one moment. I'm telling Rebraal the same thing."

Hirad swallowed his retort. "You really mean it, don't you?"

"I wouldn't say it otherwise. The demons are not this lame. They're in charge here, never mind what just happened. It is inconceivable that we've broken them."

"If you say so, General."

"I do."

Hirad chuckled. "Lucky we didn't have you join us for your sense of humour."

"I see nothing to laugh about."

"Exactly."

An hour later and barely under attack at all, the Julatsan wagon train rolled through the north gate of Xetesk. The imposing gatehouse edifice, sorely damaged though it was, was the first of many ideal ambush points. Nothing.

"Still sure, General?"

"Don't tempt fate, Hirad. They only need one place, one chance. Keep looking."

The instant they cleared the gatehouse, the atmosphere changed. The cold intensified. Breath clouded in front of faces, and with no breeze to disperse it, hung in a cloud around the train. The city stank with the scent of fear, death and decay. The quiet set Hirad's teeth on edge. Not even a demon made a sound. Nothing came from the buildings around them, the streets that ran away into the city or from the college. Not a bird sang or a dog barked. All Hirad could hear was the creaking of the carts, his own breath and the sounds of hoof on stone.

Turning into Norgate Road, the buildings seemed to climb so high into the cold blue sky. Bleak timbers and shuttered windows glowered down on them. Unconsciously, the pace slowed.

"Keep it up ahead," said Darrick, voice unnaturally loud.

"Can you feel it?" said Hirad.

"It's why we're all whispering," said Denser. He shuddered.

"Watch for any movement," hissed Darrick. "Rebraal, put the word out. Concentrate."

The demons had gone from the sky. Not a one tracked their progress. The empty shell above them was almost unnerving after so long under attack. On the second wagon of the lead pair the Xeteskians, Suarav and Sharyr, his arm in a makeshift sling, were indicating ward positions. They were pointing ahead at the first crossroads which the train would traverse on its way to the playhouse. That building stood in the middle of the tight Seamstone Square. Once on the square, they would be at their most vulnerable.

Approaching the crossway, Hirad could feel his heart thumping in his chest. He readjusted his sword grip constantly, wiping sweating hands down his trousers. Every hoof fall was a clarion call for a demon rally. Every nervous whinny or snort an invitation to attack. But still no demons. Darrick's frown deepened still further.

"Where would I do it?" he muttered. "Where?"

His voice was the only one puncturing the edgy quiet. More than three hundred elves and men travelled the dead streets. Hirad felt his earlier bravado draining away.

"Just one place, you think?"

Darrick nodded. "And with everything they have got."

Hirad swallowed on a dry throat. The Al-Arynaar at the head had just entered the junction. To either side, FlameWalls, deep and scorching, sprang up, fifty feet and more high. Drivers fought with suddenly panicked horses. Shouts of alarm rang out in the enclosed space. Hirad swore. He could feel the heat on his face.

"Scared me half to death," he said.

On the adjacent wagon, Sharyr managed a smile.

"They got the wards out further than I thought. That's good."

"Would have been nice to have a little more warning."

"Hmm." Darrick shrugged then raised his voice, scanning about him to check all horses were back under control. "Let's keep this tight. Maintain your pace, maintain your focus. Do not give those bastards opportunity."

Hirad could see the response to the voice of authority. Postures straightened, calls of encouragement bounced around. Swords and axes were gripped with more belief, back to the ready position. The trotting of feet and hoof took on a military rhythm.

"That's more like it," breathed Darrick. "Nothing like a little purpose."

The wagon train drove on up Norgate Way. The detritus of two years' neglect lay underfoot. The collected filth of decay powerful in the nostrils. At the playhouse, they turned right in response to Sharyr's promptings and the FlameWalls burning to the left, obscuring that part of Seamstone Square.

The playhouse was a circular structure with entrances at the four major points of the compass. Around its edge, the square was packed with darkened eateries, inns, shops still displaying gaudy clothes, all topped by two or three storeys of rooms and lodgings.

The sound of their passage was amplified here, echoes reverberating across the enclosed space. It was a sobering counterpart to the silence covering the city. The gargoyles and carved faces gazed down at them, laughing, crying, enraged, desolate. Monitoring the passing of the last desperate attempt to wrest control of Balaia from their nemesis.

Hirad bit his lip. The quiet was picking at their nerves and courage. Every doorway, every window could conceal an enemy. The sky could fill at any moment. There was no safety among the buildings that had once provided security for so many.

"Where are the Xeteskians?" he said, unable to speak at more than a whisper.

"Out of the way," said Denser.

The train turned left and right to exit the square and start along King's Approach. Nicknamed "The Thread," the street wound its way to the heart of the city. They could see lights burning in Dystran's tower in the college, beacons still almost half a mile distant.

Alleys and side streets ran off The Thread all along its length. Some were barely the width of a man. Others as wide as a wagon. All were silent, all deserted.

A short distance further on, The Thread narrowed and twisted around the rear of the central grain store. The Al-Arynaar vanguard closed form. The Unknown, Ark and Kas dropped back and hitched rides on the sides of Erienne's wagon. Hirad noticed Sharyr look behind him and curse.

"Problem?" asked Darrick, noting it too.

"The wards should have triggered behind," he said. "Something's dropped out."

"Or been interfered with," said Hirad.

"Unlikely," said Sharyr. "We—"

The rear of the grain store burst out onto the street, engulfing Sharyr's wagon. The noise, a crack like thunder followed by the bass rumble of an avalanche, pressed on the ears, juddered through their bodies. Huge blocks of stone smashed into the wagon's flimsy side, crushing the roof frame, battering into the horse and its driver. The two helpless Xeteskians were thrown aside. The wagon was driven sideways across the cobbles. The axles collapsed under the pressure and the splintering mass collided with The Raven's wagon in a squeal of torn metal. Standing on its left sideboard, Kas took the full force of the impact. Darrick, Hirad and Denser were jerked violently left and then away, tumbling onto the ground and into the traces and horses.

Now the air was full of screams and the sudden roar of demon cacophony. Hirad scrambled to his feet and grabbed his sword from the ground, trying to take it all in. He skipped out of the way of the horses which were bucking and trying to drag their wagon forward, though its wheels were blocked by fallen stone.

There could be no survivors inside the other lead wagon. Suarav and Sharyr were getting to their feet but they were all there was moving. Karron were streaming out of the shattered grain store. Ahead, the Al-Arynaar and Auum's Tai were already engaged in fierce fighting and half cut off from the wagon train. They weren't making any real headway. It was obvious why. The crushed wagon had been carrying ColdRoom mages. The demons were protected.

The situation was quickly becoming desperate. Al-Arynaar had rushed to stem the advance of karron from the grain store but were outnumbered and fragmented. An alert group of elven mages was crouched in the open, casting, but above them winged demons were heading into the attack.

"Darrick, Denser. Up, up. Wall side, now." Hirad led them, coming across a groggy Unknown Warrior being helped to his feet by Ark. "We've got to get Erienne away. They'll want her."

The storm of demons thickened, strike-strain barrelling down on them. Hirad led The Raven to the rear of the wagon. Thraun appeared with Erienne in his arms, blood streaming down the side of his head.

"Get her back inside the ColdRoom shell. Run, Thraun, we're right behind you," ordered Hirad.

The first strike-strain were on them, reavers closing in.

"We need to get Kas," said Hirad.

"You cannot help him," said Ark. "He is released."

The Raven ran hard. Hirad came to The Unknown's left to help Ark. Demons flew around them, reavers landing in front and stalking into the attack.

"Go," said The Unknown, his head running with blood, voice a little slurred.

Hirad nodded and ran on, streaking round Thraun's left, Darrick mirroring him right. Both men sheathed their swords but while Darrick drew his mace, Hirad had another idea. There were too many of the reavers for them to take quickly. Al-Arynaar were flooding in to help but weren't going to be fast enough.

Dagger in hand, the barbarian barrelled straight into the clutch of reavers, taking three of them to the ground with him. He landed on top of them, hearing Darrick join the attack and Thraun shout a warning.

The reavers were strong. Hirad took a punch across his face that knocked him half away. He felt hands scrabbling to get purchase under his chin and over his heart, searching for his soul. He blocked a clawed hand and jabbed his fingers into the eyes of the demon struggling to rise from beneath him. The creature howled. Hirad's next thrust took the creature under the arm. It spasmed and was still. Another pushed him away. Thraun ran by.

"Keep going!" shouted Hirad.

A hand clamped around the top of his head and jerked him backward.

He fell onto his back, fists flailing out to either side. His vision was full of demon flesh. There was a flash of steel. One of his assailants was flung aside. He turned onto his stomach and pushed himself to his haunches. Ark stood above him, The Unknown on one arm, his mace in his other hand.

"Down," he said. Hirad ducked his head and the mace swept by again. There was a squeal. "Go."

Hirad came back to The Unknown's side. "Not without him. Come on."

They set off again, Darrick taking up station ahead of them and Denser, a ForceCone directed ahead, clearing a path. Al-Arynaar had surrounded Thraun and were shepherding him back down the train. Demons were flying in all along The Thread now, attacking those within the still-functioning shell. Behind, the fighting was intense. Elves falling back in control. But the way ahead was blocked. The two ruined carts and tons of stone were strewn across the way. Just back inside the shell, Hirad took the time to look hard. He dragged strike-strain from his back as he did so, crushing their bodies in his fists or underfoot.

The two surviving Xeteskians ran past him. He could still make out Auum, leading the Al-Arynaar. There was a huge density of the squat karron in between the TaiGethen and the remainder of the train. He would survive, he always did. And the train had troubles of its own. Under heavy attack from above, there were still efforts to turn it around but in the tight space and with frightened horses it was proving almost impossible.

Thraun, with Erienne crushed close to him, was heading toward the nearest wagon. Denser was by his side. Darrick had run further down the train to oversee the turning of the wagons. The Unknown, coming to his senses, pushed Hirad away.

"I'm all right."

"You're as bad a judge as me."

"What's the situation?" asked the big man.

"Auum's cut off but he's all right so far. Darrick's back there. We have to turn this train around, get out of the east end of the playhouse square. The rest of us are here but Kas has gone. I haven't seen Eilaan or Rebraal. We're in trouble."

"Very astute," said The Unknown, smiling through the blood slicking his face.

They paused. Al-Arynaar ran around them. Reavers were beaten back while The Raven headed for relative safety. And Hirad heard a voice that gladdened him. Strong, authoritative, elven.

"Let's get those wagons turned!" shouted Rebraal. "Move, Al-Arynaar. Yniss protects us."

Wagons began to move with more purpose, elves and humans goading terrified horses into action. Hirad could see Darrick directing those turning the rear wagons. The General's mouth was moving but he couldn't hear him over the din around them. But whatever he was saying it was generating instant organisation. He smiled and grabbed Denser's arm.

"Look at Darrick. Can't really stop being a commander, can he? I—"

At the back of the line, buildings were burst from the inside left and right. Rubble flew in a storm, tattering the rear wagons, destroying them both and collapsing the rear ColdRoom. Demons poured into the street and from above, driving their advantage home while the Al-Arynaar struggled to regroup. The sound of the collapse slapped into their faces, drained their spirits.

Hirad stared, mouth hanging open, his sentence never to be finished. Darrick was gone, buried under the deluge of rock. Gone. For an instant he thought he saw the General through the dust, struggling to rise, but it could only have been the demons storming into the attack, a trick to torment him.

"Darrick. NO!"

Hirad started to run but Denser got in front of him.

"Hirad, stop."

"Out of my way, Denser. Darrick's down there."

"He's gone, Hirad, you know what you saw."

"I saw the building fall, I saw the demons come out. Get out of my way."

"Hirad, he's dead. And if we don't do something very quickly, we'll be joining him. Please."

Hirad looked into Denser's eyes, saw the tears forming there, the desperation for Hirad to understand, to accept. Biting back his anger, he nodded his head.

Around them demons shrieked their delight. Karron roared and pressed their attacks harder. He could hear Rebraal bawling orders. Elves and the few surviving men outside of The Raven fell back toward the centre of the train from both sides. Strike-strain rained in on the closing space. He looked to The Unknown who was wiping blood from his face and looking left and right, disbelief in his eyes.

Darrick was dead. The wagon train was stopped for good. They were trapped.

CHAPTER 35

Seeing the broken bodies of Al-Arynaar, Xeteskians and the Protector Kas, Auum had time for a whispered prayer while he led his Tai into the fight against the karron.

"Tai, as one."

Al-Arynaar were streaming in, arranging themselves around the flanks of the TaiGethen cell. The karron were being hampered by the rubble they had created. The TaiGethen, born to the treacherous surfaces and obstacles of the rain forest, had no such problems.

Auum hurdled a block of stone, ducked a support strut and launched himself into his first enemy. He landed both feet on the creature's chest, driving it onto its back and into the massed ranks behind it.

His balance sure, Auum stepped right, pivoted and lashed a roundhouse kick into the next, knocking it sideways and buying him all the space he needed. Evunn followed up his attack, sliding into the arm of the first downed karron, dragging it away from its body. Duele, sweat beading on his brow, dealt the killing blow. Neither elf stopped moving, coming fluidly to their feet and pouncing on their next victim. Auum didn't need to look to know they were with him. He heard the touch of their feet and the power of their strikes. And he heard the cursyrd die.

He rose in front of a karron, breathing hard, feeling the exertion and seeing the tide of enemy still before them. The creature grunted and swung both arms inward. Auum blocked right and left, feeling the shudder through his body. He locked eyes with the lesser cursyrd and saw its incomprehension of his strength. He butted its eyes. It squealed, arms rising. Duele's knife snapped in.

Auum stepped left and glanced right. He flat-palmed a karron in the chest, pushing the creature out of his way. His Tai ran around his flanks, knives catching the morning sunlight. The karron was stretched and killed.

But while the Tai fought going forward, the Al-Arynaar were being forced back. More karron were pouring into the line, hammers and spikes whirling. The squat creatures had no care for their own and no coordinated attack pattern. Each called its own guttural squawk while it bludgeoned its way forward, desperate to feel elven flesh under its weapons. Auum saw a press forming behind.

"Break!"

His Tai danced back into the space they had created. Behind them, Al-Arynaar mages had deployed ForceCones to keep the winged cursyrd busy.

The karron surged out of the shattered grain store. Auum saw creatures batter each other in their haste. Deep-coloured blood sprayed into the air. To the right, the elves hadn't retreated quickly enough. The wave of karron beat into them. A spiked arm drove left, catching a warrior in the side of the head. The karron squawked its pleasure. The elven body was tossed aside. Hammers fell fast and dense. Auum poised to strike back, identifying targets.

"Hold!" he called. "Let Tual guide your hands."

But down the train, the winged cursyrd were flooding the street. There was precious little movement from the remaining wagons. Auum had to buy more time but the karron were strong and determined. Not enough mages could be brought to bear to break the line without allowing the reavers to attack their rear. The warriors had no choice but to stand.

The right side of the elven line fractured. Karron trampled elves underfoot, crushing skulls and bodies with hammer limbs, splitting flesh with spikes. The Al-Arynaar responded and closed the line but seven karron were through, threatening the thinly guarded mage defence.

"Tai, we move."

Auum slammed the heel of his palm into the chest of an advancing karron and turned to run at the loose enemy. He didn't take a single pace toward them. In the line beside them, an elf missed his strike. The spiked arm of a karron swung, splintering his skull. The dead elf was flung back and sideways, colliding with Duele. The TaiGethen half fended the body away but stumbled to his knees on slick cobbles. The karron stepped through and struck its hammer limb into the elf's chest.

"No!" Auum saw Duele flung across the street and was already on the move to his side. Evunn swept the karron's legs from under it and delivered a blistering attack to the creature's body. Its squawk of triumph clotting in its throat, Evunn's short blade buried in its armpit.

Auum reached Duele just as the Al-Arynaar line collapsed. To the right, mages were attacked, ForceCones dispersing. Winged cursyrd stormed into the space, cutting them off from the wagon train. He had no time to care. He scooped his Tai into his arms. Blood ran from Duele's mouth but he was still breathing.

"Yniss protect you, my friend," he whispered, his limbs shaking. He raised his head and voice. "Break. Run for the college."

And with the pounding of the karron vibrating cobbles underfoot and the shrieks of winged cursyrd loud in his ears, Auum led his people in a desperate run for sanctuary.

There was a single explosion to mark Darrick's death, a Xeteskian ward triggered way too late to stop the carnage. A handful of karron were caught in its blast and tongues of flame brought demons down from the sky but it didn't stop their advance.

Karron smashed the shattered wagons and allied bodies aside, driving up The Thread toward the one remaining ColdRoom casting. The sky darkened with strike-strain and reavers, their chittering and taunting reverberating from the blank faces of the buildings. Al-Arynaar rushed to form a fighting line within the ColdRoom but the tide was going to sweep them away.

"We've got to get to cover," roared The Unknown into the tumult. "Denser, I need an option."

Denser was ahead of him. He indicated a narrow alley ahead and right. "The playhouse. It's our only chance for this many people."

"What'll it do for us?"

"Buy us time. Here, we're all dead."

He was right. The back of the train was lost completely. Demons were diving into the shell, karron battering into defenders on the ground. Hirad turned to the head of the column in time to see the Al-Arynaar line fold.

"Fuck." He ran to Rebraal and grabbed his shoulders, his own limbs quivering with rage. "I want ForceCone mages down that passage now. We're heading for the playhouse. Disengage your forward line. Do it now. Don't let those bastards get anyone else."

Rebraal nodded and began barking commands. Hirad swung back to The Raven.

"Thraun, behind me with Denser. Ark, don't drop the big man. Look out for Pheone and the Xeteskians. Rebraal, it's now. Raven! Raven with me!"

Rebraal had been quick and his mages accurate. Three strode down the passageway, warriors at their backs. Hirad went after them, hearing The Raven in his wake. In The Thread, the bodies of man, elf and demon littered the ground. A Raven was amongst them. The four remaining wagons emptied and the last ColdRoom dispersed. The demons surged, pushing the routed Balaians before them. The tight entrance to the passage was quickly becoming a bottleneck.

"Dammit." Hirad broke into a run and shouted ahead in elvish. "Too slow. Drop the Cones and let's move."

It became a headlong dash, mirroring that led by Auum to the gates of the college. Strike-strain fell about their heads, nipping, biting and scratching. No sooner had he pulled one away from himself or Thraun beside him than three more cackled and attacked. Others threatened Erienne. Thraun ignored his own pain to keep her as safe as he could. Hirad could hear the sounds of karron in the buildings either side of the narrow alley, running through thin walls, trying to get in front.

"Left ahead!" shouted Denser.

Hirad relayed the message forward. A few yards behind The Raven, karron beat a wall into the passage, spilling out after it. He risked a glance and saw elves driving through the sudden barricade, kicking, punching and butting. There wasn't time for artistry and the only saving grace for the runners was that the alley was too narrow for all but the smallest reavers.

The leading elves turned the corner flat out. Hirad and Thraun were falling back a little. Hirad could see light that indicated Seamstone Square and the playhouse. It flickered like the light above them. The sky was filled with demons.

Hirad chewed his lip. In the square, the enemy would be waiting. They needed spell cover but the incessant picking of strike-strain and the force of numbers running through the alley wouldn't give mages much opportunity to cast.

"We need a safe corridor," he said, panting a little. "Mages, get the nearest door open. Swords and maces left and right. Pass the message back. Thraun, stay in the passage. You too, Unknown."

"Forget it."

They reached the square. The nearest playhouse door stood less than ten yards across the open street. Reavers crowded the entrance. Hirad heard prayers and the Al-Arynaar went to work. Unable to kill without using Auum's move, the elves chose containment for the moment and all used blade and fist to quickly force a small space. Hirad ran into the centre of it.

"Let's go, Raven!"

In front of Hirad, an Al-Arynaar backhanded his blade into the chest of a reaver. It skittered backward, squealing. The elf moved left allowing Hirad in. He accepted, powering his mace through in an upward arc, connecting with his enemy's face and following through. The demon's head snapped back and it staggered into those behind it.

"Pressing!" yelled Hirad and then Rebraal and The Unknown were beside him.

The elf's mace pushed end on into the gut of his enemy. The Unknown's carved left to right, clattering his aside in a flurry of claw and wing. Ark led more Al-Arynaar from the passageway, strengthening the breakout and driving further across the street. The demons, surprised at the ferocity and organisation of this attack sprung from the ashes of a rout, struggled to maintain any cohesion.

Strike-strain descended. Hard to ignore, their claws like sharp frost, they flittered over the heads of elves and men, trying to get into their faces where they could be most effective.

His mace in his right hand, Hirad ducked a claw to his face and whipped in a blow of his own, seeing the spikes rip into flesh and drive the demon back. Strike-strain locked onto the back of his head, scuttling forward. He grabbed at one with his free hand and jerked it clear and flung it away, feeling blood begin to trickle from his scalp.

His limbs felt leaden. He roared to clear his mind and wiped a hand across his sweating face. He had to keep going, had to drive them all. He knew his arms were fatigued and his back sent pain through his body with every pace, every blow. They had no choice but to push on. Blocking aside another blow, he took a pace into the shadow of the playhouse. Their goal was only three yards away. He heard the dull rumble of falling stone and the crack of shattering masonry topped by the exultant squawks of demons. The karron had reached the square.

"What the fuck is going on!" bawled Dystran at his mages and Chandyr, ranged around his balcony.

Demons were clouding in two areas of the city. He watched them dive into the attack and soar high, cackling. He could hear fighting and screaming. Men's voices sounded out when the demon cacophony lulled. Dust clouded the air in the direction of the playhouse.

"The ward grid has failed," said Chandyr.

"Oh, do you think so?" Dystran rounded on his commander. "And do you also have in that incisive mind of yours the memory of my request for a contingency?"

"You know I do, my Lord." Chandyr's face was unreadable.

"Care to enlighten me, my esteemed commander?"

Chandyr nodded. "Prexys, would you be so kind?"

The old Circle Seven mage closed his eyes briefly. "He is coming," he said.

"Well he'd better be quick," said Dystran. "Our new friends are getting slaughtered."

From the centre of the city, one shape detached itself from the mass and sped back toward the college. The familiar, one of only three that still remained at the college, landed lightly on Prexys's shoulder.

"Master," it said, drooling slightly, its chest heaving in and out.

"You know it occurs to me that we should have persuaded these things to leave the college earlier. They'd have made useful spies."

Prexys calmed his tired familiar. "It is risky enough now," he said. "And enemy attention is diverted from us. Speak. Tell us what you saw."

And the familiar related everything. The attacks on two fronts. The elves approaching at speed and the larger group trying to get into the playhouse. The lack of any real watch on the college and the breaking of the ward grid. It was enough for Chandyr.

"We can get the elves inside," he asserted. "We can also trigger the rest of the wards but they'll all go up at the same time."

Dystran looked heavenward. "Yes, I mean there are a few buildings that haven't been damaged yet. And how do you propose to get the elves in?"

"Well," said Chandyr. "I don't want to bore you with the fine detail but in essence, we open the gates and rush the demons. There's more to it than that. I mean, every mage knows position and casting for a run up The Thread. It was always the most likely route into us. It'll work."

"It had better."

"It will."

"And another thing," said Dystran. "Will somebody please tell me what in all the hells has happened to our other new friends the Wesmen?"

Auum knew every approach to the college of Xetesk but he felt lost for the first time in his life. Duele was dying in his arms. Every pace he took seemed heavy, referring vibrations through his stricken Tai's body. He held on as gently as he could but surely his arms were like bindings, constricting more and more. His very breath crushed his friend and all his prayers would not be enough.

It was Evunn who retained his purpose and direction and would lead them all to safety. They ran at the head of around fifty Al-Arynaar warriors and mages. The karron would not catch them and many of the strike-strain had chased after The Raven. But enough reavers remained in the sky to threaten them. He could hear them above, harrying him, and he could see them in front, landing and challenging, aware of the relative vulnerability of their quarry.

Evunn was an elf possessed of a focused rage. He led a dozen Al-Arynaar hard at the reavers, snapping out orders and signalling positions. Auum ran in behind the crescent that formed, defended on both flanks and to the rear by more of the elven elite. His Tai did not break his stride under the torrent of taunts and the confusion of wings and cursyrd bodies advancing on him or dropping from the sky. He had his own way to respond.

Auum muttered a short prayer. Evunn struck low, foot sweeping into the ankles of two enemies. They went down even as he bounced back to his feet, snapping kicks into either face and coming down hard on bodies stunned to the ground. Auum heard his voice, indistinct words in the clamour. The Al-Arynaar responded. Blades flicked out. Fists and feet blurred. Cursyrd were driven from their path. Wings were sliced and torn, their owners tumbling from the sky.

Ahead, Evunn faced a powerful, black-skinned reaver. He leapt at it head first, turning onto his back, a move Auum had seen before. In the last instants before impact, the Tai reached forward, grabbed the creature's shoulders and pivoted around them. The cursyrd didn't know how to react. Evunn's momentum brought him slamming down behind the reaver, ripping it from its feet. They landed hard. The cursyrd squealed its frustration and flailed its arms to try and break Evunn's grip. It was the last mistake it ever made. An Al-Arynaar blade drove into its armpit.

Auum increased his pace. More cursyrd were flying at them from the direction of the college. He ducked under a reaver that flew at his head. It came back for a second pass. He crouched again. This time, the reaver landed ahead of him, sensing his slight isolation and seeing his burden. It hissed at him, spreading its arms and wings in challenge.

In Auum's arms, Duele moved weakly and coughed blood. He was broken, his soul a mere touch away from being taken. Auum felt the disgust on his tongue. Duele was being targeted like the weak of a herd by its predators. Not Duele.

"You know nothing of our strength," said Auum, covering the space between them, accelerating all the way.

He planted his right foot, half turned and struck out with his left. The blow caught the cursyrd on its extended knee, driving the joint backward. He felt sinew snap and bone crack. The creature screamed, collapsing to its right. Auum followed up, his knee thudding up under its chin as it fell, forcing lower teeth through upper lip.

He didn't pause. Those behind would finish it before it had time to heal. He ran on after Evunn. Scant yards ahead, the fighting was growing more intense and Auum feared they would be overwhelmed. Cursyrd flocked, tracking the elves' movement. Near them, a tentacled master floated, observing the chase. They had not managed to slow Evunn's pace. The wedge he had forged through the cursyrd on the ground was reinforced by those flanking him and Auum, leaving the TaiGethen to run with his cargo.

But the demons would not allow the situation to continue. Dozens, hundreds of reavers had now gathered, interspersed with strike-strain. They curved up into the sky, turned and dived, along the length of the street.

"Yniss preserve us," breathed Auum. But not even Yniss could counter this. "Evunn!" he called. "Shelter. Get to the sides, get inside."

The Al-Arynaar scattered left and right but they were all going to be too late. Auum prayed again. This time, his plea was answered.

Spells washed across the sky, dashing cursyrd into the sides of buildings. Cold air swept above his head, shattering wings and freezing bodies. Reavers and strike-strain plummeted down. The attack disintegrated. And then the buildings started to erupt. Huge sheets of flame grabbed at the sky from the rooftops. FlameOrbs sheared through clusters of cursyrd trying to regroup. Detonations rocked the ground under his feet. Across the street, a building buckled under the strain of the spell it held and began to crumble.

"My brothers, we move!" yelled Evunn.

He led them, this elf. The light that even Auum needed in this darkest of hours with his friend fading in his arms. Through the smoke and ash they ran. Through the acrid stench of burning and the rubble bouncing down into the streets they went. Heedless of demon attack now that their enemies had a far greater immediate threat to counter. Auum stared through streaming eyes at the figure of Evunn leading the elves to sanctuary. It wasn't only the smoke that brought his tears.

The Xeteskians. At last the Xeteskians had fought back.

"Hang on," he whispered to Duele though he doubted the elf could hear him. "Please hang on."

More IceWind howled above his head. ForceCones battered great swaths through the demon attack force, driving them high and distant. Auum would have laughed aloud but for the clogging dread in his throat and the burning of exhaustion in his lungs, his arms and legs. He pleaded once more with Tual to keep his friend alive. And with Shorth to stay his hand and wait a little longer.

He felt Duele breathe, coughing again as the smoke touched his lungs. But it was life that they could save if they could get him to a healer quickly enough.

Rounding a bend, he saw that the gates of the college were open. And this time he couldn't suppress the shout of triumph.

CHAPTER 36

Hirad stood in front of the two mages and swept his mace ahead of him again. Strike-strain were flung right. He brought the weapon down sharply, connecting with the claw of a reaver, sniping in from the left. Beside him, The Unknown stood, a massive presence. Mace in one hand, long sword in the other, he fought like the Protector he had once been. Hirad at once drew strength from him and feared for him. The blow to his head had slowed him. Blood ran freely over his face and slicked his arms. And his old hip wound was locking his right leg periodically, threatening his balance.

Hirad spoke over his shoulder at the mage crouched at the door's heavy lock.

"We don't have much time," he said.

"I am aware of that," came the testy reply.

"I am not losing any more of my friends."

"Then leave me to work."

The second mage swept his ForceCone back out over the elven-wrought pathway through the throng of demons, scattering the enemy from the sky. On the ground, three steps below, the situation worsened by the heartbeat. Demons were pressing in hard from both sides. Karron were at the fore, backed by reavers. The Al-Arynaar were fighting a desperate rearguard action, trying to keep the pathway open for those still in the alleyway.

The elves barely had room to fight now. They had been forced into close quarters and most had dropped swords for knives and daggers. In the midst of them, Ark battered away, oblivious to the strike-strain covering his huge body. He used his mace in both hands as a ram, relying on the elves flanking him to keep away the flailing limbs of other karron.

Back in the alley, Thraun held Erienne and was ready to run. With him, Denser, Pheone and the two surviving Xeteskian emissaries. All three mages had ForceCones deployed. Hirad knew that without that trio of spells, they would all have been killed already. But even so, inch by gradual inch, the demons were forcing the elves back into each other. Already, the pathway was barely two men wide and it was closing visibly.

At his back he heard the plop of molten metal and felt a brief wash of heat.

"Come on, come on," he whispered.

There was a click. "Got it."

"Well done," said Hirad. He thudded his mace into a reaver's face, feeling its skull crack. The creature shrieked and flew high, straight into the path of the elven ForceCone that drove it across the street to slap into the part-rubbled wall of the building opposite. "Both of you, get inside. Ward-Lock the other doors. Go!"

He didn't look round. Instead he drew in breath and roared: "Mages! Mages to me."

The chaos was instantaneous. Al-Arynaar warriors ran to fill spaces in the wall left and right as their mage companions withdrew. They rushed from the alley under the protection of Denser and Pheone, neither of whom made any move to leave Thraun. Suarav and Sharyr began to run, the latter with his ForceCone playing over his head, shielding those that came with him.

To either side, the demons surged. The Al-Arynaar held firm, Ark in their midst, bellowing his defiance. Hirad saw the hammer of a karron crush the skull of an elf, driving his body into the ground. Standing next to him, Ark's face darkened and he grabbed the creature by its throat and crashed his mace single-handed into the top of its skull again and again before flinging the squat body into the press behind it.

The first mages reached the stairs and the door to the playhouse. The Unknown and Hirad made space for them to pass, the barbarian issuing orders to each as they went.

"We need light inside. Globes to rid every shadow. I want ForceCones on every window above head height. Let's start investing WardLock in the stone. These karron do not need to use doors. Prepare IceWind, hold it in reserve. Not one demon gets in before I do, understand?"

Elves were pouring through the decreasing gap. At the alley end, karron had forced the Al-Arynaar back, threatening the rest of The Raven.

"Unknown, stay here," he said. "I've got to get back for the others."

"I'm not going anywhere."

Hirad jumped off the steps and pushed back toward the alley, roaring on the elves that passed him. He found Rebraal in the line and pulled him back.

"Get to the steps. We need the defence marshalled inside."

Rebraal, blood dripping from his nose, nodded and moved away. Hirad pushed on. Just seven yards.

"Thraun! Get ready. Denser, keep that Cone up."

Hirad clattered back into the action at the mouth of the alley. Karron had killed two Al-Arynaar. Their broken bodies were dragged clear down the narrow passageway giving Hirad room. He swung his mace down, striking a dripping spiked limb, and immediately up into the throat of the same karron. The demon staggered and Hirad helped it back, driving into its body with his, regaining a little lost space.

"Faster. You have to move faster."

His voice echoed into the alley. Still the Al-Arynaar poured out. At the back of their number, the battle continued as it had since they ran from The Thread. Karron poured in from all sides through shattered buildings.

Hirad pushed away, feeling revulsion at the writhing body matting. He brought his mace down on its head, keeping it back. From his left he saw the swinging spike of another karron. He blocked it aside. The limb struck him on the upper arm, spikes just grazing his back. His left arm numbed under the blow which shunted him sideways and into the alley mouth.

He heard a satisfied squawk. More karron pressed in. Hirad levered himself from the wall, striking out with his mace. He felt it connect with flesh but couldn't see where in the confusion. Al-Arynaar drove in again. Kicks swept low, unbalancing the enemy. He heard the roar of falling stone. A cloud of dust erupted from the alley. He shuddered.

"Thraun, Denser, move!" yelled Hirad.

And so it began. Denser came first, hanging onto his ForceCone and still sweeping it above their heads. Thraun was after him, Erienne still in his arms, with Pheone in his footprints.

Hirad rocked back and thudded a straight kick into an enemy midriff. In the moment's space, he glanced down the alley. Through the clogging dust, he could see Al-Arynaar fighting the karron. Just a handful against the storm, unaware of the situation at their backs.

"Disengage," he called. "Run."

He didn't know if they really heard him but one looked back, saw the space and brought his brothers with him. He led bruised, bleeding and shivering warriors into the light, still moving only because the adrenalin kept their exhaustion at bay a few moments longer. The last of them exited the alley. Karron were pouring down it at surprising speed.

"Dear Gods," breathed Hirad. There was no one left to stop them. "Fall back in turn. Disengage by pairs."

The order was passed back down the line. Hirad placed himself in the centre of the collapsing pathway. Elven hands on his shoulders guided him backward. All around him he could hear the cries of demons and the thud of weapons. He gripped his mace in both hands and watched the karron stream on. He wondered if he could hold them long enough to let the elves escape into the playhouse.

Demons piled into the space they were leaving. Hirad backed up, swinging his mace in a figure eight. It did nothing to halt the tide. They'd be on him in heartbeats. He glanced up. Reavers were massing to dive.

"Shit," he muttered.

He was only four yards from the doors. It was too far through the crowd of elves at his back. Those guiding hands left him but another squeezed his shoulder.

"Duck."

The word in his ear was like cold ale in a summer-dry mouth. He grinned mirthlessly at the advancing demons. And he ducked. The air froze. IceWind seared death into the mouth of the alley. Simultaneously, a ForceCone swept over his head, driving the flanks clear, and FlameOrbs dropped left and right.

For an instant the demons' triumphal voices were stilled and all that could be heard were the shrieks of the burned and frozen, punctuated by elvish orders.

"You are coming with us," said The Unknown from his left.

Rebraal was on his right. Behind was Denser.

They were all backing away slowly, the elves disengaging with them. The moment's pause ended. The demons attacked again. With renewed pride swelling his heart and strength filling his body, Hirad called out over the heads of the enemy.

"Raven! Let's see our people inside!"

With Pheone's ForceCone still deployed and sweeping above, The Raven fought the rearguard action. Hirad snapped a karron hammer aside, stepped inside the spike and smashed his mace high into its forehead, splitting its front eyes. The creature staggered and raised its arms to cover itself. Rebraal skewered its nerve ganglion.

Left, The Unknown held a mace in either hand now and both dripped with demon gore. He cycled them in quick ovals, striking out at body and limb, yelling his challenge. He caught a reaver on the side of the head sending it skittering into the pack. The karron that took its place took blows to its gut and neck before it could marshal a strike. The Unknown's attack was relentless, forcing it into desperate defence.

Rebraal's quick hands kept the attackers at bay to the right. His mace in both hands, he weaved a complex defensive pattern that confused the karron facing him. Above them, reavers screamed exhortations to attack while they tried to get themselves under the Cone. And all the time, The Raven backed off. More FlameOrbs fell, relieving the press of bodies. Rebraal grunted under a karron blow, his mace taking its full force but still it unbalanced him. Another blow came in, Rebraal quick enough to duck. And on the next pace, he stepped back into the shadow of the playhouse.

"Almost there, Raven!" called Hirad, feeling his heel against a step. "Al-Arynaar step it up, get inside."

He moved up a step. More spells flashed out over his head to crash into the defenceless demons, spreading fire and chaos. Karron rained in blows, desperate to take anyone they could in the final flurry. The Unknown's maces whirled defiance. Hirad slammed his mace again and again into heads and limbs. Rebraal took another blow to his side, half blocking it and recovering to defend.

Hirad felt for the last step. The ForceCone snapped off. Reavers dropped into the attack. Hirad raised his arms to strike out but felt hands dragging him back. He was pulled unceremoniously into the playhouse. The door was slammed against the demon pack. WardLock fizzed across its timbers and not even the hammers of karrons could break it. Not for a while.

Hirad dragged himself to his feet, his limbs quivering, his mace discarded for the moment. The gloomy playhouse was full of noise, activity and dust. Outside, the demons were hammering on doors, walls and roof, the sound reverberating dully through the heavily draped space. He counted off The Raven. There was a gaping hole in their ranks. Thraun and Denser were kneeling over Erienne who was lying where the injured were being gathered in one part of the standing area that circled the stage.

Rebraal was with Dila'heth on the stage which rose from the centre of the playhouse. He was already snapping out orders to his warriors, she organising her mages. Spells crackled away, disturbing dust during their otherwise invisible progress across the open space. Al-Arynaar warriors ran to all corners, checking for unforeseen access ways. LightGlobes hung over the scene, casting gentle light that slowly lifted the gloom.

The Unknown was making for the stage and Hirad followed him, aware of the aches washing over his body. His left arm was still tingling where the karron strike had been blocked and his head itched interminably from the sweat mingling with the scratches inflicted by the strike-strain.

"Gather all the wounded on the north floor. Pheone and Denser are assessing them," said Rebraal. "ColdRoom teams to the stage, please. Prepare and wait for the casting order. Let's hope we don't need you."

His smile was grim and weary when he saw Hirad coming toward him. He grasped the barbarian's shoulders.

"You saved a lot of lives," he said. "Thank you."

Hirad shrugged. "Not quite enough, eh?"

"You know what I mean."

"Difficult space to defend," said The Unknown.

Hirad could see what he meant. The standing area around the circular stage was flat ground ten yards in all directions. It ended in a rail beyond which a series of fourteen rows of benches were bolted onto steep steps. Gangways led from each of the bolted and WardLocked doors and a thin path ran all around the periphery of the playhouse. Stairs ran up the side of the outer wall to the left of each door, leading to the ornate and overhanging boxes for the rich of Xetesk. Empty windows now, drifting with the memories of privilege. Strange. He could all but hear the applause and smell the expectancy of the crowd. As if the walls retained the atmosphere of past triumphs.

"We need numbers, stamina and sustainability estimates now," said The Unknown, bringing him back to himself.

"We also need a way out," said Rebraal, wheezing.

"First things first," said The Unknown. "Dila'heth, what have you got?"

Dila blew out her cheeks. "It's not a good picture," she said, biting back her emotion. "We left Julatsa with one hundred and eighty mages not three days ago. And now"—she began indicating as she spoke—"I have six mages keeping ForceCones on the ceiling. I have thirty investing the walls with WardLock constructs. I have nine ready to cast ColdRooms, five are on healing duty and the other seven are injured too badly to cast. That's fifty-eight including me."

"We've all lost people," muttered Hirad.

Dila let the figures sink in. Hirad looked about him. It had seemed such a throng when they had run for the playhouse but now, in the enclosed space, the scale of their losses was all too clear.

"And what about the warriors, Rebraal?" asked The Unknown.

"Less than a hundred," he said, face drawn and pained. "We can't know the numbers Auum still has with him but at worst we've lost well over half our sword and two thirds of our mage strength. And it gets worse, I suspect. Pheone?"

The Julatsan High Mage looked up from her search of the wounded.

"How bad is it?"

Pheone's face was a picture of despair. Her face was streaked with fresh tears and she was shaking, the fear setting into her body. She took a moment to compose herself and walked onto the stage, the mage Geren at her shoulder.

"I've lost almost everyone. There's only ten left. Pathetic isn't it, but Geren and I are the only human Julatsan mages left. Everyone else is dead or a nonmage."

"There'll be others, Pheone," said Hirad. "Hidden and scattered. Blackthorne has Julatsans in his employ. You can rebuild."

"From this?" blurted out Geren. "You talk like it's over and we've won. Look at where we are. We've just swapped one trap for another. There's no way out, is there? Nowhere for us to go."

"There is always a way," said Hirad, his tone ominous and stilling

Geren's outburst. "That's what we do. What you do is go back and get our people fit to fight again. And I will do the same with mine."

Geren nodded.

"And Geren?"

"What?"

"We're all tired and scared," said Hirad. "But fear is a disease. And it spreads where it shows. Remember that when you look into the eyes of those you are healing or you're no good to us."

Geren backed away, Pheone laying a comforting hand on his arm as he retreated. The battering on walls and doors was incessant and intensifying. Loose plaster fell from the balcony-box carvings and from the pillars which were hung with dramatic deep red drapes.

The Unknown spread his arms. "So, what's the prognosis? Presumably we're at a stage where we can keep them at bay. The question is, how long can we maintain it?"

They all looked at Dila'heth.

"There's no easy way to say this. Even if I cycle the ForceCone mages and rest the WardLock casters now, we can't keep this up until nightfall." She shrugged. "Three days in the open and under attack. We just didn't come in here with enough stamina. Then they'll break in and all that we'll have are the ColdRooms. I'm sorry."

"Looks like Geren might have been right," muttered Pheone.

Hirad looked at her sharply but didn't have the heart to rebuke her. Part of him agreed with her. He could still see walls collapsing and Darrick disappearing beneath them, helpless. He shouldn't have died that way. Not him. Outside, the demons were baying for their souls, sensing the parlous state in which their captives found themselves. The endless thudding on the playhouse was giving Hirad a headache. There would be thousands of them out there, most of them just waiting for the inevitable while reavers picked at the roof and karron thrashed at the walls and doors. Far too many for them to hope to break through.

"Anyone know a secret way out of here?" he asked.

Rebraal shook his head. "We've checked. The trapdoors just lead to dressing rooms and closed storage. There are only four ways out and none of them is appealing."

Over on the north floor, Denser slapped Thraun on the back, the ghost of a smile on his face. On the ground in front of them, Erienne was stirring.

It would probably have been better for her had she stayed unconscious.

CHAPTER 37

They had run into the tower complex under a guard of ForceCones, Xeteskian warriors flanking them. The cursyrd had pulled away when they had entered the dome, shrieking their anger and frustration, promising lingering death.

Auum had barked for healers, for a place to lay Duele. Evunn shadowed him. The Tai was cut and bleeding, his eyes fierce and furious. Someone had shown them the path deep into the catacombs he remembered so well. Through multiple turns and antechambers to where the Xeteskian mages slept under guard to replenish their mana stamina. It was empty now. Just an anonymous chamber with bare walls, a single table and rolls of bedding.

Al-Arynaar had followed them through the maze and immediately began to prepare. Auum laid Duele on a bedding roll on the table. The Tai moaned feebly, blood bubbling from his lips. Auum smoothed his semiconscious frown and kissed his forehead.

"You have come so far, my Tai," he said. "Stand with us again and we will complete Yniss's work." He turned to the elven mages. "Save him. And if you cannot do that, see he suffers no more pain. Evunn, we pray."

The Tai knelt at Duele's feet while the Al-Arynaar worked on him, doing whatever they could.

"Yniss, our Tai lies before you, broken. His fate is in your hands. It is you who will call upon Shorth or keep him behind you. We are ever your servants and do your work without question. Keep Duele with us. Let Shorth wait for him. We will let your wisdom guide us and will never turn from the path. But . . ." Auum breathed deep. Evunn's arms were about his neck pulling him close, their heads on each other's shoulders. "Do not take from us the best of us, we beg you. His soul is pure. He must run with us, not the ancestors, not yet. Save him. Do not let Shorth take him. We are your servants, Yniss. Hear us in our time of direst need. Hear us."

Auum rose to his feet, Evunn supported him. He wiped the tears from his face and felt the weight of despair crushing him. He knew before he looked into the eyes of the healers what he would find. But Duele was still breathing. Indeed his eyes blinked open. Auum's heart raced with brief hope.

"He is dying, isn't he?"

The mage nodded and Auum's heart faltered. His mind was suffused with a rage he had little desire to control.

"His chest cavity is crushed beyond repair. His lungs are ruined and his heart is pierced. He should have died when he was struck but his will is so strong," said the mage. "Had we been standing over him then, we could not have saved him. I am sorry."

"Do not be so," said Auum. "You are blameless."

"He feels no pain. You should talk to him now. There is little time."

The mage moved aside, ushering the others with him. Auum and Evunn stood together in Duele's eyeline, watching his deliberate movements. He raised his hand a couple of inches. Auum grabbed it and squeezed hard. Duele licked his lips, smearing drying blood. His eyes opened, lids flickering a little. He frowned again, trying to focus.

"Yniss takes me for another purpose," he managed through wheezing breaths. Every word stung Auum with its optimism. "Shorth is waiting. I can feel him."

"So it is, my Tai," said Auum. He swallowed hard.

"Don't grieve," said Duele. "I go to the ancestors."

"It is a journey we had pledged to take together. All three," replied Auum. He gripped Duele's hand harder. "You were always the best of us. Yniss sees it. Do this for me. Seek the one who seeks Rebraal and Hirad. Seek Ilkar. Shadow him. Protect him. Show him the path."

"I will, Auum." Duele coughed blood and smiled. "Always orders."

"Not orders. A request. A hope." Auum leant in and kissed Duele's lips. "Goodbye, Duele. Until we meet, be strong. Serve Yniss. Find Ilkar."

He withdrew, letting Evunn take Duele's hand.

"Forty years TaiGethen," Evunn said. "Forty years as one."

"And not a day's regret," said Duele, his voice faint and rasping.

"There should have been forty more." Evunn's voice quavered. "This is not right. This is chance."

"It is all Yniss's design. We are his servants."

"Yes and we—" Evunn paused. Auum saw his shoulders sag. Evunn leaned in to kiss the Tai. "Shorth show you the glory you deserve, my friend." He laid Duele's hand by his side and turned to Auum, his voice breaking. "He is gone."

Auum moved back to Duele, standing opposite Evunn. He took the pouches of paint from his belt and the two of them reapplied the hunting colours to Duele's face, taking exaggerated care over every detail, leaving no part uncovered. Auum drew Duele's twin short swords and placed one in each of his hands while Evunn unsnapped his jaqrui pouch and laid a whisper crescent high on his broken chest.

"Where you go now, you go armed," said Auum.

"Fight well," said Evunn. "Fight strong."

In silence, the surviving Tai painted each other's faces, speaking quiet prayers to Yniss to watch over them all, for Tual to keep them strong and for Shorth to take their enemies quickly. Eventually, Auum addressed the chamber; three Al-Arynaar mages and a Xeteskian warrior.

"No one will touch him until we return. He will remain as he is with no covering. He is of the TaiGethen elite and he still performs the work of Yniss. Evunn, come. We have the memory of our Tai to honour. There is cleansing to be done."

They ran through the maze, their direction unerring. In the dome, Dystran moved to stand in front of the great doors. Outside, Auum could hear the shrieks of countless demons. Their calls of triumph and mastery; and their promises of failure and enslavement. Auum recognised Dystran instantly. He had no quarrel with the man. Not now in the moment of the greatest need of all Balaian races. Another day he would have killed him for his crimes against the elven nation.

"Move," he said.

Dystran smiled indulgently. "I understand your pain . . ."

"No you do not, human."

". . . but I cannot let you out there. You will be killed."

Auum felt the blood drain from his face. He took a pace forward.

"Move," he repeated.

Dystran held up a hand to stop his guards closing in. "Idiots. How close do you think you will get?"

"We have prayed," explained Auum, fighting for the words and to retain his calm. "Now we honour our dead and cleanse our minds."

"How?" asked Dystran. "There is nothing outside but death and demons."

"Leave open the doors and watch," said Auum. "Move."

Dystran clearly knew he would not ask again. He shook his head and stepped aside, nodding to his men. The doors swung gently open.

"Tai, we move. Tual will guide our bodies."

Auum walked calmly out into the cold fresh air. Cursyrd cavorted in the air over the courtyard. Karron had beaten down the gates and were gathered by their shattered remains. A tentacled master floated serenely overhead. All eyes fixed on the TaiGethen pair moving into their midst.

Auum walked to the edge of the steps, well beyond the periphery of the ColdRoom shell. He spread his arms wide, his head was cocked to the heavens. He felt the desire then, the craving for absolution. Duele would be watching them.

"I am Auum of the TaiGethen. I stand with Evunn and in the presence of Duele. You know us and you know our calling. Today, you took from us.

And for such action, there must be recompense. Which of you will offer your-selves to honour our dead? Which of you will journey with Duele to face the judgement of Shorth? Which of you will send us before him? I, Auum, am waiting."

"I, Evunn, am waiting."

Screeching with pleasure, the cursyrd descended.

The pressure on the ForceCones was intensifying. Reavers had torn away win-dows and ripped timbers and stone from the roof. Only the spells kept them out now. At ground level the situation was no less difficult. WardLocks and investitures bowed under the incessant hammering of the karron. Yellow mana light crackled across groaning joints. Plaster castings cracked and crumbled, thudding to the floor.

The Al-Arynaar waited, their calm spreading to all but one corner of the playhouse. Hirad wasn't hearing the roar of the demons gathered outside, baying for their souls. He was stalking around Rebraal, whose leather and shirt lay on the floor nearby. Denser and Pheone were studying him. Both had hands on his right arm and chest, their eyes closed as the mana probed his badly bruised body.

"You didn't think it something we needed to know?" Hirad couldn't believe it. He fought to keep his temper, aware that they needed focus for what was sure to come. "What if we needed you in the line?"

Rebraal faced up to him, expression set. "Organisation had to be done. We had to be secure above anything."

"We're capable, Rebraal. Or hadn't you noticed? I can speak elvish."

"I wanted to be sure."

Hirad shook his head. "How bad is it?"

"Ribs, arm, shoulder . . ." Rebraal shrugged and half smiled. "The rest just aches."

"Anything broken?"

"Of course there is," said Denser, opening his eyes. "And of course he also knows that to fix it we'll have to put him to sleep. Fractured collarbone, three cracked ribs and one broken and leaning on his lung."

"Bloody hell, Rebraal," said Hirad. "What good do you think you're going to be like that?"

Rebraal's eyes flared. "More than if I'm lying over there asleep. I am not in your Raven. I will fight beside you and with my people if I choose."

"Perfect," growled Hirad. "Want to tell me how you propose to tie up the right-hand side when you can't hold a mace?"

"I have two hands," snapped Rebraal. "I'll fight on the left instead."

"And who's on my right, Sirendor Larn? Only he's been dead for eight years. Want to be joining him today?"

"Hirad, enough," said The Unknown, striding over from the healer mages. The cut on his forehead had been closed by a WarmHeal. It glowed unnaturally red and was edged dark yellow, almost gold in the Globe light. "Let's get thinking."

"That'd be a novelty."

"Coldheart, stop it."

Hirad leaned into Rebraal. "Fight with us, but withdraw if you're weakening. Promise me. We can't afford to lose you too."

Rebraal nodded, a reluctant gesture. To their left, a six-foot section of the outer wall gave way to the accompaniment of roars from the massed demons outside. Above the tear, a balcony box teetered and collapsed, thundering to the ground and sending up clouds of plaster dust. Karron moved in, wading through the rubble.

"Get a Cone on that hole!" ordered Rebraal.

"Gheneer, do it," said Dila'heth.

Gheneer moved forward quickly and swung his spell from the ceiling to the ground.

"Clear!" he shouted.

Elves ran left and right. The Cone caught the karron, driving them back outside.

"I need another Cone on the roof now," said Dila. "Afen'erei. Sorry but I need you."

The weary Al-Arynaar mage dragged herself to her feet. There was not the slightest hint of discontent in her expression. She began to cast.

"Whatever we're going to do, it had better be fast," said Hirad. "These investitures aren't going to last."

As if to confirm his words another gap, longer this time, was dragged in the walls. Dila'heth called for more mage backup. Healers left their charges and ran to the defence. Pheone moved up to the stage once again, urging greater concentration and efficiency.

"Thraun, all of you, get over here," called The Unknown into the growing din. "We're forming up. Someone help Rebraal on with his armour."

"Gods falling," said Hirad. "They're going to bring this place down on top of us."

"The ForceCones will keep the roof up," said Dila'heth.

"Not for long," said Pheone. "That's a lot of weight and pressure."

Thraun led Erienne, Denser and Ark over. Around the playhouse, elven warriors readied themselves. Mages prepared offensive spells and led prayers.

Demons howled and shrieked. Reavers gathered in the sky, visible through the tears in the roof. Strike-strain clustered. Another gash was ripped in the playhouse wall. Timbers collapsed bringing more balcony boxes down.

"We've got to make a decision here," said Denser. "When to drop the spells and use the ColdRoom so at least we can kill some of them."

"Only when we have nothing else. We're holding for now," said Pheone.

"Raven, form up," ordered The Unknown. "Rebraal, my left. Thraun, switch to the right by Hirad. Ark, far left. Denser, you know where you need to be. Erienne can you cast?"

"I don't have much choice, Unknown," she replied. "I'll be all right."

"Use the weakening casts," said The Unknown. "We'll do the rest."

"Whatever you say." She sounded tired. Frail.

"Ready to move, Raven," said Hirad. "Where's Eilaan?"

"Injured but recovering," answered Pheone. "I'll back you up."

"ForceCone overhead," said The Unknown. "And thank you."

Two men ran over to the stage, flinching at the sound of falling stone from behind. Another tear, another weak point. They stopped in front of The Unknown.

"Captain Suarav."

"Sol," said the captain, a man already in the Xeteskian college guard when The Unknown had been prepared as a Protector. "Brynel is gone but we aren't done. It would be an honour to fight in your line."

The Unknown smiled mirthlessly. "How the world turns, eh? You're welcome. Our right, by Thraun if you don't mind. Sharyr, I suggest you prepare something suitably lethal. Stand in the mage line."

"My pleasure."

"Maces, Raven," said The Unknown. He raised his voice, cutting across the cacophony, Rebraal translating his words. "Waiting. Remember, we need to force a viable breach if we're going to break for the college. Al-Arynaar, you have to shore up the flanks and rear. Just keep a holding pattern. Dila, Pheone, we need someone near the wounded to bring them out of sleep if we have to."

"You want to break out?" asked Pheone.

"Not if we don't have to. If we can hold them, that's what we'll do."

"And then what?"

"Pray for assistance," said The Unknown grimly. "Because if we do have to break out, we'll lose a lot getting to safety."

"Let's hope it doesn't come to that," said Denser.

The Raven watched the increasing desperation of the Al-Arynaar mages. Hirad's heart thumped in his chest. He felt the adrenalin wash away his aches, hiding them from his body while he prepared for battle. He took a long look at Rebraal. The elf was clearly hampered by his injuries. He stood left-side-on and held his right arm across his chest. He was pale and sweating.

"Leave the line, Rebraal," said Hirad. "You aren't fit to fight."

"I'll be the judge," said Rebraal. "I do not desert my friends or my people while I can stand."

"You aren't in the rain forest now, Rebraal," said Hirad. "We need you for later."

"Think there's going to be a later, do you?" he asked. "Listen to the noise. Look out through the holes. We need everyone fighting just to survive for whatever help The Unknown thinks is coming. The Al-Arynaar must see me here in the front line."

"Be ready," said The Unknown.

He indicated a buckling area of wall behind the raft of injured. The Raven began to move. The WardLock cracked and protested. Plaster burst from the binding. Timbers groaned and splintered. The tear would be at least six yards wide and there weren't enough mages to keep ForceCones in place.

"Not too close," warned Hirad. "It's time to complete those spells."

Al-Arynaar moved up on either flank, covering the route to the injured. To Hirad's right, Thraun snarled. His yellow-tinged eyes were wide but the set of his body calm and composed. Beside him the Xeteskian, Suarav, gripped his sword tight in his right hand. He was determined but in the shake of his body was the memory of the horrors he had suffered to get to this new place of danger. His soul would not be easily taken.

The investiture failed. The stone and timber of the playhouse wall burst in, tumbling across the gangway and sweeping aside benches. Balcony boxes fell across an area of thirty yards. Dust and debris billowed toward them where they stood at the edge of the standing room, clouding around the edges of the ForceCones. Karron bellowed and squawked. They charged in, reavers behind them.

"Spells away!" roared The Unknown. "Raven, let's use what we learned on board ship. Suarav, take our lead. Steady. Steady."

Pheone's ForceCone blazed overhead, slapping into the reavers flying in behind the karron. Deep blue FlameOrbs leapt from Denser and Sharyr's fingers, arcing over The Raven and dropping into the pack still outside the playhouse. Hirad felt the heat when they passed, saw the detonations and heard the screams. Mana fire splattered across the defenceless karron. It had the desired effect. Those in front of the fire clustered in.

"Casting," muttered Erienne.

The air dried out all around them. Dust dropped from the sky, clearing the scene dramatically. The One casting, otherwise invisible, struck the karron in the front rank and over a wide arc in front of The Raven. These lesser demons, far more reliant than their better-evolved reaver brethren on the density of mana, sensed the linkage to their life force shorn from them.

Hirad sensed panic spreading through the karron but another set of FlameOrbs from Denser focused their attention once more. They came on again urged on by the reavers but vulnerable with Erienne's casting settling on them.

"Ready, Raven!" The Unknown's mace tip tapped rhythmically on the floor of the playhouse. The first karron reached the standing-room floor. "Stepping up, let's take them."

The Unknown double tapped his mace. At the left-hand side of the line, Ark took a pace forward and left. He thundered his mace through in an upward curve, following up with a downward slash with his blade. The karron was knocked backward, its stomach opened up, spewing its internal organs to the ground. The Raven all followed suit in order, a heartbeat apart. Blows catching karron on limbs, heads and torsos. The ferocity of the attack stopped the demons in their tracks, confusing them with its direction.

Suarav hadn't followed the move and had gone straight forward, many Al-Arynaar likewise. But the space it left between him and Thraun was bait the karron in front of it could not resist. It stepped forward and flailed its limbs outward.

"Thraun, go."

Ahead of The Unknown's order, Thraun had ducked and moved right, coming up under the karron's strikes and crushing its skull with a massive overhead strike. The creature collapsed and Thraun paced forward and right again, leading the line this time. Suarav had anticipated too and moved with him. His blow was caught by the karron ahead but still the demon was pushed back. The Raven's line drove hard, maces aiming at gut and chin, beating a space in front of them.

"Down," ordered Denser.

They dropped to their haunches, Thraun dragging Suarav with him. IceWind wailed into the space. Simultaneously, Sharyr dropped more Flame-Orbs outside the playhouse. The elven flanks moved up left and right, forcing the karron into an ever tighter area. Abruptly, the lesser demons broke and fled into the teeth of screams of rage from the reavers.

"Hold!" bellowed The Unknown.

Outside, the demons massed again. Strike-strain bunched and clouded. Karron jostled and reformed. Reavers landed and began to run.

"Plenty more work to do, Raven. Good start but they might not fall for that again."

The Unknown tapped his mace once more and The Raven paused for breath.

Flanked by guards and with Vuldaroq next to him, Dystran watched. He tried to take it all in but didn't really believe what he saw. Tried to understand and follow the speed of strikes. It was all but impossible, a fact that the demons were finding out in far more brutal fashion.

Auum and Evunn stood back to back and about a yard apart. Stances slightly crouched and feet planted at shoulder width, they fought with an effortless grace that was simply breathtaking. Dystran couldn't see exactly how they tackled the enemies that came at them on the ground and in the air. They barely seemed to look. But their strikes were efficient and unerringly accurate. He focused on Auum as the reavers flew in. Not in great numbers. Perhaps fifteen and accompanied by dozens of the tiny strike-strain. Karron grouped and moved up but did not attack.

Auum had logged his immediate targets. The first approached on foot, three others in the air around it. Auum dropped and swept its feet from under it, bouncing back and striking out and left with his knife hand at his next target, dragging the point deep into wing membrane. The demon flittered clear. Auum ignored it. The next had whipped out its tail. Auum caught it in front of his face, looped it around his wrist and dragged the reaver from the sky. It bounced onto the ground. The TaiGethen dropped onto its chest and drove his knife up under its arm.

Never stopping, he rose and turned, sweeping his right foot high over the head of Evunn, scattering the strike-strain that dived on him. His momentum carried him round and he planted his foot before delivering an extraordinary series of strikes that Dystran couldn't follow. The first downed demon had got to its haunches in time to catch a boot in its face, sending it sprawling. Auum's arms were a blur. Dystran could see the flash of his knife in the sunlight. He saw reavers beaten aside, he saw them die in spasm and he saw strike-strain flung far and wide. He saw Auum block the odd strike and deliver a riposte before he had any right to be balanced. His limb speed was simply awesome. As if it was being directed from elsewhere.

Seven reaver bodies lay on the ground around the two TaiGethen. The others gathered and dived straight down. The elves waited. Without a word, they dived left and right in concert, cartwheeling back onto their feet and running back into the space they'd vacated. The reavers had landed hard and were in some disarray. The TaiGethen ploughed into them. Evunn took the lead, his punches designed to cripple temporarily. His knife sheered wing membrane, his fists and fingers crushed throat and thumped into chest, nose and temple, his feet denied them balance.

Behind him came Auum, sliding into their prone forms, knives in both hands driving home. His body was a shadow across the courtyard. And where he went, demons died. Fifteen reavers were downed and strike-strain littered the ground before the karron attacked too.

Auum and Evunn stood to face them, bowed fractionally and walked calmly back toward the tower complex. The two elves strode past Dystran without saying a word. Their bodies were covered in small cuts. Evunn had a long gash down one arm and Auum's left leg was dripping blood.

Dystran ordered the doors closed. Heavily invested with protection, they would stand massive bombardment by the karron should the need arise, and Dystran had no doubt that it would.

He watched the elves return to the catacombs.

"Extraordinary," he said.

"But even they knew when to stop," said Vuldaroq. "A handful of demons are dead and tens of thousands still fly."

"If only we had a few hundred more like them, eh?"

"Shame that you killed so many of them with the Elfsorrow, isn't it?"

Dystran glanced sharply at Vuldaroq but there was no blame in his expression, merely statement.

"And all for nothing," he said, feeling suddenly weary. "Would that I could have that time over."

CHAPTER 38

The karron attacked again, backed by reavers on the ground, underneath Pheone's ForceCone. They swamped the space inside the playhouse, driving hard into The Raven and taking on the Al-Arynaar flanking forces. Erienne cast again, rendering the enemy vulnerable. But without offensive spell backup, barring Denser and Sharyr, the demons slowly made ground.

"Firm up left," barked The Unknown.

Rebraal took a glance. The Al-Arynaar had faltered. They were distracted by the rubble and broken benches around them and the slope of the auditorium. Reavers, floating a couple of feet from the ground, were hitting them hard.

"Gheneer," he called. "Bring up defence."

But he knew there was very little of that. He struck out at a karron's hammer limb. The spikes of his mace dragged gouges in its flesh. It reared and fell back. Ark followed up and drove his sword deep into its gut. In the heartbeat's space, Rebraal assessed their situation. It was becoming ever more forlorn. The cursyrd were pressing on every casting, keeping the pressure up on the ForceCone mages, not letting them have a moment's respite. In five areas around the playhouse and all across the roof, reavers and karron launched themselves at the constructs. And every time they did, more plaster and loose stone was dislodged and a degree of stamina leeched from the caster. It was only a matter of time.

In front of him, more cursyrd poured through the gap which they widened at every stroke. Overhead, the timbers supporting the roof shifted, seeking new solidity they'd never find. The walls of the building were seriously compromised. Without the ForceCones overhead, Rebraal wasn't sure the roof would hold.

They had been forced a few paces back across the floor toward the stage. Rebraal felt tired. His right arm ached up at the shoulder where the collarbone was cracked and every breath sent a skewer of pain through his chest. Sweat dripped down his face and he had the first inklings of a shake in his left arm. The mace felt too heavy.

Pheone swept her ForceCone above their heads once more. Strike-strain were dispersed to all points, squeaking frustration. Rebraal blocked a spike arm and reversed his mace across the neck of a reaver following up. The cursyrd reared into the air and was pinned against the wall by the Cone. Ark battered the skull of a karron, sending the creature back into the lines behind. The Unknown jabbed his mace into the eyes of another and he could hear Hirad's shouts clear across the floor. The barbarian demanded more effort. He demanded strength and unbroken will in Darrick's name. All those around him gave it without question.

Taking Ark's lead, Rebraal drove forward. He ducked a flailing limb and struck left to right. His mace caught the karron on the side of the head, sending it sprawling across the line. The disruption was used instantly. The Unknown moved up and split his next enemy groin to chest. Hirad swivelled and kicked out high, taking his on the chin. Planting his foot he smashed his mace in under its arm, killing the creature instantly.

"Pushing!" he shouted.

Reavers flew low into the line, blocking any move of the allied forces. Rebraal saw a claw rip out and scratch three lines down Ark's face. Strike-strain followed in, buzzing in their faces, distracting their focus. One bit Rebraal high on the right arm. He jerked with the sudden pain, ice flowing into his cracked collarbone. He moved to snatch it away. A reaver saw its chance and lashed in its tail and a claw simultaneously. Rebraal tripped and went down hard on his right side, his mace just about blocking the claw.

He roared in agony and for a moment thought he was going to pass out. He heard The Unknown shout an order and saw the big man's mace flash across his eyeline and bury itself in the reaver's side. Rebraal pushed himself back and away. Gheneer hurdled him to take his place in the line, sword in hand for now.

He dragged himself to his feet.

"Still standing, Rebraal?" called Hirad.

"Still standing," he confirmed.

Erienne was at his side. "You should leave the line. Let me dull this for you."

"No time," said Rebraal.

"Down," ordered Denser.

IceWind again, forcing the cursyrd back, killing them in their dozens. How much stamina he had left was open to debate but it would be plenty. He was the most efficient mage Rebraal had ever seen. Sharyr, though, looked tired. Inexorably, the battle was turning the cursyrd's way.

Rebraal moved back to the front. Gheneer noted him, savaged a cut through reaver wing membrane and ducked backward. Rebraal moved into the fight once more. His next strike killed the reaver Gheneer had crippled.

"Press!" The Unknown sounded off. "Erienne, another casting if you can. We have new blood coming in."

"On its way."

To the left, a massive section of wall disintegrated inward. Al-Arynaar were trapped under rubble, others knocked from their feet. Karron poured in through the new gap, reavers at their backs. Rebraal heard Gheneer shout orders. The Unknown joined him.

"Alter the angle of defence, Raven. Let's give them some breathing space."

The pain in Rebraal's chest was intensifying. His right arm was completely useless now and he held it hard across his chest, trying to account for the lack of balance it created. The Unknown ordered the move and right to left. The Raven angled toward the new attack. The right-hand flank of the Al-Arynaar followed suit, keeping up the pressure, denying the cursyrd freedom to press home on the left.

But the battle front was too wide to hold for too long. Rebraal wielded his mace in front of his face while he thought hard about how they could turn the tide. Above the noise of the cursyrd that reverberated around the playhouse, and the sounds of orders and struggle, Rebraal could hear something else. Like approaching thunder carried on the wind. He fancied he could feel it through his feet too but dismissed the thought.

"Unknown!" he shouted. "We need to relieve the pressure left. Orbs and IceWind to the gap."

The Unknown concurred. "Denser, Sharyr. Redirect. Pheone, keep those strike-strain away."

The cursyrd were pressing hard on the left. Gheneer had been quick, organising a new defensive line, yet he had lost ten or more warriors. The line hadn't actually broken but it was perilously stretched. Mages from the holding areas behind turned their attention front. FlameOrbs landed in the gap, detonating plaster dust and incinerating enemies.

Rebraal ducked a tongue of fire that scoured into the cursyrd ranks. The air was hot and choking. He followed Ark into a fresh attack, feeling his mace biting deep into exposed cursyrd flesh. The reaver howled and lashed out, catching the top of his head. He felt cold blood flow. He staggered back. Ark was with him, fending off the next attack while he regained his balance.

"Drop back," said Ark. "You are not fit."

But that noise of thunder was getting louder. Something was happening. If it was cursyrd, they would be washed away. If it was help, they had to hold out. Whichever it turned out to be, there was nothing to be gained by pulling himself out.

"I'll be fine." And to prove it, he struck out right to left and slightly upward, splintering a karron jaw. The strike it had thought to put in died with it. "Can you hear the thunder?"

"Yes." Ark's blade blocked a hammer limb, the return severed it. "It is not thunder. It is singing."

Rebraal fenced away a reaver claw and thrashed above his head at a strike-strain. The kitten-sized cursyrd was dashed to the ground. Ark was right. It was singing and it was definitely getting closer.

"Let's keep them back!" roared Hirad. "Help is coming."

Hirad's words were taken up all across the line, giving tired limbs more strength. Rebraal felt invigorated. Hope flowed through his veins. The ache in his arm seemed to diminish. But if they thought the enemy would crumble, they were mistaken. Reavers set up a dreadful cacophony that bounced around the confined space.

The effect was instant. Strike-strain withdrew and bunched just outside the playhouse. Rebraal frowned, wondering why. The karron backed up a pace, some a little further. It was the first concerted move he had seen them undertake.

"Steady!" roared The Unknown. "Watching."

A handful of Al-Arynaar moved up. Rebraal and The Raven barked them back. Three were too late. The karron, under the spell of the reavers' voices, whirled back into the attack at astonishing speed. Limbs cycled twice, three times as fast blurring in the air in front of the allies. Those too late and cut off were battered dead in moments, unable to raise a defence in isolation.

Two karron broke through and ran straight at Erienne. Rebraal saw them coming.

"Erienne, your left! Left!"

But she couldn't hear him, lost deep in her casting. Denser too was preparing, unaware of his peril. Al-Arynaar detached and chased. Others moved up from the back but all would be too late.

Rebraal turned left-side-on. The karron in front of him rushed on. Next to him, Ark with his longer reach dismembered the first creature that came into his range and swept his mace at a second. He moved his sword to Rebraal's defence, deflecting the hammer limb. Rebraal fended away the spike and knew he had to detach.

"Ark, cover me."

He danced back a step, turned and raced into the gap to protect Erienne. The karron squawked, their limbs flowed fast. Rebraal gripped his mace in both hands and felt the pain flooding his shoulder and chest. He drove the weapon through hard and low, taking the first creature across its hammer limb and deep into its chest cavity. The karron reared and flashed its spike limb across its body. Rebraal fenced it off but didn't have the balance to deliver a counter of his own. The speed of the limb beat him. The karron's hammer limb thudded into his defence, hurling him from his feet even as Al-Arynaar blades tore through its body.

He felt the sensation of falling. It was a weightlessness combined with a roaring in his ears and deep inside his mind. Somewhere distant, a voice called his name. He felt no pain until he struck the ground. Darkness closed over him.

"I ask you this as an adversary for whom I have developed a certain respect," said Ferouc.

His hands clicked together and his skin flowed from a deep green to a livid blue, his emotions clashing while he spoke. Blackthorne stood alone before him on the steps of his castle keep, far enough away that he could turn and escape should Ferouc attack. But he didn't think the demon would. Not that he trusted his enemy. Ferouc simply didn't have to risk himself or any measure of humiliation. Ranged behind him were hundreds of the demon strain he called karron, destructors. Hovering above them a similar number of reavers. The strike-strain were gone. Not needed now.

"Respect is a long time earned, Ferouc," he replied, choosing not to irritate the occupying commander with his nickname. "But understanding of the spirit of humans would take you a lifetime. We have been so long resisting you that the thought of surrender can never now enter our minds. And even more so knowing what that surrender would mean. This is not mere captivity and subjugation, after all."

"But you are beaten," said Ferouc.

"Not so, my enemy," said Blackthorne, enjoying the reaction his words provoked. "We accept that we cannot beat you. Your numbers are vastly superior. But we are not beaten. One does not necessarily follow the other."

"The instruction has changed," said Ferouc. "I am to bring about the end of your resistance and if that means taking your lives but not your souls, so be it. You may be relatively few but you are dangerous and I am required to the north to aid in our final victory."

"And hence these . . ." Blackthorne indicated behind Ferouc. "Karron."

"They are a race not suited to any but the most mana-dense atmosphere," said Ferouc, and there was a note of disdain in his voice. "It is a measure of our inevitable victory that we are now able to use them in Balaia."

"We will kill them as we will kill any who come against us."

Ferouc's colour distilled into a bright blue, his anger surfacing strongly. "I had wanted to taste your soul, Baron Blackthorne, but now I would laugh over your soulless corpse. The karron will tear down your walls and expose you to us. And while they might fear your ColdRooms, we no longer do. Ask your people. Life even if it is brief under the rule of the demons is preferable to ignominious death beneath the rubble of your own castle."

Blackthorne laughed. "Oh Fidget, you will never understand. No, it is not. Do you not see that every moment we resist you, our friends in Xetesk close in on the way to beat you and The Raven get ever closer to your beating heart? Before you came we were a divided nation. It took you to bring us together, to give us the will to fight again as one. And for that, we will always be grateful.

"One day, you will be beaten. You do not believe it I know but that is where your weakness lies. Come, attack us if you will. Taste death in your hundreds and frustration over the days we resist you."

Blackthorne turned and strode back into his castle, knowing he had to deliver the speech of his life to stop his people being overwhelmed before nightfall.

Hirad thrashed his mace through waist high. It tore across the karron's hammer limb and into its midriff, ripping flesh away. The knife now in his left hand jabbed into its face. Across the line, the karron were slowing dramatically. They hadn't forced the breakthrough they wanted. The Raven had held firm and the Al-Arynaar had responded with typical courage to the change of pace of the karron attack. But the attack wasn't fading fast enough and Hirad burned with the frustration.

"Someone get to Rebraal. Now!" He battered his mace into a karron skull. "Get the fuck back." Every muscle burned. He felt the sweat pouring from his body. "Erienne, see to him."

He had glanced around as the Al-Arynaar's leader had taken the blow from the karron, saving Erienne as he did so. He had landed unmoving. The Unknown had led The Raven on the counter, defending until the whirling limbs began to slow. After that it had turned into carnage. Al-Arynaar forged into the karron lines, driving them back toward the holes in the playhouse walls. Reavers shrieked and strike-strain dived but ForceCones kept them away. FlameOrbs crashed again and again into the back of the demon horde already distracted by what was coming up behind them.

"Pushing," shouted The Unknown. "Don't lose your focus, Coldheart. Put these bastards down."

Hirad let the rage settle on him like Auum had taught him, using it to give him clarity. He kicked the legs from a karron and broke its neck with his mace when it fell in front of him. He straightened and jabbed out with his knife, feeling it connect with flesh. The karron reared. Hirad butted it in the face and struck it under the chin with his mace. From his right, a laboured spike limb strike curved his way. Thraun had switched to his long sword and took the spike off at the wrist.

Outside, the sounds of approaching running feet and chanting were filling the air. Panicked calls went up from the demons around the playhouse. Hirad watched reavers darting into the air. He saw karron falter and stop at the back of the line.

"Let's break them," he growled. "Raven with me."

He moved and knew he wouldn't stop until they were running or he was dead. His mace crashed again and again into bodies rendered weak through exhaustion and Erienne's casting. His knife licked out, inflicting pain and frustrating riposte. Next to him, The Unknown wielded sword and mace in tandem as did Ark nearby. The karron had no answer. Their ploy had failed. Their enemies too skilled. And with the new threat almost on them, they were called off, broke and ran.

"Holding!" called The Unknown. "No one move after them."

Hirad saw the first of the relief pouring into the square. Banners flew, axes and swords glinted in the sunlight and the songs echoed from the louring buildings.

"Gods falling, Wesmen," said Hirad. "Now there's something I never thought to see."

"Let's hope they're offering help," said Thraun.

"Oh they are," said Suarav. The college captain had fought quietly and effectively next to Thraun. He was cut and bleeding but still very much alive. "We'll make the college now."

Hirad remembered and his relief turned to fear. He spun on his heel and ran to where Rebraal lay near the stage. Erienne and Denser knelt by him. Denser was casting. Hirad could see Erienne's hands shaking. He prayed it was with exhaustion and not grief. He joined them, crouching at Rebraal's feet.

"Oh dear Gods, no," he said. "Not you too."

A trail of blood ran from beneath his head. His face was pale. His mace lay twisted by his side, his left arm underneath his body and his leather torn, buckles broken. At least he was breathing.

Denser finished his casting. "This is one lucky elf. He's got a cut on his scalp and no doubt a concussion from the impact. But his mace took the force of the blow, deflected it along his leather here. It only glanced him or it would have burst his stomach, surely. But when he wakes he's going to be in a lot of pain."

"Dammit, Rebraal, what did I say to you?" whispered Hirad. "Why did you have to stay in the fight?"

"Because he's Raven at heart," said Erienne. "Because that's what he knew you'd do in his place. What any of us would do. He saved me, Hirad. Think how close we came to losing everything."

Hirad reached out and smoothed his hair. "Well done, Ilkar's little brother. Well done." He looked up to the sky. "We won this one, General," he said.

All around him the Wesmen songs filled the air. From the corners of his eyes, he saw warriors pouring into the playhouse and through the gaps he saw them surrounding the building. He heard voices shouting orders and the calls of demons, more distant now.

He became aware of a presence in front of them, standing a respectful distance away. He raised his head. In front of him stood a man with a middle-aged face but whose furs and leather covered what was plainly a powerful body. That face was crisscrossed with scars and fresh cuts. His greying light hair was braided and long, his eyes fierce. He exuded an aura of authority and power. Yet he waited for them to acknowledge him. The huge axe gripped casually in his hand dripped demon gore. Hirad had never set eyes on him before but there was no doubting who he was.

"Lord Tessaya," he said.

Tessaya inclined his head. "The Raven. It has been a meeting long in the making." He frowned and looked hard at Hirad. "We have all lost brothers. Your loss pierces you. It is written on you as plain as script. Which of you has fallen?"

"A great man," said Hirad. "General Darrick."

"Ahh." There was genuine regret in Tessaya's voice. "He, I respected above most men though his actions caused the Wesmen such pain. I wish we could have spoken together. I am saddened by his passing. The Spirits will keep him."

"His body is still on the street. We can't leave it there," said Hirad, turning to The Raven. "We need it. We have a ritual to perform."

"No," said Tessaya. "You cannot."

"You don't understand," said Hirad, keeping himself firmly in check. "He's Raven. We owe him respect."

Tessaya placed a gentle hand on Hirad's shoulder. "No," he repeated. "It does not matter where he fell, you cannot get to him. The demons are gone but merely to regroup. They will be back and we must make the college grounds before they do. If you stray they will take you."

"Unknown?" Hirad looked to the big man. "He's only on The Thread. Just a little way north." The Unknown bit his lip and shook his head.

"Then he is behind us and he is lost," said Tessaya. "The demons have the north of the city, everything beyond this building." He glanced around him. Most of the Al-Arynaar were standing still, plainly without the energy to do anything else. "Your forces are exhausted. Consign his Spirit through prayer and he will find his way. But you must come now. The storm is building again outside. The Wesmen will guard you all. Run amongst us. And have your mages keep the demons from over our heads." He allowed himself a small smile. "I may detest magic but I concede it has its uses. Particularly today."

"Unknown?" asked Hirad again. "Darrick's so close."

"Not this time, Hirad," he said. "We can't risk losing more of us to find him. Look inside yourself. Remember why we are here and what we have to do. You know I'm right."

Hirad rubbed a hand over his chin, determined not to break in front of Tessaya. "I know, I know," he said, though the words dragged reluctantly from his mouth. He could feel his cheeks burning. His fury, pent up. His frustration at boiling point. "Tell you something, Unknown, I've had it with these demons. I've had it with enemies destroying my country and killing my friends. Think I was angry before? That was nothing. Nothing. Let's make these bastards regret the day the first of them ever dared breathe our air."

CHAPTER 39

The attacks had been incessant ever since the Wesmen and their charges had burst through the rubble and broken timbers of the college gates. Tessaya had seen The Raven, the wounded and the exhausted back into the heart of his former nemesis, leaving his tribal commanders to organise and defend.

He had received unexpected but very welcome help from the elven mages who began by keeping overhead their defensive shields and then delivering the castings they called ColdRooms.

Tessaya didn't know how they worked. He didn't much care. What he did know was that the spell rendered the demons vulnerable to sword and axe and his warriors could kill at last.

The realisation had fired the tribes and the first battle had been a short, intense slaughter. The quick winged demons were more resilient than the lumbering karron but all fell to the released frustration of a Wesmen army previously impotent to inflict anything more than temporary disability.

Gallons of demon blood had washed the stone flags of the college court-yard, mixed with mere splashes of their own, before the demons had withdrawn. The Wesmen songs had begun then and had barely let up since. This was not just victory over the demons, this was the knowledge of where they stood as masters. Tessaya slapped his Shaman, Arnoan, on the back and laughed as he listened.

"Hear that? Today, we have met our destiny."

"You are being a little premature," said Arnoan. "We have not beaten the demons yet."

"But when we do, we will be standing as victors in the heart of the Dark College. It is surely a matter of time."

Arnoan frowned. "The Spirits would have it another way. They are scared and under threat. There is more to this than you or I can see."

Tessaya looked above him at the towers of Xetesk where his erstwhile enemies gazed out over the Wesmen in their midst. He turned his eyes to the sky where the borders of the invisible ColdRoom shell were marked by the demons that travelled its outer surface. There were those that waited their moment to attack at speed; and those who sought the location of the casting and directed the attacks on the mages they divined.

Four incursions were under way that he could see from his part-covered position near the barracks. All from reavers trying to snatch the elven mages. His warriors guarded them. Dragged the enemies from the sky. Split their skulls and tore off their wings. It was the Wesmen way.

On the ground the karron stood mute. Tessaya could see them through the holes they had torn in the walls and the gates they had destroyed before the ColdRooms had pushed them back outside the college grounds. They were strong in attack but weak in body. They succumbed so quickly to the effects of the ColdRooms. "Lesser" the elf Rebraal termed them. Tessaya agreed.

"You worry too much," said Tessaya. "The Spirits are far from us and their minds are confused more than they are clear. Look at the demons now. Futile, isn't it? Why don't they use all their force to attack, do you think? They outnumber us by ten to one at the very least. It's because they know that in here we can beat them. They don't fight well. They rely on fear and we are not afraid."

Arnoan shook his head. "Perhaps, my Lord. Perhaps."

"You disagree?"

"I think we have merely been contained. While they grow stronger. How long will the karron remain so weak they are barely able to enter the mage casting? They have all the time in their hands and we grow weaker."

"I think not."

"I mean them." Arnoan pointed at the towers. "When the mages are gone, we have no weapon. Why else do you think they have not tried to attack us until today if not that we can be kept until all meaningful defence is gone?"

"We will prevail," said Tessaya.

Arnoan raised his eyebrows. "I need to pray."

"Try and calm your Spirits, my Shaman."

Tessaya watched Arnoan go to the shrine he had created in the barracks' officer quarters. The attacks had broken off for the moment and Wesmen jeers chased the demons out of the casting. Drenoul was up there too, gazing down on the mistake he had made by leaving the Wesmen unchallenged. A movement in the tallest tower caught his eye and he glanced up. Arnoan's words returned unbidden to his mind and he frowned.

The atmosphere inside the tower complex was one of relief, not victory as it was outside, and he found himself doubting his confidence. He wondered what news The Raven had brought to Xetesk and what his part in it would be. He had asked not to be involved in their debate and was beginning to regret that decision though it had seemed the right one at the time. His presence would have been inflammatory both among the tribal lords and high in the towers he detested so much; and for now at least, they had to be a united force against the common enemy.

Finally, he stared through the gates at the karron. Thousands of them. Waiting. He had to accept the fact that Arnoan might be right and so instead of taking to his bed for an hour as he had thought to do, he barked for his commanders to attend him. There was defensive planning to be done.

Hirad wasn't sure if Dystran or Vuldaroq had listened to a great deal of what The Unknown said. Both men could barely take their eyes from Erienne. She sat leaning on her husband, the grief evident in her face and her hands still shaking from her One castings, still so recent.

Enough to know what was being asked of them but little more. Hirad was feeling tired and sore. His mind was full of images of Darrick. He was furious that he hadn't been able to save him and he wasn't in the mood for anything but the answers he wanted. He barely waited for The Unknown to finish speaking.

"Either of you know who's been talking?"

His voice, loud and sharp, brought both their heads round.

"I beg your pardon?" said Dystran.

"It's just that The Unknown is sitting beside me and you barely looked at him."

"Your point being?"

"That we're offering the one chance all of us have to beat these bastards but the pair of you are eyeing up Erienne like a prime steak. Let me make a couple of things absolutely clear."

The Unknown tensed but didn't speak.

"We have fought our way in here to do what has to be done to save our country from the problems you have caused it. And not just our country but probably countless other dimensions in addition to those we know about. Already, we have lost Ry Darrick in the struggle and Auum has lost Duele. We have lost those we sent to try and warn you what was coming. All because of you. But this isn't the time for revenge and recrimination. If it was, you'd be dead already. But what it also means is your desire to control Erienne is also behind us, for the good of us all. Erienne is Raven. She will be coming with us. All you have to worry about is what The Unknown has just asked you. Assuming you were listening. If you can't put aside what is past and gone then none of us have any future. What is it to be?"

Dystran stared at Hirad as if composing a suitable retort. But something in the barbarian's expression changed his mind and instead a wry smile crossed his face. He spread his arms.

"No one underestimates the problem we face or the losses you have suffered. But at heart we remain mages. Erienne, please forgive us but what you are is a unique fascination."

Erienne shrugged. "Whatever makes you happy."

"But as to what you ask . . ." Dystran shook his head. "We have no way of sending you or anyone to the current demon dimension. Our link to them was all to do with focused mana trails and nothing to do with their location. I'm sorry, but we're going to have to think of another way to beat them."

"There has to be a way to get us there. It's the only chance to close the tear, stop any more of them coming here and to disperse the mana. Without it, we're all as good as dead, you know that."

"Yes, we know that," said Vuldaroq wearily. "And believe me we're sure there is a way but we just don't know it. We scoured every text we managed to steal from the library for anything useful. And we found something incredibly important. Unfortunately, it speaks of a religious punishment based on an ancient magic that died with a race called the Charanacks. Find one alive and no doubt we'll be fine."

"Because?"

"Because according to a note in the margin of one of our demonology texts, they, whoever they were, had a link to the demons. That was the punishment apparently. Banishment or some such." Dystran paused and looked past Hirad. "Something funny?"

Hirad turned. Rebraal was smiling despite the prevailing mood and Auum wore that curled-lip expression that denoted utter contempt. The TaiGethen spoke.

"Humans are so stupid," he said in elvish that Rebraal translated. "Always you ignore your past enemies because you think them unimportant by the mere fact of their apparent passing. And yet you wonder why it is you have no future."

"Care to enlighten us?" said Dystran.

"Charanack is a play on an ancient elvish term," said Rebraal. "Chorun-y-ayck. It means man of the west. I trust I don't need to make further connection."

Hirad exhaled a breath he hadn't realised he was holding. Shaking his head he pushed himself to his feet and walked stiffly over to Dystran's balcony doors where Thraun and Ark stood on guard. He was exhausted. Gods drowning, they all were. Erienne and Denser practically spent. All the warriors carrying cuts, muscle tears and the aches of a long time out of the routine of battle. Like all of them, Hirad couldn't wait to get his head down for a few hours. Perhaps even feel the benefit of a WarmHeal from someone. For now, they were as safe as they could get on Balaia. He only had to look down to know that to be true.

The doors were open and he strode outside and looked down on the reclaimed college. The courtyard was crawling with Wesmen. They had clearly just repulsed another demon attack. Around two thousand warriors and their Shamen had brought a quite extraordinary optimism to the college. Their songs echoed into the sky, their cook fires burned bright and the smells of the provisions they had brought with them were driving the taste-starved Xeteskians to distraction.

They had occupied the open spaces, the stables, the barracks, three of the long rooms, and liberated the library and mana bowl. They had access to the courtyard and stable wells and they were using the surfeit of water to wash demon slime and corpses from the stones toward the edge of the ColdRoom shell. They seemed to have no fear of the enemy gathered scant yards from them though as he watched, Hirad saw Tessaya stride into the centre of the courtyard to begin marshalling something or other.

An extraordinary man and one of the few to live up to Hirad's expectations. He watched the Wesmen forming into more cohesive defensive units in front of the gaps in the walls through which they could see the karron. The lesser demons hadn't attacked the ColdRoom so far but clearly Tessaya's distrust of magic wasn't appeased.

"So," he said. "Before we all fall asleep, who's coming with me to ask the great man a big favour?"

He felt the pulse of pure panic through them all and the massing of the malevolence close at hand. They pushed and tore where the fabric between the living and the dead was stretched. Gone were the feelings of light and warmth, of closeness and joy. Replaced by a marauding dread and a chasm opening to an eternity of absence.

Those others that he sought for communication had gone with the mass pressed as far from the threat as they could be. Though distance held no real meaning. But he would not run. There was nowhere safe. The threat had to be removed. He sought again the light of those he loved through the thinning fabric. How had the malevolence gained such strength? He had no conception, no answer. Time was a meaningless measure.

He felt a presence near him. Strong. Calming. Reminiscent but not loved. How would he describe it . . . respected. Revered. He felt urging and saw the images of running feet and fast-flowing water. He felt the words too. They signified security.

I have found you.

He communicated, still moving toward his goal, his impetus increased. In his mind the blurred began to focus. He felt clarity and direction such as he had not developed in the presence of any of the others.

I will show you.

The presence by him dominated his mind now. It held disdain for the malevolence nor did it fear the threat. He saw images. Blood flowing and a body hitting cold earth. He saw arms raised in triumph. He saw a building and felt the burgeoning of that power he knew had to be shut off. The feelings of urging intensified.

The living have little time.

Who are you?

A friend.

He journeyed on toward the place of greatest threat. Comforted. Justified. Near him he felt the brief touch of a bright living light. Alien. He tried to connect with it but it shied from him, seeming to glow brighter when it turned toward the mass. Ilkar felt the spring of a new thought. But all around him, the helpless fear only deepened. There was sudden and enormous pressure. Light dimmed. Feelings chilled.

They were inside. It was not just the living for whom time was short. He thought of the name and shouted for help.

Hirad would have pitched down the stairs but for The Unknown's broad back breaking his fall. He turned and caught the barbarian, ignoring the sharp pain in his hip.

"Hirad? Hirad!"

The Raven clustered around him. He was holding his hands clamped to his head. His eyes were wide and searching. His mouth, initially clamped shut, began to move. A frown deepened the lines of his forehead.

"Let's get him to the next landing. Thraun, take his legs."

They moved off. The Unknown backed down the spiral, using the outside wall and rail to guide him.

"What do you think. Sha-Kaan?"

The Unknown shook his head. Sha-Kaan's presence caused a relaxation in Hirad's body. This was more like a seizure. Hirad's eyes held a deep anxiety he hadn't seen before. He experienced similar misgivings as they laid the barbarian down on the landing, a cloak under his head.

"Ilkar?" suggested Erienne.

The sound of the elf's name seemed to echo in the enclosed space. The Unknown felt a shudder pass through him.

"Let's hope so," he said. "But it's never been like this before."

"No indeed," said Rebraal, coming to Hirad's side. "Listen to him, my friend. Listen hard. Try to understand."

The sounds of renewed battle filtered up to them. The Unknown ignored them. He clasped one of Hirad's tight-bunched fists.

"All right, Coldheart," he said. "We're all here with you. Breathe easy."

But he wasn't. His chest was fluttering and his face pale. The Unknown looked to Erienne who was stroking Hirad's hair back across his head. Her expression reflected his concerns.

"Can you do anything?"

"I daren't," she said. "Look at him. It's deep in his mind. This is all physical symptom. I can't stop it. I wouldn't know how."

"And you mustn't try," said Rebraal.

"Just checking."

Erienne smiled. They all looked back at Hirad. His eyes still jerked and his mouth moved. He was whispering. The Unknown put his head closer.

"Where are you?" Hirad's voice was very quiet, his breath shallow and pained.

"Right here, old son," said The Unknown.

"I can't see you. Can feel you, Ilks."

The Unknown glanced up.

"It is Ilkar," he confirmed.

"Let me through." Dystran's voice was overloud. He shouldered his way through his guards and more gently eased Denser and Thraun aside. "What's going on? Why did no one think to tell me? I could have walked out there alone. Hardly fitting."

"Hirad's got a contact. Just be quiet," said The Unknown.

Dystran inhaled sharply.

"Don't disturb him," said Rebraal. "It would be dangerous for both of them."

"A contact. Who with, that damned dragon?"

The Unknown looked up into Dystran's face and saw the arrogance still there.

"No, Dystran," he replied, his voice deliberately cold. "Ilkar. In another dimension you've placed at risk."

"But he's dead, surely?"

"Yes," replied Rebraal.

"Yes but—"

"Just accept it," snapped Erienne. "Leave us alone."

The Unknown became aware of a growing noise from outside. Below them, in the complex, men were shouting.

"You have to run," shouted Hirad.

They all jumped.

"Gods," said Denser. "You think he means us?"

"No," said Rebraal. "He's not aware of us at all." The Al-Arynaar leader looked strained.

"Please. Make yourself safe. We are coming," said Hirad.

"I take it this is unusual?" said Denser.

"Impossible," said Rebraal. "He should not be understanding Ilkar so clearly."

A colossal roar split the air. Wesmen voices raised in song and call. Xeteskians in the dome were running. They heard the doors cycle closed, the boom reverberating through the tower.

"Ark, go and find out what's happening," ordered The Unknown. "Come on, Hirad, I think it's time you were back with us."

The former Protector moved away and out of sight. Auum and Evunn went after him. The Unknown could see Thraun sniffing the air. He watched the shapechanger's face. His forehead pinched and his jaw tensed. Their eyes met.

"The hunt has begun," said Thraun.

"What?" said The Unknown.

From below, Ark was shouting for them. Dystran was on the move, closely followed by Vuldaroq and their guards. The Raven held station, willing Hirad to regain consciousness.

He obliged, his eyes snapping open. He gripped The Unknown's arms and pulled him close. The barbarian's eyes were bloodshot and desperate.

"We have to go now," he said. "They are inside."

Arnoan gasped. He wrenched himself from his prayers and fell flat on his back. His chest heaved and his pulse raced. His head throbbed and pounded. Shards of pain speared his forehead and temples. The clouds of incense further fogged his damaged vision.

He lay where he was until he was sure he wasn't about to join those he had so recently contacted. Slowly, his heart calmed, the incense suffusing his blood and forcing him to relax. Residual pain like a pulled muscle remained. His breathing eased, his vision began to clear and he unclenched his fists. It seemed there was little he could do about the thrashing in his head or the sweat running from every pore.

The old Shaman hauled himself to a sitting position against the wall facing the door to his shrine. Anxious faces looked in. He waved them away feebly.

"I'm all right," he said. "All right. Some time, please. Some privacy."

The faces withdrew. Arnoan placed shivering hands on quivering legs. He closed his eyes, fighting for control. He tried to recall the Communion. It had in so many ways been like any other. The gateway had opened in his mind. The physical expression of it in the hardening of incense smoke. He had stepped to the open portal through which his body could not pass and he had knelt. He had travelled with his mind and almost lost it.

First, the touch of something fresh. Bright and new and almost apologetic. He had ignored it though, seeking the Spirits of the ancients. The force of their emotion would have overwhelmed a lesser Shaman. Left them lost in themselves. But it had spoken loud and unequivocally; a coalescence of all the tendrils of anxiety he had been feeling for so long.

Terror. Helplessness. Desperation. Pleading. The expiration of time and opportunity.

Arnoan opened his eyes and pushed himself to his feet. He staggered and clung to the wall, waves of nausea sweeping over him. Outside, the sounds of battle were taken up once more but the noise was intense and alien. The old Shaman, his heart rattling painfully in his chest, waited for the sickness to pass. He pushed himself away from the wall and bustled toward the barracks door.

"Where is Tessaya?"

The warrior at the door turned frightened eyes to him. "Out there," he said. "Leading the tribes."

"Shadow me," ordered Arnoan. "I must speak with him."

The warrior drew in a deep breath. "Yes, my Shaman."

Arnoan gestured him aside and strode out into the freezing late afternoon. The demons were attacking on multiple fronts and from above. It was to be expected. Tribal banners flew proud, the songs of the Wesmen reached beyond the ColdRoom shell and the warriors fought bravely.

It was several paces before Arnoan's confident stride into the courtyard faltered. There were the bodies of demons on the ground but too many Wesmen lay with them. He saw Al-Arynaar elves running from the dome complex, splitting into two large groups and running toward gates and long rooms, the latter where elven casters were protected.

The atmosphere was wrong. The songs weren't those of victory but those of struggle and grit. The songs that kept scared warriors together and fighting against the odds. Ahead of him, he could see the Paleon banner flying high. Tessaya was underneath it, fighting against reavers and strike-strain. Immediately in front of the Wesmen lord, the walls of Xetesk crumbled and burst in, scattering rubble into the courtyard. The walkway above collapsed along a forty-yard length. And through the gap came the karron. Transformed.

"Spirits preserve us all," said Arnoan.

CHAPTER 40

The Raven followed the Al-Arynaar out of the dome complex while the Xeteskians were still organising themselves. The elven warriors and mages split, heading for the ColdRoom casters. The Unknown brought The Raven to a halt on the steps to take stock.

The courtyard was in upheaval but the reason for the roar they'd heard beginning from inside Dystran's tower was high in the sky above the college. From the slit in the deep blue sky, white clouds billowed and jetted into Balaian space. It was mana, pouring in at a hugely increased rate. The temperature, already low, was dipping fast toward freezing and there was no doubting that the colouring of the cloud was ice crystals. Those crystals were warming just enough as they fell to drop as chill rain onto the combatants below.

Down on the ground, the Wesmen and Al-Arynaar were under a blistering attack. Reavers had stormed the ColdRoom shell with strike-strain clouds backing them. Karron were battering on the walls in a number of places and fighting to try and gain access through the sundered gates. So far, the two thousand Wesmen warriors were holding comfortably enough but they were suffering casualties. Hirad, still feeling bleary after his frightening contact with Ilkar, couldn't work out why but felt the scene didn't quite ring true.

"Is it just me or are the reavers quicker and stronger?" he asked.

"Definitely," said Rebraal. "Tell me what Ilkar told you."

"He said they had broken into the spirit dimension. He said they were fighting but that they only have their belief to defend them and their links to us to sustain them and give them strength. We have to go and close off the demon power now or they'll be overwhelmed."

Hirad set off down the steps.

"Hirad wait," said The Unknown. "I'm sorry but I don't see the connection."

"And how did they break in?" asked Erienne. "I understood that to be possible only if they broke either the elves or the Wesmen."

Hirad rounded on them, feeling suddenly hot. "Do you think we've got time to debate this? Look around you. The demons are pressing like never before. Isn't it obvious what's happened? We have to go or Ilkar will be lost and so will we."

"Hirad wait," said The Unknown. "We have to approach Tessaya the right way. We have to be sure of our ground. We're about to use a centrepiece of his religion. He's hardly going to just wave us goodbye."

"Well why not? We'll be saving his dead too. Gods drowning, why are you all being so cautious? Look!"

He pointed up into the sky. Reavers plunged on the Wesmen and Al-Arynaar. Tired warriors fought hard. From gaps in the shell elements, elven mages cast IceWind into the sky. He backed up the steps to stand with The Raven. So far, they had been ignored but it wouldn't last for long. Hirad could see the masters floating high above, directing battle. The noise was growing. The walls groaned under the battering of the karron. Abruptly, a five-yard section gave way, bringing down the parapet on a long stretch either side.

The karron stormed in. Or at least, they began as karron. These were striding into the ColdRooms apparently unhampered by the lack of mana within. And they were growing with every stride. Seven and eight feet high now and they weren't finished. Bodies filled out with new muscle. The hammer and spike limbs lengthened a little, weapons developing, building. Halfway down their torsos, under their arms, more limbs were sprouting. Sinuous, long and pincered. True monsters, facing which the Wesmen sang defiance and courage. Unwavering in the face of a new and deadly threat.

"Gods burning," breathed The Unknown.

"Reckon we've got time to have a little chat now?" asked Hirad. "Darrick died to get us all in here. Let's not waste what he gave us."

"Right," said The Unknown. "Rebraal, Auum, we need their head Shaman. And find Eilaan. Raven, with me to Tessaya. Meeting at the barracks, that's where their shrine is. Go."

The Raven ran down into the maelstrom. They took up their classic angled chevron but with Thraun at Hirad's right-hand side now Darrick was gone. The Unknown and Ark formed the forward muscle to the left. Behind them, both Denser and Erienne had blades in their hands. Al-Arynaar came to their sides, providing a flanking defence.

"Tessaya!" shouted Hirad. "We need Tessaya."

They could see the Paleon banner fluttering in the breeze toward the front of the line where the boosted karrons were engaging the Wesmen. Warriors turned to see The Raven approaching. Orders were shouted. Ahead of them, a path was created somewhat reluctantly.

Reavers dropped in front of The Raven. Strike-strain gathered overhead and dived.

"Keep moving, Raven!" called The Unknown.

"No problem," said Hirad.

Holding his blade in both hands, he ran on. The first of the reavers were engulfed in a storm of Wesmen axes but others were heading in. Hirad, head cocked up, saw three coming in.

"Upward, Unknown!"

Hirad ran on a pace, spun on his heel and whipped his sword in a circle above his head. The blade caught reaver feet, sawing through claw and bone. The demon screeched. It tried to regain some height but its momentum brought it on down. Thraun's blade chopped through its left wing, bringing it to the ground.

To the left, The Unknown had heeded Hirad's warning. The big warrior's mace dragged through reaver flesh and his sword took off its tail. Unbalanced, the creature crashed to the stone where Ark crushed its skull. The third flew in at a shallow angle, aiming for the mage targets. Hirad left Thraun to finish the first and moved fast.

"Erienne, down!"

She dropped to her haunches. Hirad's blade swept through, cutting to the reaver's spine. Gore flew and splattered. The reaver flew on a couple of beats and fell among the Wesmen.

"Moving on, Raven!" The Unknown's voice kept them focused.

Strike-strain rained down on them. More tenacious than they had been before but carrying no greater threat in reality. Hirad kept his sword up and forward, watching for reavers. He kept his free hand in front of his face, warding off the strike-strain trying to take out his eyes. Wesmen and Al-Arynaar closed in around them. He could see the Paleon standard at hand.

Scant yards ahead, the new karron were deep in the fight along an expanding front. They moved at frightening speed against an unmoving Wesmen wall. Lord Tessaya's voice sang out, giving his people strength. Axes rose and fell. Warriors screamed. Karron died.

Hirad saw through the crowds a glimpse of the power of the boosted demons. A Wesmen axe flashed into a karron face. It fell back but another was in so quickly. A pincer limb whipped out, grabbing the warrior's axe arm. The spike limb thrashed across his undefended body and his corpse was hurled aside.

"Hold!" said The Unknown.

The Raven stopped and formed up to defend. Ahead of them, Tessaya roared more orders. Hirad saw his axe take the head from his enemy. The Wesmen pushed forward, halting the karron advance. Hirad could feel their pure ferocity like a shivering in the air. He dragged a strike-strain from his shoulder and crushed it under his heel. By the time he looked up, Tessaya was standing in front of them.

"You come to stand with the Wesmen?" he asked.

His face was cut and bleeding but his eyes shone with his determination and energy. Warriors around him took the strike-strain from the air near him much as the Al-Arynaar did for The Raven.

"No," said Hirad. "Our fight is elsewhere but we need your help and that of your Shaman."

Tessaya frowned. "I do not understand."

"We'll explain but not here. Please, come with us to the barracks where your Shaman is waiting."

"I will not leave the battle with the ul-karron," he said. "I must stand and fight with my warriors."

Hirad watched him square his shoulders. His eyes had barely left the fight to his right.

"Just for a few moments," said The Unknown. "It concerns the future of us all."

Tessaya sized them up. Hirad felt like he was in a bubble. He was aware of the fighting all around him. The desultory spells working across the shell and the sound of reaver and strike-strain attacks. The chants of the Wesmen as they drove hard at the ul-karron. But it seemed distant somehow. Almost unimportant compared to the workings of the mind of the man in front of them.

Tessaya turned and spoke quickly to his lieutenant. He nodded at Hirad.

"You have my attention," he said. "Don't waste it."

Al-Arynaar and Wesmen rushed their charges to the barracks. The move had not gone unnoticed by the master demons and already the focus of reaver attacks was switched. It bought the Wesmen in the front line some respite but posed a new problem. Wesmen reserve were already organising themselves to ring the barracks building while Rebraal, standing at the door, was overseeing his people scaling the walls to stand on the flat roof.

They were ushered inside to the officers' quarters. Arnoan was already there and with him were Auum, Evunn, Pheone, Dystran and Vuldaroq. Eilaan stood in one corner, looking nervous. With The Raven, Rebraal and Tessaya completing the complement, the incense-heavy room was crowded and hot. Hirad felt a rush of nerves combined with a sense of excitement and history. In this room were the men, women and elves on whom the fate of the entire dimension rested.

Tessaya, his presence the single greatest in the room, laid his axe on a table by the door and strode across to Arnoan. He took in the assembled company and was clearly impressed despite himself.

"We have a battle to win outside these walls," he said, speaking in eastern Balaian for the benefit of those around him. "Explain to me what is proposed."

Arnoan had the look of a haunted man close to panic. His hands were shaking and his face was grey with exhaustion. Tessaya gripped his shoulders and his expression softened.

"My Shaman, calm yourself," he said. "I understand we have more problems than those immediately without. What has happened?"

"I was on my way to find you, my Lord," said Arnoan. "The demons have broken into the Spirits' resting place. They fight but they have no real weapons. The attack is confirmed by the elves. We have to act or our ancestors will be lost to us. We cannot let this happen."

"How can this have happened?" demanded Tessaya. "The Spirits are inviolate."

"The incursion is as yet small but it will grow," said Arnoan. "I fear one of our Shamen must have been taken by demons."

"Then we will find him and rescue him. Close this breach and continue our fight against the enemy on our own terms."

"That is not possible," said Dystran. "Xetesk is a big city. The demons control both it and all the surrounding lands. You can never hope to find him."

"But there is another way," said Hirad. "The Raven's way."

"The only way," added The Unknown.

Tessaya's head swung round to The Raven. "Speak," he said.

Hirad nodded at Denser, best able to make the explanation.

"My Lord Tessaya, the demons attack us on multiple fronts. What we must do now was always a certainty but we are forced to act sooner than we would have wished. The only way to stop the enemy is to close the gap in the sky above the college. Cut off the flow of mana and the pathway to this dimension before the density of both enemies and mana becomes overwhelming.

"With the breach in the spirit dimension, that time has drawn much closer. You can already see the strength it has given them and that strength will only grow. We have to travel to the demons' dying home and shut off the power, close the gap. Force the demons to defeat. We had thought Xeteskian knowledge of dimensional magics would be able to send us there but it cannot. You can. Your religion and your Shaman's powers allow for travel to the heart of the demon lands. You must agree to send us. You must or we will all perish under the power of our enemies."

Tessaya's doubt was evident in his expression and mirrored in his words. "This is preposterous," he said. "The ceremony you speak of is the severest punishment we can hand down to a warrior. It is banishment and damnation without possibility of resting with the Spirits." He shrugged. "It is death alone without salvation."

"Nevertheless, you must agree," continued Denser. "It is a gamble but one that we must take. It is the only thing which can save us."

"And to take on this mighty responsibility, we send a few exhausted Easterners? If it is so important, then the Wesmen will undertake it. Why send a few when there is an army outside?"

"Because, my Lord, if your army travels, then Xetesk has no defence and will be overrun. Julatsa is abandoned, Dordover has fallen and Lystern must be close to failing too. If Balaian magic dies then it will not matter if we close the gap or not. The demons will rule Balaia."

"The Wesmen will never bow to demons."

"Damn you, Tessaya, but you remind me of me," growled Hirad. "If there is no magic there are no weapons. You cannot kill demons without it, and you know that. So stop the posturing and do the right thing."

Tessaya's head snapped round. "Never speak to me in that fashion, Raven. I am Tessaya, Lord of all the Wesmen."

"I know," said Hirad. "And I admire and respect you. But you will be lord of an enslaved race if you do not let us attempt this."

"What do you have to lose?" asked Erienne. "If you don't believe us, so be it but don't stop us doing what we believe to be right. Listen to your Shaman, Lord Tessaya. Give the order."

"Arnoan? Speak."

"My Lord, I cannot say if they will succeed but I, like you, know where they will travel. No Wesman will go there willingly and to be forced to do so would weaken them. We cannot afford to take an army. We have to defend while they make this attempt. I would say let them go. And should they not come back, we will still be here to fight. The Wesmen will prevail."

Tessaya considered again. On the roof above them, the Al-Arynaar fought reavers trying to gain access to their prizes. A demon fist smashed a hole in the roof, scattering tile and plaster.

Hirad indicated above his head. "The demons know we are a threat. They may not know what we intend but they want our souls. While we live, they cannot win because the will of our country cannot be broken."

Tessaya chuckled. "Your arrogance matches my own," he said. "But you are asking me to agree to something in which I can see no benefit. I agree the demons think you a threat. So surely you should fight by me. Show enemies and allies alike that we are unbowed."

"Not this time," said The Unknown. "The Raven have a different path. You are critical to the worth of it. You must hold the college. Keep magic alive."

This time, Tessaya laughed out loud. "Save that which I despise. That I should stand here and be forced to agree with such a sentiment." He sobered. "You really believe this to be our only hope?"

Hirad nodded. "And we will not be alone. While we have no army of Wesmen, which I would welcome, we have allies who will travel the dimensions to safeguard our path. Dragons, Lord Tessaya. You know their power and you met only three. This time, I can call on thousands."

"A powerful ally. Perhaps they should be here with us."

"They are not because they know what must be done. Their battle will not be fought here."

Tessaya turned from Hirad to the quartet of elves. "And you?"

Auum inclined his head. "There is but one solution. I travel with them."

And finally he settled on Dystran. "And you, my Lord Dystran. How do you see this folly?"

Dystran smiled. "I have learned over the years that The Raven are seldom mistaken and always victorious. I do not pretend to understand the links between the living and the dead and will be fascinated to research them at a later date. But for now, I need to know I have a chance of living long enough to indulge myself in a world free of demons. If The Raven feel this is the way, I will not dissuade them."

Tessaya nodded. "Very well. Travel where you will with the help of my Shaman. You have my blessing and my hopes travel with you though I believe you travel to your deaths. It is a wasted opportunity. I would have welcomed the chance to see you fight by my side."

"We also," said Hirad, the relief at Tessaya's acquiescence warming his body.

"When you return, there may still be time," said Tessaya.

"No," said Thraun, quiet until now. Until the reality of their decision had to be faced. "I think we all understand that while your Shaman can send us to the demon dimension, he cannot bring us back."

There was a pause. None of them could look another in the eye but the determination remained.

"Raven?" said Hirad. "Unknown, you have family."

"That is precisely why I am here," said The Unknown.

"None of us will turn," said Denser. "Isn't this the ultimate ride for The Raven?"

"All the way there," said Hirad, not afraid. "No coming back."

"Then my grief for the loss of General Darrick extends to you all. May the Spirits welcome you to your rest." Tessaya picked up his axe. "Now, I have a battle to win or as I understand it, your sacrifice will be meaningless. And that would be unforgivable."

CHAPTER 41

The attack halted so abruptly that it was far too long before anyone spoke. The pressure was so intense in defence that it was hard to break out of the mind-set.

"Stand down, stand down," said Heryst.

He lowered his own dripping sword and felt the shivering in his arms and legs and the heaving in his chest. Again they had beaten off the demons. Reavers had stormed through the windows and doors of the grand council chamber and tried once more to take out the two last remaining ColdRoom teams. The battle had been desperate but it had been successful.

Yet the cost, like always, was far too high. Bodies of demons and Lysternans mixed in the hall and would have to be cleared aside. The floor would have to be washed again of the blood and gore but the stench would inevitably grow. And the sickness would intensify in its wake. He stopped the thought. He saw the chamber afresh and knew there would be no time for new sickness to develop.

How quickly real hope was extinguished. So recently, they had been contemplating a breakout. They had laid plans to steal their wagons and their route from the city was known inside out by them all. They had bagged up provisions and filled waterskins. They had been set to go.

And then quite without warning the demons had launched an attack with numbers Heryst hadn't thought them able to bring to bear. It had been short but devastatingly effective before it was beaten off. Three successive attacks later and it took too little time to count up the survivors. They were less than fifty now.

Heryst looked around his people and still their spirit hadn't been broken though with every moment their inevitable deaths drew closer. He studied each of them in turn, seeing in their pale faces and their bloodied expressions the knowledge of their impending doom. Arabelle, Makkan, Terol, Renarn . . . all still lived, all still fought. From soldier through mage to cook's runner, they stood proud but exhausted. All wondered how many more attacks they could resist before the ColdRoom mages were taken or killed.

"Why did they break off?" asked Arabelle. "They had us, you know."

"Perhaps they didn't realise," said Renarn. "Perhaps they were called to another battle."

Heryst chuckled in spite of their situation. The filth, cold, hunger and thirst. "Ever the optimist, Renarn. There is little else, I suppose. I think that no matter their overwhelming numbers, they are still wary. They know we can hurt them as we have proved. They are many but finite."

Heryst beckoned them all to him, but for the guard that stood on the council table and over the mages that gave them their remaining glimmer of hope. He felt a curious elation.

"My friends," he said, and he meant that term with every fibre he possessed. "We have held the enemy for so long. We have bought time for those who are stronger and who can damage the demons more severely. We have occupied so many and that has kept them from the souls of others. Never forget what you have achieved. Nothing you have done has been wasted.

"When next the demons come, we can expect it to be the last time. They have merely gone to report. Those who wish to surrender to them now, you have my blessing. It may be that you will survive with hope for your liberation. All I do know is that there is no hope for you if you stay here."

Not a single person moved. Heryst nodded.

"I expected as much. It would be like betrayal, wouldn't it?"

Murmurs of agreement greeted his words.

"We want nothing but to stand by you until the end," said Arabelle.

"Then now is the time to make your peace with the Gods if you believe in such and to say goodbye to those you have come to love. There won't be the opportunity later. I will see you all individually but you know where I must begin."

Heryst walked to the quiet corner of the chamber. One of the five who lay on makeshift beds there was Kayvel. His old friend and mentor was close to death and that was a blessing. He had lost his sight in the last day and his skin was sallow and cold to the touch. Heryst knelt by him and wiped the mucus from his mouth and nose.

"You heard what I said?" he asked, voice gentle and quiet.

"It was a fitting speech," said Kayvel, his voice dry and cracked. "You always did pick the right moments."

"Then you know why I'm here."

"I am honoured to be your first port of call."

"Where else would I begin, Kayvel?"

Kayvel grabbed at his sleeve, catching a grip at the second attempt. "Then listen to me one last time. You and the remaining mages must leave and leave now. Lystern cannot be allowed to die. Drop the ColdRooms, cast ShadowWings and fly anywhere."

"I will not leave my people."

"You know I am right," said Kayvel, breath rasping in his throat. "We have no more time for sentimentality."

Heryst was silent. Of course Kayvel was right but it was an impossible course to follow. He'd struggled with these people for so long. How could he possibly look down on their deaths from beneath ShadowWings?

The unmistakable rumbling of advancing karron was heard through the shattered windows. It had purpose about it. And in the sky, reavers called and strike-strain chattered. It was beginning. Heryst turned to Kayvel to say his last words.

"Don't let them take me," said Kayvel. "I will not lose my soul."

"Whatever your wish," said Heryst.

A dull thud resounded through the tower's foundations. Then another. More. In moments, a constant pounding reverberated across the building. Plaster was dislodged, remaining window glass rattled and timbers squeaked at their joists. The pounding intensified quickly. The council chamber rumbled and shook. Doors rattled in their stays.

"Dear Gods," muttered Heryst.

Kayvel's grip hadn't loosened. "Do what I say, Heryst. Soon you'll have no choice."

Heryst leaned in and kissed the dying man's forehead. "Goodbye, old friend. Don't worry about me."

"Goodbye, my Lord Heryst. It has been an honour to serve you."

Heryst swept to his feet and looked back into the chamber. The karron were taking the tower apart from the bottom upward. Arabelle was organising the remnants of the defence. On the table, the guards looked down anxiously on the casting mages. The whole table was vibrating. The mages, all seated, were juddering. It was only a matter of time.

"Arabelle!" called Heryst. The chamber shifted violently. "Arabelle!"

She shouted more orders and ran over to him. "Get ready to go."

"Where?" he asked.

She pointed straight up. "You know where. I was listening to Kayvel. We agree with him. We'll hold them off for long enough."

Another juddering series of impacts. The tower rocked in its broad foundations.

"Arabelle, they aren't going to come up here again. They're going to bring the tower down."

"I know," she said. "We're going to distract them. You take the mages."

The sound of falling stone echoed up the tower. A timber in the roof cracked and crashed to the ground. His people scattered. It fell square on the table, crushing two of the guards.

"ColdRoom down!" shouted one of the casting mages. "We're defenceless."

Arabelle grabbed Heryst. "It has to be now, my Lord. The windows are open, you can cast."

"No."

"The college must survive. Don't argue with me."

Heryst looked past her at all the faces staring back at him. Every one of them was behind Arabelle.

The first reaver appeared at the windows to look inside, checking on the state of the Lysternans. Below, karron took great gouges out of the tower. The floor was cracking. More timbers groaned overhead.

"Fly well, fly safe," she said.

Heryst, the tears forming in his eyes, nodded his thanks and admiration. Arabelle turned to the defenders.

"To your positions. Go!"

The reaver backed away as the tower shifted and angled. Timbers split and began to fall. Heryst ran to his mages on the table.

"With me, my mages. ShadowWings and fly."

Seven. Seven mages. Two more than the flight from Dordover if he did but know it. The casting complete, the Wings at his back, Heryst flew for a shattered window. Below him, the bravest people he had ever known bought him the precious time he needed.

He whispered last words to his friends and flew hard for the clouds.

Arnoan was deep in concentration performing the banishment ritual while the demons tore at the barracks roof and fought the Al-Arynaar. Wesmen warriors had filled waterskins and provided provisions sacks. Now all they could do was wait for the Shaman to be ready.

"Where does it draw from?" asked Erienne. "I mean, it is magic, isn't it?"

"Plainly," said Vuldaroq. "But there is no mana usage."

"It's a conversation for another time," said Dystran. "Dear Gods, look at you all. Some last-hope group you make."

Hirad thought to round on him but stopped. He was right. Hirad himself felt like sleeping forever and around him none of The Raven were in any better condition. Both Erienne and Denser had to be close to their stamina limits, The Unknown was limping heavily on his bad hip and Thraun, like Hirad, had suffered so many demon cuts he had a constant shiver. Only Ark looked anything like ready. Even Eilaan looked tired. Beside him, the TaiGethen were impossible to gauge. Decked out in their paints, they had completed their prayers and were standing silent, betraying nothing.

"We're the only choice you've got," said Hirad.

"But even so, the human is right," said Auum, breaking his silence. "Rebraal, you will fight with the TaiGethen."

Rebraal all but jumped out of his skin. "Auum, my place is here, with the Al-Arynaar. They need their leader."

"Tessaya will use them effectively." Auum turned to Dystran. "See the message is relayed."

Hirad waited for Rebraal to protest but the elf's expression was not one of irritation, it was one of honour and pride. He simply nodded and joined them in new prayer.

"Will you look at that," breathed Denser.

Arnoan's incense smoke was taking on form in the air. Grey wisps gathered and appeared to harden into a long shallow oval. Inside it, the view of the barracks room faded to be replaced by a flat grey. It rippled once and was still. The Shaman's eyes opened.

"The gateway is prepared," he said. "Use it quickly." He paused. "I think it is traditional for Easterners to wish each other luck. So, good luck."

"Thank you." The Unknown shouldered his pack. "Come on, Raven, no sense in delaying."

"Keep in physical contact with one another," said Arnoan. "Or you will be lost on the journey, scattered about the banished lands."

Vuldaroq helped Erienne on with her pack. She nodded at him curtly.

"Could have all been different you know," she said. "All you had to do was leave me to educate my daughter in my own time."

Vuldaroq raised his eyebrows. "Sad history now." He moved away to stand by Dystran. "Tell me one other thing. At Triverne Lake when you passed through it. There was no one there?"

"There had been," said Hirad. "But whoever they were had been killed by demons. Why, people of yours?"

"We had to try," said Vuldaroq.

"Try what?" demanded Dystran.

"Later, my friend. Much later."

The Raven gathered in a line two abreast. Behind them were the elves.

"What happens in here?" asked Hirad.

"I don't know," said Arnoan. "Often the warrior screams but I suspect that to be more in anticipation of the arrival than the journey."

"I hope you're right."

The Unknown spoke. "Remember. We're going somewhere we know nothing about. We don't even know we'll be able to breathe. But presuming we can, we first need a place to hole up so Hirad can call in the dragons. I need to know if mages have access to the mana spectrum for casting. Erienne, your condition is vital to us as you know. Don't keep it a secret. We're relying on all three of you to tell us where the mana is flowing out because that's where we're headed."

"Let's just hope we appear somewhere relatively close by," said Denser.

"If we don't we have ShadowWings and we have rope. We can ride dragons." The Unknown paused. "Are we set?"

He and Hirad locked their arms around each other's shoulders. Behind them, the other pairs did the same and with free hands grabbed the belt or wrapped around the waist of the person in front.

"Keep fighting," said Hirad. "We aren't doing this for nothing."

"Don't fail us, Raven," said Dystran.

"One thing, Dystran." Hirad couldn't help himself. "I have not and will never forgive you for the death of Ilkar and every other elf you sentenced to death when you unleashed the Elfsorrow. So let's get this straight. I am doing this for him, then for the elves, then for the rest of Balaia. Even Vuldaroq. But not you. Understand?"

"If it makes you happy."

Hirad laughed. "It's almost a shame we aren't coming back. At least then I'd have the opportunity of killing you myself."

"Good luck, Raven," said Vuldaroq. "Make me proud, Erienne."

"Don't push your luck."

"Raven! Raven with me!"

Hirad stepped into the gateway.

He felt the drag almost at once. It was like the tide, slow but undeniable. There was an absence of anything and yet it wasn't dark. A pale light surrounded them. He tried to look in the direction they were being taken but could see nothing. He looked down too. It was the same. He noticed he was moving his legs as if he was walking but there was nothing solid beneath him. He stopped.

"We all here?" His voice sounded muffled but at least he could speak.

He heard murmurs and presumed they were assent. He tightened his grip on The Unknown and felt the reassuring tug on his belt that meant Erienne was behind him still. It was an odd sensation. A controlled fall. It was just a pity he couldn't see the destination. But perhaps stranger than that was the realisation that he wasn't at all fazed by the experience. His life had been punctuated by extraordinary events. Dimensional travel, links with dragons, speaking with the dead . . . and this was just another. To be endured and remembered.

Abruptly, their path was buffeted. They were flung from side to side and only then did they realise they were within walls.

"Hold on, Raven!" he called.

He heard wind whistling outside the confines of the tunnel, as he now thought it to be. And he fancied he could hear the calls of demons but it was probably just his imagination. He fended off the wall once more, feeling it give like taut cloth, and felt a surge of energy through his body. He jerked.

"Hirad, you all right?" asked The Unknown, his voice distant despite his proximity.

"I think so, I . . ."

There was a presence in the tunnel with them. No, two of them. Hirad had the sense that they were floating ahead. He fancied he could see something in the pale light, like shadows of shadows. Indistinct yet with purpose. He felt a warmth, like the touch of one thought lost.

"Do you see it?" he shouted. "Ahead. Do you see it?"

Clearly, no one did. But the voice was something all of them could hear.

"You're going the wrong way, Coldheart. As usual."

Hirad heard laughter behind him. Erienne closed and hugged him with her free arm. Her lips were at his ear. "It's him. It's really him."

Hirad wiped at eyes suddenly brimming with tears. His heart surged in his chest and he was infused with pure elation. He could feel him too. Almost smell him.

"Where are you, Ilks?"

"You're looking straight at me, idiot," said Ilkar. "I am a little insubstantial as far as you're concerned but I'm hurt you don't see me."

"A little? I can see a ghosting ahead. Nothing more."

"Well, it'll have to do. I've brought a friend. He hasn't worked out the talking bit yet but I'm showing him. Thanks for sending him, Auum. I wouldn't be here without him."

"I said for you to get somewhere safe," said Hirad. "This doesn't seem much like it."

"Begging your pardon but I thought dead would be safe. But apparently, the living have screwed that up too."

"Xeteskians," said Denser.

"Might have known. Never trust a Xeteskian, eh? That's why I'm here. Gods, Hirad . . . Raven . . . but we're in trouble. The enemy are inside. We know the source of their energy but we can't reach it. So far we can hold them off but they're growing so fast."

"Well, that's why we're here," said Hirad.

"I knew you'd come. I knew you'd help. The Raven never leave their own to suffer. But you have to be quick."

Hirad felt the emotion wash over him. The relief and the love mixed with the fear of threat.

"Hey, Ilks, we're going as fast as we can. Haven't tried this sort of transport before."

"And like I say, taking it in the wrong direction. Gods drowning, but I can't leave you alone for a moment without you taking a wrong turn, Hirad."

"Ilkar, if it is you, stop this and tell us what to do. What do you mean wrong direction? We weren't offered a choice."

"Ah, Unknown, although I feel I should call you Sol now. It is me. And believe me, this is as weird for me as it is for you. This isn't possible, you understand, but for the fact that the fabric of my world is weak and I can feel you enough to be with you. Now you're here, anyway. Don't think it'll last."

"And where are we?" asked Erienne.

"At the junction of every dimension, or three of them at least. Yours, mine and the demons." The Wesmen portal sends you to a single point in the demon dimension but you don't want to go there. They'll be waiting for you like they have all the lost souls banished there."

"So take us where we need to go," said Hirad.

"With you it is always so simple, Coldheart," said Ilkar. "Lucky really, that your outlook mirrors your intellect."

"Dear Gods, but I've missed you. Denser is no substitute on the abuse front."

"I am peerless," said Ilkar. "Now listen, all of you. Rebraal, are you there?"

"You know I am, my brother. I can feel your strength through the touch of our souls."

"Yniss provides for us all that which we need in the direst of circumstance." Ilkar paused and for one awful moment Hirad thought he was gone. "Rebraal, remember to keep hold of the knowledge of the ancients. It will bind you all."

"I understand."

"What are you talking about?" asked Hirad.

"It's not your concern. Now listen. The path you're taking will drop you right where they expect you. You don't want that—"

"Always the gift for understatement," said Hirad.

"I learned it all from you. Now, we can break the path before you arrive but it'll be a little rough. It'll drop you beyond their immediate influence but they'll sniff your souls or magic quickly and be onto you."

"So what's the catch?" asked Denser.

"While I can get you nearer the energy source, I can't guarantee where exactly you'll appear."

"So long as you land us on something soft," said Hirad.

"I'll see what I can do." Ilkar's voice was full of doubt.

"How do you know all this?" asked The Unknown.

"Ah well, Duele and I caught a demon and, you know, asked it."

Hirad laughed. "You never change, Ilks."

"Yniss did indeed have a greater destiny for you, Duele," said Auum. "Why did I ever doubt him?"

"When is all this going to happen?" asked Thraun.

"Pretty much right now," said Ilkar. "It's been wonderful, my friends, but it's time to go. I doubt we'll have this sort of contact again. But hey, Coldheart, you know where to find me."

"I'll drop by as soon as I can."

"Not too soon, eh, old son?"

Ilkar was gone and they were falling. The light had changed from its pale tint to a startling blue and it grew in intensity around them. Hirad closed his eyes but it made no difference. He felt suffocated for a moment, a huge weight crushing down on his chest. He fought to breathe but nothing came into his lungs. He tightened his grip on The Unknown, seeking what solace he could from the big man's presence. Around him he heard screaming and realised it was all of them, the sounds torn unbidden from their mouths. Momentarily, he experienced the sensation of his skin being dragged from his body. The pain was extraordinary. But at least it was brief.

Freezing-cold air hit his face and a sour odour drove into his nostrils. He opened his eyes.

"Oh, shit."

They weren't on the ground but they were about to hit it. Hard.

Chapter 42

"Break! Break!" yelled The Unknown.

He pushed himself hard away from Hirad and felt the loosening of the grip on his waist. They plummeted groundward toward a glistening green some twenty feet below. A stench arose from it that assaulted the nostrils and fogged the mind. He hardly had time to register what it might be before he struck.

Just about turning his shoulder against the impact, he ploughed into the fetid mud, water and reeds. He rolled for what seemed like an age, keeping his mouth closed tightly and forcing air out of his nose to keep the stagnant slime from driving up his nostrils.

He slowed to a stop and came quickly to his feet, checking his weapons as he looked around him for the rest of The Raven. His mace was still in its bracket and his sword in its sheath. One of his belt-sheathed daggers had broken and his pack had torn from his back. It lay a little further back along the path he had dragged through the swamp.

He flicked his wrists to shake off the worst of the stinking mud then wiped down his arms and legs with the back of his hands. The Raven were scattered around him, all in various stages of coming to their feet.

"If he wasn't dead, I'd kill him myself," muttered a voice alongside him.

He looked round. Hirad was smeared from head to toe in black mud. His eyes peered from his face like stars in the nighttime sky and the ooze dripped from his braided hair. He wiped at his mouth and nose with one filthy sleeve.

"Yeah, but at least it was something soft," said The Unknown. "Come on, let's help everyone up."

"Do I smell as bad as you look?"

"Probably."

The Unknown reached down a hand and Erienne grabbed it, pulling herself to a sitting position.

"Terrific," she said. "Where's Denser?"

"He's here."

"You all right?"

"Yes, love, never better. Nothing I like more than bathing in putrescence."

The Unknown scanned around him in more detail, seeing the four elves and Thraun making their way over. Ark was shaking his head to clear it. At least no one was hurt. At least not badly.

"What have we got?" asked Hirad, coming to his shoulder.

"You know, I'm not at all sure," said The Unknown.

Up above him, the sky was loaded with deep-grey cloud. A dull light was cast on ground that in some ways was little different from parts of Balaia. There were hills to their left and an open plain that ran away to their right. A quick look behind revealed shale running up gentle slopes with steeper ground beyond. Directly ahead, the land levelled out and what looked like it might have been a settlement lay at the edges of his vision.

But it was dead. All of it. Silent. Still.

The Unknown looked down at his feet, ankle deep in sludge. What he had thought were reeds were long ribbons of algae floating in the stagnant water. Underfoot, the mud was soft and yielding. They had had a lucky landing. Less fortune would have seen them on the shale and their mission would have been over before it had begun.

Everywhere, the colours were drab. From the grey of rock to the dull brown of the plain sprinkled with the odd patch of palest yellow. He couldn't see the petal of a single flower anywhere he looked. There were no cart tracks, no animal trails. There were no trees. Not as far as the eye could see. But for the undulations of the land, it was completely featureless. And it was cold, very cold.

The breath clouded in front of their faces and dissipated upward. Tracking it, The Unknown looked into the empty sky. No birds, no insects. No demons either and that was a blessing. He wondered how long that would last. He glanced left and right. Erienne had her arms wrapped around her and was shivering. Denser was doing the best he could to warm her but his own nose was pale with the cold and there were only tiny dots of colour on his cheeks.

A wind blew at them from the direction of the hills behind. It mourned over the rock and sent icy gusts into their bodies. It wasn't exactly the popular vision of hell but it would do just as well.

"We must be the only souls still here," said Erienne.

"Which should worry us," said Thraun. "Ours will be like a beacon fire to the demons." He sniffed the air. "I can't smell anything above this stench."

The Unknown nodded. "We need to get out of sight and into some shelter. Not just because of the demons. We're cold and we need to warm up and dry off."

"Can't see much firewood lying about," said Hirad.

"There are other ways of providing heat," said Denser.

The Unknown turned to the elves and raised his eyebrows. While Eilaan had a good covering of the cold mud and slime, the warrior trio had little more than splashes up their trousers and over their boots.

"You need to know how to land when you fall hard," explained Auum, seeing his expression.

"You never taught me," said Hirad.

"You could never be with us long enough to learn," replied Auum.

"What can you see?" asked The Unknown.

Auum pointed ahead of them. "Tumbledown settlement. All but dust now. Just a few stones. The plain is broad and barren. Behind, there will be shelter. The land is folded. If we are lucky, we'll find a cave."

"That would be very useful," said The Unknown. "That way it is, then."

He stooped and dragged his pack out of the mud and icy water. One strap remained and he slung it over his left shoulder. He felt a great stiffness in his hip and shook his head.

"I'm too old for this."

Hirad clapped him on the back. "Don't worry, big man, it'll all be over soon."

"Hirad, you are no comfort whatsoever."

Auum and his Tai led the way, clearly ill at ease. The stagnant water continued for over a quarter of a mile before they began to travel up slope. The drier ground beneath their feet was a welcome change and the slope afforded some protection against the biting wind. Even so the elves set a cruel pace, driving up the shale at close to a trot. And while their every pace found firm purchase around the loose stone, The Raven slipped and slithered continually, adding grazes and bruises to their shivers and aches.

"Whose idea was this?" grumbled Hirad, picking himself up and brushing shards of stone from his now gauntleted hands.

"Yours, I think," said Denser. "Unless my memory fails me, it was you who arrived on Herendeneth and said that something had to be done."

Herendeneth. The Unknown felt sudden sadness welling up. Every day, his wife and son would stand on the rock overlooking the anchorage awaiting his return. He brought images to his mind of Diera's smile and the wind blowing her hair about her face. And of his son, shouting with wild excitement as he toddled toward his father's open arms. And there really was no going back.

"It's for you," he whispered. "This is all for you."

They continued to climb. Beyond the slopes they could see from the swamp, others revealed themselves, giving the truth to Auum's assessment of the land. The higher they went, the colder and more barren it became; and after an hour's walk, there was no vegetation around them whatever. It was a desolate scene. With their backs to a damp crag that towered hundreds of feet above their heads, they stood or sat to rest.

The Unknown crouched by Rebraal, the two friends looking back over the way they'd travelled.

"Just look at this place," said The Unknown.

"Small wonder the cursyrd covet Balaia," said Rebraal.

"Well, for Balaia's vistas today, substitute this glorious view in a few years' time."

"Unless we put a stop to it."

"Right." The Unknown turned to him. "So, what do your eyes tell you?"

Rebraal shrugged and gazed long out over the decayed landscape. "It meets exactly the expressions of desolation in the texts in Aryndeneth. This is what the cursyrd do and it is why the sanctity of the dead must be maintained. If it is not, all dimensions will ultimately fall to this state.

"There is nothing out there, Unknown. The settlement we could see that is just so much dust and rot is the only one as far as any of us can see or sense. The only break from the wind that we can gauge is the hills at our backs. So the topsoil is eroded and the vegetation has died because it has no purchase. There are no trees. Unknown, there are *no* trees. So the low-lying land will flood as it rains and more and more is leeched from the earth. And so it dies. As will the air because the vegetation provides the last part in the cycle of life." He shook his head. "If this scene is repeated across this dimension then soon it will not be possible to breathe here. And where is the power source my brother said he would set us near? It is not out there."

"Then we must hope it is behind us." The Unknown looked down at Erienne and Denser. Both were struggling with the cold. "Come on, let's move on. Can't have The Raven's mages catching cold." He helped the pair to their feet. "Not far now."

"I hope you're right," said Denser. "My cloak wasn't made to carry this much mud."

"I'll have a servant clean and dry it the moment we arrive."

Denser smiled. "And have him draw a bath too, would you?"

Auum trotted down a shallow slope to the right of the crag. Beneath his paint, the elf's face was impassive but The Unknown thought he could detect the ghost of a smile.

"What have we got?"

"Shelter," said Auum. "This way. But quick and quiet. The cursyrd are beyond these hills."

Hovering behind his new karron force, Ferouc berated Blackthorne for his stupidity and cursed him for the time he was wasting. It merely served to fire his spirit. He led his warriors out of the castle keep and down the steps, driving headlong into the karron taking lumps out of his walls. He carried long sword and kite shield, his armour was his ceremonial chain and in his belly his anger was a cold knot.

Blackthorne thundered his shield into an enemy, knocking it backward. It flung out a pincer but didn't connect. The Baron stepped after it and drove his blade into its gut, wrenching it sideways before dragging it clear. The beast died at his feet, belching dark blood.

He roared his approval and swung hard at the next. Its hammer limb sheared off.

"Yes!" His shield blocked a pincer and he reversed his blade into its face. "Keep them moving backward!"

Twenty men had run out with him to stop the destruction of his castle. The shields half of them wore represented all the armoury had to offer. But all carried swords sharpened or maces that gleamed in the half-light.

At his right-hand side, one of his men struck out, catching a karron on the side of the head. Its skull was crushed but still it came at him. One pincer gripped his shoulder and the spike limb flashed in, driving straight through his chest. The man was flung back to slide on the marble floor of the keep. The karron died under a welter of blows.

Blackthorne cursed and struck out again. His shield thumped into a karron left and his sword flicked out right, nicking a pincer limb. Gore sprayed into the evening air. The limb coiled quickly and snapped out at him, glancing into his side. He felt the air knocked from him but his armour held. He rebalanced quickly, fending off a hammer and striking right to left, carving into unprotected flesh.

Above the karron, reavers screeched their displeasure.

"Beware overhead," warned Blackthorne.

To the left of his tight line on the steps and under the overhang of the grand door stones, one of his men took a hammer in the side and was flung into those next to him. Three men went down. The karron, moving faster than they had any right to, bounded up the steps and slaughtered the trio where they had fallen.

Blackthorne's eyes narrowed. He flung himself left. His sword drove through the chest of a karron rising from its bloody task and his shield jabbed up and took a second under the chin, the force snapping the creature's neck. A third swung at him but he caught the blow on his shield, bracing his feet and chopping down through the karron's shoulder.

Reavers prepared to dive on them. Left and right now, the karron attack was faltering. More were massing but Ferouc hadn't ordered them in.

"Back off!" ordered Blackthorne. He pointed his sword at Ferouc. "One day it'll be you, Fidget. For every man that dies, we take six of yours. Sound familiar, you bastard?"

"You fight against the inevitable, Blackthorne. Two days and you are crushed."

Blackthorne made sure he was the last man inside. Five of the twenty lay dead. Some of their weapons had been snatched away but their bodies would have to lie where they fell.

"Your ambition is not matched by your ability, Fidget. You won't beat us. You don't have the will."

He stepped back inside the castle and the doors were swung shut behind him. He handed his sword to a footman and clapped the man on the back.

"Another bloody nose, eh Daniel?"

"Yes, my lord," agreed Daniel.

But Blackthorne could see in Daniel's eyes the futility of their actions. He wrapped his arm around the boy's shoulder and walked with him back toward the kitchens, the only place they were truly safe.

"Don't lose faith, youngster. We have very determined friends out there. They won't let us down."

It wasn't much of a cave but they could at least get out of the worst of the chill sweeping across the land. The space was dank, dark and cold but sitting close together they shared warmth. The indent in the crag that Auum had found went back no more than ten feet but was overhung by a further six, making it reasonably defensible from air attack. He and Evunn stood just in shadow at the entrance, looking out over the bleak landscape and searching the sky for evidence that they had been discovered.

Just within earshot and above the wailing of the wind, they could hear the low rumble of demon activity. It was the sounds of calls and orders mixed with the whip of thousands of wings and the tramp of innumerable feet.

"So he did get us close then," said Hirad.

"Very," said Rebraal. He smiled. "He did well."

"Except we all smell absolutely terrible."

"Makes a change from it just being you, doesn't it, Hirad?"

"My, my, Xetesk-man, I admire you for still trying. But like I said to Ilkar, you have a long way still to go."

Under his right arm, Erienne was shaking. "Still cold?"

Erienne snorted. "No, Hirad," she managed. "It tickled me, that's all. I think Ilkar would have been proud of that one. Remember those furs you used to wear?"

Hirad nodded. "They weren't the most fragrant."

The Raven laughed.

"All right," said The Unknown. "Let's get serious. We need to do several things. Hirad, you have to contact Sha-Kaan, bring him here as soon as you can. Eilaan, confirm that the mana is concentrated where we think it is. Denser, do what you do best and warm this place up a little, would you? We might as well be comfortable. Thraun, Ark, see about preparing some food. Erienne, get yourself some sleep when the temperature goes up. We're going to need you."

She looked up at him and all the doubt was back in her eyes. "I hope I don't let you down."

"No chance," said The Unknown. "Now listen, everyone, we seem to have been fortunate up until now but if there's one thing guaranteed to bring on demons, it's spell casting. I don't see there's any harm them knowing we're here. A ForceCone will keep them out of the cave until the dragons arrive. But if any of you want to empty bowels and bladder, I suggest you do it now. We don't know what length of wait we'll have. Denser will pause until you get back. Any thoughts?"

There were no dissenters.

"Good, then let's get to it."

The group broke up and immediately the biting cold returned. The Unknown put his back to a wall and beckoned Erienne over. He held his arms out and she moved gratefully into his embrace.

"Gods falling, but I hope people aren't too long taking a leak," she said.

"You don't feel the need?"

"Too cold to be out there," she said, snuggling in closer. "Good job my husband's not the jealous type."

"How do you know he's not?" Denser's voice carried back to them from just outside the cave.

"It's just the impression I get."

"I see." Denser buttoned his fly back up and walked back inside. "Convenient how The Unknown organises everyone else to work and leaves himself free to get fresh with you."

"Perk of the job," said The Unknown.

Denser chuckled. "I'll set about this spell then. Make yourselves comfortable. Don't think to help or anything."

"We won't," said Erienne.

The Unknown watched Denser collecting stones from outside and arranging them in the centre of the cave. He was very precise in the shapes and sizes he chose and in the way they were arranged.

"It's all about reflecting the heat from the spell," said Erienne in answer to his question. "The mana will bounce around for longer if the stones are placed right. Keep the heat in for longer, you know."

"I see." He paused. "How are you feeling?"

"Warming up."

"That isn't what I asked."

"I know." She sighed. "Look, Unknown, I know I can do it. In the playhouse, I had no doubt. But look how many of us there were and how relatively few of them. We could afford a mistake and so I didn't make one. Now the stakes are higher. One slip and it isn't just us that's gone, it's everyone. That's a burden."

"I understand. Look, if it's any help, we're all scared about who we'll let down if we fail. But that's how it's always been, hasn't it? The Raven united does what it has to despite how we feel individually. Draw strength from us."

"I'll try. Thank you. Hmm. Can't really imagine Hirad being scared." They looked across at him, seated with his hands in his lap, searching for his dragon. "And you . . ." Erienne trailed off and The Unknown felt her shoulders sag. "Oh, Unknown, you poor soul."

The Unknown knew what she was talking about. He smiled grimly and shifted in his position, swallowing hard. "We have all had to make sacrifices."

"But you're the only one of us for whom family waits on your return."

"Diera knew this time I was unlikely to come home."

"And this time you knew all along, didn't you?"

The Unknown nodded. "We all did, didn't we? When we thought about it in the quiet of the night, there was never any chance of us surviving what we have to do."

"There's always hope," said Erienne.

"You listen to Hirad too much. The hope we have is for the survival of our dimension, not for ourselves."

"And are you handling it all right?"

The Unknown blinked away the moisture in his eyes. "Erienne, it guts me every time I think about it. The last things I said to my family were lies. How long will it be before Diera finally gives up hope of me ever coming home? How long will she be forced to grieve?"

"Then do what you would have me do. Focus on The Raven and our strength. Know that what we do now will mean that your family has a future even if it is without you. When the grief has faded, they will rejoice they had you for as long as they did. Believe me, I know."

"Thank the Gods you're here, Erienne."

"That we're all here."

"All right, I'm ready," said Denser. "All of you done the necessary?"

The Unknown jogged out of the cave briefly but could hear Denser speak.

"Eilaan, as soon as I begin to prepare, we can assume the demons will be onto us. We need a flattened Cone ready right away. You up for it?"

"I know what to do."

"Good. Well, it may bring the hordes down on our heads but at least we'll be warm and dry. Unknown, may I?"

"Be my guest."

Denser closed his eyes and developed the FlamePalm construct. The simple casting was complete in moments and he played the flame over the stones in a circular motion. They began to emit heat. Smoke curled lazily upward. The blue of Denser's spell played over their exposed surfaces and took on a cycle of its own, bouncing and reflecting as Erienne had described. The warmth began to fill the shallow cave.

But from all around them, the sounds of the demons changed and a new call grew. It was a call of fury and it was taken up by myriad throats, gaining quickly as it neared.

The demons had found them.

CHAPTER 43

"I have your signature, my Dragonene. We are coming."

Sha-Kaan broke the contact with Hirad Coldheart and wheeled in the air. In the day since their last contact, he had probed the human's mind and found it stressed and active, denying him safe access. And during that same time the damaging battle in the skies of Beshara had finally burned itself out but the cost to the dragon population and that able to travel with him had been severe.

Almost four hundred dragons had perished in flame and fall, taking from him more than a fifth of those who had originally assembled on the plains and offered such hope. Now, they numbered a little over fourteen hundred. It would have to be enough.

Around him, the Kaan and most of the Naik circled, guarding against further trouble. Yasal was on the ground, talking with representatives of the recently warring broods while those that had taken no part were flying distant defensive patterns. It would take time to gather them all and Sha-Kaan was not confident that all would come.

He rose high above the circling Kaan and Naik and gouted flame long into the clear sky. He roared and dived, pulsing out his message, demanding their attention and their respect.

"Our time is now," he sent. "Gather in the skies, my allied broods. Put aside your petty squabbles. We are already weakened and we cannot afford further diminution of our strengths. The battle for our futures and for all those of our melde dimensions begins for us.

"Fly, my friends. Fly to me."

Sha-Kaan dipped below his brood who were forming up as they had drilled. Around them, Naik did likewise. From the ground, he saw the dust flood the air, a thousand wings beating skyward. The pulse message would be passed out among the Stara, Veret and Gost. Soon those that still believed would come.

Yasal-Naik barked his relief that the call had finally come through.

"So your human has survived and made his journey."

Sha-Kaan pulsed feelings of warmth and pride. "Did I not tell you he was tenacious? I never doubted him."

"Then you were alone."

"I alone understand his capabilities." Sha-Kaan turned his head to Yasal as they flew side by side. "And what were the results of your diplomacy, young Naik?"

"I have salvaged much of the support but none will fly with the Skoor. They are dismissed and with them must go an equal number of Kaan and Naik to ensure they do not abuse their temporary advantage in our skies."

"It is as much as I could have hoped," said Sha-Kaan. "But it leaves us a further eighty mouths short. We take with us barely more than thirteen hundred to do battle with our enemy."

"Then we must all fight as hard as two," said Yasal.

Sha-Kaan inclined his head in respect. "You have grown, Yasal. It makes me almost glad this crisis fell upon us."

"And I, Great Kaan." Yasal's mind pulsed regret. "We have lost so many to each other over the cycles. Perhaps our future will be more productive."

"We can rule the skies together."

"Yes, we can."

The two master dragons flew into the centre of the gathering. Though they were much reduced in number, the acreage of wing and scale remained truly awesome. The days of drills and organisation had benefited them in structure in the sky. Each brood was formed and solid. The outlying patrols swept and dove and the mass was prepared.

"Now is the time of greatest risk," said Sha-Kaan. "Now we will know whether our talk was believed."

"Does it matter if it is not? If you see what I mean."

"I do and to us perhaps it does not. But it matters to Hirad Coldheart. He expects and we must deliver."

Sha-Kaan led Yasal high above the massed ranks of dragons. Beshara's last and only hope.

"Now is the moment of trust. You know me and you know my honour. Yes, many of us have battled in the past but now that must be consigned to history. Now we fight for our survival. And for that I give to each of you the trace signature of my Dragonene who sustains me." He pulsed the signature.

"And now, I exhort you all to follow me. Save us, save every dimension we hold dear. Be ready to fight."

He switched out of Beshara and drove through the void to Hirad Coldheart.

Tessaya's warriors were holding but only just. Elves were with them, their fast blades and skilled movement disrupting the ul-karron attacks. Reavers and strike-strain concentrated on attacks from above, quick-fire strikes that dealt swift death to those snatched but cost the enemy more than the allies.

The Lord of the Wesmen, flanked by four lieutenants, strode into the tower complex and demanded audience with Dystran and whoever else commanded the eastern forces, such as they were.

"They are in conference," he was told by a callow youth, barely strong enough to hold the sword scabbarded at his waist. "They cannot be disturbed."

Tessaya hefted his axe meaningfully. A silence had descended on the complex, punctuated by the muted sounds of battle without and the rhythmic dripping of demon blood from his axe to the marble floor.

"And on what do they confer, boy?" he said quietly.

"The defence of the college," said the youth. His face was red with anxiety and he couldn't keep his hands still.

"The defence which I alone conduct while they cower in their towers!" Tessaya's voice rang around the complex. In front of him, the youth jumped backward. "Get them down here now or so help me, boy, I will take my warriors and leave the demons to feast on your rotting souls."

The youth hesitated.

"GO!"

The youth ran through into a curtained passage. Tessaya let his gaze travel around the people sitting in the complex. Some with swords resting on walls beside them. Some plainly mages, wringing their hands in their impotence.

"Is there not one of you with the desire to stand by me and live or die a hero? Yes, that's it . . . turn away. Block your ears to what happens beyond your cocoon. The Wesmen are dying for you. And this is how you demonstrate your gratitude?" Tessaya shook his head. "There are those who have travelled the path of banishment by choice because they believe it the only way to victory. Each one of you I would gladly consign there as cowards in the face of battle."

There was a rustling of bodies and the odd mutter.

"So prove me wrong," said Tessaya. "Stand with the Wesmen. Fight for your lives."

Movement from the passage revealed itself to be Dystran and the Dordovan, Vuldaroq. Behind them came two women, one an elf, and two more men, both soldiers, both scarred from battle. Tessaya recognised both women and one of the men. All three should have been resting after their ordeal in the playhouse and before on the road from Julatsa. He had heard their stories.

"Lord Tessaya, you asked to see me," said Dystran, smiling and opening his arms in welcome.

"I need support out there," said Tessaya. "You have men and mages idle. Give them to me. Right now, Wesmen and elves are keeping you alive. You have had your rest. It is time to fight."

"Now we need to keep reserves and ensure the sanctity of the Heart. Our involvement will and must be on need alone."

"That need is now," growled Tessaya. "My warriors die to protect you."

He pointed at Dila'heth and Pheone. "Their people die to protect you. Be visible or we will leave you to your fate."

"And what exactly do you suggest?" asked Dystran.

Tessaya sniffed. "Spells will kill more enemy than swords ever will. We have seen that. Warriors will occupy their ul-karron, you must cast to destroy their commanders and their reserve."

"My Lord Tessaya, you must know that we cannot cast inside the Cold-Room shells," said Dystran.

"You must think me an ignorant savage," said Tessaya, carefully holding onto his temper, "if you think that pathetic excuse will impress me."

"Now listen—"

"The elven mages stand at risk in the spaces between the castings they have made so we can fight and they do what they can. But they are not enough. Mages must travel outside the college. Come into the back of the demon lines and kill them where they wait the order to attack. Defence alone is no longer enough. It will not give The Raven time enough to act, should they be able to do so."

Dystran paused and held up his hands in a placatory gesture. "Now let's not get carried away. What you suggest sounds plausible but surely mages scattered outside the college will be committing suicide, not supporting the defence."

"And is what we do for you any different? It is slow but we will be overwhelmed eventually. That is, unless we disrupt their chain of command and damage their morale and belief now. Now."

"I'm sorry, Tessaya, but I will not commit my mages and warriors to battles they cannot win. Their souls are vulnerable in a way yours are not."

"Vulnerability is no excuse for cowardice." Tessaya took a pace toward Dystran, feeling his anger infuse his body. "And that is what you are. You and all those that follow you and do your bidding. Cowards deserving of nothing but my contempt."

"I will not stand by and let that slur stain me," said the soldier Tessaya didn't recognise.

"And who are you, hiding behind your ruler's platitudes?"

"I am Chandyr, commander of the Xeteskian armies, such as they are."

"Then stand by me, Chandyr. Fight for your freedom. You are clearly no stranger to battle. And you, Captain Suarav, my words do not apply to one such as you."

"Chandyr, you will not walk outside of this complex without my express permission," spat Dystran. "I will not have this man making demands in my college."

Chandyr walked calmly in front of Dystran. "Go ahead and hide, Dystran. I will not do so. The fact is that Tessaya speaks wisely and you know he does. All stood here know that your decisions are based on your fear of the order of power should the demons be defeated and you will risk all of us to hang onto that power."

"Commander Chandyr, I will say this just once," began Dystran.

"Save it for someone who will listen," said Chandyr. He tore the insignia from his chest and arms. "I resign my commission and fight as a free man. And I encourage any who despair of your weakness to do the same." Chandyr smiled. "What of your power now? To cast to stop me you will have to place yourself at risk. I would like to see that, I really would. At least it would show some courage."

Behind Chandyr, Tessaya nodded, knowing this man had true spirit. Here was a man he could respect and trust to fight next to him. Chandyr turned to him.

"Lord Tessaya, I place myself at your command."

"As do I," said Suarav.

"And already you are heroes. Come, let us do that which your leader dare not and try to save us all." He jabbed a finger at Dystran. "You have until dawn to schedule your remaining warriors and mages to the defence of this college or I will do it for you. Pheone, Dila'heth, I urge you, work with me."

He turned and strode from the dome, his heart swelling with new belief and his brain racing with the possibilities. Should they defeat the demons, he would be the most powerful man on Balaia. He roared a battle cry and charged back into the fray in the dying light of a freezing day, his warriors at his back.

"How long is the journey?" asked Denser.

"I don't know," said Hirad. "But they are coming. We'll have warning, I'm sure."

He turned his head to the scene outside the cave. Demons crowded the entrance. Some strains he recognised, some he did not. In the darkening sky, he saw reavers hovering, screeching orders at the lesser demons in front of them. He saw ul-karron beating on the face of the Cone; and there were other, smaller wingless demons, completely hairless and pure white. Their thin fingers leeched into the Cone, trying to disrupt the construct. So far it was holding but there were signs of stress on Eilaan's face.

"How long can he hold on?" asked Thraun.

"Hard to say," said Erienne. "He will let us know if he comes under serious threat."

The cave was quiet and warm. They were trying to relax. Erienne had slept for a long period and looked a little refreshed. Ark and The Unknown also slept as did the elven warrior trio. Outside, the cacophony would be undimmed but Denser's casting of a SoundBell had shut off the din, leaving them in a bubble of relative calm.

"We know Denser can cast the same spell. What can you do?" asked Hirad.

"Something similar but I'd be loath to try it. I need my strength, Hirad, and I don't need to experiment with new castings right now."

"But if we had to call on you?"

"Hirad, do you really have to ask?"

The barbarian smiled. "No. Just making conversation. All right, let's try something else. How far does Eilaan reckon the power source is?"

"Close. Probably no more than a short run," said Denser. "It's impossible to say after that."

"What will it be?"

Denser scratched at his beard. "Gods, Hirad, how the hell do you expect me to know that? All we can tell is that it's a massive mana construct and it is driving mana out of this dimension and obviously into ours. There's still a significant density here but it's interesting that where we landed there was a relative lack. Whatever it is they have done, it is attracting mana into a huge concentration to pump it out."

"What's interesting about that?"

"Well, that as far as our writings are concerned, what is happening is impossible. That makes whoever is doing this very powerful indeed. And we have to kill it or them. And that's after we get through the hordes waiting outside our front door."

"Should be fun."

"I very much doubt it," said Erienne.

"Now, surely it's your turn to get some rest, Hirad," said Denser.

"What makes you say that?"

"Because your inane questioning is setting my teeth on edge."

Hirad thought to retort but when he considered it, was too tired. The hours they'd had behind the ForceCone had allowed Denser and Erienne to deliver a few key healing casts and they were as fit as they would ever be. But nothing was going to take away the raw fatigue.

Hirad lay back on his pack, punching it into an acceptable pillow and trying to ignore the stink. He closed his eyes and was immediately suffused by feelings of warmth and speed.

"No time for rest, my Dragonene. We are come."

Hirad shot to his feet. "Game time, everyone. Hope you're feeling good. We're about to get help."

CHAPTER 44

"Maces everyone, we aren't going to have spell backup on the run. Mages, do whatever you can, just don't risk yourselves."

The Unknown's words were bawled into the tumult from outside the ForceCone Eilaan still held. The Raven were formed up to run. Packs were discarded at the back of the cave, empty waterskins with them. The demons knew they were ready to break out. Their excitement had reached fever pitch and the thudding on the ForceCone reached new pressure. Eilaan grunted.

"Just a little longer," said Rebraal, his hand on the young mage's shoulder. "You'll make a fine Al-Arynaar."

"They have no idea what's about to happen," said Hirad. "No idea at all."

He could feel the closeness of Sha-Kaan. The great dragon brought with him the largest assembly of his kind ever to fight together. It was going to be some spectacle. They were all homing in on Hirad's position and they all knew what they had to do. The only question remaining to be asked was whether they would prove to be enough.

They were just about to get their answer.

"Ready, Raven," said Hirad. "Here it comes."

Hirad felt the jolt through him as Sha-Kaan entered the demon dimension. He heard the bark of the Great Kaan taken up by a thousand throats and the dragons joined the fight for survival. Shadows passed over the darkening landscape. Demon voices stilled then raised in alarm. Flame swept across the mouth of the cave and in a swath forty yards at least down the slope away from them. The demons in its path were simply obliterated, scorched to ash by the extraordinary heat. Never mind their mana protection, nothing withstood dragon breath.

"Yes!" Hirad punched the air. "Come on Sha-Kaan."

His mind warmed again. "We are with you. You have safe exit."

"Raven! Raven with me!"

Rebraal squeezed Eilaan's shoulder and the mage dispersed the Force-Cone. He was dragged to his feet and the run began. Auum and Evunn sprinted from the cave and turned immediately right and away. The Raven followed in standard formation with Rebraal and Eilaan bringing up the rear.

The noise outside the SoundBell was a shock but not as much as the heat. Dragons had fired the air hotter than inside the cave. Rock was scarred black and smoking, dirt and stone had fused and where any vestiges of plant life had clung, they had been snuffed out in an instant. The ground was hot underfoot.

Of the demons who had been massed outside the cave there was no sign.

Nothing at all. Hirad had time to shudder at the power the dragons generated and thanked the gods they were on his side.

Up in the skies the battle had already commenced. The heavens were darkened further by the mass of scale and wing that had appeared in the dimension and the element of surprise was being used to the full. Hundreds of reavers were in the sky with them but were being taken apart by flame and claw, crashing to the dead earth. And on the ground in front of The Raven, the demons were being swept aside as flight after flight screamed overhead, fire gushing from their mouths. Beyond the hills too, and out of sight, they could see the flare of flame brightening the sky. Dragons climbed above the horizon, chasing packs of winged demons, panicked into misguided attempts at escape. They might have been masters on Balaia but everywhere dragons went, they were undisputed lords of the skies.

It was glorious.

"Keep the pace up," called The Unknown. "They'll get themselves together sooner or later. Come on, Denser. This is what Darrick had you swimming round the ship for."

They were heading up a steep slope. The stone was smoking from dragon fire and presented a hot and slick surface.

"Don't put your hands down," warned Hirad. "Keep moving."

"Sound advice," said Denser. "You'll be sure and tell me when we get there just in case I don't realise."

"Concentrate," snapped The Unknown. "No accidents. Not now."

Reavers had gathered in the air ahead and they plunged. Forty winged demons diving headlong, heedless of their lives, desperate to kill those that threatened them. Hirad raised his mace to a defensive position knowing it wouldn't be enough. He slipped almost immediately, planting the weapon in front of him to break his fall and push himself upright. He looked back to where the reavers were coming, saw the flash of scale to his right, and a blast of flame brushed them from his sight, squealing as they died, tumbling helpless from the sky.

The dragon pulled a tight circle and flew close, head snaking down.

"At the top of the next rise," said Sha-Kaan. "Where your elves have reached already. Wait for the signal. There are many enemies."

And he was gone with a beat of his wings that almost knocked Hirad over. He reached flatter ground and looked after the mighty dragon, still in awe of his grace and speed. He ran on up the shallow slope to where Auum and Evunn waited, looking down.

"Right," he said, reaching them ahead of the rest of The Raven. "What have we . . ."

His voice trailed away, caught in his throat. He sensed the rest of The Raven come to his sides and he felt their hearts sink.

"How the hell did we ever think we could achieve this?" asked Denser.

Hirad would have berated him for his lack of faith but couldn't find it within him to disagree. Stretched out below them, across a plain maybe half a mile long and four times that in width, was a carpet of demons. Tens of thousands, perhaps hundreds of thousands, it was hard to tell in the half-light. It was a shifting mass, ordered and with one purpose. It moved toward a massive low edifice on which stood hundreds of spires angled out like the spines of a hedgehog. Each spike glistened and flashed at its end, and closer to the roots a maelstrom of colours danced and clashed.

The entire front of the edifice was open to the air. Hirad could see light within it and watched as demons entered its shadow and were lost in the brightness. Countless karron moved across the plain. Reavers flew in complex patterns overhead while strike-strain cavorted amongst them. The long-fingered albinos issued slowly toward the edifice, trailed by the mana gliders. And around the periphery masters floated on their tentacle beds, directing the remorseless advance.

But there was consternation in the ranks of the enemy. Not every demon was intent on its goal and eyes had been turned behind from where a threat had risen quite without warning. Even now, cohorts of karron were racing for the rise on which The Raven stood. Great clouds of reavers chattered and grouped, flying high to assess, and strike-strain bunched and flocked.

"Dear Gods," said Erienne. "At least it'll be over soon."

Above, the sky darkened and a wind blew straight down on their heads. Hirad looked back and a smile crossed his face. There they were, moving serenely across the heavens in drilled formations on two levels. He recognised Kaan colouring in the vanguard with Naik red flanking them. He saw Veret blue in the upper skies mixed with sand-yellow and deep green from broods of which he had no knowledge. They were poised.

"It's never over," he said. "Raven. Once again. Let's be ready to run. But first, I think we should crouch or we'll be blown away."

The dragons attacked. Sha-Kaan's bark echoed loud and was washed away in the beat of three thousand wings. Hundreds of dragons power dived down the slope, passing just a few feet above their heads. Fire belched from their mouths left, right and always down. The karron approaching up the slope were destroyed in the blink of an eye but the attack did not pause there. Sha-Kaan led his legions onto the plain and the demons scattered before them.

Fire gorged again and again. From every mouth, heat singed the flesh from demon backs, blew them aside in their hundreds and drove an expanding wedge all the way to the edifice. Above them, the second wave stormed into the attack. Keeping high, they took reavers and strike-strain from the sky, the bodies falling like rain on the packed earth.

Hirad could only stand and stare at the extraordinary force ranged above him. Flame banished the dark, orange after-echoes ringing his vision. The sky was full of the huge bulk of dragons, the roar of a thousand mouths and the panicked cries of demons being slaughtered in their homeland. The fight in the sky waged as far as he could see in every direction until the dark swallowed it. The stench of burned flesh assaulted his nostrils.

On the ground the demon armies were scattered and running; and watching it all, The Raven and a handful of elves. Pitifully few looking for a way through this battle of ancient enemies. Two species locked in war across dimensions and the centuries, facing each other in mass conflict for perhaps the first time.

Hirad felt indescribably small. He shivered despite the heat beating in from all around him and brought himself back to their immediate situation. Reavers were flying in from every point of the compass, rising from hiding places surrounding the plain. And despite the dragons' awesome power, their flame without fuel was finite. The time to move was now.

"Go! Go!"

The Raven and TaiGethen surged down the slope at full tilt. Ahead, the dragons had reached the end of their run and already the demons were crowding back into the centre of the plain, running for the only safety they could see. The Kaan led the glide up into the air and down they swooped again. More fire, more death, more screams of demons echoing unheeded into the air.

Hirad felt the heat on his face. His legs and arms pumped and his eyes scanned the ground ahead, looking for anything that might trip him up. Occasionally, he glanced upward and each time he did, he saw the fight beginning to balance. Reavers had organised themselves into attack groups and were falling on dragons from above and behind. Ten and twenty on a single back, clawing and biting. They tore scales out by the root while strike-strain confused their prey, clawing at muzzles, necks and softer underbellies. He saw his allies begin to falter, attack runs break up as thousands more reavers appeared from hiding behind the edifice, screaming challenge.

They hit smouldering flat ground. Sha-Kaan and his wave soared over their heads and climbed again, themselves the targets of reavers now. Karron closed on the ground. Albinos sprinted in front of them, scampering stride driven on by powerful hind legs.

"Don't look back!" yelled Hirad, doing exactly that.

The ranks had closed behind them but above, dragons were coming in. Sha-Kaan had broken his wave into three. One shot straight overhead, scouring the path clear once more. The beat of wings weighed down the runners, the heat from dragon fire burned into their lungs. Each of them stumbled more than once but always there was a Raven hand to keep them up and forward.

The second and third waves passed by left to right, one in front, one behind. Fire lashed across their path and Hirad felt the heat bloom behind them as well. He didn't risk a glance back this time, imagining the carnage that would have been created in an instant.

They were closing on the edifice but now the dragons were beginning to fall. A mournful roar to their right and a Veret thudded into the ground, sending vibration through their feet. Nearby another flew low, spiralling in the air, trying desperately to shake off the reavers that tore at its body and wings. It failed, ploughing into the earth and sending up a spray of mud, stone and demons. A third plummeted straight down, landing just off the path ahead. Too many, too regular.

The flame was guttering now. Less and less, the night was lit by new fire from dragons' mouths. More and more they were fighting with tooth, tail and claw. And that was a fight they would not necessarily win.

Hirad upped his pace, gaining a little on Auum and Evunn who ran at the periphery of the fire-blasted path, blades out and held against an onrushing enemy. Again, the dragons came in. Fewer this time as more were tied up in the battle overhead. Sha-Kaan was still there. Hirad saw his mouth open and fire lash ahead. He saw demons flung burning into the sky, others disappear in the melt of the flames and still more dive aside, rolling and burning.

He could make out the detail of the edifice now. Its open front was crowded with demons, looking out at the destruction wreaked by their enemies. The stone above the wide entrance was decked with swirls and scratches, as if some great claws had raked across it while it was forming. The spines atop it throbbed and glowed, attracting mana to them. He could see clouds of the fuel coalescing in the air and felt swaths of cold in between the heat of dragon fire.

But one thing was absolutely certain. They weren't going to get inside.

"Sha-Kaan!" he yelled, pulsing simultaneously, trying to hang onto his limbs and keep running. He stumbled. Thraun caught his shoulder and steadied him. "Sha-Kaan! The entrance. You have to clear the entrance."

Karron closed in. Ahead, Auum swayed left and struck out, sending an enemy sprawling. On the next pace he leaped into the air, coming into a full tuck and rolling over the karron's head. He landed behind it, spun and kicked out, catching the back of its head. It fell flat on its face and the TaiGethen turned and ran on. In his wake came Hirad. The karron raised its head only to take the barbarian's mace square-on. He felt the satisfying crush of bone.

"Don't stop. Keep running!"

Hirad felt a warmth spread across his mind.

"Be ready to duck," came the voice of the Great Kaan.

Six dragons flew overhead, Sha-Kaan leading them. His fire scorched the ground and he pulled up, the last remnants of flame shrivelling spines on the roof of the edifice. But the other five had no such intentions. They drove on, unflinching. Mouths open, disgorged killing fire into the entrance. And in they followed it. Wings caught in stone, bodies connected with the massive lintel and they crashed hard, sliding inside, bellowing pain. Stone shivered and fell. Wrecked spines were shaken from the roof to shatter on the ground. Dust filled the air. They had almost done too much. Five Kaan all but sealed the entrance. Up in the sky, Sha-Kaan barked respect for their sacrifice.

"Do not let it be wasted," he toned in Hirad's mind.

"Raven let's go!"

More fire swept across and behind them. Right above his head he felt the beat of wings and the snap of jaws. A Naik dragon soared away, reavers in its mouth. It bit down and spat the pieces to the ground. But while it flew free, so many of its brethren were weakening under the concerted attack of many thousands of reavers.

Auum and Evunn had made the entrance. They found a path through broken dragon bodies and picked their way through the fires that pitted it. Inside, Hirad could see demons moving but he wasn't sure how many.

"Mages, we're going to need you."

One last glance behind. They were all with him. The Unknown and Thraun either side of Erienne. Rebraal with Denser; and Ark, a flap of skin hanging from his cheek, shepherding Eilaan. Hirad ducked inside the edifice. He squeezed by the flanks of two Kaan, letting his hand trail across their cracked scales, feeling their lives ebb away. He whispered words of thanks but had no time to stop to pay them proper respect. The Raven followed him in.

Inside, it stank of burned flesh and dragon, sharp oil and wood. It was thick with smoke and he coughed each time he drew a heaving breath. He took quick stock of direction but there was only one way to go.

The edifice was one huge room, dominated by the shimmering brightness they had seen from the rise. It cut a slash clear across the bedrock floor, wall to wall. Light danced in the air and off the crude murals that adorned every vertical surface. He didn't need to be told what the shimmering was, that much was obvious. All he cared about were the two stone pathways that crossed its centre and the sight that greeted him on the other side.

"My friends, you are in big, big trouble."

He turned and yelled for Erienne but behind her every demon left standing was trying to get inside.

The light was fading but the ferocity of the demon attack had not abated. The Wesmen had been driven back across the courtyard and were now in possession of just half of it. They had lost both barracks and long rooms plus the ColdRoom mages therein and now the library was once again threatened as was the mana bowl on the other side of the complex.

Dystran watched from his tower while his fury turned to admiration and his arrogance to shame. Down in front of the steps, Tessaya, Chandyr and Suarav fought side by side. The Wesmen lord was indefatigable. His axe in both hands, he chopped an ul-karron in two, shoulder to waist, and had turned to strike at the next before it had directed its pincers to hold him.

Suarav was a man possessed. His head was a mass of blood but he fought like a fresh entrant. His sword snaked out, piercing karron eyes, his dagger weaved in front of him, chopping at pincers. He ducked, twisted and swayed, defying hammer or spike to touch him, and he roared his disdain at them. Put furs on him and you would have sworn he was a Wesman.

And lastly Chandyr. He was the skilled fighter. The one in Ry Darrick's image. He and three other Xeteskian soldiers fought as a tight quartet, each targeting a separate point in the enemies they faced. Chandyr focused on the killing thrusts while his men blocked pincer and limb with axe and mace. It was mesmerising but ultimately it would be futile. Above the shell, the masters floated, directing their forces in ever more focused attack. Reavers were taking their toll on the back of the lines now, looming out of the gathering darkness to split skulls, rake throats and steal souls. And outside what was left of the walls, ul-karron paced forward while more of their number spilled from the gap in the sky to glide quickly down on gossamer wings that stowed in folds of flesh as they landed hard.

A single shout of alarm echoed up the tower. It was Chandyr's voice. Dystran's gaze snapped round and down. One of his men had taken a spike through his head. He was stuck on the limb and his corpse was thrashed through the air. It swept into another of Chandyr's men not fast enough to duck. Cruelly exposed, Chandyr bounced to his feet, blocked away a second enemy but, with Tessaya's axe slicing through the air to his defence, was unable to escape the third. The hammer came down on top of his skull and drove his body to the ground. The ul-karron exulted; and died.

Dystran tensed. "All my fault," he muttered.

He looked across to his left around the balcony where Pheone and

Dila'heth stood. Their mages were already outside the college backed by elven warriors. He had seen spells light up the evening. IceWind and FlameOrb destroying enemies only for more to take their place. No, something more drastic was called for.

Dystran looked right instead. "Sharyr, who's the heavier, me or you?"

Sharyr dragged himself from the fight below. He was living every sweep of Suarav's sword. "You, I think."

"I agree. Then I will carry you. Pheone, go and tell the ColdRoom casters to lower the shell to below the level of this balcony. Just for a short time. Dila'heth will tell you when it should be reverted. Sharyr, we're going flying. I'll take you places, you kill what's in front of you. All right?"

A smile spread across Sharyr's face. "Yes, my Lord."

Pheone was already on her way. Dila'heth raised her eyebrows.

"Are you sure that's wise?" she asked.

"Never order that which you would not do yourself," said Dystran. "That's what Tessaya says, as I understand it. Time to admit he was right, I think. Sharyr, stand in front of me."

Mana played over his face and imbued his veins with energy. He felt awakened. Free. He cast quickly, the wings at his back in moments. He put an arm under Sharyr's knees, the other across his back and under his arms, and took off, hearing Dila'heth shouting Pheone's name as he did so.

"Time to bring down one of the big bastards," he said to Sharyr. "You comfortable?"

"It'll have to do."

"Focused Orb, my friend. I'll get you in close. Tell me when you're ready."

He flew straight up and looked all around him. Even though Sharyr was lighter for the lack of food over two years, he was still a weight in Dystran's arms for the same reason. They were only going to get one chance at this. He could see no one rising to attack him. It was hardly a surprise. Every demon eye was focused on the battle they were winning in the college courtyard. He circled, picking out the demon master, Drenoul, silhouetted in the light of Wesmen fires below him. Perfect. He wondered why they hadn't thought of this before but then Tessaya hadn't been in the college grounds before.

"Ready."

"Cast on my command then we're away. We'll drop to the balcony. It'll hurt but at least we'll be alive."

"You're in charge."

"Correct."

Clutching Sharyr as tight as he could, Dystran moved almost directly above Drenoul. Still unseen, he dropped, feet first and fast, coming to an abrupt halt next to the demon master.

"Surprise," he said. Drenoul swivelled, eyes widening. He reached out his hands but Dystran was carefully out of reach. "Tut, tut," he said. "Now. Die."

Sharyr cast. The deep blue focused Orb seared across the short distance and took Drenoul in the face. He screamed and shot straight up, the flame spreading quickly over his body. Dystran was already powering away back toward the tower when Drenoul's tentacles caught fire and he plunged to the ground, howling all the way.

CHAPTER 45

"**O**ver the bridges!" roared Hirad. "Now. Don't look back."

He saw them all past him. Outside, the dragons swept by again. Every time, less flame touched the ground and more was expended in midair as the reavers took their toll. Demons were slaughtered in sight of the edifice but so many were still advancing. He turned and ran after The Raven. Eilaan had managed a ForceCone and had beaten a few of the survivors of the dragon suicide flight against the left-hand wall. Denser played an IceWind right and forward, taking out some more. The rest of them were sprinting for the bridges and the prize beyond.

Hirad stormed past the still-breathing hulk of a dying dragon and swallowed hard at the scene before him. Across the shimmering light, two figures stood on a raised dais. Their shapes were hard to discern beyond tall and slender, with long arms raised palms upward toward the sky, because of the light that bathed them, head to foot. They stood thirty or so feet apart and between them spanned an arc of light. And from that arc a canopy of shimmering luminescence flowed out, feeding down into the gap which led back to Balaia.

That they were alive was never in doubt. He could see them shuddering and through the light he thought he saw eyes burning into him but it could have been his mind playing tricks. He ran on and across the nearest bridge. The power roiled and sucked below him, threatening to pluck him from a path only just wider than his shoulders. He fixed his eyes dead ahead and reached for The Unknown's hand.

He turned, his heart pumping painfully in his chest. His breath came in huge gasps and he felt like dropping to his knees. But instead, he dragged himself around to face the hordes coming after them. Desultory fire played outside the edifice, lighting the demons within in harsh relief. Reavers, too many of them, floating in and joined by more every heartbeat. Ul-karron paced up to the bridges, albinos scampering around them.

"Kill those fuckers behind us," said Hirad. He brought his mace to the ready.

Denser's spell was quick and sure. A focused Orb lashed out, plunging into one of the demon conduits. There was a flare, then nothing. The reaver advance stopped. The karron ceased their pacing. Denser cast a second Orb. Eilaan followed with IceWind. No effect.

"What is happening?" demanded Hirad.

"We can't harm them," said Denser. "Magic won't do it."

"Magic has to," said Hirad. "It's the only way."

"It must be the One," said Auum. "The Al-Drechar saw it."

"Erienne?" asked Hirad.

"I'll try." Erienne's voice was weak with the exertion of the run.

"You can do it."

The Raven formed up one more time in front of her. The demons watched them, moving closer by degrees but convinced they were no threat. More and more were crowding in. The Unknown came to Hirad's side, Thraun the other. Behind him, Eilaan and Denser prepared once more and encasing Erienne were Auum's Tai.

Hirad felt a presence in his mind. "We are weakening," pulsed Sha-Kaan. "Our fires are spent. The reavers are many and strong. You must be quick."

"One moment," said Hirad to his friends. And he pulsed out the message he had to. "Go home, Sha-Kaan. You have done all you can. It's up to us now."

Warmth flooded him. "Skies keep you, my old friend. You will prevail. I can feel it." Then a pause. "Expect my touch one more time. I will not abandon you here." And he was gone. Hirad smiled. There was always hope. But first, there was a job to be done. Preservation could come later.

"Erienne, over to you."

She began to cast. The demons screamed and attacked.

Reavers flew over the gap. Karron ran for the bridges, albinos in their wake.

"Brace!" called The Unknown. "Remember the ship. Let's do honour to Darrick!"

There were fewer of them than had organised the mock defence on board ship but the principle was the same. The reavers came at them quite low, dictated by the height of the carved stone ceiling. Each man stood his ground, half crouched.

"Now!"

Maces flew low to high. Hirad connected with a reaver groin, beating the creature back over the shimmering light. Beside him, The Unknown had battered his target high. It collided with the roof, only just steadying itself. They had all the space they needed.

"Down!"

They dropped to their haunches on Denser's command. IceWind howled away. Reavers froze in flight. Wing struts shattered, membrane frosted and bodies were whipped away into the shimmer to fall into the Balaian night.

Again they rose to punch hard with maces. Hirad ducked a flailing tail spike and crashed his mace into the reaver's side. It slewed away and came again, this time slicing down with its arms. Hirad brushed aside one but felt the other rake into his right arm. He felt the ice gather there and grunted in pain.

"Down."

Eilaan this time and a ForceCone drove the reavers away.

"It's a good idea," said The Unknown. "Denser. ForceCone. Keep the reavers off the both of you. We have other problems."

Eilaan and Denser backed away to the dais, ForceCones playing out over the heads of the Raven warriors. Ul-karron came on, pincers snipping at the air, writhing in front of the weapon limbs, searching for purchase.

"Two to a bridge. One sword, one mace," ordered The Unknown.

It made perfect sense. Hirad flung his mace at the nearest karron and dragged out his sword, running right with Thraun. Only able to come across one at a time, the karron were severely hampered. Hirad grinned fiercely, feeling the aches grow in his tiring body.

"Let's send these bastards on a journey, Thraun."

Thraun howled like a wolf from his human mouth and the two joined battle, the ex-Protector duo mirroring them four yards away.

Behind the fight at the bridges, Rebraal watched the reavers and strike-strain trying to evade the two ForceCones. Beside him, Auum and Evunn stood in silence, waiting for the inevitable. Kneeling by them, Erienne tried to form the casting that would break the light cycle and close the gap.

But she seemed to be struggling. He heard her gasp and curse, berate herself and slap the ground.

"Easy, Erienne. Plenty of time. We are with you."

"Shut up, Rebraal."

Ahead, Hirad shouted in triumph as a blow from Thraun's mace sent a karron tumbling into the pit. But simultaneously, two sets of reavers worked out the flaw in the Raven defence. Left and right they came, under the Force-Cones, and there was nothing either mage could do to stop them without striking their own people.

"Eilaan, Denser, disperse and defend, it's your only chance."

Rebraal could only hope they had heard him. The reavers were amongst them.

"Blades," muttered Auum.

He blurred. A reaver died. Short blade in his right hand, Rebraal dragged at a reaver's legs as it dropped toward Erienne, pulling it across his body and onto the ground. The creature lashed out with its claws, ripping into his thigh. He gasped and dropped hard onto its chest. It choked and spat, lashed in again. This time he rocked backward, ducked under its claw and drove his blade high up under its arm.

He turned as he rose. More were coming at them, targeting Erienne. Auum and Evunn stood either side of her, hands and feet moving in harmony, knocking enemies from above her head, dragging their blades through wing membrane, hurling strike-strain toward the pit to be swallowed to Balaia. But even they would not be enough.

"Raven," called Rebraal. "We need you here!"

He saw Hirad turn his head and mouth a curse at what he saw. Ten, twenty, fifty reavers circling and darting in, each needing only one strike to disrupt her concentration. Hirad dropped, swept the feet from under a karron that plunged left. He called to The Unknown and ran into the maelstrom.

Erienne screamed in frustration.

"You can do it!" shouted Denser.

He and Eilaan joined the fray. Both mages held FlamePalms. Denser leapt at a reaver pacing along the floor, bearing it to the ground. He took a claw across the face but buried his palm in its mouth. The mage fire took hold quickly, bursting from its eye sockets. He stood and turned, the next creature punched him from his feet.

All sense of cohesion had gone now. The room was full of wings and screams. Blades flashed in the shimmering light. Rebraal saw Hirad grappling with a reaver, plunging his sword into its side and ripping it clear only to see the creature come back at him and backhand him across the floor. The Unknown and Ark had one by the arms. Ark savaged his mace across its face. The Unknown stabbed it through the chest and up into its nerve ganglion and they threw it aside.

Rebraal ducked a tail, stood and straight-punched his assailant in the gut. It doubled up and dropped to the ground. Eilaan's hand clamped around its neck and charred the veins in its head. At his feet, Erienne's arms moved in slow motion. A strike-strain appeared in front of her but Auum's hand was faster and it bounced from the wall right and spun into the gap.

Evunn was bleeding from a cut on his neck. The reaver in front of him ducked his blow and landed its tail on the side of his head, knocking him off balance. It reared to strike Erienne but Hirad's body flashed across Rebraal's vision and the scream of frustration was all he needed to hear.

He turned toward Evunn. The TaiGethen was scrambling to his feet, Auum guarding him, his hands and feet doing the work for both of them. Reavers still flew in. Ark and The Unknown had moved closer to Erienne now and The Raven had formed a circle around her. She was still casting, her movements fluid now, but still she had not released.

Rebraal lashed out at a strike-strain pair, catching them both and beating them aside. One disappeared back over the gap, the other struck something far more solid.

"Karron!" he yelled.

They had stormed across the bridges and were running hard at The Raven. Hirad had killed the reaver he had dived on and stood in time to block the first hammer strike. The Unknown and Thraun flanked him, sword and mace thudding home, sending the creature stumbling back.

Auum drop kicked another in the chest while Evunn fenced away pincer limbs as best he could, blood running from his neck and temple. Above them, reavers gathered for one more attack.

"Now would be a good time, love," said Denser, staggering back into the circle, a bruise the size of an egg coming up under one eye. He held his sword at ready but the reaver coming at him wasn't going to worry about it. The demon lunged with its pincers but had failed to notice either Eilaan or Ark. The former Protector chopped down hard on the searching limbs and Eilaan drove FlamePalm into its chest.

Ul-karron by the dozen were streaming into the attack. The Raven backed away, the circle around Erienne tightening ever further. With blood running into his eyes, Evunn missed a strike and took a glancing hammer blow in his thigh. He went down. Auum stepped across him. His hand whipped out and grabbed a pincer, his foot speared low into its abdomen and his blade sliced into its spike.

"Keep it steady, Raven!" called Hirad, but his voice was weary. "Just a little more time."

But they had no more time. The reavers screeched and dove, the karron charged. A reaver claw connected with the back of Erienne's head but with a scream of pure release, she cast.

Green luminescence fountained from her hands, face and chest, boiling into the space around her. It coalesced into multiple spears that shot away, each targeting a demon heart. Reavers and karron were impaled, their bodies sloughing flesh while the spears dissolved inside them. Rebraal saw one pass straight through him and sink deep into an ul-karron forehead. The creature fixed him with a stare of incomprehension as its mouth collapsed and its face fell like slime over its chest.

More of the light pulsed from Erienne. Stronger and stronger it came, each pulse jolting her body and drawing shuddering cries from her throat.

"Erienne, stop," shouted Denser but she couldn't hear him.

The spears still rattled away across the gap, seeking their targets, but around Erienne a coil formed. It gained in intensity at frightening speed. Rebraal shielded his eyes from the glare but was captivated by what he saw. Where they stood, the demon conduits started to moan and shiver. Their bodies bucked and twisted as if they were trying to break shackles far too strong for them. All too human faces stared out of the light, eyes imploring mercy.

The coil around Erienne tightened and flew away. It struck the nearer demon, travelled up its body, across the arc and into the second in less than a heartbeat. It bled into the canopy of light and down into the gap. The conduits struggled, suffocating as the coils pulled tighter and tighter. Eyes bulged from sockets and breath was forced from tortured lungs. They pleaded for the pain to stop and stop it did.

Erienne opened her eyes, closed both fists and uttered a single word.

The world went black and the wind began to howl.

The karron were coming. Blackthorne could hear them pounding on the doors that led down to the kitchens. It hadn't been two days. Ferouc had beaten them. Too many demons, too few defenders and no respite. Incessant and draining, the karron had attacked. He had lost men in the grand hall, in the cloisters by his council chamber and in the banqueting hall. He had fought the enemy all the way down the stairs to the armoury and around the corner to the quartermaster's stores. He had held them at the servants' chambers and driven them back briefly but the result had never been in any doubt.

And now he and the thirteen that were left with him were holed up with no place left to run. Blackthorne was tired beyond belief. His left arm was broken and bound to his side so he could still strap on a shield and his left leg bore deep cuts raked by a karron spike.

But still he stood in the middle of the line, waiting for them. Still the ColdRoom was in operation and he could take some of them with him. He heard timbers splinter and the sound of karron feet tramping down the stairs. He knew Ferouc would be behind them, far enough to avoid harm himself.

The first hammer on the kitchen door sprang a hinge but the second barely made an indent. The third was more a gentle knock and there was no fourth. He heard squawks and shrieks echo about his castle. And then he heard nothing at all.

He took a pace toward the door and stopped, wondering how long it would be before he dared believe that they had won.

Hirad found that there was light. It came in from the fires surrounding the entrance to the edifice and from those that still burned around the mouths of the dead Kaan dragons. He opened his eyes against the gale. The conduit demons were screaming in terror that had no end. Their bodies were being stretched into the arc that joined them. Little by little, they were picked apart. Their heads distended, their legs split and their bodies twisted and elongated. How they still lived he didn't care but that sound they made cut him right to the bone and he prayed for it to stop.

From the gap he heard a sucking sound. Above, the darkened canopy bowed inward, its centre drew closer and closer to the gap. It touched and shattered and for a moment the room was filled with a dazzling light. The conduit demons wailed their last and were sucked into the arc which fed at dizzying speed into the canopy which in turn was snapped up by the gap. The howling of the wind reached a crescendo, then with a bass thud that slammed through Hirad's skull the gap closed.

He lay where he was for a moment, listening to the sound of his heart and feeling the energy drain from his body. He had no more to give but then, there was no more he had to give. And yet he felt no joy, no victory. Instead he felt cheated. They had closed the path to Balaia and cut off the demons' power. The mana would dissipate through the Balaian dimension and the demons would not be able to sustain themselves for long. The Raven had saved their world and yet for them there was nothing. Sha-Kaan was silent.

It wasn't right.

Hirad dragged himself to a sitting position and let his eyes become accustomed to the darkness. There was movement around him and the sound of sobbing near him. He pushed himself to his feet and found The Unknown helping him up. He swayed. Blood was running from his face, his hands, his left shoulder and his right leg. The big man was in little better condition. He limped heavily and reaver claws had left his right ear flapping and pumping blood.

But it was as nothing to Erienne. She lay sprawled at the scene of her triumph. Denser was sitting at her bloodied head, stroking her face, and the shake in his shoulders told him everything. He knew he should move to comfort the Xeteskian but he couldn't bring himself to break into his grief. Perhaps it was better that way.

"We won, then," he said to The Unknown.

The big man shook his head. "No, Hirad, we lost. Balaia won. We have nothing. And Denser has lost everything."

Around them, people were forcing themselves to their feet. Auum supported Evunn who was clearly barely conscious. Thraun was staring at Erienne, his head shaking, his lips moving in denial and his feet taking him gradually closer to grim truth. Ark was wobbling on his feet but found Rebraal's shoulder on which to lean. All of them gravitated slowly to Erienne and Denser.

Hirad could see her stillness. Her eyes closed and her chest unmoving. She lay on her back, her arms thrown above her head.

"I'm so sorry, Denser," he said.

Denser didn't move. "Not you as well," he whispered. "Not you as well."

They all spun at a sudden infuriated din from outside. Hirad's heart pounded anew. The noise grew and grew, the voices screaming revenge, promising purgatory.

"Not again," said Thraun.

"What did we expect?" said The Unknown.

Karron, albino, reaver and master walked, flew or floated into the edifice. Strike-strain buzzed around them. The mass grew and grew. They advanced across a floor wide and unblemished. They took their time. After all, The Raven had nowhere to run.

"We have to keep fighting," Hirad said. "Sha-Kaan might still be able to save us. If he can make it back to Beshara he can open the portal to me. We can make it."

But those that faced him plainly did not believe him. They couldn't conceive of hope, they just wanted rest. And even as he uttered the words he didn't really believe them himself. Demons were crowding the space and Sha-Kaan was going to be too late.

He glanced over his shoulder. "Sleep well, Erienne. Best you didn't live to see this."

CHAPTER 46

Tessaya shuddered under the blow from the hammer limb, pushing it aside with the flat of his axe. He was running with sweat despite the frost of late evening. He drew in another exhausted breath and worked his axe back, fending off the spike from the same karron. The creature writhed its pincers, looking for a hold. A blade flashed across in front of him, severing the sinuous limb. The strike continued up, connecting with a reaver diving overhead.

Tessaya pulled his axe back across his body and buried it in the ul-karron neck. He glanced sideways and nodded his thanks to Suarav. The old soldier still stood though he had no right to. A spike had torn a gash in his left shoulder and reaver claws had dragged the armour from his back, missing his soul by a hair. He had refused to leave the line and rest. Tessaya could see his point. The end was upon them. Better to die in defence than be taken in your sleep.

More karron, backed by reavers and a cloud of strike-strain, were heading through the main wall breach. They crowded behind those already pressing against his faltering warriors. The ul-karron had wreaked dreadful havoc, weakening even their traditionally indomitable spirit. Tessaya opened his mouth and began to sing again.

He battered his axe through the next karron attack, taking off both pincer and spike limb. His song was taken up by throats all around the college. It was a song of defiance that spoke of endurance and the glory of death. It didn't allow for fear.

Tessaya raised his blade to strike again. A flaming body fell screeching from the sky, landing among the karron just ahead of him. Even through the curtain of fire, he recognised Drenoul. For a moment, the attack faltered. The demon master's squeals upset their rhythm, disrupting the flow of calls from the reavers.

Tessaya didn't care why Drenoul had died. He saw opportunity. Yelling a forward order he ploughed into the confused enemy. The karron, dull of mind, had stalled completely.

His axe swung, taking the head from an enemy. He used the purity of the cut to set up an unstoppable rhythm of pace and strike. Spells erupted outside of the college, mages taking advantage of the moment.

The Wesmen roared, sensing the change. They advanced quickly, chopping through an enemy that didn't back off before them. Overhead, reavers circled but their calls were altered. It couldn't just be put down to Drenoul's death.

Tessaya paused and stepped back, wiping gore from his face. He took a breath. Around him, his lieutenants signalled the halt. Overhead the wind picked up, blowing around the courtyard. Abruptly, the slit in the sky guttered. A green light flashed within the white. The wind blew harder, like the gales of the One magic. But only for an instant. With a report like the crack of an avalanche breaking, the slit blanked out.

Silence but for the sound of reaver wings. It lasted only for a few heartbeats before the winged demons set up mournful cries. They spiralled skyward toward the glorious emptiness that had been the basis of their power. They cried in panic and loss, flocked with the strike-strain and keened across the heavens rudderless.

In front of Tessaya the karron stood mute. Limbs hung limp, resting on the ground. Eyes were dim and confused. He could hear their rasping breathing. They didn't even have the sense to try and run. Around the college, his warriors engaged in slaughter. Songs of triumph reverberated around the grounds. Chants of victory, voices of conquest.

Tessaya didn't join them. He stepped away from the carnage and turned to Suarav, a great weariness settling on him.

"I didn't believe they'd do it," he said.

"Never underestimate The Raven," said Suarav.

Tessaya laughed and clapped Suarav on the back. "Or a Xeteskian soldier who fights like a warlord."

"It was an honour to fight with you, my Lord."

"And I with you, Easterner."

The two men walked together toward the tower complex. At every pace, Wesmen roared his name and raised their weapons in salute. He acknowledged them all but though he smiled, he couldn't accept the triumph. Not yet.

The scene around him was charnel. So many warriors lay dead. So many elves lay with them. And the Xeteskians who had come to join the last defence lay among them, most of them. It left every faction so weak. None of them had the strength to push onto dominion now. Tessaya wasn't sure he had the will left anyway.

Dystran and Vuldaroq were coming down the steps toward them. Both wore expressions of exhausted disbelief.

"Congratulations, Lord Dystran," said Tessaya. "A late entrance to the fight but effective."

Dystran inclined his head. "The plaudits are all yours, Lord Tessaya. I am shamed by my outbursts."

"You'll learn," said Tessaya. "If you live long enough."

"I wonder if it's really all over," said Vuldaroq.

They all followed his gaze. Demons still thronged the sky. Wesmen and mages destroyed those unable to take sanctuary in the air.

"Inevitably, time will tell," said Dystran.

"Meantime," said Tessaya. "We all have a great deal to discuss."

"Yes," said Dystran, his smile almost sickeningly grateful. "Indeed we do."

Thraun had pushed Denser aside and scooped Erienne into his arms before anyone else blinked.

"Put her down," ordered Hirad over his shoulder. "You can't help her now."

The demons closed on them quickly. The Raven backed off across the floor and over the dais, at least denying their enemy rear attack. Still, there was no way out.

"She's not dead," growled Thraun.

"Don't be stupid, Thraun," said The Unknown.

"Honour her," said Rebraal. "Take down some of those who brought about her death."

"She's not dead."

Hirad glanced again. He saw her eyelids flicker.

"Oh Gods be hanged, he's right. Denser, get in line and get casting. Let's buy ourselves some time."

"What difference will it make," muttered Denser.

Hirad turned back to face the enemy that already outnumbered them at least thirty to one.

"Because for one thing, The Raven is not going anywhere meekly and for another, every beat we give her means she might wake. And if she does, anything is possible."

The Unknown tensed and took a pace forward and shouted into the growing din.

"Form up, Raven!"

New hope pulsed through them. Hirad stood by The Unknown. Thraun laid Erienne down behind him and snarled at the advancing demons. Ark took up his position left. The TaiGethen paced to the right-hand side, affording Erienne more protection, Rebraal with them. And behind, Eilaan and Denser prepared.

The demons were close now. Karron spread across the floor. Reavers, their skin rippling with colour and vein, chattered and called to marshal their forces. Albinos loped to each flank. They moved in, desire for vengeance almost a taste in the air.

"Well," said Hirad in The Unknown's earshot. "It gives us something to do."

The Unknown smiled down at him.

"One more time, Hirad Coldheart?"

"One more time, Unknown. Sol."

The two men touched gauntlets. The Unknown's blade tapped against the floor, metronomic, comforting. It echoed around the edifice.

"Ready, Raven," he called. "Pick your targets. Mages, tell us when to duck. Good luck everyone. Let's leave them with a few bad memories, eh?"

The karron hung back, leaving the reavers to attack alone.

"Bastards want our souls," said Hirad.

"There's a lot of pain between now and then," said Thraun.

"Down," said Denser.

They complied. Both mages cast. Eilaan's FlameOrbs described a shallow arc to land in the midst of the karron. Denser's IceWind blew straight into the first of the advancing reavers.

In the enclosed confines of the edifice, the wails and screams tore at Hirad's ears and the stench of burned demon flesh assailed his nostrils, over-powering the clean frost of Denser's supercooled air. Reavers dropped to the ground in front of them, shattering on impact. The mass packed and surged backward, leaving a hole where the karron burned.

Hirad grinned. "We're The Raven, bastards!" he shouted. "Who's next to die, eh? Who really wants us?"

"Tell me you've got more of those, Denser," said The Unknown.

"One or two."

The demons gathered. Reaver calls bounced from walls and ceiling. Albinos scampered past the karron. Strike-strain massed and flew in and the mages cast again. Eilaan's ForceCone swept a swath of strike-strain from the right-hand flank. Denser's second IceWind ripped into the reavers. But this time, the rest didn't pause. While the karron blocked any hope of escape, reavers and albinos attacked.

The Unknown's blade ceased tapping and the final fight began. Hirad thrashed his sword into the body of an albino, sending the creature spinning backward. He stood tall as reavers crowded in. A tail whipped into his legs. He responded with a circular strike that dragged through wing membrane and sinew. The reaver crashed down but already the wounds were healing.

By him, The Unknown operated a figure-eight defence, blade in both hands. Thraun was howling, cloaked in strike-strain, while further right Auum, Evunn and Rebraal blurred into action, beating back the over-whelming weight of enemy.

Inexorably, the demons forced further in. Hirad could taste their breath. He fenced off claw and bite, snatched a knife from his belt and drove it into the nearest albino face. The demon reacted, neck extending, jaws agape. It sank its teeth into his leg, drawing a cry from his lips.

A reaver fist caught him square on the jaw, knocking him over. Immediately, The Unknown stepped half a pace right, slashing his blade across the open space, denying the reaver access. Hirad struggled to his haunches, blood dripping from his chin. familiar warmth flooded him. Sha-Kaan. Their words came at the speed of thought.

"Where are you, Sha-Kaan?"

"I am home. I can feel your pain."

"Get us out of here. Use the Klene."

"I am coming. Did I not say you would feel me again?"

Hirad surged to his feet and waded back into the fight. He carved his sword down into an albino skull and up into a reaver groin.

"Raven, with me. Fight on. I told you. Sha-Kaan is coming. Fight."

To their right, beyond the press of reavers, a pure white horizontal line appeared in the air.

"Right!" roared Hirad. "Right."

He clattered his blade through a reaver's claws and kicked out straight, catching an albino in the side of the head. He moved into the space.

"Drive. Drive."

The line described the outline of the door to the Klene. To Hirad, it appeared desperately slow and terribly distant.

"Down."

More IceWind, blasting a path halfway across the edifice. The elves rushed into the gap. Reavers closed in left, karron blocked them head-on. The winged soul stealers dropped on the trio, obscuring them from sight. Kicking out at albinos, Hirad saw Auum drag a reaver from Evunn's back. His knife flashed under its arm, killing it instantly. But more dropped down. Auum danced among them, Hirad saw reavers fall. He saw fists and feet fly, knocking them back, keeping open the merest of gaps.

"Move, Raven, move!"

Thraun, with Erienne in his arms again, dashed forward. The Unknown was in front of him and past Hirad, crashing into the reavers and karron ahead, intent on forcing them back. Ark came behind Thraun, his axe slicing left and right in a fluid motion. Strike-strain were about his face and neck. He ignored them.

"Eilaan. ForceCone over the doorway. Keep the reavers back. Denser, keep the rear clear. I'm with you."

ForceCones played out ahead and behind. Reavers were swept aside just to rise and run or fly back in. The pressure to the rear eased just a little.

"Hurry, Great Kaan."

The doorway drew down the air inch by tortuous inch. At the front of the fight, Evunn was in trouble. Auum's roundhouse kick cracked a reaver from above his head but another two rushed in, one lashing claws into his side though he ducked the other. The Unknown savaged his blade through waist high, scattering albinos from the group around the elves. Evunn blocked away tail and claw. Reaver jaws closed on his shoulder. Auum's fists flew faster than Hirad had ever seen them. Strike-strain circled. Evunn thudded his knife again and again into the reaver's head, dislodging it. But so many were on him. Claws dragged into his back. Strike-strain were about his head, forcing it back. A reaver tail tore out his throat.

Hirad saw Rebraal and Auum diving on the collapsed body of the downed Tai; the next he heard were the screeches of agonised reavers.

The Raven line was compromised along its length now. Reavers fell on Thraun. Ark's powerful defence not quite enough.

"Unknown, behind!"

Nearly overbalancing on his damaged hip, he turned and chopped hard down, taking the arm from a reaver which collapsed, nerve ganglion punctured. Simultaneously, karron forced a blockade across them, cutting Hirad and Denser off. Hirad could barely see as strike-strain poured down from overhead.

From the left, reavers crashed in feet first. Eilaan was struck side-on and sent sprawling into the karron closing in right. Hammer and spike rose and fell. Blood fountained into the air.

At the doorway, the loss of Eilaan's ForceCone left the reavers free to attack in even greater numbers. Karron shoved their way forward. From the mass, Auum and Rebraal shot back to their feet, drenched in demon blood. They stood back to back, defending themselves from the onslaught.

"Unknown, get forward!" yelled Hirad. "I'll cover Thraun. Denser, clear these bastard karron. We need to get to Erienne."

"Got you."

The barbarian fenced away a ferocious reaver attack and ran headlong into the karron left while Denser switched his ForceCone half forward. Hirad thrust his long sword deep into the creature's gut. The two fell. Hirad leant on his sword. The blade screamed against the stone, bent and snapped. The karron howled in agony, thrashing uselessly. Hirad searched for the opportunity to kill, the creature's stench filling his head. He pinioned its spike limb away for a beat and drove his dagger in deep.

He rolled away, abandoning his shattered blade. A hammer struck the karron carcass where he had been lying. He scrambled to his feet, spun and smashed a kick into the karron's face, hurling it back. He ducked a reaver flashing over his head; it missed by a claw. Straightening, he stabbed the karron through one baleful eye, dragged his knife clear and moved a pace closer.

The doorway was complete. Light flooded the edifice as it opened.

"Inside. Inside."

Denser's ForceCone drove demons back left. Hirad ran into the space by Thraun.

"Go, Denser. I have to be last. Go." He took in the situation in the moments he had. They weren't moving fast enough. "Defend the door. Go, Raven."

It became a headlong charge. The Unknown battered a karron aside. The elves fought with controlled rage. Auum backhanded a reaver in the face with his knife. Rebraal followed up, delivering the killing blow.

Denser was just ahead of Thraun now. Ark covered the shapechanger still, his axe cleaving into enemies right, but the karron were pressing hard now, filling the gaps, narrowing the path.

"Thraun. Down!"

The shapechanger dropped to his haunches. Reavers whipped overhead. The last of three flicked out its tail, catching him on the temple. He sprawled, clutching Erienne to his chest. A karron hammer came down on his legs, dashing his right knee. He roared in agony and tried to get up. The spike followed up and raked up his back. He fell again, Erienne spilling from his grasp; reavers pounced, claws poised to slash into her helpless body.

"No!" shouted Hirad. "Denser, clear the karron left. Unknown, get inside. Ark, let's get them."

Ark barrelled into the reavers threatening Erienne and stood astride her. Hirad forced a path to protect Thraun and his charge. Ahead, Rebraal and Auum were at the doorway, keeping it clear. Denser's ForceCone scattered demons from their left in a wide spread. He backed away, The Unknown shadowing him.

Hirad glanced down at Thraun. The shapechanger was still alive, clutching at the hem of Erienne's cloak. He was trying to drag himself nearer to her. Blood puddled on the floor beneath him. His face was grey.

"All right, Thraun," he said. "We've got you."

"Go," said Thraun, blood dribbling from his mouth. "Can't move, Hirad."

"We'll take you."

But he looked around and it was clear that he could not hope to fulfil that promise. Denser was trying his best to keep the demons away left and right but he could do nothing about the mass that packed in behind, out of the compass of the ForceCone.

"Hirad!" bellowed The Unknown. "Come on. It's your only chance."

"Hang on, Thraun," he said. "Ark, get Erienne away."

"It is done."

Hirad turned to face the enemy. Karron and reaver pressed in.

"Go," said Thraun. "Please." Hirad felt the tears running down his face. "Go."

He turned and started to run. Reavers flocked down on Thraun. He died without a sound.

Hirad felt the demons closing in on his back. Ark and Erienne were just a few yards from the doorway. He could see The Unknown and Denser beckoning them all on. Rebraal and Auum kept the edges of the doorway clear.

"Run!" yelled The Unknown. "Don't make me come out there. Run!"

But there was such despair in his voice. He made to move but Auum shoved him back hard. Hirad frowned. The claw of a reaver ripped up his back and into the base of his skull. He was pitched from his feet, tumbling head over heels. He scampered to his feet, a wave of nausea sweeping across him. He staggered, ran on a couple of paces. He heard the beating of wings close, so close. They were all around him. He felt the lash of a tail into his legs, claws grabbed at his back and shoulders and the hot breath of a reaver fired right in his face.

"Hirad!" cried The Unknown. "Hirad. Get up. Get up."

He tried to push past Auum but again the elf knocked him back. Hirad dragged himself to his hands and knees. They were all over him.

"Do something!"

Ark was moments from the doorway. A reaver exalted and buried its hand into Hirad's ribs. The barbarian gasped. He locked eyes with The Unknown briefly, favoured him with that damned smile and collapsed to the ground.

The doorway snapped shut.

Ark slithered to a halt as the doorway disappeared, clicking out of existence as if it had never been there. All that was left was a memory of it in the air. In his arms, Erienne's breath was ragged and faint. He closed a hand over her nose and mouth until it ceased altogether. He laid her on the ground and stood astride her, snapping his sword from its back mount. He turned, saw the faces of reavers look up from Hirad's body and the whole room of demons focus on him and move in.

He lifted one hand toward them and beckoned them on.

"No," said Denser, panic spearing his voice. "No. Open the door, open the door."

He scrabbled at the blank wall. The Unknown fell back a pace, swaying. Rebraal and Auum were next to him. Supporting him.

"Open this fucking door!" screamed Denser. "She's still out there. Sha-Kaan. Please open the door."

"Oh no," said The Unknown. "Not him. Not him. If one of us deserved to live it was him. Oh, Hirad, not you."

"Please open the door," mumbled Denser.

But it would not open. Hirad was dead and the link was gone. Denser slumped to the ground by the wall and was leaning against it, desolate, his body wracked with sobs.

The Unknown, his tears flowing free, shook off the elves and knelt by Denser, enveloping him in his powerful embrace. Behind them, the elves joined in prayer. And from the chamber behind them, they all heard the wailing of a dragon lost in grief for his Dragonene.

"Please make him go back."

"They've gone, Denser. Dear Gods burning, they've all gone."

The Unknown had no idea how long he sat with Denser. How long until he stopped crying and he could take control of his shuddering body. But when he did release the mage, when the poor man had sobbed himself out, he looked up into Rebraal's eyes and saw the light of relief there.

"You can feel them, can't you?" he said "Sense them."

Rebraal nodded. "The fabric between worlds is thin here, I can feel so much of those I love who are dead. And he is with my brother even now. The spirits rejoice. They are only lost until we travel to be with them again. And he will be there, sensing you, with you. All the time."

The Unknown managed a smile though it tore at his heart.

"You know, Rebraal, that is a truly scary thought."

He pushed himself to his feet, Auum stepping in to help him up. He was covered in blood and his body felt like he was still being attacked.

"Thanks. I think it's time we went and saw Sha-Kaan. Shared some memories and found out where it is this Klene is taking us. His world for now, I expect, until he can find himself a new Dragonene."

He reached down a hand which Denser took and hauled himself upright. The Unknown threw an arm around his shoulder and looked into his eyes.

"Raven," he whispered. "Raven with me."

EPILOGUE

Sol unlocked the door of the Raven's Rest in response to the insistent knocking. He cleared his throat irritably.

"We aren't op— Oh, if it isn't the Lord of the Mount elect."

"Very funny," said Denser. "Mind if I come in?"

"Be my guest." Sol stepped aside and let him in out of the chill rain. "Fancy a glass of wine? Just had some excellent young Blackthorne red come in."

"Sounds ideal."

"Hungry?"

"I could eat a scabby horse."

"Sold out of that at midday. Still, I'm sure I can find something. Sit yourself down if you can find a seat." He gestured around the big empty room, clean for the evening traffic. He limped around the end of the bar and took a bottle from the racking beneath it. "Jonas, you in the kitchen?"

"Yes, father."

"Bring in some bread and ham for two, there's a good lad. Denser's here."

"Oh, great."

Sol fished in his pocket for a corkscrew. He watched Denser walking around the walls of the tavern, looking fondly at the paintings of The Raven hanging there. And like always, he lingered at the portrait of Erienne, reaching out to touch it, brush away an imaginary hair.

The cork pulled with a satisfying pop. He sniffed the bottle then set it on a tray with a couple of glasses.

"You know," said Denser. "I've wanted to ask this for a while but don't you think we should think about taking these down? You know. Let them fade naturally in memory?"

"You cannot expect me to answer that question when you ask it wearing an expression like that. Besides, they bring in the punters."

"I'm not really sure what I'm trying to say. I don't mean don't display them at all. It's just that The Raven isn't for everyone. They're ours."

"There are plenty who would dispute that," said The Unknown. "Are you saying that I shouldn't profit from them?"

"It's not even that. Gods drowning, but everyone alive still owes us . . ."

Sol set the tray down and sat beside Denser. The dark mage had chosen a high-backed leather chair; one of four grouped around a low table and large open hearth. Same as always. It reminded him of their back room at the Rookery. Long demolished now of course. Gone along with Tomas, Maris and Rhob. Like the loss of so many friends on that cataclysmic day in the demon dimension, the fact still haunted Sol sometimes. At least with Tomas and family he didn't have the nightmare memories too. The unwelcome recollection brought a shake to his hand as he poured the wine.

"See what you make of that," he said, sitting in the next chair.

"The nerves never really recover, do they?"

Sol shook his head. "Some days it's worse than others. Yesterday, I couldn't have poured the wine for you." He felt the familiar sickness twist his stomach. "That's really why I keep them up here, you know. How their souls escaped the demons I don't know or care but we need to . . . I need to remind myself every day about their sacrifice. I actually find talking to one or other of them a comfort. Keeps me sane."

Denser chuckled, a laugh born of intimate understanding. "You talk to pictures to keep yourself sane."

Sol smiled and the two men chinked glasses.

"Good health."

"Oh, now that's very good," said Denser, savouring the taste. "And tell you what, when that slight sharpness softens in a year or two, it'll be phenomenal."

"My thoughts exactly."

"Have you seen him recently?" asked Denser.

"The Baron? No, not for a couple of seasons," said Sol. "Funny the effect all this has had on people long-term. Blackthorne doesn't often leave his town these days and you know what he used to be like."

Jonas walked in from the kitchen carrying a tray of bread and meat. He set it down on the table. The Unknown ruffled his blond hair.

"Thanks."

"Hello, Denser," said Jonas.

"Good to see you, young man. How are you?"

The tall and very solid lad shrugged. "All right. The Julatsans ask too many questions. I'd rather be riding my horse."

"Good points. Pheone is up at the college now. I think she was planning on dropping in to speak to the young man here," said Denser.

Jonas sighed dramatically. "Do I have to?"

"It won't last forever," said Sol. He patted Jonas's backside. "Go on now, see if your mother wants anything then you can go and take the horse out if you want. But don't be out after dark."

"All right."

Jonas trudged wearily away. The two friends watched him go.

"How old is he?" asked Denser.

"Eight."

"Five years . . ." Denser shook his head and looked again around the bar at the pictures. "Is he finding it difficult?"

"Some days," conceded Sol. "He's reached a stage where he understands how important he is but he doesn't really understand why. After all, he's only ever seen Sha-Kaan as a friend and protector, never as a key interdimensional link."

"He is only eight."

"Exactly. He's a quarter the age of the next-youngest Dragonene and like Hirad he's not a mage. It confuses him. It's bound to." Sol took another sip and then reached for a hunk of bread. "When you see Pheone, tell her to go easy, will you? Sometimes she forgets herself, I think."

"I'll certainly mention it."

Jonas clattered down the stairs and ran out of the back door toward the stables.

"I take it she didn't want anything then?" called Sol after him. He didn't get a reply. "Children." He shook his head.

"How's Lady Unknown, then?" Denser cut a thin slice of bread and loaded it with ham.

"Bearing up, thanks. She's due in ten days so she doesn't get around too much but her health is good. Thanks for keeping an eye on her. She's pleased it's going to be another son, by the way. We both are."

Sol refilled their glasses.

"Have you decided which name, yet?"

"I could only really call him Hirad, couldn't I?"

"It'll be good to hear that name echoing round again."

"He'll have plenty to live up to."

Sol leaned back in his chair. He looked over at his friend, who scratched his grey-flecked beard then reached into his pouch for his pipe and weed. He'd been a tower of strength in the intervening years when Sol had found it very difficult to come to terms with what he'd lost. He'd managed his own grief so much better and been able to sit with Sol night after night until the horror and pain began to fade.

"So, Denser. What really brings you down The Thread from the Mount this wet afternoon? I seriously doubt it was merely social."

"Ah, glad you asked," said Denser. He tamped down his pipe, brought a flame to the end of his thumb and lit up. "I've got a job for you."

Sol tensed. "See this fist? Do I have to point out again that I own and run a bar?"

"Hear me out," urged Denser.

"I'm not leading any more demon-hunter teams into the Blackthornes. I've told you."

"Sol, no one is asking you to. Suarav and that Wesman with the long and involved name are doing what's necessary. We've not had a raid in Xetesk for, what . . . a season and a half? Like I said, hear me out."

Sol shrugged. "All right. Sorry."

"I've just come from the Balaia reconstruction council meeting and we're starting to run into some problems. With Dystran being forced to step down, there's a vacuum building. Whether or not I take over is neither here nor there. The trouble is that some of the Barons are talking about reinstituting the Korina Trade Alliance. While that's not a bad thing in itself, it starts to divide eastern Balaia.

"Tessaya doesn't like it and neither does Rebraal. I can see their point. After all, Tessaya speaks for the whole of the Wesmen, Rebraal for the elven nation. But here, we're all of a sudden going to have mage and nonmage power blocks. It smacks of the past."

"So find yourselves someone to unite you. Everyone respects Blackthorne. He's perfect." Sol drank more wine, washing down his bread.

"But like you say, he doesn't really like to leave Blackthorne and we have to be honest, he's not quite the man he once was."

There was a long pause. Sol didn't like the way this was heading at all. He stared at Denser, daring him to speak.

"Sol, don't make me say it." Denser had read his expression.

"You want me to speak for Balaia? Come on, Denser, I'm no diplomat."

"No, you're not. You're thinking too small. I know you see yourself as the quiet man running his bar with his family in Xetesk. But to everyone of influence in Balaia, and for that matter, the Weslands and Calaius, you're the voice and presence of the East. You survived the demon dimension; you've led the hunt into the Blackthornes; you've been at the centre of so much of the reconstruction planning; you aren't a mage. And you were the centre of The Raven. There's not a man or woman that wouldn't accept you."

"All right, all right, enough massaging of my ego. You're making me blush. Accept me as what?"

Denser leaned forward and placed his glass down on the table.

"I've been asked to come down here after a unanimous vote of the council meeting. Sol, this country doesn't need a diplomat or a representative. It needs to follow Calaius and the Wesmen. For the first time in our history, we need a leader. You."

Sol almost dropped his glass. He felt his face flush and his heart race.

"That's quite a step up from bar owner," he managed.

Denser didn't smile. "I'm not joking, Sol. Balaia needs stability. We're in danger of reverting back to the old schisms. We have to be united or what we've been building will be wasted. What The Raven achieved will be wasted."

"Don't you bring The Raven into this," snapped Sol.

"Doesn't stop it being true. You are the man who can keep it all together. You know you can. Come to the Mount. Talk to us. Please."

"I've got a bar to run and a wife to look after. I have a new child on the way and a son who needs me by him right now, I don't have the time and I don't have the energy."

"And they all need to have a secure future." Denser poured more wine into Sol's glass. "Talk to us. See what we have in mind. Think about it."

Sol looked at Denser and allowed a smile across his face. Anyone else and he would have dismissed the notion out of hand. To this man, though, he owed more than to anyone alive.

"Tomorrow," he growled. "Now drink up and get lost. I've got to open up in a couple of hours."

"Thank you, Sol. You won't regret it, I promise you."

"Denser, I already am. What the hell do you think I'm going to say to Diera?"

"You'll think of something suitably pithy and persuasive, I feel sure."

"Go."

Denser drained his glass and walked back to the door, opening it on the rain sheeting down, pounding on the street. Sol wondered if Jonas had actually gone out. The two men shook hands and Sol pulled Denser into a brief embrace.

"See you tomorrow," said Denser.

"After lunch, when I've closed."

Sol watched Denser walk away up The Thread and back to the Mount of Xetesk, pulling his cloak close about him. He shut and bolted the door and walked back through the bar toward the stairs. He paused by Hirad's picture. The barbarian gazed back at him, eyes intense and full of belief, that damned smile on his face.

"What on earth would you think, Coldheart?" he said. "Probably nothing. Too busy laughing I expect. How does it sound . . . Sol, The Unknown Warrior, Ruler of Balaia. Daft, eh?"

And as he turned away, he could have sworn he saw Hirad nod.

Acknowledgments

At the risk of repeating myself for the sixth book in a row, I'd like to thank those who have supported and cajoled me through the writing of this book. Peter Robinson, John Cross, Dave Mutton, and Dick Whichelow for their criticism, suggestions and encouragement. David Gemmell and Rob Grant for sound advice at a time of great change. Robert Kirby for helping me to another level, and Nicola Sinclair for keeping my feet firmly on the ground.

And my family for just being brilliant.

ABOUT THE AUTHOR

J AMES BARCLAY is in his forties and lives in Teddington in the UK with his wife and son. He is a full-time writer. Visit him online at www.james barclay.com.